# THE MIDWIVES

Duncan Ralston

SHADOW WORK PUBLISHING

This story is a work of fiction. Names, characters, places and incidents are either the product of the author's imagination or are used fictitiously. Any resemblance to actual persons, living or dead, is entirely coincidental.

# Praise for THE MIDWIVES

"Get ready for a roller coaster ride of terror as once you arrive in Barrow's Bay, you might not be able to leave! Five stars for one hell of a ride!"

— Book Nook Retreat

"I'm adding this to my list of favorite books and I have no problem giving *The Midwives* my highest recommendation!"

— Char's Horror Corner

"If you want a modern day, twisted fairy-tale type of story that is both dark and gripping – this is the one."

— Proud Book Hoarder

"If you are looking for your next creepy read, I highly recommend giving Midwives a chance."

— Bookaholic Reviews

# Contents

"You can't go home again."
—Thomas Wolfe

"Better the devil you know than the devil you don't."
— Richard Taverner

"There is no truth beyond magic."
— John Fowles, *The Magus*

# PROLOGUE

## MOTHER

*BARROWS BAY, 1978*

THE GIRL LEFT a trail of blood behind her, glistening as she passed under streetlamps lighting her apparently aimless trek. Blood flattened the blonde hairs on her slender legs and pooled in between her toes. Her bare right foot tattooed red on the ragged pavement over and over, like a stamped signature falling back into dark oblivion.

Sunken within bruised pits of flesh, her green eyes stared frantically ahead through tangles of wet and straggly hair. Fresh blood dribbled from a rope of purplish flesh dangling below her pink nightgown, soaked through the crotch with a dark, wet stain.

In the distance, the ocean sound beat against the shore. Here, on this lonely stretch of island road closed in by skeletal black pines, a baby cried joylessly.

Closer by the second, the old women stalked her.

She felt their invisible presence in the darkness surrounding her. They had yet to show themselves since she'd dashed from the house with the baby in her arms, but she knew they were close behind. She heard the intermittent scuttle of their feet out there in the dark.

*My name is Rosalee*, she'd told the old woman, and the old woman had nodded and said, *We know who you are, dear child.*

She could have hidden from them in the woods, if not for

the boy. It would be impossible to keep him quiet. His cries were much louder than they had any right to be, considering his size.

He was premature. Purple and slimy and fresh from the womb, his wriggling limbs so small and frail. She held him away from her body, as if in offering to a nameless god watching from the darkness.

Up ahead the county road sign, a single 8 in a white shield, rose out of the dark like a glimmering beacon.

From there the road forked three ways. One road gave way to gravel and eventually plain dirt the further west you traveled. The other widened as it led east toward town. Both weaved through pine and spruce and cuts of sheer granite on either side, pitch black under the starless sky.

Eventually, both led to the ocean, as did most roads on the island.

County Road 8 continued its northbound trek until it reached the ferry docks. The last ferry was her only chance to escape. If she could just flag down a passing car. She didn't know how late it was, if the ferry was even still running. But she had to try.

A knife-wound throb between her legs doubled her over. She caught her breath, focusing on her breathing.

Not on the pain.

Not the old women gaining on her every moment she wasted standing still.

She knew they would tear little Stephen from her arms. She couldn't let them.

Everyone knew what happened when a young girl got pregnant in Barrows Bay. Hadn't they all heard the rumors? Hadn't they witnessed firsthand how much Yolanda Macken changed when she returned from her birthing? Yo was a cheerleader before Kenny Simms knocked her up in the bed of his Chevy during the Hallowe'en dance two years back. After the birthing, she no longer had any use for cheers, for the school or herself.

The baby girl was being raised by her grandmother in Narragansett while Yolanda finished school, though there didn't seem to be any point in it. She was depressive, lethargic, her beautiful blonde hair, often compared to Farrah Fawcett, now stringy and falling out in clumps. She barely scraped by with a

D average. And the parents of Barrows Bay did not ascribe to "the cult of pharmaceuticals and psychiatry the rest of the country does," at least according to Rosalee's father.

Rosalee's right foot painted the yellow line red. As Stephen continued his plaintive wail, she pulled him close to her small breasts and shook him lightly in her arms.

"Hush little baby, don't you cry," she sang tonelessly. "Shhh. Shhh. 'Cause Grandpa loves you and so do I. Shhhhh."

A sharp *snick!* of metal against metal stopped her under the blazing yellow light of a streetlamp. Night bugs flitted on its cover, drawn by the light.

She peered out into the blackness. Heart racing, pumping blood that maintained its steady course down her legs.

She knew the sound. Everyone in Barrows Bay knew that terrible sound by heart.

The knitting needles.

*The Midwives.*

An elderly woman's laughter. Echoed by a second.

*Them.*

She whirled, concrete biting into the soft pads of her heels. Her wide, tear-rimmed eyes chased the sound as she whipped herself round and round, the dizziness barely noticeable above the pain between her legs and the creeping dread.

Squinting into the darkness, she finally saw it. Two glints of light in the black. A hungry animal, lured by the smell of blood to prey on her helpless child? Or the cold, murderous eyes of her pursuers?

The light became wider, brighter. She heard the engine. Not eyes, but headlights. A car up ahead on the road—*coming this way!*

She laughed, joyful laughter for what might be the first time since she saw the dark brown ring on the in-home pregnancy test she asked Auntie Jean to purchase on her behalf, so as not to alert her father.

As she waved her free arm, the headlights caught her for a moment like an actor on a stage. Blood a stark contrast to her ghostly pale skin.

The station wagon swerved. It was still far enough away it seemed not to be caused by her being in the road but something else. One of *them*?

She waved frantically. "Please! Please help me!"

The engine grew louder, close enough she could hear the crunch of gravel under its tires.

In those few seconds as the familiar station wagon passed by, Rosalee recognized the look of sheer terror in his eyes and knew, she *knew*, he wouldn't stop—even though it was his duty to help her, as one of God's children, this man of the cloth, his white clergy collar visible in the streetlight as the young reverend's station wagon blew past.

Rosalee screamed after him, a desperate scream of fear and frustration. Having never let up his cries, Stephen became her chorus.

Laughter filled the silence left by the retreating vehicle, coming from all around her, several voices at once, filling her ears and entering her mind, a cackling chorus echoing between her ears.

She pulled Stephen close to her bosom, his tiny presence like a talisman against evil. She was afraid she was losing her mind.

"You can't have him!" she shouted at the darkness. "He's mine!"

A woman's voice, thick and gruff, called out, "You're wrong, sister! He belongs to the Mother!"

"*I'm his goddamn mother!*"

The heavy *clunk!* of wood on asphalt made her turn.

A figure in a white hooded cloak stepped out of the darkness into the circle of streetlight, materializing as if from the black void of a distant galaxy. A face made entirely of darkness and little glints of light in the eyes was bathed within the hood's shadow.

Another *clunk!* of the cane—Rosalee knew it by its actual name, *shillelagh*, because her grandfather had one much like it held up by nails on the wall by the front door. The cloaked figure held it clenched in one withered, spider-veined hand.

When she spoke, her voice was much different from the first woman's, soothing and very Irish. The others had called her *Mother*, as if they were her daughters, though they all appeared to be the same age.

"Give us the boy and all will be forgiven," Mother said. "You belong with us, dear child. You'll catch your death out here."

Rosalee hugged Stephen tighter. His wails grew more desperate, as if sensing the danger they were in. "No. *Please*. This is unfair! *Can't you see this isn't fair?*"

"Fair's got nothin to do with it, girl!" the gruff woman barked.

A shrill voice this time: "Hand over the boy!"

More figures emerged from the shadows. Five in all, dressed in the same pristine white cloaks. Rosalee thought she could make out more in the darkness beyond, closing in around her.

Dozens more. Maybe *hundreds*.

She was surrounded. *Trapped.*

In her desperation a pet phrase of her father's came back to her: *If you're short on options, go with the flow.* He said it when the stomach cancer finally took her mother back to Jesus. He said it again when Rosalee finally admitted her predicament to him. Being Catholic, the "flow" dictated she carry the baby to term.

Seven months ago, she would've given anything to get rid of the alien presence growing inside her. She'd thought of it as an annoyance, something like the tumor that ended her mother's life and possibly worse—it was a farting, kicking, living thing that would end her life as surely as the tumor ended her mother's.

During those seven months she hadn't felt a single twinge of what her aunt called the "mothering instinct."

It wasn't until the old women lifted Stephen from the birthing pool, a wriggling little creature struggling for air, that she found herself understanding everything Auntie Jean said about having a child of her own.

This baby was *hers*. His name was Stephen and *she* was his mother—not this old hag. She would protect him with her life.

*Go with the flow.*

Those words again. Ringing in her ears as the old women circled her.

It took a moment for their meaning to sink in. She was no use to Stephen dead. Alive, she could plead with her father to get a lawyer, to fight these evil bitches and win him back. In her confusion and terror and all of the other emotions swirling around in her mind, it seemed like the most reasonable choice.

If these women—*these hags*—wanted Stephen, she would

give him to them. They would take care of him, as they took care of several children whose mothers had abandoned them or died, according to rumor. Offered them to good families on the mainland who gave them a better life.

By the time she was finally able to win him back, she'd be an appropriate age for motherhood.

Suddenly this plan seemed more than reasonable. It was the most mature, rational decision she'd ever made in her life.

*Go with the flow, baby girl.*

She could almost feel her father's voice in her ear, prickling the hairs on the back of her neck. The image of the coiled black snake lunging at her from the pulsating stones came to her bright and clear, like a movie flashing before her eyes.

*Entering* her.

The shock of pain.

The terror and confusion.

The blood—so much blood.

She whimpered. The memory of the standing stones made her decision easier.

With great care, she held out the boy, still tethered by the fleshy umbilical cord which had nurtured him into being.

The ancient woman whose face Rosalee had yet to see, even during the birthing ceremony—always in shadow, ever watchful—tucked the shillelagh under her arm and snatched the boy up in her crepe-paper hands.

"Please don't hurt him," Rosalee said, her voice a hoarse whisper.

"You know what must be done," the ancient woman said.

And she did. She supposed she'd always known, just as every living soul in Barrows Bay must, in their hearts.

She knew what must be done.

For the good of the people. For the good of the *town*.

Stephen wouldn't be given a good home. He'd be *sacrificed*. A profane ritual older than the town itself. A gift of blood to appease the caretakers of this godless island.

"Please," she said. "Please, just do it quick. Don't make it hurt him."

The lady to the old woman's left removed her hood. Beneath was a gorgeous mound of beehive gray hair that had gone out of style before Rosalee was born, set atop a pleasant, rosy-cheeked face with penciled-in eyebrows. She could easily have been a grocery store clerk or a secretarial temp. The others had called her Helen.

She removed something from her purse. A knife with a wavy blade, a green medallion in its shaft. Greener than Rosalee's eyes, which widened as they caught its reflection. It twinkled with a glint of streetlight.

"No..." she said. "Not now, please not now. I don't wanna *see...*"

"How would *you* have us remove the cord, dear child?" the ancient woman with the shillelagh asked. "Shall we gnash it with our teeth?"

She demonstrated, clacking her ancient yellow teeth together: *clack-clack-clack-clack-clack!* They gleamed in the unnatural light, the rest of her face still awash in darkness. All but those terrible, all-seeing eyes.

The other women laughed hysterically.

Rosalee joined them, startled into it, *bullied* into it, looking around at all their laughing faces and wondering why she was laughing with them when she was terrified to her bones.

Helen reached out and pinched the umbilical cord with one hand, carving with the dagger. Dark fluid oozed out onto her Mary Janes. "Yech!" She stepped out of the dribble.

"Hush, you ninny!" the ancient woman said, holding Stephen under his tiny arms, her bony fingers encircling his narrow chest.

With a final cut, the cord snapped against the blade.

"About blessed time," the ancient one said. She passed the boy into a gray blanket held by another. This woman swaddled him in it, folding it like origami with her dainty white gloves. Military-style, the way Rosalee's father made his bed. At the birthing, the others had called her Geraldine.

Finally, *mercifully*, little Stephen stopped crying.

It was only then that Rosalee realized how eerily quiet the night was. Not a croak of a frog, a chirp of a bat, nor the mournful howl of a loon to be heard. As if the animals themselves were afraid to make a sound in the presence of these hags.

And how *cold* it suddenly was, as though it wasn't midsummer at all but the dead of winter.

"There," the ancient one said. "Safe and swaddled. Isn't that better, child?"

Shivering and uncertain, Rosalee still managed a nod.

*Snick!* She turned at the sound. *The awful sound. The deadly sound.*

A fourth woman approached, holding a pair of silvery knitting needles like weapons. She was ruddy-faced and plump, her eyes full of mischievous glee. During the birthing, she'd been wearing a fancy hat. They called her Mavis.

The ancient woman said, "Deal with her."

Helpless, Rosalee backed away. She tripped. Her legs tangled in the umbilical cord still spooling from her insides. She landed on her butt with a startled exhale.

Baby Stephen resumed his cries.

Rosalee looked back over her shoulder, watching the ancient woman's white robe recede with her child into the darkness. Clarity returned. Sanity. She couldn't let them take him— how did she let them take him?

"No, please! *Please!* Don't hurt him! *Don't you hurt my Stephen!*"

Swollen, weeping from the pain and the loss of her son, knowing she would soon lose her own life, Rosalee turned to face her adversaries.

Eight menacing eyes fell upon her, their lined and wrinkled faces scarcely visible under the hoods. Each woman scraped a knitting needle over and under the other like sharpening knives as they approached.

Rosalee crawled backwards on her hands and feet. The slippery, veined umbilical cord dragging along beneath her, slithering like a snake, chasing her like the memory of the thing that ravaged her among the stones.

Someone grabbed her by the hair. Her scream echoed. A white-gloved hand covered her mouth, smothering her cries. Baby powder-scented silk against her lips. She struggled, kicking out at them with what little strength remained.

No use. Despite their age, they were far stronger.

"Hold on, kiddo," Helen said in her ear. "This is gonna hurt like hell."

A knitting needle swished out in the gloved woman's hand, glinting as it caught the light.

Rosalee's pretty green eyes—eyes her father described as

"perfectly Irish"—widened in sheer terror. The needle pierced the soft tissue of her left temple, gouged through bone and into the tender meat of her brain.

She slumped sideways on the asphalt. Blood trickled down her cheek into her Irish eyes, the left bulging against the pressure of the needle.

Rosalee looked up with her remaining eye, not at her killers but past them, past the insects flitting against the streetlamp to the dark cosmos beyond.

Blinking blood from her good eye, she searched the heavens for any sign of the God children who grew up in Barrows Bay knew had turned a blind eye toward them.

All she saw was an endless galaxy of lifeless, indifferent stars.

As her vision waned along with the last of her breath, the Midwives broke the circle, vanishing into the chilly midsummer night.

# PART ONE

---

MAIDEN

# CHAPTER 1

## TRUE CRIME

$K$*ILLER*. THE GIRL actually called him *Killer*.

She looked him straight in the eye, grinning suggestively, expecting him to sign something nice in the copy of *Mirror Man* the stamp on the inside identified as property of Carnegie Library's Homewood branch. Not even a hardcover—she held a heavily abused paperback, likely salvaged from someone's private collection, read once and tossed to the curbside or willed to the library in a deceased widow's estate.

All that and she had the nerve to call him "Killer," the insult Martin Savage despised more than any other. It took every ounce of willpower to twist the lower half of his face into a smile. "Who should I make it out to?"

"To Tish." Excitement caused her to bounce on the balls of her feet. An ankh necklace jingled on its chain between the curves of her breasts. "I'm a *huge* fan."

Martin stared at them for a moment, pressed together under the stretchy fabric of her low-cut top. He wasn't sure if he was staring at her tits or the shiny silver trinket dangling from her necklace.

Something about the ankh made him uneasy, had him cringing behind the card table at the front of the store, behind stacks of his nonfiction books and a standee ad for his first fiction novel, *Dead Weight*.

He swallowed hard, forcing himself to resume eye contact. "Huge, huh?"

She raised her arched eyebrows. "*Major* huge."

Martin knew her type. She wasn't so much a fan of his writing as the genre. True Crime junkies like her were the bane of his career. They wore black clothes and dour, I've-seen-it-all expressions. They carried worn copies of *Mirror Man*, never his latest book and never *Witch Hunter*, not even the subpar collection of short stories he vanity-published fresh out of college.

Not these types. These so-called fans were ghouls. Serial killer groupies. Drawn to Martin because of his close contact with maniacs. As if that evil, that *danger*, might rub off on them by proxy.

They were self-harmers or drug addicts and most often women, the type who'd make a prisoner into a pen pal with the potential for conjugal visits. He suspected some might be hybristophiliacs, masturbating to signed photographs of Richard Ramirez or burnt hairs belonging to Ted Bundy, plucked with tweezers from the floor under the electric chair and sold for fifty dollars a pop on eBay. Some might even assist their psychopathic crushes, committing crimes and violent acts for them, to prove their love.

The only thing these so-called fans ever wanted to know about him was how it *felt*. And if it came down to him or "them," would he do it again?

Martin had no idea what he would do if he came face to face with another serial murderer in the outside world. He could hardly believe he'd been able to get the upper hand with the Mirror Man, though his just sitting here proved it.

He supposed he just had to hope his instincts would spare him, as they had in Nico Damiani's antique shop. The tinkle of glass could have been wind chimes, a crystal chandelier, virtually anything within the shop. It was just blind luck he assumed the worst. And when Damiani turned, the lower half of his head still visible below the mirror mask—

Everything after that went red.

He'd gone over and over it with the police. They asked all the same questions these ghouls asked him. The same questions he asked himself.

*How did you end up drenched in the killer's blood?*

*How did you get the knife?*
*How did it feel?*

He'd never answer any of these so-called fans who dared to ask. What he would do was smile and ask, "Who should I make this out to?" and sign their goddamn book. Because if he wanted to keep his fucking Lexus and fucking condo in fucking Greenpoint, he needed to climb down into the fucking trenches. This advice came courtesy of both his publisher and his agent, who seemed to be working in tandem to drive him insane.

*Fuck this*, he thought.

He scrawled *To Trish, Kindly go fuck yourself* in big block letters very unlike his normal handwriting and he didn't sign his name. He closed the book and slid it across the table with a phony smile.

She smiled back and sighed wistfully, pressing it to her chest, her tits threatening to burst through her shirt as she stepped aside.

A large woman in a lumberjack jacket quickly took her place, holding out a twenty-dollar bill. "I want that one," she said, jabbing a stubby, dirty finger at the last few *Witch Hunter* hardbacks—the twisted tale of James Barclay, self-styled killer of "witches," a *New York Times* Best Seller for nonfiction eight weeks in a row. *Mirror Man* may have propelled him into stardom, but *Witch Hunter* still paid the bills.

Only a few copies of his novel sold today. *Dead Weight* could easily describe how the book landed on the shelves. The true crime books that allowed him to turn his hobby into a career sold far more. All told, he'd made about three-hundred bucks and possibly a handful of new readers. Not bad for a few hours' work. With the hotel, gas and per diem paid by his publisher, he supposed he was doing all right.

He peered over the lumberjack woman's shoulder, saw the girl frowning over his dedication. Probably deciding what to do about the offense.

He took the woman's money, signed a copy of the book—*nicely*, because although this woman was curt, she was no ghoul like Trish—and handed it to her with her change.

A man in a denim jacket thrust a hardcover of *Dangerous Curves* forward with autumn-chapped fingers. The story of seductive murderess Margaret Abbey, whose modus operandi was tampering with the brakes in her ill-fated lovers' cars. Abbey was currently serving three consecutive life sentences in Bedford Hills. It wasn't a very good book, but it had titillated the right people at the right time, when everyone was very into femme fatales and their lurid crimes of passion.

"Is it true what they say?" the man in the denim jacket asked with a shy downcast of his eyes. Behind him, the low early-March sun peeked out between two rotting rooftops in the town's decrepit business district. Martin felt a twinge of guilt taking money from people who likely lived paycheck to paycheck, but such was the business of art. Not like he could make a living by giving his books away.

"Who should I make this out to?"

"Oh. Uh, Juh-Jason?"

"Jason. Great." He scrawled a dedication. "Is what true, Jason?"

"That, uh... that James Barclay... th-that he escaped?"

The pen slashed across the page mid-signature with an audible scratch. "What's that?"

"Es-escaped. I, uh... I just heard it over the r-radio."

Martin was about to tell this man how implausible it was, but suddenly there wasn't enough air in the small bookstore to speak. His vision blurred. Blood thudded in his ears, dulling the voices in the room.

*A trail of blood, Marty.* The killer's words echoed in his mind. *A trail of blood right to your front door.*

His surroundings swam back into focus. Juh-Jason no longer stood in front of him. The lovely Trish had pushed him out of the way.

"Okay, first of all, it's *Tish*, asshole. Not *Trish*."

She slammed the book down on the table. Its wonky leg shook, threatening to spill everything to the floor in a virtually perfect metaphor for how the stutterer's news turned his life upside down in an instant. Torn down the entire delicate façade in a single sentence.

"And *second*—" She leaned over the table, gripping its edge. "—I'd much rather fuck you than fuck myself."

Her words drew looks of shock from the next few people in line, and a *tisk!* from the blue-hair standing directly behind her.

Tish whipped around, her auburn horsetail flipping over her shoulder. "Oh, like you *wouldn't*."

Martin was still too distracted to react. He needed to check his phone. Most mornings he'd watch the news, catching up on the latest celebrity gossip and "weather system" that was supposedly going to kill everyone. He hadn't today. He slept in—he did a lot lately, drinking too much and not writing nearly enough—and was almost late for his own book signing.

He missed the news.

James Barclay. The Witch Hunter.

Escaped. On the loose.

*Trail of blood, Marty.*

Barclay would come for him. Hunt him down. The Witch Hunter had threatened Martin's life several times and Martin couldn't blame him. He'd played fast and loose with the truth to bump up his sales. It worked for Capote, the granddaddy of the genre. It almost worked for Capote *twice*.

He and Barclay had each made a promise. Martin promised to tell the Witch Hunter's unvarnished side of the story. The truth, exactly as Barclay saw it. No matter how crazy it might sound.

The killer only agreed to be interviewed by Martin because of what he called their "kinship." During those several weeks of interviews, he'd been allowed special visiting privileges in the psychiatric facility because of his own infamy, his own special relationship with death.

"Just don't kill this one, pal," a guard said one day with a dry chuckle.

It was meant as a joke, but it hadn't been to Martin, nor to Barclay.

This was their kinship. Martin had taken a life with his own hands, so James Barclay held him in high regard.

In the end, he published things Barclay hadn't agreed to, things which might be considered libelous if they were written about anyone other than a convicted murderer. Additions the publisher may have requested, but mostly he'd decided to add on his own, because he was aware of the requirements of the market.

Readers of true crime books were savvy, with reality television and procedural crime dramas and 24-hour news. They expected not only to read about *motivation* but *criminal profiling*.

They wanted to hear about the killer's troubled childhood. His bedwetting, his shyness around women, his propensity to torture small animals.

Sheila Tanner, the criminal psychologist who testified during the Barclay trial as an expert witness, had given Martin plenty to work with. But he'd known his readers would want more.

They wanted to hear about molestation and cigarette burns and mothers who prostituted themselves to pay the bills. Things that might not exonerate the murderers of their crimes, but had shaped them into the monsters society deemed should be kept behind bars for the rest of their lives, or put to death.

He gave his readers what they craved. Much more than was necessary. He'd spoken to Barclay's childhood bullies and his estranged mother, his teachers, the men he'd served with in Vietnam, the local police where he'd grown up.

What James Barclay had promised Martin was a sequel. During the last visit, after the promotional book tour and all the TV interviews, Barclay guaranteed enough material for a second *Witch Hunter* book, which Martin would write with a knife at his throat.

It would be Martin's curtain call, the killer said. A posthumous success.

"An' while the ink's still dryin," Barclay told him, presumably thinking Martin wrote his books with a pen or a typewriter, "I'll cut off yer balls and choke you to death with the cord."

Martin's gaze fell on the girl's breasts, swelling toward him with each hot, angry breath. The ankh shifting between them. The cinnamon smell of her gum made him think of mummification. Ancient Egyptians had used cinnamon during the process, he'd read once. The Pharaohs were believed to live forever. The ankh symbolized their belief in eternal life.

*Nobody lives forever*, he thought.

And on the heels of that: *They'll catch Barclay before he gets to me.*

Still, he needed to be cautious. The book tour dates and venues were easily accessible on his website. Each of them was only a few hours' drive from the Central New York Psychiatric Center in Marcy from which Barclay had somehow escaped.

The killer could easily be on his way to Harrisburg or Scranton or Reading while Martin sat here peddling his wares to the rubes.

He could be lying in wait in some cheap hotel room—much like the one Martin's agent had booked him in, a mere six blocks from the bookstore—waiting to spring his trap.

Would Barclay cut off his balls, as promised? Would he use them as a garrote to throttle the life out of him? Or would he use whatever was handy—a tire iron, a candlestick, a pair of scissors—as Martin had when the Mirror Man slipped on the mask and turned to reveal himself?

He wouldn't know until the moment came. It was the not-knowing that filled him with cold dread, like a man on Death Row never told how or when he'd be executed.

Just one day—*surprise!*—death by emasculation.

*That's life though, isn't it? You never know when you're gonna buy a ticket. Never even sure what the ride's gonna be until you're at the top about to plummet.*

He made a mental note to jot down that thought—or something with a touch more gravitas—into his phone.

Then he answered the girl.

"Give me a minute."

---

MARTIN LAY on his back on the ugly covers of the hard, springy hotel bed, wearing nothing but his wristwatch. He needed a distraction from his thoughts, and as distractions went, Tish—whose full name was Letitia May Cotton, just about as *Hee Haw* as you could get—wasn't half bad.

They made out in the litter-filled alley behind Eugene's Magic Beans and Books. She kneaded his balls—still happily intact—as he drove them back to the hotel.

More sloppy kissing and fondling in the stairs up to the room, interrupted by the sudden presence of a maid carrying a vacuum in the hall, who looked like she'd rather be anywhere else in that moment. Inside the room, they dry-humped on the bed until Tish tore her lips free and announced she had to "tinkle."

He was getting antsy, watching his hard-on dwindle, and was about to reach for his phone to check the news when the bathroom door finally opened.

"I've got a surprise for you," she said in singsong, still behind the bathroom door.

*About fucking time*, he thought.

She stepped out sideways, one bare leg kicked out like a chorus girl's. Just the sight of her lean, tanned profile got him throbbing back to half-mast. One tit pressed against the door, ass against the jamb, she slipped something over her head.

*What is that, a stocking? A latex hood?*

He was never big on kink, but at least one part of him was intrigued, stretching to its full length.

Something glittered on the surface of the—*hood? mask?*—while her face was still hidden. She raised her head to show him his surprise.

His own shocked face reflected back at him on the dozens of tiny mirrors covering her face.

He tasted blood. Must have bit his tongue as he crawled backwards on the mattress and struck his head on the wall.

"Take that fucking thing off!"

"Oh, come on, silly!" The mirrors moved with her lips, though her mouth wasn't visible beneath the mask. "It'll be fun. You could wear it instead, if you wanna."

"Take it *off*," he said again, not daring to look at her, to see himself reflected in the contours of her head. To see his guilt reflected back at him.

She slipped off the replica mirror mask and shook out her hair. "Party pooper." She almost laid it on the dresser, then reconsidered. "If you let me wear the mask, I'll let you put it wherever you like."

"I'm not gonna put it anywhere with you wearing that—that *thing*."

"Fine."

She laid the mask on the dresser, beside his portfolio bag and the hotel bible. It tinkled like a swinging chandelier, the same sound it made when Nico Damiani slumped face-first on the rolltop desk in the antique shop's back office.

The girl climbed over him and hovered over his groin, a sly grin curling her lips. Like she had something over him now that she knew how scared the mask had made him.

He pushed her head downward to avoid her scrutinizing gaze. She put up no resistance, taking him swiftly into her mouth. Her scalp was clean and pale. Auburn hair parted in the center. His mind relaxed as his body stiffened.

His cell phone made a chittering buzz like an insect against a still-wrapped condom on the bedside table. He sat up abruptly, unintentionally shoving himself hard down Tish's throat.

She gagged and fell back on her calves as he snagged the phone. If she expected sympathy, he had none to give. And maybe she deserved a little pain after what she'd put him through with the mask, which he could still see beside the bible. He was just glad she hadn't instinctually bitten down.

"Sorry," he said. "I've gotta take this."

He slid his thumb across the screen and put it to his ear while the pain in his groin subsided to a dull, not-entirely-unpleasant throb.

Tish wiped her lower lip and sat up with an angry animal grunt. She lit the joint he'd left half-smoked on the bedside table.

"Savage," he said into the phone, passing an irritated glance at the girl, who was sucking down his best shit as eagerly as she'd sucked on him. A long silence passed. "Hello?" The sudden edginess in his voice made him sound like a nervous old woman.

"They let him escape, Martin. *They let him escape.*"

He recognized Sheila Tanner's voice straight away, could even tell she was drunk. *I should've called her first. She should be here instead of Trish or Tish or whatever her name is.*

"That better be your mom," the girl said behind him, sullen with jealousy. Martin raised a finger very close to her face to shut her up. She slapped it away.

"I heard." He spoke calmly into the phone, though his heartbeat had quickened at the fear in Sheila's voice.

James Barclay had murdered three pregnant women, each in a different state, each the victim of a rape months prior to their deaths. No evidence had linked Barclay to the rapes, though it had been deemed inconsequential in the jury's eyes since the larger crimes were the murders of mother and child.

The state of New York put Barclay away six years ago. His lawyer had convinced him to plead not guilty by reason of insanity. Based on Sheila's expert testimony, the jury had believed Barclay was insane. Rather than serve out his sentence in prison, he'd been placed in the Central New York Psychiatric Center, instead of the "S" block of the Mid-State Correctional Facility just down the road, where Martin believed he should have been sent, insane or not.

"Do you know how it happened? How he got out?"

"He just never showed up for his meds last night." Her voice was thick with tears. "He just vanished."

"Last night? When did *you* hear?"

He struggled to keep from sounding shaken. To not accuse her of withholding life-and-death information, particularly since he could be accused of the same.

He'd never forgotten Barclay's promise. And Sheila hadn't forgotten the promise Barclay had made her.

"An hour ago." She let out a big, shuddering sigh. "Two, maybe. I've been drinking—"

"I could tell."

A pause on the other end.

"Do you need me to come back?"

The girl slapped his shoulder hard enough to sting. He threw a fierce glare over his shoulder and she shrank back against the pillows. The ankh rattled between her perky breasts.

"I don't think that's a good idea, Martin," Sheila said some two-hundred miles away. He knew what she meant without her having to say it. She was vulnerable. In such a state, anything could happen between them.

Not that he wanted things to change. The way they'd left things after *Witch Hunter* was finally released, he couldn't imagine ever falling back into that easy, comfortable and somehow still crazy-hot relationship they had during the trial and the few months afterwards. It was only by the skin of Sheila's teeth they were able to remain friends after the book launch.

Their unique bond, that Barclay wanted them both dead, kept them on speaking terms.

"Finish the tour," she said resolutely.

"I've only got two more shops," he said, meaning he could easily cancel if she needed him. "These shit-pit towns, Sheila. You wouldn't believe the wackos I've met here."

Tish gave him the finger, pressing it right up against his nose to be sure he saw it.

"Are you sure you'll be all right?" he asked, using the absolute last of his patience to ignore the finger until she pulled it away out of boredom.

Sheila uttered another trembling sigh. "I'll be fine. Stay safe, okay?"

"You too."

Before he could say goodbye, he heard the click of her cradling the phone.

He put his cell back on the dresser and snatched the joint from the girl's pursed lips. He dragged deeply, aware the high would only amplify his paranoia and not caring, only craving a temporary release from the jangling of his nerves.

"Asshole," Tish muttered, her eyes red and glassy.

He took another long pull. Held the smoke in his lungs, feeling his heartbeat slow to a dull thud.

"So who was that bitch, anyway?"

"The asshole repairman," he said, exhaling a lungful of smoke. "Apparently my warranty's up."

# CHAPTER 2

## CHAPTER AND VERSE

PENNSYLVANIA IN OCTOBER and another snowy, relatively busy day, this time at the Dusty Corner bookstore in Reading—pronounced Redding, not as Martin thought, which possibly explained the small turnout.

Every time the door chime rang—*tinkled*, he thought, remembering what Tish said before she used the bathroom—he imagined Barclay stepping in, his country swagger more pronounced by the limp allegedly caused by shrapnel he caught in Vietnam. He'd be wearing dirty blue jeans, an open-throat, Roy Rogers-style Western shirt and an off-white sport jacket, a dusty rose handkerchief folded neatly in its breast pocket. He'd likely have on something heavier for the weather over top, probably a thick corduroy jacket with a wide shearling collar. A miasma of English Leather aftershave and cigarettes would precede his entrance.

He scrutinized every tall, slender man who walked through the door with dread, limp or not, until the face became visible in the overhead lights. Only then would he allow himself a sigh of relief.

After little over an hour, signing autograph after autograph, scanning every unfamiliar face in the crowd, a wiry, wild-eyed man in the front of the line held out a copy of *Witch Hunter*. "I like your book," the man said. "S'good."

Martin sized him up. Dead incisor on the right side of his mouth, tobacco-stained fingers, long, neat fingernails, and a single long hair below his Adam's apple the razor hadn't caught, suggesting dirty mirrors, bad eyesight, or just plain indifference.

"Thank you. That's the most concise literary acclaim I've ever received. Do you mind if I quote you on the cover of my next book?"

The man considered what to say, then shrugged. "Nup."

"Great. You know, if brevity really is the soul of wit, you could be the next Dave Barry."

"My name's Dave."

Martin laughed gregariously and scribbled *Dave, Such a rare pleasure speaking with you!* He signed his name below and handed it back.

The man puzzled over it. He looked up with his brow furrowed. "That s'posed to be a joke?"

Martin held up his hands, playing innocent. "Just being nice."

"*This* is not nice." The man held up his book, jabbing a yellowed finger at it. "This is fuckin *smarmy*. And if it's a fuckin joke, I don't think it's very funny, either."

"You're holding up the line, sir," a young Asian guy with messy hair and a Gor-Tex hooded coat said.

Dave slapped the book down and gripped the table's smooth sides with his thick, yellow fingers, leaning in very close.

Martin cringed, not out of fear but from the man's breath, its sweet chemical reek of ketoacidosis and charred tobacco. He was rubbing the thumb of his right hand on the palm of his left in concentric circles, a nervous habit he'd had as far back as he could remember. When he noticed it, he stopped, ashamed, like a child caught sucking his thumb in public.

"You think you're so fuckin smart 'cause you strung a few words together I coulda just looked up on the innernet?" Frothy saliva pooled at the corner of his lips. "*Huh*, funny man?"

"You're holding up the line, sir!"

"I wuddn't askin you, shithead!" He didn't even bother to turn, but the kid in the Gore-Tex coat shrank back as if dodging a blow. Angry Dave shook the table. Stacks of books slid and toppled. "*Is that what you think?*"

The crowd gasped. Nobody knew what to do aside from

looking at each other to see if anyone would be brave enough to intervene. The rest stared stiffly at the altercation.

Martin racked his brain, looking for a way out without ingratiating himself to the man. He'd poked the bear and gotten its teeth, but he still had a reputation to live up to. Some of these people thought of him as Martin "Killer" Savage, and despite his hate for the insult it did carry a bit of cachet.

Suddenly, the man began to shake and jerk as if he'd been struck by a seizure. His eyes bugged out, his Elmer Fudd hat flaps flopping until the hat fell off his head.

Martin marveled for a moment, wondering if he'd done it with his mind the way he used to think he could kill ants just by looking at them. Then the man buckled at the knees and fell sideways onto the floor.

Tish stood behind him, gawping at the Taser in her hand with shocked amusement as if she hadn't expected the result she got.

"Security! All clear!" She turned to the stunned crowd with an all-business attitude, the arms of her big winter jacket swishing. "Y'uns probably wanna step back. He's gonna be pissed when he gets up."

Martin stood and started a round of applause that traveled to the back of the room.

When Angry Dave stood up shakily, with Tish's hand at his elbow, the man was so stunned and confused he started clapping himself as she walked him right out the door.

"That chick just straight-up Katnissed his ass," the kid in the Gore-Tex coat said, setting his hardback copy of *Mirror Man* on the table. "You get to hang around that every day?"

Martin peered through the shop front windows, where Tish was placing the man's hat back on his head and speaking very close in his ear. Angry Dave nodded, and nodded once more at whatever she said next. Then she sent him on his wobbly way.

When she caught Martin's eye, she twiddled her fingers at him in an ain't-I-cute way.

"Apparently, I do," he told the kid.

A FEW HOURS after the signing in Reading, they lay naked and sweating on the covers of yet another uncomfortable motel bed, this one in Bethlehem. Tish had followed him since she heard about James Barclay's escape. She caught the news while on the late shift at her local hospital, what she called "working a night turn," doing her internship for Duquesne University's School of Nursing.

She caught up with him in Harrisburg. "Worried to hell," she said. She'd taken a couple of days off, making it her mission to protect him. Whether she'd followed him in spite of the way he treated her or because of it, like a beaten puppy too loyal or too stupid not to come running when its master needed help, he didn't know.

*Daddy must have done a job on her*, he thought.

"Where'd you get that thing, anyway?"

"What? Tansy?"

"You gave your Taser a name?"

"You named your dick, dintcha?"

He grinned. "Fair enough."

"This friend of mine got raped on campus one time." She took a puff off the joint he'd rolled. "After that, it seemed like girls were getting ascared of their own shadows. I didn't wanna be afraid all the time like them all. I asked my daddy what to do, so he got me Tansy."

"It's pretty cool of your father to do that for you."

"That's what dad's do, isn't it? Protect their kids?"

He shrugged, faking indifference. In his house Aunt Norma had protected him. He supposed if his father had been around, it might have been different. But his father had left long before Martin was born, and he'd grown up without a paternal influence at all.

*Daddy did a job on me*, he thought.

He meant it as a joke but it felt more like self-pity.

"I'm gonna tinkle," Tish said, pushing up from the bed.

He watched her walk, enjoying the sight as the folds beneath her ass cheeks vanished and reappeared. He got up and padded over the coarse carpeting to the bottle of bourbon he'd left beside the two complimentary plastic cups provided by the motel. He thought about throwing on a towel and getting some ice from the machine outside, but his hard-on would be difficult to miss even under the plush fabric. There were at least two families staying here at the Firefly Motor Court.

He poured two fingers and sipped it casually, glancing at Tish's clothes scattered on the floor. The lacy purple bra and mismatched black thong. The black tights and gray wool winter socks. Her boots, long, flat-soled black things she'd kicked off at the door, lying beside his brown leather jodhpur boots.

He turned to the dresser and saw the Gideon's bible had been opened.

It was in the top drawer when he left for the bookstore. He always checked for the Bible. Made sure the phone worked. Checked if there was cable. These were small rituals he performed in every hotel room. Rituals that helped provide the illusion of safety. A sense of home and place.

Whoever left the Bible open had underlined several passages. The motel pen lay on the motel stationary, where they'd scribbled to be sure the pen worked before marking up the Good Book:

*10 There shall not be found among you any one that maketh his son or his daughter to pass through the fire, or that useth divination, or an observer of times, or an enchanter, or a witch, 11 Or a charmer, or a consulter with familiar spirits, or a wizard, or a necromancer. 12 For all that do these things are an abomination unto the LORD: and because of these abominations the LORD thy God doth drive them out from before thee.*

Color flushed his cheeks. He went to the bathroom door, a twinge of fear gnawing at him. "Tish?" Water was running inside. He thought of Leviticus's "unclean woman" as he rapped on the door.

"Just having a li'l warsh!" Her Pennsylvania accent made him wince, like when she told him she'd "redded up" the previous hotel room instead of tidied.

"Did you move the Gideon's?"

"*The what?*"

"The Bible."

"Why would I move the Gideon's?" she said over the pattering water.

He returned to the dresser. Picked the phone and dialed for the front desk.

"Firefly Motor Court," a cheery male voice said. "How can I direct your call?"

"Yeah, hi, it's Martin Savage from room 6." There was a jitter in his voice he didn't like. "This might sound weird, but, uh... the Bible is open on the dresser and somebody's marked it all up."

"Oh dear." The desk clerk sounded considerably less cheery.

"Yeah. So I'm wondering if maybe the cleaning staff—?"

"Oh no, Mr. Savage, it's against company policy for our chambermaids to touch or remove anything which may belong to our guests 'til they've checked out. Besides that, Candy hasn't done your room yet this morning. Said you left the Do Not Disturb sign on your door."

"Well, somebody did it, and it wasn't me—"

*Barclay.*

An ice-cold sliver of fear ran up his spine. The hand holding the phone to his ear felt clammy, his arm suddenly very heavy. He wanted nothing more than to be done with this call, curl up in bed with the warm bottle of Heaven Hill. He fumbled with the receiver, the front desk clerk apologizing until he finally hung up.

Tish stepped out of the bathroom just then, making him jump. She wore a towel around her torso and a smaller one twisted on her head. "Who walked over your grave?"

He pointed to the Bible. The bottle sloshed in his hand.

She bent at the hips to look. She read the passages, mouthing the words. When she'd finished, she said, "Think it was him?"

He swallowed a swig from the bottle, grimacing as it burned its way down his throat. "Who else would it be?"

"Motel staff?"

"Front desk said nobody's come through."

"Some prankster then."

He shook his head with an annoyed huff.

"Well, I don't know, Marty, *jeez*—"

"Don't call me that, okay? I hate it when people call me that."

"Sor-*ry.*"

"It was *him*, Tish. You know it could only be him."

She squinted out the curtains.

The parking lot led to the highway. Beyond was an industrial park, a series of low buildings, brown grass and intersecting roads, everything dusted with snow. Transmission towers stood in the distance below a gray scud of clouds.

Tish turned back, looking him in the eye. "Then it's a good thing you're leaving." She patted his ass to get him moving.

———

He put Pennsylvania in the rearview in under an hour, driving the Interstate to avoid city traffic in Allentown and Bethlehem, crossing the Delaware into Jersey.

Instinct took over as he drove, his conscious mind already miles ahead, eager to get back to his desk. Writing was a compulsion for him, as much as booze and sex. Likely more.

Another small town fell behind him in the rearview. Their Anglican church came up on his right, its white barnwood façade lit by the last dim glare of the sun. The sign out front quoted the famous line from the poet Alexander Pope: *TO ERR IS HUMAN TO FORGIVE DIVINE.*

*Could they forgive Barclay?* he wondered, his gaze returning to the darkening road before him, white lines bright against the winter sunset. *Could they forgive* me?

He often thought about the families of Jessica Renault, Tina Wozinski and Paula Danlon. During the trial, they were vocal in their hatred of James Barclay. They declined to be interviewed for *Witch Hunter*, but he wondered if they'd have something to say to him now.

Only Paula Danlon's mother had spoken out about the release of the book, calling it "salt on a wound," and "the Devil's book." He respected her for it and wanted to tell her, but she would never give him the chance. Not to the man who'd had her daughter's corpse "strung up on a flagpole and paraded" across North America on book tours and daytime talk shows.

And what would telling her accomplish besides clearing his own conscience?

His phone rang on the dash. He answered it hands-free: "Savage."

"Martin! My favorite fucking writer!"

The last person he wanted to hear from was his agent, Qurban Youssef. The man was damn good at his job, but he drove Martin crazy sometimes with his badgering and special requests.

"How did you make out, my friend?"

"Hey, Qurban. Made out okay. Got a trunkload of empty boxes and a nice fat wallet full of cash."

"That's good, that's good." Without a pause, he added, "Even *Dead Weight*?"

"Every copy." In truth he paid out of pocket for a stack of ten hardbacks and left them in a box outside a library in Reading. But Qurban didn't need to know that.

"Amazing!"

"Don't act like I made the Statue of Liberty disappear."

"Ha ha, yes, I knew you could do it, Martin. I knew it." He left a pregnant pause.

"What's on your mind, Qurban? I hear the gears turning."

Qurban sighed heavily. "I suppose you've heard—"

"I know. Barclay's sprung the joint."

"'Sprung the joint'? What is this, an Americanism?" The agent clucked his tongue. "I don't like it. It sounds—I don't know. Too Dashiell Hammett. Vulgar."

"Leave the critique for my editor."

The agent laughed. "Yes, okay. Listen, my friend. You know I would take the bullet for you myself, if I could. You know this, right?"

"You're being a little melodramatic, aren't you?"

"Okay, I wouldn't take a bullet. But I'd thrust you out swiftly of its path. I bet he's not even worried about you. He's on a bus to Tijuana right now. Over the border and out of mind, with any luck."

"With any luck," Martin agreed.

"Listen, Martin, I know this may sound opportunistic, but this situation could be the best thing to happen since you met that crazy prick with the mask."

"What do you mean?"

He knew full well what Qurban meant. He'd thought it himself less than an hour ago. If fresh blood were to run, it would mean more meat for his hungry public. Enough to fuel a sequel. Two books. Three.

*Witch Hunter* had been his most profitable book right out the gate, even somewhat well-received critically. Something about the murders of unborn children appealed to people on a gut level. Maybe because it was a safe space to continue the Great American Abortion Debate without provoking too much partisan fury on either side.

Only a psychopath could believe the deliberate murder of a child *in utero* without consent of the mother, and the murder of the mother herself, was anything less than an abomination. Atrocities like that put food on the table for a good many people, from journalists to lawyers to the people who built the caskets.

"*Witch Hunter* was a pretty successful book, Martin," Qurban said playfully. "Successful? Shit, it put braces on my youngest. It's paying my eldest's way through college. He'll be a doctor soon because of that fucking book."

"You must be proud."

"You're damn right I'm proud! I'll be even more proud when they finally make it into a movie. Several hundred-thousand dollars proud."

"And now you're hoping there could be a sequel."

"Hey, you said it, Martin. I didn't say anything, did I?"

"You do realize what he intends to do to me, right?"

"Not to *you*, my friend! Just a little murder. One or two." Martin could picture his agent bobbling his head from side to side noncommittally. "Maybe if we're lucky he kills himself when he's done, or perhaps the police gun him down in a shootout, and it's broadcast all over the networks and the video goes viral, you never know—"

A horn blast startled Martin. The road had been empty, but a black car with a monster grill crept up behind him during the call, and now it was riding his tail.

It moved jerkily back and forth like a big black insect. The headlights were off, but there was still enough light in the sky to see. The dome light illuminated the hooded silhouette of the driver through the tinted windshield. Its only occupant. Gloved hands gripped the wheel.

"Hit some traffic?" Qurban asked.

Martin sped up. The car behind matched his speed, an old Lincoln Continental or a Grand Marquis. The type of car only old men drove these days. It was as if the car had attached itself to his rear bumper.

"Some asshole on my tail," he said distractedly. "Road's empty, I don't know why he doesn't just—"

"*Oh no.*"

"It's *not* Barclay."

But that was exactly what he'd been dreading: that Barclay had caught up to him in a moment of distraction. That he'd run him off the road and fulfill his promise, strangling him to death with his own severed testicles. He wasn't even sure such a thing was possible, but he didn't want to be first to find out.

"Don't be an idiot," he told himself. Of course, it wasn't possible.

"Idiot? Why? What are you doing?"

"I'm gonna flag him past."

"Are you crazy? What if it's *him*?"

"It's *not* him." Martin rolled down his window. He eased off the gas and threw out his left arm, waving for the driver to pass.

"What's happening?"

The driver fell back, swerving back and forth, big black tires spinning on the snowy road.

"Relax, Qurban. You're making me crazy as catshit."

"'Crazy as catshit'? Another silly Americanism. Don't make jokes, Martin, this is serious business."

The Lincoln jerked out into the other lane. The engine roared as it crept up alongside the Lexus. The passenger window zipped down and the driver, a bald man creeping toward old age, duded-up in a hooded winter coat, threw Martin the middle finger before ripping by, tires spitting clods of gray slush.

Martin relaxed his grip on the steering wheel and slumped back a little in his seat. He let the speedometer drop into the low 40s.

"Martin? Are you dead?"

He jumped at Qurban's voice. His shoulder caught on the seatbelt, tearing into his skin. The agent sounded terrified. As if his one and only meal-ticket had just driven off the road in a fiery crash, though he had several high-profile clients.

"Please tell me you're not dead."

"Jesus, Qurban! You would've heard something if I was dead, wouldn't you?"

"Not if he used a silenced pistol. Or what if the car was a distraction, and the real Barclay was crouched in your backseat waiting to spring his trap?"

"I'm hanging up now."

"Hey, these are great ideas I'm firing at you, Martin. Don't discount them. Let's do lunch when you get back to the city. The Writing Room? My treat."

"Why the hell not? Your optimism always puts me in a sunny mood."

---

His keycard was missing.

He kept it in his wallet, nestled behind a thick stack of business cards from people he barely remembered. Easy enough to slip out of his pocket and swipe at the door, the elevator.

But it wasn't there. The business cards were, but the keycard was gone.

*Must've fallen out somewhere.*

*Stolen,* his paranoid amygdala countered. *You know it was stolen. Don't be obtuse.*

He knocked on the glass. Inside, a security guard he didn't recognize rose from a chair behind the desk and looked at him quizzically. Martin pointed at the maglock and the guard shrugged indifferently. The door clicked, and Martin pushed his way inside.

"You live in the building?" the guard asked. He was mid-fifties, salt-and-pepper hair, with a diamond crucifix earring that seemed oddly out of place against his grizzled face

"Savage, Martin."

The guard looked it up on the terminal.

"That's a nice earring."

The guard looked up, seemingly mystified, then grinned sheepishly. "Got it pierced in the service. I lost the stud the other day. Thought I'd keep it from closing up with one of my granddaughter's."

"It's a good look."

The guard chuckled. "Go on up, Mr. Savage. I'll buzz you through."

"Thanks."

The elevator doors opened as he approached. He thumbed the button for his floor. As the doors closed, he saw the guard look up expectantly. Martin waved, and the man gave him an amiable nod.

His condo was done in a spartan style, all chrome and eggshell-white plastic and black leather. He'd never been much on interior design, and let the man he'd hired do pretty much whatever, even hang the wire chandelier Martin hated that looked like a bright, fuzzy ball over the dining room table.

He sat on the sofa and watched the news, eating breakfast for dinner, until a story came on about Barclay's escape. Then he turned off the TV and went to the liquor cabinet. Poured a generous glass of bourbon and took it to bed.

It was early still, but after the morning sex, the long drive, the scare at the bookstore and another on the road, he felt okay about crashing before the evening news.

The tour had been short, but had taken its toll. He wasn't a salesman by nature. The job required it, but he found it draining. Faking geniality all day took a lot out of him, yet another thing he had in common with the killers he wrote about.

He was under the covers, getting toasty warm, when something he'd noticed but hadn't had the mental fortitude to process came back to him like a kick in the guts.

As he'd entered the condo he'd dropped his keys, kicked off his boots and struggled out of his jacket, but he hadn't paid attention to the objects on the side table by the door.

The mail to be redirected. The bills to be paid. The little dish he'd put there for pocket change, the pen left in it. The book.

Not simply *a* book: *The* Book.

He flipped the covers off and jumped out of bed, crossed the plush shag rug to the long, white hall with its bare walls—so unlike the homes he'd shared with his aunt Norma, even with his mother before she'd lost her mind, covered with photographs and paintings—and out into the living area.

The book was still on the side table: the *Good* Book. *His* Good Book.

Raised by superstitious Aunt Norma—who was actually his mother's good friend, not a blood relative—he'd grown up be lieving in angels and demons and the eternal fires of Hell that awaited him if he chose to step off the straight and narrow path.

These days he considered himself more an agnostic than a lapsed Catholic. Either way, he no longer believed in Aunt Norma's fairy tales. If pressed, he couldn't pinpoint an exact incident that led to this change of heart, nor if it had been a conscious decision at all. The countless childhood hours spent dreading an Omnipotent Man in the Sky, who saw and heard everything, *knew* everything, even his darkest secrets and thoughts—at some point in his life between then and adulthood, he'd decided he no longer had the need nor fear of a God.

The Bible he kept on a bookshelf with technical manuals and his old encyclopedias was for research. It came in handy in his dealings with serial killers, particularly James Barclay. Checking for bibles in motel rooms was a holdover from his youth, before he and Norma had settled down in Connecticut, a habit he often wondered if it was ironic or superstitious.

Now here was his own bible on the entry table, opened to Deuteronomy.

And there were the same three passages underlined as the Gideon in the Firefly Motor Court: *son, sorcerer, dead, abomination.*

# CHAPTER 3

## WITCH HUNTER

MARTIN DIDN'T CALL the police. He called Sheila Tanner.

He buzzed her up to his condo a little over half an hour later. While she cabbed from Manhattan, he washed off the stink of fear sweat and threw on a plush robe. He was half drunk when he opened the door. Her overcoat was much too thin for such a brisk night, her high cheekbones flushed from the cold. She was beautiful and unattainable and looked him over briefly with a scowl.

"Don't say it," he said.

She grinned, flipping her long, dirty-blond curls off her shoulders to remove her coat. The many bangles on her wrists jingled. "You know me too well." He took her coat and threw it on a hook. "Well?" she said. "Where is it?"

He tipped his head toward the entry table, where the King James Bible lay opened to the page Barclay had marked. Sheila knelt to study it. She knew better not to kneel in front of him, particularly when he was half-naked. It almost felt like a dare.

"Uh-huh. This is exactly his style." She reached to flip the page. Martin snagged her arm. She tensed, throwing an anxious, upset look up at him.

He let her go, shrugging. "They've already got one set of prints to rule out. Better not make it two."

She let her arm relax and returned her gaze to the table. A ballpoint pen lay in the change dish. "Was this pen here?"

"I think so. Sometimes it's there, sometimes it's in the kitchen."

She snatched the bottle from his hand and placed it on the table. "You've had enough. We're gonna need at least a few working cells in that brain of yours to sort through all your junk."

He led her to the bedroom, though she already knew the way. "You remember the last time we walked down this hall together?"

She sighed behind him. "I didn't come here to talk about things that ended a long, long time ago, Martin."

He grinned over his shoulder, trying to provoke her. They continued down the hall, to the closet that had been mirrored until shortly after the incident with Nico Damiani, when looking into mirrors in the dead of night had gotten to be too much for him.

The wheels squeaked as he opened the closet door. He kept meaning to oil them but had never gotten around to it. On a high shelf were several cardboard boxes of old research. He reached up and snagged one down, then set it on the floor with a jangle of plastic.

"This one's all James Barclay. It's everything I've got on the sick little puppy."

Sheila gave him a look. She saw right through his false bravado. He was terrified and she knew it.

She didn't even need to tell him. She knew that too.

Martin found it both comforting and terrifying to be known so well. To know someone as well as he knew her. He'd spent his entire life keeping people—especially women—at arm's length. He'd never even visited the same barber twice. During one of their last arguments Sheila had suggested it was his fear of abandonment. Martin wasn't so sure, but he'd let her have the win if only to stop from fighting all night.

Diving into the box, he pulled out photocopies of Barclay's criminal records, including the mug shots they'd taken the two times he'd been arrested prior to his multiple murder charges. One for DUI and another for assault and battery, both when

Barclay was much younger. He'd worn a real slick wide-collared shirt in one of them. Looked like a carbon-copy Roy Rogers.

Beneath these was a stack of small cassettes held together with a rubber band, copies of Sheila's interviews and originals of his own, along with pages of court transcript. He brought his notebook to the bed, rubbing his right thumb on the old scar on his left palm in a circular motion while leafing through it.

"'Juvenile record expunged,'" he read. "Is it true about serial killers and bedwetting? I only ask because I know a certain someone who wet the bed until she was eight."

Sheila swatted his leg with a manila folder. "I never should have introduced you to my parents."

"'No signs of sexual contact on the bodies,'" he continued. "'Three different modes of death: vehicular manslaughter with victim's own car—'"

He thought about the car earlier that night, the big old Lincoln, and he shivered despite the bedroom's warmth. If it really had been Barclay, he wouldn't be sitting on his bed with Sheila Tanner at his feet. He'd be dead in a ditch, one of Aunt Norma's favorite phrases, as in: *For all I knew, you could've been dead in a ditch.*

Suddenly Barclay's jocular Southern twang filled the room: "Sixes and nines, the yin and the yang. The man eats the woman and the woman eats the man—"

Martin leaned over her shoulder and flicked off the tape player, his heart drumming staccato. He knew he'd eventually have to listen to that voice again, but he hadn't been prepared for how he would react. He tasted blood. The bite on his tongue from earlier must have split open.

Sheila looked up at him from the floor. "You okay?"

"I'm fine. Just give me a second, okay?"

"I know how you feel."

"Barclay didn't threaten to *kill* you."

"No, that's true. But he did say he'd send me your genitals in a box, and that's a pretty frightening image too."

"Ha." He nodded toward the tape player. "All right. Do it."

She thumbed the Fast-Forward button, then hit Play again. This time it was her own voice, relaxed and comforting. A therapist's voice if he'd ever heard one. "And you believe you had the right to kill those women."

"It's my *purpose*," Barclay said. "It's what I was put here to do."

"Meaning?"

A long pause. The tape whirred. Cold wind from the river whipped against the outside of the building, thumping on the windows.

Finally, Barclay laughed. Cackled, really.

"Well, I don't know. I ain't particularly religious. My mother was Southern Baptist, I believe, but Daddy... he didn't need no church to be spiritual. I b'lieve my daddy always looked down on Mama for that. I 'member one time he told me she was weak. A weak-minded woman, he said. That she needed Jesus to carry her like she was a cripple. Only the way he meant it was *emotionally* crippled, y'understand. Not handicapped."

Sheila murmured noncommittally.

"I s'pose some of her old-time religion musta rubbed off on ol' Jimmy, though," he said, speaking in the third person as he often did. "Ol' Gimme Jimmy. Apple don't fall far from the tree, they say, even if that tree is crazy as catshit."

*Crazy as catshit.* Qurban had asked Martin if the phrase was an Americanism when he'd said it in the car.

But it wasn't. It was a Barclayism.

*And I didn't even remember where it came from*, he thought. *It's a part of me now.*

"Yeah," Barclay said thoughtfully, responding to something Sheila must have said. "Yeah, you're not like most women, are you, Doc? You *understand* things. You git it. See, most women, they think with their emotions, which means they ain't *thinkin* at all. Women feel. Men reason."

A slight pause, filled with an off-mic response from Sheila, barely a murmur. Sitting at Martin's feet, Sheila shook her head derisively.

"Oh, you can sneer, but it's a stereotype because there's some truth to it. We're built that way, ain't no fault of our own. It's in our genetic make-up. Our *DNA*," he said with a sarcastically reverential vibe. "But we aim to deny that. See, women want equality, but they don't want the price that comes with it. Don't expect chivalry with equal rights. And there's no battered woman syndrome, not 'less there's a battered man syndrome, which I'm liable to think there *ain't*. And *girls*—you look at the schoolyard these days and tell me they aren't just about as messed up as you ever seen a boy. How's *that* for equality, huh?"

"As women rise into positions of power," Sheila said, audible now, as though she'd moved closer to the recorder, "it's natural they should share the same afflictions as men. There are studies that show a significant portion of both men and women in the business and political world suffer from a range of sociopathic tendencies, from narcissism to delusions of grandeur. Even paranoia."

"I don't know about that," Barclay said dismissively. "What I do know is that this idea people have, women in particular, that we'd all be better off if women called the shots..." He fell into a high-pitched impersonation: "If women were in charge, there would be no war. There would be no poverty, no famine, and we'd all live together in peace and love and harmony."

He laughed, reverting to his normal voice, suddenly furious. "Well, I call bullshit! Where's the proof of that, Doc? I defy you to show me a matrilineal culture that's not just as fucked up, if not more fucked up, than any phallocentric society in the history of the world!"

"I'm not an anthropologist."

The sound of him rising from his chair was as loud as a car crash. "You're goddamn right you ain't!"

"Again, Mr. Barclay, I'm going to have to ask you to sit down."

"All right, all right. No need to get emotional."

Martin could just make out Barclay's snicker under the sound of his shackles jingling, the chair scraping against the floor as he righted it.

"I mean, that's what this is all about—this feminization, this *gynefication*, this Lorena Bobbitting of society. And you, Doc, you're the heart of the beast: you and your colleagues. *Psychiatry*," he said with unrestrained contempt, "is the huge swingin Mother's teat of the Modern Age, coddling and pacifying these —these *children* in grown-up bodies. You talk it over, you dispense the medicine and you kiss all the ouchies away. But we never really *learn* nothin for ourselves, do we? We always need more help. It's an addiction. It's *chiropractic for the soul*."

"Say what you will about him," Sheila said from the floor, "his sermons could give Charles Manson a run for his money."

"You mentioned earlier—" she said, this time on the tape. A pause as she leafed through her notes. "You said it was your *obligation* to murder those women. Your purpose. Do you think you can tell me about that now?"

"I s'pose you heard of the Bantu. Them African folk?"

"I believe that's a derogatory term now."

"Be that as it may," Barclay scoffed. "There's this old tradition—musta read about it in a book when I was a young feller, cain't say fer sure—anyhow, there's this tradition where all the females of the tribe, the women and the girls, they all gather in a circle shakin and hollerin, an' this old woman with a big ole headdress on and a long, bloody spear, she's standin in the middle, big brown eyes all bugged-out like a cow 'fore the slaughterhouse, flickin at all them girls with a swatch, dancin and shakin and *leapin* out at em all. Now this tribe calls her the Witch Smeller. And whoever she touches, they drag her off right there an' then an' slaughter her just like an animal."

"A tribal witch hunt," Sheila said, her voice cracking. It was clear the image had shaken her. "A brutal relic of ancient superstition."

"*Not* superstition."

Another brief pause. "You believe these were real witches."

"I ain't *stupid*, woman. There may have been a witch or two among em, but the majority was just reg'lar old scapegoatin. Just another poor little lamb slaughtered to ease the—the *hearts and minds* of the tribe."

"So you think, despite the massive cultural gap, not to mention the huge physical distance between you and these—" She said what followed patronizingly enough for Martin to notice it, and surely enough to rile Barclay. "—these *witch smellers*, that somehow you've acquired this ability, and that the women you've *murdered*, Mr. Barclay—Jessica Renault, Tina Wozinski and Paula Danlon, three *innocent* young women and their unborn children murdered in cold blood—that these girls were in fact *witches*?"

"That is what I believe, correct."

Martin felt his skin crawl as Sheila flicked off the tape and took it out of the player. He knew well enough there were no bogeymen, no witches, warlocks or demons. The true monsters of this world were flesh and blood—men and women who struggled against the darkness in their own hearts and all too often gave in to temptation.

But something about Barclay's tirade had shaken him. It scratched at him, a truth just beyond his reach. He tried to clear his mind, to get a handle on what it was that bothered him, but an image from an old fairy tale popped up in its place: Hansel and Gretel gnawing away at the gingerbread house, oblivious to the ravenous old hag at the window, ready to fatten and then gobble them up.

"The scarf was hers—Paula Danlon's," Sheila said, reading from Martin's notebook. "Forensics pulled a ton of dead skin off it matching her DNA. It was a printed, kind of Jackson Pollack-y thing, splotchy and multicolored." She looked up, firing a hard gaze at him. "I remember Barclay told me the 'deathblow' had to be dealt by something these women owned, that it was the only way they could be..." She squinted, looking toward the Manhattan skyline. "...how did he put it?"

"Vanquished," Martin said, remembering.

"Right. Vanquished."

"You think he literally believed these women were witches? It wasn't just some bullshit he conjured up to stay out of prison?"

"Oh no, these were full-blown delusions. The oddest thing about it was, he considered himself a white knight. The way he saw it, he wasn't trying to eliminate those women at all. He felt he was *releasing* them."

"Meaning?"

"In his mind, they were mercy killings. He told me something that particularly stuck in my head, something that still bothers me. He thought of these women as 'unclean.' He didn't think of them as witches in the fairy tale sense of the word, but in the medieval sense. He believed they'd been..." She looked off for a moment in thought. "That they'd been *defiled* by the Devil."

"The Devil?"

"As in Satan. Mephistopheles. Beelzebub."

The realization struck Martin with the force of a remembered trauma. "So Barclay wasn't after those women at all."

Sheila nodded, grave-faced. "Exactly. That's where you got it wrong, Martin. He was killing their *children*."

# CHAPTER 4

**TRIGGERS**

AFTER SHEILA WENT home, Martin drank himself into a stupor. Thoughts of his impending death—not just a possibility now but a fact—circled his head like water in a drain. He had to flush them out if he wanted to get any sleep at all.

He puked on the Berber shag on his way to the toilet, and passed out around three in the morning on the cold bathroom floor. When he came to just past noon, his right upper arm and cheek were marked with red diamonds from the ceramic tiles.

While espresso brewed in the kitchen he stood under an ice-cold stream from the showerhead. He downed the espresso like a shot before making a second, which he sipped by the living room windows, squinting down at tugboats zigzagging the sun-dappled East River, at yellow cabs crisscrossing the bustle of Manhattan.

He'd have to brave a trip later this afternoon for a magazine interview. The interviewer refused to come to Brooklyn. For now, he had some free time to cure his hangover with carbs and coconut water. Maybe even a nap if he could manage it.

He felt like he could sleep for days, even after the influx of caffeine. But Barclay was still on his mind.

*Enough for a sequel.*

Part of him hoped Barclay was already cutting a bloody

swath on his way to Mexico. That he was anywhere but here. But he knew—he *knew*—the killer was hiding out somewhere in the city, in the tunnels, under a bridge or a byway or in the sewers like a rat. Biding his time, waiting for the police to widen their search upstate and down into Jersey, Maryland and West Virginia, where a man could easily disappear in the Appalachians or the Catskills.

He was waiting for Martin to get complacent. To feel like he was safe.

Then he would resurface, bringing a trail of blood to his door.

The cell phone rang. He crossed to the kitchenette to answer it.

"Mr. Savage," the baritone voice said.

"Speaking."

"It's Detective Lumsden, NYPD Major Crimes. We met before. During the Barclay trial?"

"I remember you."

Lumsden said nothing for a moment, as if waiting for Martin to continue. Then: "I suppose you've heard what happened?"

"Of course, I've fucking heard. Frankly I'm surprised you didn't call me sooner, considering."

"We've had a lot on our hands, as you can imagine." Lumsden sounded on the verge of losing patience. "Nationwide manhunt and all. I just wanted to touch base with you. Let you know we've stationed a man at your building."

"That's not necessary—"

"Look, don't try to be a hero, Mr. Savage. This time the judge might not let you off the hook so easy."

He felt the anger returning. It was Lumsden who'd given him the nickname "Killer," as in "Killer Savage," and once the candid video hit the internet the name stuck. "It was self-defense and you fucking know it," Martin said. "He was wearing the fucking mask—he never would've put on the mask it he wasn't planning to kill me."

"Wrong place wrong time, I get that. And of course, you have every right to defend yourself. You *had* every right. But if you find yourself in a tight spot, you call me. Not 911. *Me*. This is my personal number. Put it in your contacts. Put it on fucking speed dial. Do *not* attempt to confront this man on your own. He is a dangerous psychopath, and he will not hesitate to put you in the ground." He left a pause. "Do you hear me, Mr. Savage?"

"I hear you."

"Good. Stay out of trouble, Marty."

"Yeah, fuck you, Detective."

He hung up and tossed the phone on the sofa.

Lumsden had been the lead detective on Barclay's case. Antagonistic toward Martin after the trial, and tightlipped about everything. Lumsden believed Martin had been too close to the Damiani investigation. That when the police had been stumped, when the detective handling the case had run out of leads, Martin had withheld key information in order to take the Mirror Man down himself.

But he never would have gone to Damiani's Bed-Stuy antique shop if he'd known the man was a serial murderer. He'd gone to discuss one of Damiani's employees, a key suspect in the eleven homicides committed by the Mirror Man. He'd believed Damiani could provide the last piece of the puzzle linking small-time hustler Ray Robinson to the murders and had nearly gotten himself killed for it. For a fucking book.

*I was so wrong. Just like I was about Barclay. It was the kids he wanted. The poor fucking kids.*

Again, the image from Hansel and Gretel appeared in his mind. The children gorging themselves. The old crone lying in wait, sharp-nailed fingers curled over the white frosting windowpane. He couldn't place the memory and he didn't understand the connection. Was it a book from his childhood? Something he'd seen on television?

Whatever it was would have to wait. Bed was calling. He needed to catch a nap before driving into the city. With a police escort.

He had the distinct feeling the tail was more for Barclay's protection than his own.

---

THE DRIVE into Midtown was unremarkable except for the police car constantly in his rearview mirror. Not that he'd had any urge to smoke a joint with the hangover still lingering, but it would have been nice not to have to worry about the baggie in his glove compartment.

He parked in a lot near the bistro the journalist suggested and took a corner table on the patio in the sun. He chose the seat not because of the unseasonable warmth but because it was in direct view of cameras set up in the windows of the electronics store next door, displaying passersby on multiple monitors.

Barclay was reckless but he wouldn't be stupid enough to strike in broad daylight with a whole city block watching. Especially with the cop twenty feet away.

Leaning against the hood of his cruiser, Officer Tanaka unscrewed the lid off a Thermos. He looked young, couldn't have been out of police school long. His hair was crew cut, polarized sunglasses on a lanyard around his neck.

Martin raised his bourbon in a toast. The cop grinned. He returned the toast before taking a swig.

The first sip of bourbon took the edge off the residual hangover. The second got him lightly buzzed.

He hated interviews. They always asked questions about a childhood he couldn't remember, and he'd have to recall the lies he'd made up during previous interviews, hoping to H-E-double-hockey-sticks Aunt Norma wasn't reading this stuff.

He always felt one lie away from some eager beaver discovering the truth about Martin "Killer" Savage, the shy boy who grew up without a father, without a mother after the age of five, once they'd locked her away in an institution.

A boy raised by an older woman who wasn't even a blood relative, just a friend of his mother's.

A boy with very few memories of his past, like a child who'd suffered traumas so profound he'd had to bury them so deep in his subconscious no one could ever possibly dig them up.

"Martin?"

He'd zoned out, staring at a young mother at the far end of the patio. She'd been texting for the past two minutes, earbuds in, not looking up once to check on the baby in the stroller beside her. The little boy had dropped his plush dinosaur toy on the concrete to get her attention.

The interviewer looked just like her headshot, minus the

white background: black leather jacket with a white, wide-collared blouse beneath, long dark hair, olive complexion, slender neck, soft brown eyes and sharp eyebrows, thick-rimmed black glasses. Too young to date—he had a self-imposed cut-off at thirty—but not too young to turn his crank.

"Izzie Medina." She held out a hand with rings on several fingers. He stood partway to shake it. "Pleasure to finally meet you."

He agreed it was. She had a slight accent he hadn't noticed over the phone.

"I hope you haven't been waiting long."

"Just a few minutes," he said, smiling.

She returned the smile. Across the patio the young mother looked up from her phone and finally noticed the baby had dropped his toy. She bent to scoop it up, wiped it off, scowling slightly at the child, and tucked the toy into the stroller. Then she went back to texting.

"Don't you just love kids?" Izzie Medina said.

"Not particularly."

She narrowed her eyes. "Not a paternal type?"

"Bad genes."

"Huh. Well, I guess that's a valid reason. Me, personally—"

The server approached their table. "Can I get you something to drink?"

"What are you drinking?" Izzie asked Martin.

"Bourbon."

"Drink of champions. I'll have the same. Thank you."

The server went back inside. Martin sipped his drink, watching the reporter root through her purse until her ringless left hand emerged with a slim silver voice recorder. She set it down on the wrought-iron table.

"So," she said, scooching her chair closer. "I should ask, do you mind if I record this?"

"That's what I'm here for."

"Great." She thumbed the Record button.

"You don't want to wait for your drink?"

"I had one before I left the apartment," she said with a slightly embarrassed grin. "I've done hundreds of these and I still get nervous, you know?"

"Even with a nobody like me."

"Aw, come on." She touched his arm lightly. "You're some-body. If you weren't, I wouldn't be here."

The server reached over Izzie's shoulder with a tall glass of bourbon, mostly consisting of ice, the paper straw and a lime wedge. Izzie thanked her, removed the straw and the lime and set them on the coaster before taking a healthy gulp. Then she let out a gasp of satisfaction. "It's hot today, isn't it? Such a great day."

*A great day to die*, he thought.

"It was snowing in Pennsylvania yesterday."

"Ugh. I never leave the city these days. Everything I need is right here. So... brass tacks, as my dad used to say."

"Brass tacks," Martin agreed. Aunt Norma used to say the same. "I'm an open book—Izzie, was it?" He knew damn well it was Izzie. He was just baiting the line.

"That's right. Can I call you Martin?"

"It's my name."

"Well, Martin, as I said over the phone last week, I meant for this piece to be about your transition from true crime to literary fiction. But considering what's happened, I guess I should ask you this first..." She cocked her head at an angle, the glasses shifting on the bridge of her nose. "Are you scared? I mean, I would be. I get death threats on Twitter like ten times a week, but this is different. It wasn't internet tough talk. He literally said he'd cut off your—"

Martin crunched ice between his teeth. "I remember what he said. I was there."

"And you're not worried?"

"Look, I'm not Salman Rushdie. I'm not gonna go into hiding. I'm just a writer, like you."

"Except you're not like me. I've never killed someone."

"We're not gonna talk about that, are we? I've been over it and over it—"

"I'm not interested in that. I've read your statements. I've read the police reports. That's old news." She leaned over the table, gripping its edge. "James Barclay is out, though. He's *escaped*. I mean, I was so nervous about being here with you I almost ghosted."

"You're not in any danger." He nodded toward the cruiser up the street. "I've got a police detail."

The journalist flashed him a dubious look before turning. "Ooh." She sat back and regarded him, sipping her drink. "That's kind of hot, actually."

"I'll get you his number."

"I meant the danger. You're a marked man."

"Marked since birth," he said.

The offhand comment struck him as oddly as it did her. But a memory surfaced of Aunt Norma shaving his head during a lice epidemic at school. She'd smoothed away cut hair from his shorn scalp and said, *Hmm. It got bigger*. And when he'd asked what got bigger, she'd told him about the ruddy brown birthmark on the back of his crown.

He'd forgotten all about his birthmark until just now. Aunt Norma had called it his "mother's mark." This was after his mother had already been taken away. Ruby had mentioned it when she was in the institution—his little "fairy mark," she'd called it. Just what a boy his age had wanted to hear.

The young mother at the table across from him was breast-feeding now. The boy suckled away while his mother continued to text.

*They do say women are better multitaskers*, he thought idly. *No wonder kids these days grow up glued to a screen.*

"Anyway," Izzie said. "Let's forget about James Barclay for the moment. Tell me about your childhood. I've read just about every interview you've done and you always skate around anything prior to your mid-teens, your Stratford years. But I did some digging and it turns out you weren't born in Connecticut."

"That's right."

"You were born in a small town nearby," she said, reading from her cell phone. "An island settled by the survivors of a ship carrying dozens of Irish immigrants. It sank in the Rhode Island Sound in... 1847... during the Potato Famine. Back then they called them 'coffin ships,' because of how many people would die on board. But this ship, the *Ruby*, they called it—that's your mother's name, isn't it?

Martin narrowed his eyes. He couldn't recall having mentioned it to anyone. As far as he knew, his mother's identity was a deep, dark family secret.

"It is," he said.

"Nearly everyone died on this ship, the *Ruby*, because of an 'unusually vicious storm system,' is what the town historian called it. The few survivors settled on the shore, where they buried their dead. In burial mounds. What the English sometimes called *barrows*."

She was pausing intermittently for dramatic effect. He nodded for her to get to the point.

"They named the island and the town after these graves," she said, "which I thought was kind of odd but it maybe explains a lot about your morbid fascination with death. You grew up in a town literally named after it. The town of Barrows Bay," she said, holding his gaze with her dark eyes, as if gauging his reaction.

He wouldn't give her the satisfaction. "You did your homework."

Izzie smiled proudly. "I did. And what I also discovered was that you weren't raised by family. A woman by the name of Norma Higgins raised you—who I noticed in a few other interviews you called your aunt, even though she's not a blood relative. This was after your mother, Ruby Savage, was committed to a mental facility for—"

The glass shattered in his hand.

He hadn't even realized he'd been squeezing it. Shards slashed his fingers, his palm, the ice and bourbon burning the wounds. He stood abruptly, instinctively sucking on the deeper gash in his palm. Blood filled his mouth disconcertingly fast as he stared down at the mess.

Izzie pushed her chair away from the table and was eyeing him with fear, as if she thought he might take a chunk of the glass and cut her throat with it.

"What the fuck?" she said.

"I'm sorry." His voice was small, like a child apologizing to his mother. "It was... I'm on edge. It was an accident."

Already she was gathering up her things: wiping bourbon from her purse, shaking off her recorder and slipping it into the bag. "No, it's my fault. I should have asked about your moth—"

"She's not—!"

He caught his anger, tried to calm himself down. The young mother with her cell phone and her suckling baby watched him, eyes wide. The hipster bros at the next table looked poised to intervene. All he needed was an accusation of abuse haunting him. He needed to dial this back without looking like a psycho.

"Aunt Norma raised me," he finished, as calmly as he could. "Ruby was a sick woman. And I don't like to talk about that part of my life, if that's okay."

"I can see that." She stood, holding her purse to her chest like a frightened child might hold a stuffed animal. "Let's, uh... let's pick this up at another time, okay? You're obviously under a lot of stress."

"It's Barclay. I'm sorry."

She was already leaving. His hand dripped blood on the table. He grabbed a napkin from the stack and pressed it to the open wounds. It soaked through quickly. He grabbed the whole stack and held it there, focusing on the pain screaming up his wrist and down to the tips of his fingers. He'd have a pretty good scar there soon, one to match the old pale scar on his left hand.

*A fucking stigmata*, he thought.

"Hey, nice arm there, killer," one of the bros at the next table said.

The guy couldn't have known who he was, just picked a random word and happened to land on his trigger. Either way, Martin wasn't about to pick a fight against three bearded gym rats. Not after he'd already scared Izzie Medina half to death. Not with Officer Tanaka sitting half a block away.

"Fuck you, pal."

The muscular guy in his too small V-neck T-shirt threw up his hands in mock surrender and he and his bros laughed uproariously, cheersing their microbrews.

At the bar he discovered Izzie Medina had paid for her own bourbon. He apologized to the server and stepped out onto the street. On his way to the lot, he stopped by the cruiser. Tanaka zipped down the side window.

"Everything all right, Mr. Savage?"

"Everything's fine. Just had a little accident."

"Cut yourself pretty good. You should probably get that looked at. Might need stitches."

"I'll be fine."

Tanaka nodded. "Heading home then?"

"Got a stop to make first, Officer, if that's okay."

"Hey, I get paid whether I'm sitting here or sitting somewhere else."

"Great. Then I'll see you on my six."

Tanaka chuckled. "Ten-four."

---

MARTIN PULLED the Lexus out of the lot and headed for Hell's Kitchen, dialing Qurban Youssef on the way.

"Martin! How's my favorite fucking writer today?"

"Not good, Qurban." His hand throbbed dully. He wiped away a spot of blood from the transmission with his thumb. "Hey, uh... do you remember that thing you told me about last year? Do you still have it?"

"Last year? Martin, you don't mean...?"

The pause came just as Martin hit gridlock. He glanced in his rearview. Tanaka's cruiser was four cars back. Could he lose him if he needed to? It might be difficult, unless he could somehow get ahead of this truck.

"I think we're on the same page, Qurban."

"Hey, if you get into trouble, you know that shit is going to trickle down on Qurban."

Martin swung into a sudden gap in the right lane. "You said you'd take a bullet for me." He tried to sound hurt. His agent took the bait, seemingly offended by the accusation.

"Martin... that was a metaphor! I'm no Kevin Costner, much as he might wish he was me. Hey, if you think you need it, I can get it for you. But we have to be discreet. I'm your agent, not a small arms dealer."

He swerved in front of the truck. The driver laid on the horn. Martin threw up a middle finger and glanced in his mirrors.

Tananka's cruiser was out of sight, hidden behind the truck. All he needed to do now was swing left at the next opportunity and he'd lose the guy.

"Just tell me when and where, Qurban. I'm gonna get you that sequel, I promise."

"HEY, HEY!" the literary agent cried, throwing out his arms as Martin stepped out of the car. Qurban was a big hugger. Martin wasn't much of one himself but it kept his agent happy. If Qurban was a happy man he'd make sure his favorite fucking client was even happier.

Qurban squeezed him, enveloping him in thick arms and fresh-scented cologne, clapping his back vigorously. Martin patted him back halfheartedly until Qurban let go.

The agent regarded him with narrowed eyes. His wavy black hair with silver wings glistened under the streetlamp between the backs of a sushi restaurant and a repair shop. The alley stank of the Hudson and axel grease and the nearby NYPD horse stables, making Qurban's cologne a godsend.

"You look terrible, Martin. Have you been sleeping?"

"Some."

"Are you getting laid?"

Martin laughed. "I'll tell you all about it at our next meeting."

The agent smiled. "Hey, I'm a happily married man, Martin. You know I live for these stories."

Martin glanced toward the mouth of the alley, expecting to see Tanaka's cruiser pull up on the street. A few pedestrians walked by but it remained eerily quiet.

"Can we get down to brass tacks? I'm in a bit of a rush."

Qurban frowned. "'Brass tacks.' I don't like that expression. Let's get down to *business*. That's a phrase I can appreciate." He led Martin to his silver Porsche 911 and popped the trunk.

"Why didn't you just keep it in the glovebox?"

He gave Martin a look of disappointment. "Martin. I'm not a common street thug. I don't ride dirty."

"'Ride dirty' you like, but 'brass tacks' is a no-go."

"What can I say? I'm a man of many contradictions."

Qurban bent and scooped up the gray blanket nestled beside the spare tire and tire iron. He unrolled it, revealing a black pistol. It looked small in his large hands. "This is a Glock 19. I was assured by the very respectable gentleman who sold it to me that it has quite a lot of *stopping power*, which I was subsequently assured is quite important."

He handed it to Martin. It felt lighter than Martin had expected.

"Hey, what happened to your hand?"

Martin looked at it. He'd made a quick stop at a Duane Reade and gotten some gauze and wrap bandages. Blood had soaked through both. "It's a long story."

Qurban waggled his eyebrows. "Kinky stuff?"

Martin laughed. He studied the pistol while Qurban ducked back into the trunk. There were several things that looked like switches but none like the safeties he knew from other pistols. But there was a small lever on the trigger itself.

"You'll need these." Qurban handed him a box of 9mm Luger bullets with a bald eagle on its face. "And they're called *rounds* not *bullets*. You don't say *bullets*, not unless you want the respectable gentleman with a van full of assault rifles to laugh at you."

Martin slipped the box into his coat pocket. "I'll bear that in mind."

"Now, Martin, you must be very careful. There's no traditional safety, the respectable man assured me. That's why it's so good for protection. If you need it in a hurry, Martin, you just pull the trigger. It won't fire unless you pull the trigger."

"That's reassuring."

"Do you know how to load it?" Martin admitted he didn't, and Qurban took the gun from him. "*Weapon*, never *gun*," he said.

"Not unless I want the respectable man to laugh at me."

The agent grinned. "You're catching on."

He popped the cartridge and began loading rounds with a speed loader. It looked complicated but Martin figured he'd get the hang of it after a few times.

"That's it. Now you're *ready to rock*, as they say," Qurban said, rolling his Rs, as he handed the pistol back.

Martin pointed the pistol at the overflowing dumpster and squinted down the sight. He hadn't fired a gun since the spring-loaded BB pistol he'd had when he was a kid, stalking squirrels in the woods near their apartment. He'd been a crack shot but that was almost thirty years ago. And he suspected this gun—this *weapon*—would have a little more kick than a child's air pistol.

Qurban put a hand on Martin's arm and eased it down. "Please don't shoot anything here."

"I was just testing the feel."

The agent studied him. "And do you feel you could use it, should events force you to?"

Martin regarded the weapon. "I think Barclay won't see what's coming until it hits him."

"Allah forbid," Qurban said darkly.

"God forbid," Martin agreed, though he didn't believe in God, and a small, selfish part of him wished he could just put a bullet in Barclay and be done with it. Sooner rather than later.

"The respectable man said you should give it a name," Qurban said. "Something cool."

Martin studied the gun in his hand. He grinned. "How about Tansy?"

The agent gave him a look. "Is that an Americanism?"

# CHAPTER 5



## Enough for a Sequel

H IS PHONE BUZZED on the way across the Queensboro Bridge. Unknown Caller. He debated not picking it up. On the third ring, he slid the green icon.

"Savage."

"Heyyyyy, sexy. Guess where I am?"

Martin glanced at the screen. Tish was there, twiddling her fingers at him, the camera holding her in close-up. Her hair was pulled up, with short ringlets hanging down in front of her ears. Above the ankh necklace, she'd tied shiny green fabric around her throat in a bow.

"I'm on the road, Tish. I don't have time for games."

"You'll like this one. Look."

She turned the phone around. In quick-pan, he saw his kitchenette, his living room, his television and artwork, the living room windows with the darkening East River beyond.

"How the fuck did you get in my house?"

The phone spun back, taking a split second to focus on her wide smile. "Oops. I kinda borrowed your keycard. Was that wrong?"

She stretched out her arm, pointing the phone at her black lace cupless bra, nipples hard and poised above it, a garter belt and black stockings, her long, tanned legs and black high heels.

He couldn't help but stare as she slid her right hand over her stomach and down into her panties.

She brought the phone back up, licking her upper lip, walking through his condo now, heels clicking down the hall toward the bedroom. "Get home quick, Martin. I've been a bad, bad girl. I need to be punished."

She stood in his bedroom, the closet behind her. He regretted having removed the mirrors. Already stiffening inside his jeans, he would have appreciated getting a look at that thong in her reflection.

A familiar squeak alerted him—the sound of the small wheels on his closet door. It began to roll slowly open behind her, revealing the darkness within.

Someone was in the apartment with her.

A car honked behind him. Martin stepped on the accelerator, closing the gap, and returned his attention to the screen.

She turned, the phone remaining on her face. Her eyes had widened in surprise. Not in fear but excitement.

"Have you been hiding there the whole time, you naughty boy?"

"Tish, I need you to get out of there right now. Go to the front desk and tell the guard—"

Her lips rose in a wicked grin. Something tinkled, like the sound of a chandelier. "Hey, now. When did you get so kinky?"

"—Tish!"

With a strangled cry, she let the phone drop from her hand. It spun in mid-air and struck the pillow, tumbling over until it was aimed down the length of the bed, catching her lean, tanned body in profile.

A tall, slender man wearing a black Western shirt and the replica mirror mask straddled her, gripped the green bow in clenched fists and twisted it around her neck like a garrote.

Despite the mask, there was no doubt who it was.

"Barclay! Barclay, it's me you want, you fuck! Leave her out of this!"

Tish's eyes bugged toward the camera. Her face turning purple. Veins and cords in her neck standing out as she slapped weakly at the killer's arms.

Barclay turned his reflective face toward the phone, twisting the bow hard enough either the fabric would snap or the bow would cut right through her flesh.

Her trachea bulged. Her tongue rose from her mouth, wriggling in a soundless scream. Nipples rock hard now, and whether that was some psycho-sexual reaction or from the chill he didn't know and didn't care to pursue the thought.

*"Let her go, goddamn it!"*

She was helpless and he couldn't do anything about it, trapped bumper-to-bumper on the bridge. He tried pulling into a small gap between cars and the van beside him moved up, closing it. He slammed a fist against the steering wheel in impotent rage.

*"Fuck!"*

Tish stopped slapping the killer's arms, her hands falling limply to her sides. Her eyes were vacant, staring glassy at the ceiling.

Barclay let the fabric fall from his hands.

Her head rolled to the side. A tear spilled from each of her eyes, rolling over the bridge of her nose and down her cheek leaving black streaks of mascara.

The killer crawled over the mattress to the phone and picked it up. He peeled off the mask. The pieces of mirror tinkled lightly, reminding Martin of home—not Stratford but Barrows Bay, of the windchimes they'd had on the great big wraparound porch when he was so small the little island felt like the biggest place in the world.

Barclay grinned from ear to ear, breathing heavily. "Thou shalt not suffer a witch to live, Marty. A trail of blood lies between you and me, *mi amigo.*" The killer fumbled with the phone, looking dumbfounded by the technology.

Martin ended the call before Barclay could. Punched up Detective Lumsden's contact info and swiped.

The phone rang once, twice.

On the third ring, Lumdsen picked up. "Where the hell are you, Martin?"

"Where the hell were *you*? Where's your fucking police detail?"

"He called and said you shook him. I told him to go home. Another car's scheduled outside your building in—wait, has something happened?"

"He's at my condo, Lumsden. He's fucking inside my house, he just murdered my friend—"

"He...? Okay, I'll be there in ten minutes. Don't go up there without me, Martin. I'm serious."

Martin hung up.

Traffic thinned as he reached the exit.

Ten minutes later he was parked in front of his building, staring at his brand-new Glock 19 in the glove compartment.

He picked it up, tucked it into the back of his jeans, and stepped out of the car.

In a rush to the front doors, he left the driver door open. The same guard from the day before sat behind the desk. "Evening, Mr. Savage."

Martin blew past him. He heard the guy mutter something but he didn't care. He'd apologize later. He stopped halfway to the elevators and returned to the desk.

"Did you see a guy in a black cowboy shirt walk out of here in the last few minutes?"

"Cowboy shirt?"

"Like he was dressed for a rodeo," he said impatiently, white knuckling the edge of the desk. "Black dress shirt with fancy white embroidering."

"Can't say that I have. I've been on the door all afternoon."

Martin turned and headed for the elevators.

"If I see him, you want me to call up?"

Martin mashed his thumb on the up button. "If you see him, you better have that Taser handy."

The guard gave him a quizzical look.

The elevator doors opened and Martin stepped inside without further explanation. He kept thumbing the close button even after they already started to close.

When he finally caught his reflection in the elevator's mirrored walls, he couldn't deny the guilt on his face.

This was his fault. The girl was dead and he was to blame. He never should have let her get close to him, not with Barclay on the loose. He should have been more careful with his keycard. He never should have lost Officer Tanaka. What was he thinking, buying a gun?

*It's my fault, I didn't mean it, Ma, I swear I won't be bad no more—*

The elevator dinged and the doors slid open on the Lower Penthouse level. Right foot holding the door, he stuck his head out briefly. Checked both ways like he'd been warned to do as a child before crossing the road.

All clear toward the Bannermans' door. All clear toward his own. He drew the weapon from the back of his jeans and stepped out. Padded down the carpeted corridor toward his unit.

Either Barclay was waiting for him inside, or he'd escaped through the parking garage. Martin wasn't sure how he'd gotten into his unit in the first place. He supposed the killer could have followed Tish, slipped into the condo and hid while she "redded up" for Martin's arrival.

Not that it mattered. He'd been there, hiding in the closet, waiting to spring his trap. Now Tish was dead and Martin would be his next victim.

It was impossible to enter the unit quietly. A good thing if you weren't expecting visitors. Bad if you were trying to get the jump on a serial killer.

He used his temp keycard. The mechanism beeped and the lock unlatched with a loud click. He twisted the handle with agonizing slowness. Drew the door open cautiously and stepped in with the weapon held out in front of him.

Tish's boots lay kicked off in front of the door.

A bottle of red stood open on the kitchen counter, two glasses and the corkscrew beside it. One had been drunk out of, a lipstick stain on the rim.

The gas fireplace crackled. A black slip of a dress lay draped over the back of the sofa, a heavy winter coat beside it. The TV news on mute.

The ethereal wail of sirens floated up from forty stories below.

He followed a trail of scattered rose petals from the kitchenette down the hall to the bedroom, creeping heel-to-toe, heel-to-toe. His floors had never creaked but caution was wise. The soles of his boots crushed flower petals, leaving powdery red smears on the hardwood.

He pushed on the bathroom door, swept the room with the gun. He pulled the shower curtain aside, checked behind the door in the mirror.

Empty.

Colder down here, the further he got from the fireplace.

He opened the next door, the hall closet. Nothing but toiletries and towels and stuff from his past he'd never gotten rid of: trophies and school papers and knickknacks from trips, old short stories gathering dust, school yearbooks he hadn't looked at in over a decade.

At the end of the hall the bedroom door thumped against the jam. Open just a crack, wide enough to peer through. The sirens were louder. Blue and red flashing in the darkness beyond the door. If Barclay was still here, he already knew Martin was armed, that he was approaching down the hall.

"I've got a gun, you motherfucker! You try anything, I'll shoot!"

The door thumped against the jam.

He took two wide steps toward the bedroom.

The door creaked open slowly.

Even if Barclay stood behind it, Martin would have the upper hand. He could kick the door wide and go in blasting. Still, the spit at the back of his throat was thick with terror. His heart thudded in his ears.

He booted the door. It swung into the room without impedance and struck the doorstop with a springy sound.

The cold struck him immediately. One of the windows was shattered, curtains fluttering in the wind. He smelled the East River, which was good, because it masked the acrid copper tang of Tish's blood.

Even before he flicked on the light, he could see her in flashes of blue and red from the police cars below.

Barclay had splayed her out on the white linen, her head resting on the pillows, her limbs spread wide as if she'd collapsed on the bed after a long day of driving and fallen asleep waiting for him.

But he couldn't pretend she was warm and alive and hungry for him because he'd seen it happen. He'd watched Barclay strangle her while he was stuck in traffic, arguably the most mundane activity in the world contrasted with the most brutal, the most *savage*—the yin to Barclay's yang.

*The man eats the woman and the woman eats the man.*

As if to punish himself, he flicked on the light.

He saw everything in a single glimpse and staggered back against the doorjamb, sliding down the wall to the floor. His breath came in gasps.

None of the crime scene photos he'd studied over the years had prepared him for this, for the impact of it. She lay in a glistening pool of blood, her stomach splayed open. Bloody handprints streaked the duvet and the wall behind the bed.

Gore dripped from the thing Barclay had hung in place of the New York City skyline print, a fleshy red thing he first mistook for a ram's head painted red but realized with dawning horror was Tish's reproductive system, her uterus and fallopian tubes nailed to the chipped plaster.

And despite the repellent sight of Barclay's macabre work of art, Martin's gaze kept returning to Tish's bare throat, so constricted the ligature marks were nearly black. The bow she'd worn, the bow Barclay had choked the life out of her with, was now tied neatly in her hair.

A belated Christmas gift from the Witch Hunter for his closest friend in the outside world.

"Martin?"

Lumsden's voice seemed to come from very far away, even though the detective had already stepped into the unit.

Pulled from his stupor, Martin realized he was still gripping the pistol. He laid it on the carpet between his feet, vaguely aware of how easily this scene could be misinterpreted in an instant of confusion.

*Maybe I should pick it up. Let them shoot me. I deserve it, don't I, Ma?*

Thinking about his mother again, about Ruby. Talking to her in his mind, on the verge of delirium. He couldn't remember the last time he'd done that, probably not since he was very young, in the few years after they took her away.

Hard soles tromped up the hall, stopping at the door. "Martin, Jesus..." Lumsden's voice. "Is that—?"

"*My God*," a woman hoarsely whispered. Lumsden's partner, Detective Kline.

One of them gagged.

Lumsden grabbed Martin under the arm and hauled him to his feet. He looked down at the gun on the floor, gave Martin a look of disappointment. "You should've listened to me."

"What does it matter? She's dead. She's dead because of me."

"It's not your fault. Come on. We'll need to take your statement."

As Lumsden dragged him from the room, he looked back once more at the grisly tableau and spotted it at once, what he kept looking back for.

Her necklace, the ankh. It was missing.

Barclay had taken it.

# CHAPTER 6

## FRIGHT AND FLIGHT

"SO HE WAS leaving you messages, and you didn't think to tell anyone."

Lumsden and his partner eyeballed him, the three of them sitting in a brightly lit interrogation room in the Bowery 9th Precinct. It was the same way they'd treated him after the incident with the Mirror Man. Like he was the lead suspect in a murder investigation.

"You knew he was gonna come after me." He was exasperated and dead tired. It took all of his energy to argue. "What fucking difference would it have made?"

Detective Kline squeezed the bridge of her nose. Her hair was pulled back so severely it acted like a facelift. Lumdsen looked like a grizzled veteran in comparison. "Well, for one," she said, "we would have known he tracked you all the way to Pennsylvania. That's kind of a big deal."

"I wasn't sure it was him. I didn't want to seem paranoid. I happen to know you guys don't appreciate it when people call wolf."

"Who's calling wolf? This is an escaped serial killer we're talking about. If you had reason to believe—"

"Fine! I should have checked in. I shouldn't have bought the gun. If you're gonna press charges, just do it already so I can go home."

"Home?" Lumsden looked up from flicking through his notebook, letting the pages fall back. "You're not going home tonight, Martin. Your home is an active crime scene."

"Well, where the fuck am I gonna go then? Are you gonna pay for my hotel?"

Lumsden and Kline shared a look. "Yeah, we'll set you up at the Waldorf, Martin. How's that sound?" The two of them laughed.

"Fuck sake. Is there anything you chuckleheads *can* do for me?"

Lumsden gave him a cold glare. "We are doing everything we can for you, Martin. But you've fought us at every turn. If we'd known about Barclay in Bethlehem, we could've had him apprehended before the two of you got back to the city. But you had to play hero, just like you did with Damiani."

Martin's fist came down on the table before he could stop it. Kline startled. Lumsden didn't even blink.

"You goddamn well know that wasn't my intent!"

"You were drenched in Damiani's blood," Kline said. "Looked like that Tom Cruise movie, you know? Plays a vampire?"

"What the fuck does that have to do with anything? Have I committed a crime? There's a killer on the loose—"

"You don't think we know that?"

"We're aware of that, Martin."

"Then why the fuck are we just sitting here? We should be *out there*—" He jabbed a finger toward the door. "—looking for that fucking maniac!"

"You have no business looking for him, Martin. That's our job. What you can do, if you want to help, is check yourself into a nice hotel and try to get some sleep."

"Pamper yourself," Kline said with a sarcastic smirk. "You deserve it."

Martin shook his head and got to his feet. In the same moment he reached for his phone on the stainless-steel table, it began to buzz.

The detectives shared another look. Lumsden held up a finger.

"Put it on speaker."

Martin looked at the screen. "It's Sheila."

"Sheila Tanner?" Kline frowned. "I thought you two broke up?"

"Oh, was I supposed to run that by you as well? Jesus fuck." He answered the phone, holding it to his ear to spite them.

Kline rose partway, gripping the table. Lumsden patted her shoulder and she eased back into her seat.

"Martin?"

"Are you okay?"

"Okay? I'm okay, Martin. I'm just annoyed. I found what you left me. I just got home and there it was on my doorstep. So my question is, are you out of your mind?"

"What? There *what* was, Sheila?"

"The present you left for me? The jewelry?"

"Sheila, I didn't leave anything for—" He paused. "Wait, what kind of jewelry?"

"It's got your name on it. 'Love, Marty'? The little red box?"

"Since when do I sign anything 'Marty,' Sheila?" Lumsden and Kline perked up at this. "What was in the box?"

"Hang on." A moment later his phone buzzed. He brought up the message. A closeup of Sheila's hand with Tish's ankh necklace in her palm.

"So what's the deal, Martin? Are you trying to get me back into bed? With *that*?"

"Sheila, I want you to go to the kitchen and get the biggest knife in the drawer."

"What are you talking about?"

"I'm at the police station right now. They'll send someone to your house."

Lumsden nodded. Kline stood and left the room, leaving the door wide open. She barked orders to an officer in the hall.

Sheila still wasn't getting it. "You're what? Why?"

"Barclay killed another woman. A friend. At my condo. He killed her and he took her necklace—"

"No," she said, the truth finally hitting her.

"Yes. That necklace was hers. That means Barclay's been to your house."

"*Shit*." He heard her rummage in a drawer. The clatter of cutlery. The *shing!* of metal on metal as she pulled out a knife. "You think he's still here?"

"He could be. Stay away from the closets, closed doors."

"Why would he leave me her necklace, Martin?"

"It's a message. He said something to me when—"

He swallowed hard, not wanting to think about the video call. The struggle. The tears. Tish's bulging eyes and erect nipples. Her neck, ringed black. The awful thing Barclay had nailed to the wall like a crucifixion.

"—he told me 'Thou shalt not suffer a witch to live.' Then he repeated his threat about the river of blood between him and me."

Lumsden leaned forward in his chair, keenly interested, though he'd already told them all of this.

"*Jesus,*" Sheila said. She was whispering, afraid for her life in her own home. "What do you think it means?"

"It means he plans to kill you next."

---

LUMSDEN AND KLINE suggested Martin and Sheila leave the city for a few days. When Sheila met him at the station, she brought an overnight bag with her. She didn't want to leave, to put her job on hold, but the detectives were adamant. There just weren't enough resources to put a protective detail on both of them around the clock.

A brief vacation, just until Barclay was back in custody, and their lives could go back to normal.

Martin didn't think normal was possible, not after what he'd seen. Though he did agree getting out of town for a few days was wise.

The question was, where? It was too late to drive anywhere of distance. And neither of them thought it likely the detectives would apprehend Barclay over the weekend. A trip to Amish country or the Hamptons wasn't going to cut it.

They needed a place to hole up for what could be as long as a week, maybe two or more. Sheila mentioned her parents in Hoboken, though she didn't seem eager to visit. Martin had a few friends in Stratford he could call up, but anyone could discover where he'd spent his teenage years with a glance at his website.

That left one place, somewhere no one but Martin and his last remaining family knew about.

Frankly, he would have preferred to take his chances with Barclay than go back there.

"It's the best choice you've got right now," Lumsden said. "We need you close. But not too close he'll find you."

Sheila and Detective Kline agreed.

It was already far too late to wake Aunt Norma with a phone call. So instead of driving the full three and a half hours and a ferry ride to Barrows Bay, Rhode Island, they booked an overnight stay at a motel about a quarter of the way under assumed names, paying cash.

The Dovercourt Motor Inn was just off the New England Thruway in the relatively small beach community of Rye. From the second floor, where Martin and Sheila had adjoining rooms, the rainbow-bright framework of Playland roller coasters and the Ferris wheel were visible against the black waters of the Long Island Sound. He'd gone there on a school trip in the tenth grade, nearly thirty years ago. After his third time riding the Dragon Coaster he puked corn dogs and root beer into a nearby trash can while running to the washroom.

Standing on the balcony, swigging from a small plastic bottle of Stoli from the minifridge, he was struck with a sudden urge to stroll down to the beach, overdose on nostalgia. Who knew how long he had left to live? But it was late and the amusement park was closed. He doubted Sheila was interested in roller coasters, anyhow.

He suddenly wondered what she'd been like as a kid, if she'd been a tomboy or a wallflower or what. In the year they'd spent together he hadn't learned much about her past. Like him, there had been a period of her life she'd simply never opened up about. He guessed she'd been a nerd or overweight and wanted to leave those memories buried in the past, the way he'd buried his own. She definitely did not want to relive them by going home again, and neither did he. But that was exactly what they were doing, whether he liked it or not.

A black-and-white police cruiser with CITY OF RYE on the door was parked beside the Lexus in the street below. Lumsden and Kline had gotten them an overnight protective detail but had told them they would be on their own once they arrived in Barrows Bay. Having the closest local police watching over them twenty-four-seven would be more likely to draw attention, Lumsden figured.

Martin finished the bottle, gasping as the liquor scorched his throat, washing away the hint of blood in his mouth from a wound that wouldn't seem to heal.

His breath was visible under the parking lot lights. Winter still clung to the trees, heaped in the gutters and against buildings. The chill, salty air from the sound brought back vague memories of frigid winters and meager Christmases living in a one-bedroom apartment in Stratford with Aunt Norma. Working long hours after school to help keep a roof over their heads while Norma put in time at a nearby home for the elderly, then coming home to wolf down dinner and work on short stories until he passed out, exhausted.

Despite it all, he'd grown up in a loving home, which many weren't able to say. He'd had his problems, like anyone. But Stratford had been nothing like when he'd lived in—

—*the Gingerbread House*—

—the big old Victorian house in Barrows Bay. He still remembered very little of his life there. On the seldom occasion he thought back to that period, the feelings that arose were fear and confusion, the images blood and black smoke.

He rubbed the old scar on his palm. His right hand still stung where he cut himself with the glass. He'd changed the bandage again after a quick shower in the hotel tub. The blood hadn't soaked through this time.

"*Dammit!*"

Martin leaned over the railing. Sheila was downstairs, banging on the soda machine, dressed in a bulky green sweater and leggings.

"Need help?"

She looked up. "What I need is caffeine."

He grinned. "Pulling an all-nighter?"

"I figure if I'm gonna be awake I might as well get some work done."

"There's Diet Coke in my minibar."

"I see you've already partaken."

He raised the empty bottle. "When in Rye."

Five minutes later she knocked on the door separating their rooms. He opened it, saw that she'd removed her sweater and was wearing the overlarge gray Michigan University T-shirt she often wore to bed. He wondered if it meant anything but chose to ignore it, popped the tab on her soda and poured it into one of the clear plastic glasses from the tiny bathroom.

She took it, watched it fizz for a moment, then shrugged. "Hell, you might as well Irish it up."

"You sure?"

"After the night I've had." She glanced at the empty bottles on the dresser and her eyes welled with sympathy. "*We've* had. Martin, I'm so sorry."

"Don't," he said, crouching in front of the opened minibar. "Not tonight. Tonight, just drink with me. We've got plenty of time to rake over what happened with a fine-toothed comb."

He selected a Jameson and rose with it, unscrewing the cap. She held out her glass and he poured half into the mix.

"Make it a double, bartender," she said. He poured the remaining whiskey into the glass and stood the bottle with the others.

She sat on the edge of the bed. The TV was on, soundless. Some religious program. Save the children or something. Martin flicked it off and sat with her beside the bed, where he'd piled the pillows on the floor. The way they'd been left leaning up against the headboard reminded him too much of his bed at home—the scene he was drinking to obliterate from his memory.

He held up his Heineken. "I don't know what to toast."

"How about to not dying?"

He shrugged and tapped his can against her glass. "To not dying."

They sat quietly, sipping their beverages, staring at the peeling off-white paint behind the dresser.

"There was a man I treated, before I stopped practicing," Sheila said, finally breaking the silence. "His wife committed suicide. She'd been having paranoid delusions, terrifying hallucinations. She'd wake in the middle of the night screaming. He was worried she'd harm herself, or their daughter. He convinced a colleague of mine to prescribe her medication for schizophrenia, even though she'd never been formally diagnosed."

"Okay," Martin said, unsure where she was going with this.

"A few months later she overdosed on those same pills. Her

daughter found her. He blamed himself for her death. But it wasn't his fault."

"Oh, we're doing this."

She gave him a sympathetic look. "You think you could have prevented it. But she insinuated herself into your life, Martin. You said so yourself. She knew the risks. Hell, Martin, she *stole* your keycard. For all you know, she could have let him in—"

"Sheila, I appreciate what you're trying to do, I do, but I don't want to talk about this right now."

She nodded. Sipped her drink. Martin finished his beer and crushed the can. He returned to the minibar, got himself a bottle of tequila and twisted off the lid.

"So when was the last time you've been back home?" she asked as he sat back down beside the bed, eagerly changing the subject. "You never told me you lived in Rhode Island."

"I only lived there until I was five. We moved to Connecticut shortly after they took Ruby away."

"Your mother."

He nodded. It was difficult to admit, having never really had a mother for most of his life, at least not in the parental sense. But Ruby Savage *was* his mother. Though they looked and acted nothing alike, they'd shared a home for the first five years of his life. They shared the same name.

Ruby Savage was his mother and Barrows Bay was his home.

"You never did tell me what happened there."

"I will."

"When you're ready," she said.

"Uh-huh. But I haven't been back to Barrows Bay since we left. A part of me is scared to, I guess."

"Scared?"

He nodded. "The last time I was there, someone tried to kill me."

"What? Martin, you were five years old. Why would someone want to kill a—?"

She stopped short of saying "kill a child," realizing her error. They both knew someone intimately who murdered children as a hobby. They were on the run from him right now.

"We left town because Aunt Norma didn't feel safe there anymore. Not after Ruby left. After the fire."

"Fire?"

"Our house. Some people called it the Gingerbread House. It was winter. I remember being so cold, standing in the street in boots and pajamas watching my house burn down, huddled under Norma's big winter jacket."

He swigged the tequila, feeling the half-remembered chill creep into his bones.

"It was strange, what happened that night. I woke up. I don't know how long I'd been asleep but the moon was high and bright. I woke up because I had a nightmare—I remember that much, but not the nightmare itself. I know I'd dreamed it before. It felt familiar, when I woke up. The fear. I was terrified but somehow the fear was comforting. It was the same way I felt every time we visited Ruby in the hospital after what happened."

"Hmm," Sheila said. She sipped her drink.

"Anyway, I woke up screaming. That's what woke Aunt Norma up. Not the smoke creeping up the stairs, not the fire alarm in the upstairs hall, because it never went off. And that was weird, you know, because Norma checked those batteries religiously. It would go off if you scalded water. Later, the police said the battery had come loose. But Aunt Norma knew better. Because ever since Ruby was committed, she'd seen them watching the house."

"*Them?*"

"Aunt Norma never did tell me who she thought they were. She told me I was better off not knowing. The police claimed it was arson, but they had no suspects in mind, at least that they told us. But that night, I woke up screaming, and my screams woke up Aunt Norma, and the second she stepped into the hall she smelled it. If I hadn't had that nightmare, we probably would have died of smoke inhalation, if not burned to death. Norma came running down the hall to get me and the first thing she noticed was my bedroom door was locked. I didn't lock it. I told the police that, but I was five. I'm not sure if they believed me."

"Would your aunt have locked you in your room for some reason?"

"No. Ruby might have, if she'd still been living with us. But I don't think it was locked at all. It locked from the outside.

Even if Norma had locked me in, she had a skeleton key. The two of us tried to get the door open, her shouting at me to pull while she twisted the key in the lock and pushed on her side. It just wouldn't budge. Someone had jammed it or wedged it closed somehow. Either way, the intent was clear. Whoever set our house on fire wanted me to burn with it."

"Jesus, Martin." She shook her head. "And they never figured out who did it?"

"It's still an open case. I looked into it a few years back. There were a handful of suspects. A drifter from Canada. A local troublemaker. A weirdo who lived on the edge of the woods, liked to set fires in the county dump. But they all had alibis and not a single one of them had a motive. Whoever it was is probably in jail or long dead by now."

"No history of arson in the area?"

"A handful of fires, over the years. None that could be tied to our house. The previous one was seven years prior, the old schoolhouse. No discernable pattern to any of them that I could see."

Sheila nodded and finished her drink. She stared down at the bottom of the cup.

"I remember that night, though. Norma hugging me under her big jacket, the smell of her flowery perfume and cigarette smoke. The two of us standing there while the Gingerbread House burned, the volunteer fire department dousing it with water so cold you could see vapor coming off it the second it left the hose. And I remember Norma suddenly pointing, leaving me sitting in the back of the fire chief's Suburban. 'That's her!' she shouted, running out into the street. 'She's one of them, Chief!'"

"Them," Sheila repeated again. "Who was it? Did you see?"

"That's the weird thing. It was just some pasty-faced old lady. And when Norma shouted after her, the woman backed into the shadows until she disappeared."

"And she never told you who the woman was?"

"Never. I asked, but she'd always say 'Best you not know,' and close the subject. After a while, I guess I just forgot about most of that night. I only just now remembered the old lady standing in silhouette under a streetlight. Like she'd come to *watch it burn*."

He shivered, holding Sheila's gaze. "I remember she wore one of those big hats like the Queen wears. And when she stepped into the light, I could swear she was smiling."

---

AFTER MARTIN'S story they fell into a thoughtful funk. They each had another drink and Sheila dragged her comforter and pillows into his room from hers because the idea of sleeping alone, even with the door left open between them, didn't feel right to either of them. Martin spread his pillows out on the floor, leaving Sheila the bed.

He lay awake staring at the stucco ceiling for an indeterminate period after Sheila's light snoring began. Thinking about how good it would be to see Aunt Norma again after so many years. To finally get over his irrational fear of going back to that place, of seeing the house and his mother again.

Nobody wanted him dead in Barrows Bay. Death was behind him, in the city. Hopefully, it would stay there.

It was possible someone really had tried to kill them that night, but that was almost forty years ago. There was no longer any reason to fear that place. He'd already dredged up the most terrible of his childhood memories and it hadn't killed him. He would survive a visit with Aunt Norma and Ruby, who'd been released from the mental hospital nearly a decade ago. They could get a few rooms at a local B&B for the duration, but Norma would urge them to stay at the house, to sleep in his childhood bedroom while Sheila stayed in the guest room, and Ruby likely wouldn't put up a fuss. He supposed he might even survive that.

He almost hadn't survived the fire.

It demolished the kitchen and had only just started burning the dining room and up the stairs by the time the fire department showed up in their big red trucks. They worked efficiently, managing to save the living room and the second floor.

In 1985, two years after the fire, the Barrows Bay Historical Society funded the house's reconstruction. It was apparently the oldest house in town, built by one of the town founders. Ruby had lived there since she was a child, or so she'd claimed to Aunt Norma, who was born and raised in Stratford. Ruby's parents died when she was still in her teens. She'd lived in the big old house alone for decades, until Martin had come into her life. Her health had been spotty at the best of times. After Martin's arrival she'd brought in Norma to serve as a live-in nanny.

He'd never known his father. Ruby had never told him who the man was, as far as he could recall. Aunt Norma either didn't know or had been sworn to secrecy.

Ruby had been the oldest mother of any of his friends. Kids older than him had called him a bastard. They said his mother was a witch, an old hag, a crone. They said she found him in a pumpkin patch after making a human sacrifice to the Lord of Hallowe'en. Stupid stuff that only made sense to children. The three of them never celebrated any of his birthdays and his friends had never been allowed over to play.

He'd had a strange childhood. No worse than anyone else's, he supposed. Just strange.

He fell asleep picturing the old woman Norma had chased into the dark the night of the fire. He could remember her very clearly. Her face rosy and plump under the hat, smiling a devil's smile.

*I should write a book about it,* he thought as he drifted off. *I bet if I could find her picture in the paper or some ancient school yearbooks, I could ask around, see if any old-timers remember her, if they know anything about who she might have been hanging around at the time of the fire. It's a longshot, but maybe I can figure out who Norma's Them really was, find out who tried to kill us in our sleep.*

Thinking this, Martin finally passed out.

---

They had a somewhat late start that morning. The Rye Police officers woke them at eight, informing them they were going off duty and no one would be taking over.

Martin drank several plastic cups full of water and Sheila let him sleep it off on the bed for another few hours while she went out looking for coffee. She returned to her room, drank her coffee with a small breakfast, took a shower, then knocked on the door separating her room from his.

He woke, still groggy, his back sore from having spent half

the night on the floor. He cracked a mini bottle of scotch and drank it in one go.

"I guess I'm driving," Sheila said as he headed to the bathroom for a cold shower.

The headache lingered for another ten minutes before it became a light buzz. He drank the cold coffee Sheila brought him, then handed her the keys to his Lexus. "I'll call Norma on the way. Warn her of our impending arrival."

"The prodigal son returns." She looked at him askance. "No offence."

He shrugged. "No, I've read the Bible. That's pretty accurate."

She laughed. They headed down to the car, returned the room keys and drove off. By ten-thirty, they were back on the thruway. Two hours later they crossed the state line into Rhode Island. An hour after that, they were crossing the Sound on the small car ferry from Point Judith to the island community of Barrows Bay.

On the ferry, they got out of the car and headed up to the top deck. They stood beside a young father and son, the four of them looking out at the ocean as the boat rose and fell on the choppy water, coating them in a light mist.

They stood there in silent awe for several minutes, taking deep, invigorating breaths of the saltwater air. It brought strong feelings of nostalgia for Martin—not all of them good.

"Look, Daddy!" the little boy said suddenly, pointing toward the dark, craggy island in the distance. "The island sparkles!"

Sheila lowered her sunglasses to look, furrowing her brow in confusion. Martin blinked blearily but he couldn't see what the boy had seen, either. Even the sun's diamond-glint reflection on the water was on the opposite side of the boat.

The three adults looked at each other for a moment, mystified. The father shrugged amiably and tousled his son's hair. As the boat neared the dock, they all returned to the car deck. The Lexus was first off, after a small white delivery truck, and at just past two p.m. on a windy Thursday in early March, Martin Savage finally returned to the place of his birth.

# Part Two

MOTHER

# CHAPTER 7

## HOME AGAIN, HOME AGAIN, JIGGITY-JOG

S HEILA PARKED THE Lexus out front of a Victorian
home at the end of a cul-de-sac. Martin still looked pretty
rough as he stared up at the big old house with his forehead
pressed against the window. After everything he'd been through
in the past few days—the murder, the interrogation, fleeing the
city in the middle of the night—she supposed he could have
looked worse.

"Look at me," she said.

He gazed at her with apprehension in his bleary green eyes.
She gave him an encouraging smile, brushed his hair back from
his face and straightened his shirt collar under his pea coat.

"Better. Are you gonna be okay?"

He processed the question a moment before nodding. "I
think so. Thank you." He gave her a tight smile. "For coming
with me."

"I didn't have much choice in the matter, did I?"

He grinned sheepishly. "No, I guess you didn't."

She ducked to look up at the house through his window.
"Should we go up?"

"I'm just trying to gather my strength."

Nodding, she said, "Take all the time you need."

He took a few deep breaths. In the seven years she'd known
Martin she'd never seen him so scared. Even the other night,

when she went to his place to go over her Barclay interviews, he'd seemed relatively cool.

Sitting here now, the seatbelt still drawn across his chest, he looked like a frightened little boy about to be dropped off at summer camp. Having lived under the shadow of a woman with an undetermined mental illness during his formative years would surely have been traumatic. Terrorized by her mentally ill older sister well into her teens, Sheila knew how dealing with a relative's mental illness could negatively affect someone's life well into adulthood. She also knew how the sting of a mother's coldness or indifference could last a lifetime. But for him to be afraid of her still, after all this time, it just didn't click with what she knew of him.

"Okay," he said with a quick nod. "Let's do this, before I lose my nerve."

He unbuckled and opened the door. She stepped out and met him on the sidewalk.

"Home again, home again, jiggety-jog."

He frowned. "What's that?"

"Some old nursery rhyme. 'To market to market, to buy a fat hog. Home again, home again, jiggety-jog.'"

"I don't like it," he said, then started up the walk.

The Savage house was a two-story Victorian, all red brick and white trim, dormers over the windows on the second floor and a widow's watch, where Sheila thought it might be possible to see the ocean over the houses, trees and rooftops across the street.

Martin had called it a gingerbread house last night, and the description fit. The light dusting of snow on the crisp brown grass made her think of powdered sugar. Surprisingly, it was in good repair. As far as she could see, there wasn't any sign of the fire that caused Martin and his aunt to flee the island for Connecticut.

"You coming?"

He was looking back at her from the wraparound porch, reaching out for the screen door with his uninjured left hand. She hurried up and stopped a few steps behind him. The wind chimes above his head tinkled lightly in the chilly breeze.

He rapped on the door's wooden frame, then gave her a nervous grin. His aunt hadn't picked up the phone when he called at the ferry docks. The visit would be a surprise for both women. Hopefully, it would welcome.

"Maybe nobody's home." He knocked again, harder this time.

From inside the house came a husky woman's voice: "Hold your horsies!"

A moment later, the sound of a chain being drawn and latches pulled. It seemed like a lot of security for a town surrounded by water with a population just shy of a thousand, although she supposed with what had happened when Martin was young it made sense to keep the house locked from intruders.

The inner door opened. A husky woman stood leaning against it. She looked to be in her mid- to late-seventies, with broad shoulders and short-cropped silver hair. She squinted out into the sunlight, her eyebrows pinched in a scowl as she looked first at Sheila, then at Martin.

When she recognized him, her scowl became a pleasant smile. "Marty!" She opened the screen door. "Lord, it's been ages!"

He held the door open as she hugged him, hugging her back with his free arm.

"How are you, Aunt Norma?"

"Better now that you're here." She held him at arm's length, looking him over. "You're getting gray, Marty. And those frown lines don't suit you. You should smile more."

"I'll try."

Sheila stood a moment under Norma's gaze as the woman looked her up and down.

"And who is this pretty young thing?"

Sheila laughed. Been a minute since anyone had called her "young." She stuck out her hand and introduced herself. "Marty's told me so much about you."

"Nothing bad, I hope." The woman smiled, but when she looked past them suddenly, her brow clouded. "Come in, come in, you'll let in the devil," she said, stepping aside to let Martin in.

Sheila turned to the street as an ancient pink Cadillac on the opposite side of the road drove off, engine chugging, spewing black exhaust. She didn't get a good look at the driver but whoever it was had been wearing a large hat, the kind an elderly woman might wear to church.

---

"Where's Ma?" Martin asked, following Aunt Norma to the kitchen.

"Oh, she should be back soon. At her physio."

The walls of the corridor between the living room and kitchen were bereft of photographs, where he remembered they'd once been crammed. The wallpaper was new to him, its predecessor burned away.

He glanced up the stairs. The old varnished hardwood had been painted and the carpet runner was new. As was the stair lift, which he supposed had been put in despite much indignant protest from Ruby.

Peering into the living room, he found it very similar to how he remembered it. His mother's carnival glass reading lamp on an end table beside her favorite chair. Over the fireplace hung the painting of the *Ruby*, the coffin ship she'd been named after, a three-masted vessel sailing a rough storm.

He knew if he looked closely, he'd see her crew desperately trying to keep the ship afloat. If he looked even closer, the ghostly, terrified faces of the passengers would be just barely visible peering out through dark slits in its hull. The painting had always scared him as a kid. He remembered hurrying past it after turning off the lamp on his way to bed for fear of seeing their frightened white eyes in the dark.

The television was new, at least for the house—an old tube TV with knobs and rabbit ears opposite the sofa and his mother's chair. Ruby never had much good to say about television, from what Martin could remember. While kids his age had talked about Saturday morning cartoons, he'd nodded along cluelessly. Even at the mental hospital Ruby had avoided it, preferring her books. He supposed Norma must have convinced her to get one, since the two women shared the house alone.

The dining room furniture was antique but not what he remembered. The fire had taken the table, the china hutch, the buffet. It had burned right through the serving window from the kitchen. Not a single scorch mark remained, covered up with new wallpaper and paint, both decades-old now. It was easy to imagine the fire had never happened at all.

"They did a good job with the house," he said, following Norma into the kitchen.

Nothing was as he remembered it in here. From the cabinets to the laminate floor, the frilly curtains with terriers printed on them, the yellow wallpaper. It was like stepping into a time capsule rather than stepping into an earlier time in his life. Everything had been replaced in the 1980s, aside from the gadgets Norma had shoved on every free inch of counterspace: a breadmaker, a blender, a four-slice toaster. The gas range was a recent addition as well, shiny brushed steel with cast iron grates.

"I see you don't have to cook on a woodstove anymore. That must be nice."

Norma scowled. "Woodstove? We never had a woodstove."

"You didn't? Wasn't that where I burned my—?"

Aunt Norma's scowl deepened. He was sure they had one, but he let it go. Maybe he'd gotten it mixed up with somewhere else, a friend's house or a school trip to some living history museum. The incident that left the pale scar on his left hand was almost forty years ago. For all he knew, he'd burned it on a regular stove and the woodstove was just something he'd dreamed about.

"Burned your what, Martin?" Sheila asked, looking at him with professional curiosity.

"Nothing," he said, feeling silly.

"Well, sit down, you two. Make yourselves at home."

They sat around the kitchen table. Martin looked up at the cream-colored rotary telephone on the wall. He remembered Norma speaking hurriedly on it, a splash of blood on her face, smearing it on the receiver. Asking the person on the other end to send someone quick, *Ruby's done something bad, she's cut herself real bad*.

He tried to remember the incident itself, how it had happened, but nothing came back to him. He always assumed she'd tried to commit suicide. The long scar on her right wrist had been his only proof, as neither Norma nor his mother had spoken of it since.

Norma picked up the teapot. "Tea or coffee, either of you?"

Sheila smiled. "I'd love a cup of tea if you're having some, thanks."

"I'm fine," Martin said.

"So what brings you back here after all this time, Marty?" She spoke while facing the wall as she filled the teapot in the sink. "Not that we don't appreciate the visit."

"I guess you don't watch the news."

"Only the locals."

She twisted a dial on the stove and set the teapot on the open flame. Then she came and sat with them, grunting as she eased herself onto a cushioned chair.

She'd always seemed old to Martin but now he could really see it. Her skin looked like tea-stained crepe paper over a roadmap of thin blue veins. Folds of wrinkled skin hung from her neck below the jaw and her silver hair had thinned. When she clasped her hands on the table, every knuckle bone was white like a chicken drumstick.

"Well, spill your guts, Marty. Pardon the expression," she said to Sheila, which Sheila acknowledged with a polite smile.

If Norma had known what happened to Tish, she probably would've used a different figure of speech.

He spared her the sordid details, giving her a brief account of everything that happened since Pennsylvania. The teapot began to whistle as he arrived at their decision to drive out here and Norma poured two cups, served one to Sheila and blew on her own, nodding thoughtfully as Martin finished his story.

"Well, I can't say your mother will be thrilled to see you. If you thought she was a pill when you were a kid, she's the whole dang pharmacy now."

"Does she still...?"

Norma nodded. "She has her spells, time to time. Not like back then. Can't say there's a day goes by I don't think about walking out that door and never coming back. Glutton for punishment, I suppose."

"Punishment?" came the old woman's voice from the hallway, her Irish accent as familiar as if he'd heard it yesterday. "Is that what you call it, then?"

Martin stood, wheeling around to face his mother.

She was hunched over her walker, tennis balls on its feet to muffle their sound, her skeletal fingers clasping the grips. She looked older than time. Older than God. Her skin was so thin

Martin thought he could see every sinew, every vein, every wiry muscle beneath it. Her cheeks were sallow, her green eyes—once full of "pith and vinegar," as Norma would say—had dulled, milky from cataracts, sunken within the deep pits between her brow and cheekbones. Her wiry gray hair was done up in a single braid that hung over her bony shoulder.

"Ma," he said.

A wave of conflicting emotions washed over him and for a brief moment, just looking at her standing there in the doorway like an ancient apparition, he had to fight back tears. Whether from joy, sadness or terror, he wasn't sure.

"Yes, 'Ma,' 'Ma.' As soon as they learn to talk, it's 'Ma this' and 'Ma that,'" she said brusquely, shuffling her walker into the kitchen to get a closer look at him. "Now what's this you say about murder?"

# Chapter 8

## Mommie Dearest

"WELL, THAT CERTAINLY is quite a tale, isn't it?" Ruby said once he'd repeated a condensed version for her. "But you've always been a teller of tall tales, haven't you, Martin?"

He knew she was baiting him, and he almost bit the line.

"The question is, how much of it is true?" She turned to Sheila. Her opinion of Sheila Tanner as an "interloper" had softened since Sheila introduced herself with what, according to Ruby, was a "fine Gaelic name."

"Every word of it, as far as I know. I've never known Martin to be a liar." She shrugged. "Aside from a little white lie or two to get me into bed."

"See, Ma? Your boy made good.... Kinda."

Ruby ignored him. "And this *serial killer*? This rubbish about witches and warlocks?"

"Just witches, Mrs. Savage."

Ruby clucked her tongue, her cloudy eyes narrowing with sudden fury. "There is no *Mister* Savage, so there will be no *Missus*. Ruby will do just fine, and short of that, Miss Savage."

"I'm sorry. Ruby it is. James Barclay is a very dangerous, very troubled man. He believed in some highly unbelievable things, but in my professional opinion that makes him more dangerous, not less."

The old woman nodded, her gaze softening. "Your professional opinion," she said, even more dubious. "But surely this Barclay is only dangerous to pregnant women and my Martin. The question becomes, why on Earth did you follow him here? Is my son courting you? Has he gotten you up the stick?"

Sheila carefully swallowed her tea, clearly trying not to laugh and choke on it.

"*Mom.*"

"Mom, what? I watch cable television now. I know what you young people get up to in this day and age, and I don't condone it in the least."

"I didn't get her pregnant."

"Well, that's certainly a relief."

"Ruby, play nice," Norma said. She set a cup of tea on a saucer in front of the old woman.

"*Play nice.*" Ruby sneered, looking from Martin to Sheila as if for assistance against Norma's tyranny. "This is my house. I'll play any way I like."

"Drink your tea, Ruby."

Ruby picked up the cup and saucer, hands quivering as she raised the cup. She sipped the steaming tea greedily, unfazed by its heat, and smacked her lips. She placed them back on the table and smiled.

"I'll have Norma make up the beds for you—"

"We don't want to be any trouble," Sheila said.

"We were planning on staying at the B&B," Martin added.

"With those *beatnicks*? I'll have none of it." She grasped the walker and hauled herself to her feet with a groan and a crackling of joints. "So long as you're in the Bay you'll stay under my roof, the two of you. Of course, you'll sleep in separate rooms. I won't allow hanky-panky in the same house I bathed you as a child."

"That's a great image, Ma. Thanks."

She clucked her tongue. "In the meantime, perhaps the two of you could take a walk into town? Norma forgot to get the shortening and I'd like to bake a pie. Is strawberry and rhubarb still your favorite?"

He hadn't eaten a strawberry-rhubarb pie since she was committed. "It sure is," he said, just to please her. "And we'd be happy to. Thanks, Ma."

Ruby nodded curtly, expressionless. "Think nothing of it." She shuffled over and placed a hand on his shoulder to steady herself as she kissed him on the top of his head. Her lips felt like sandpaper. "Have you been drinking?"

"Not today, Ma."

Her supernatural nose for troublemaking always surprised him. Sheila popped her eyes at him, obviously impressed.

"Good. Let's keep it that way. I'll not have a souse living under my roof."

"Cut the kid some slack," Norma said.

"Nonsense. Spare the rod, spoil the child."

Norma gave him an apologetic look as Ruby shuffled out of the room, the tennis balls on her walker thudding softly on the linoleum. Then she poured Ruby's tea down the sink. "That nasty old broad'll be the death of me."

"If you're lucky," Martin said.

"Well, I guess I'll show you to your rooms. Though I sure wouldn't fault you for getting in that car and driving as far away from here as possible while you still have the chance," she added with a dry chuckle.

---

It was a relatively nice day, so they decided to forgo the car and walk into town as Ruby had suggested.

His old neighborhood had blossomed in the past thirty-five years. When he was a kid, there'd only been two houses out on this side of the island: theirs and a house that belonged to the mayor. Now it was a small suburb with cookie-cutter bungalows and semis, smooth asphalt streets and neatly manicured lawns dusted with snow, the streets all named after counties in Ireland. Cork Road, Cavan Street, Kildare Avenue, Londonderry Crescent, Limerick Lane.

He pointed out his old school as they walked by, remarking how being back here made him feel tall. Small children laughed and played in the schoolyard. Older children stood outside in a huddled mass, a few of them surreptitiously vaping or dragging on cigarettes, eyeing the two adults suspiciously as they moved past.

At the entrance to the chain link fence, a young mother

pulled her weeping boy of nine or ten along by the hand toward the open door of their minivan. His shirt was torn. He had smudges of dirt on his face and elbows and skinned knees.

"You're grounded. No playing with your friends for a whole week."

"*But Mo-o-om,*" the kid whimpered.

She buckled him in and slammed the door. When she saw Sheila, she nodded at her as if she was part of the tribe. "Kids, huh?"

"Yup," Sheila said. Once they were out of earshot and the mother was behind the wheel, Sheila winked. "Tell me again why you don't want kids?"

He laughed.

Ten minutes later they stood at the foot of a monument on the eastern edge of the downtown core, overlooking the shopfronts on King Street. Statues of a man and a woman made of weathered bronze, both of them emaciated and dressed in rags, with a skeletal girl of about eight or nine clinging her father's leg. Below this, the plaque read *In memory of the victims of the* Ruby *and the families they left behind, during the Great Famine, 1845 – 1850. Go ndéana Dia trócaire orthu.*

"Is that Gaelic?" Sheila wondered.

"Fine Gaelic, even," Martin joked.

"I think Sheila's Latin, but I didn't want to argue."

"Probably for the best. I can't remember where the damn grocery store is. I guess it wouldn't hurt to wander until we find it."

Sheila laughed. "It's not like we could get lost. If we hit the ocean, we'll know we've gone too far."

They headed down the main thoroughfare. Many of the cream-colored brick buildings looked like they'd been there for decades, possibly even from the turn of the previous century. Any sign of urban decay many small towns suffered had been smothered by colorful earthen-toned paints, hanging flowers and potted trees. The shops all screamed "retail therapy," from a chocolatier and a quilting store to a clothing boutique and an antique shop that sold barnwood doors, tin-bucket planters and tables made from salvaged wagon wheels.

Martin remembered once having seen a TV ad for Barrows Bay—it took him by surprise and he'd almost jumped out of his skin. It was for something called "Women's Weekends," two solid days and nights of wine and shopping. He couldn't have imagined it from what he remembered of his hometown, but standing at the corner of King and Princess he realized this place was nothing like what it once was.

*Wolfe was right. You really can't go home again.*

Thinking this, he looked up to see himself in a shopfront window.

"Look, Ma, I'm famous."

In the window display a small space had been reserved for "LOCAL AUTHOR MARTIN SAVAGE." It featured a blow-up of his author photo from the dustjacket of *Dangerous Curves*, taken when he was much younger, a real ladykiller just like Norma said, on a stand behind several of his hardcovers placed on risers.

The Constant Reader bookstore was a warren of dark shelves lined with paperbacks and hardcovers of all sizes. There was a small reading area near the entrance. The glass on the bottom of the door had been smashed and covered with cardboard, held to the frame with duct tape.

"Looks like you've got a number one fan," Sheila said. "You going in?"

"How could I resist?"

She peered down the street. "Let's get the shortening first, huh? I don't want to make an enemy of your mom on the first day."

"Fine, fine," he said, and reluctantly allowed himself to be dragged away.

---

SINJIN'S WHOLESALE Grocery stood at the top of Princess Street on the northern edge of town. It sold everything Martin would have expected to see in a Brooklyn hipster co-op: fresh, "organic" fruit and vegetables from local farmers, a deli section with "free-range" meats and "responsibly harvested" lobsters in a giant tank, a bulk foods section, shelves stocked with non-GMO products and a limited supply of big-name brands. A small selection of local craft beers—a brand called Ravenous seemed to be most prominent—and wines were available in their own section of the store, along with staples like Narragansett and Jack Daniels.

"Technically, grocers aren't allowed to carry liquor in Rhode Island," a man said behind Martin as he perused the alcohol longingly. "So we just pretend this kiosk is a store of its own."

Martin turned and looked up. The man was a giant, with thinning black hair, a bushy black beard and black, thick-rimmed glasses. He wore an apron with the Sinjin's Wholesale Grocery logo on it and a button with "HELLO MY NAME IS" and *SINJIN* written with a Sharpie.

"Holy moly!" Sinjin said, the blinking of his green eyes magnified behind the thick lenses. "Martin Savage?"

"I sure am. Are you a fan?"

The grocer scowled in confusion. Then he grabbed the button on his apron. "It's Sinjin, man! Dave St. John. We went to kindergarten together. Wow!"

Encounters like this always made him feel awkward. He was rarely on the other end, the one remembering someone who didn't know him from Adam. It was always someone who remembered him, and the fact that he was semi-famous only made it worse, particularly if he made the mistake of thinking they might be a reader of his books.

He didn't remember Sinjin. He couldn't remember much about his life in Barrows Bay at all, let alone specific children he'd known in kindergarten. He did have a vague memory of running through the streets with two children, one a freckled girl with a shock of red hair and the other a chubby boy with black hair and glasses—

"Sinjin," Martin said, nodding. "Sure. We went to kindergarten together."

A huge smile spread across the big man's face. He clapped Martin on the shoulder. "Those were the days, huh? Wow," he said again. "So what's new and exciting? What brings you back to the Bay?"

Behind the mountain of a man, Sheila held up a block of shortening for Martin's approval. He nodded. "Hey, uh..." he started to say.

"Sinjin."

"Sinjin, it really is great to see you. I have to take off, but we should catch up some time—"

The grocer brimmed with excitement. "Yeah? Man, I'd love to have you over for dinner. Meet the wife. D'youse like lobster? Of course, you like lobster, you're a fellow Rhody."

"I guess I am," Martin said, smiling in spite of himself. "I'd love to have dinner with you. And the wife."

Sinjin caught Martin's glance at Sheila. "Hey, is that your woman? You dog!" He clapped Martin in the same spot on the same shoulder. Martin rubbed it absently with his fingertips, careful not to touch it with his injured palm.

"We're just friends."

"Well, she looks like a real catch, Martin. I wouldn't throw her back in the water without baiting that hook, if you know what I mean."

"Thanks for the advice." He gave Sinjin a hearty smack back on the forearm. The man glanced at the place Martin struck. "You take care now," Martin said.

"Yeah, you too." He chuckled as Martin began to walk away. "Same old Smartypants."

Martin turned back. "What's that supposed to mean?"

"Smartypants Marty," Sinjin said, grinning as if it was obvious. "You don't remember? That's what kids used to call you."

"They did, huh?"

"Yup. Not me and Nadine, though. The other kids."

Smartypants Marty. The nickname did have a familiar ring to it. There were no hurt feelings attached to it, just a word that rhymed with his name. And Nadine must have been the freckled girl with the red hair. The feelings that arose thinking of her made him wonder if she'd been his first crush.

"Is, uh, is Nadine still in town?"

"Oh yeah. You prolly passed her store on the way here. She runs The Constant Reader downtown. The bookstore."

Martin grinned. "You don't say. See you later, Sinjin."

"Later, brother. I'm gonna hold you to that dinner."

Martin had no intention of eating dinner with a stranger and his wife, but he said, "Look forward to it."

He met Sheila at the counter. "Do you mind running this stuff back to the house? I want to hit that bookstore on the way back."

Sheila chuckled. "Looking to get your ego stroked?"

"Or something," he said.

THE BELLS above the door jingled pleasantly, making him think of wind chimes and patio lanterns, lemonade and the sweet smell of hay in the summer.

The Constant Reader smelled like every other bookstore he'd been in over the past several weeks, aside from a whiff of fresh-brewed coffee and patchouli beneath the strong musty odor of slowly decomposing paper. He lingered by the door a moment, looking over his little shrine, hoping someone would pass by the window and do a double take when they saw him standing beside his author photo, but nobody did.

"I'll be right there," a woman called from the stacks.

"No rush," he shouted back.

The interior was dimly lit with hanging lamps from the exposed rafters and painted ductwork. On the counter a snuffed-out incense stick leaned over a pile of ashes in a wood holder. There were pamphlets and money jars for various charitable causes, from Save the Oceans to Black Lives Matter, stacks of business cards for local artists and stickers on the cash register with slogans like THE FUTURE IS FEMALE and I AM A NASTY WOMAN.

A French coffee press stood near the register, still steaming. Near the stacks, a reading area had been set up with two cozy-looking armchairs and a round table. Under a small handmade sign with *Femme Voices* painted in red, books from Toni Morrison, Roxane Gay, Margaret Atwood and Ursula K. LeGuin rubbed shoulders with Maya Angelou, Shirley Jackson and Virginia Woolf.

A woman emerged from the back holding a large sheet of Bristol board, her strawberry-blonde hair pulled up in a high ponytail, splashes of black paint on her denim overalls. Her bare feet slapped on the tiles, soles dirty, nails painted green.

She spoke with a thin paintbrush held between her teeth. "Just one more thing." If she recognized him, she didn't show it.

She spun the board around. Painted on it were the words CLOSING SALE EVERYTHING MUST GO! She held it up against the window and glanced back over her shoulder. The sun shone in her hair and suddenly Martin was five years old again, chasing her through a farmer's field.

"Hold this?"

Martin hurried over and reached past her to hold the sign against the glass. She smelled of patchouli and citrus and fresh sweat as she slipped by to the counter, grabbed a roll of scotch tape and brought it back to where he stood.

She snapped a piece off with her teeth, slapped it on the sign and rubbed it vigorously. She did the same three more times, ducking down in front of him to get the low corners, allowing him a glimpse directly into the cups of her black bra at the tops of her areolas before she turned and stood, catching him with a coy grin.

"Martin Savage, as I live and breathe."

"I wasn't sure you recognized me."

"Are you kidding? Small town boy makes good. I've read every one of your books. They're good. A tad salacious." She grinned again. "But good." She laughed, brushed a tress of hair over her ear and stuck out a hand. "I'm Nadine. You probably don't remember me—"

"We went to kindergarten together," he said, shaking her hand.

She smiled. "Wow. I'm impressed." She held his gaze a moment too long, looked down at their entwined hands and laughed again, letting go. "Look at me, gushing all over myself. I guess you must've seen my little shrine to you in the window there, huh?"

He grinned. "I could give you a lock of my hair if you need a holy relic."

Nadine laughed. "But then you'd have to worry if I'm gonna use it for a voodoo doll or to clone you from your DNA."

"Good point. You never know these days."

They shared an awkward smile.

"God, so what brings you back after all these years, Marty? I kind of thought you forgot all about little old Barrows Bay. You never mentioned it in your interviews." She rolled her eyes. "Not that I *blame* you. I mean, *gawd.* What's there to say, right?"

"That's a long story."

"Say no more. I know how the book market is." She chuckled, running the tip of a finger over her freckled collarbone. "Do I ever."

"It's not that, it's—wait, is that why you're closing up shop?"

"No, no. Business is as slow as ever. But that's also a long story."

"Well, maybe we can discuss our mutual woes in the book business over drinks."

As he said it her attention drifted toward the front windows, her brow furrowing.

"That old fucking *cunt*." She brushed past him, racing to the door, twisted the lock and jerked down the door shade.

Martin spotted the back of a mint 1959 pink Cadillac idling across the street, spewing black smoke. Then Nadine pulled the drapes down over the shopfront window, blocking it from view. Cracks of sunlight barely allowed him to see her face. She looked both frightened and angry.

"Is someone harassing you, Nadine?"

*Yeah, harassed by her local Avon lady*, he thought, berating himself.

She turned with fire in her eyes and her hands on her hips. "Do you wanna fuck me, Marty?"

"What? Like now?"

She unsnapped the buckles on her overalls and let the bib fall, exposing her bra and the slope of her breasts as she breathed quickly, anxiously. "Oh, Smartypants," she said, looking up into his eyes. "Do I really need to paint you a picture?"

He didn't need a picture. He kicked off his shoes and unzipped his jeans, then pulled them down with his boxers in one swift, practiced movement.

Nadine laughed, gave him an appreciative once-over, and leaped into his arms.

---

THEY LAY on the cold tiles in their own sticky sweat, looking up at the bare rafters and ducts. The glow of a joint illuminated their faces in the otherwise dim store.

"That was fucking great," he said, holding in a toke.

"That was great fucking," she corrected him. "And just so you know, I haven't been pining away for your return all these years like some swooning Victorian heroine."

He laughed, exhaling a lungful of savory smoke. "Oh no?"

"Oh no. This was strategic."

"How so?"

She turned to face him, rising on an elbow. "What better way to get back at a town that's fucked me over my whole life than by fucking its native son?"

He passed the joint and regarded her in the dim light. "Native son? These people don't even remember me."

"Martin Savage? Please. Just because no one talks about you doesn't mean they don't remember. That's *why* they don't talk about you. Because of what you represent."

"And what's that?"

She took a long pull off the joint. "Escape, for one thing," she said, smoke spilling from her lips. Then she scowled, exhaling the rest through her nostrils. "How old is your mother, Martin?"

"She never said. Must be in her eighties by now, I'd imagine."

"So she had you when? In her forties?"

"Thereabouts."

"How often did women have children at that age back then? Single women, in particular."

He shrugged. "I'm not a sociologist."

"What did she look like, the last time you saw her? How old would you say she looked when they hauled her off to the loony bin?"

"That's not nice."

"*She's* not nice."

He sat up stiffly. "This is taking a weird turn."

Nadine shot up beside him. "This took a weird turn forty years ago, Marty."

She stubbed the joint out on the tiles. Her ass peeled off the floor as she stood, sticky with sweat. She slipped her feet into a mismatched purple G-string and pulled it up over her hips.

"What do you know about midwifery?"

He watched her get dressed. Was she serious? A minute ago they were fucking like long-lost lovers and now she was asking him about midwives? He scooped up the torn condom wrapper from the floor, glad he'd thought to use it.

"Do you know there hasn't been a birth in this town for

decades that hasn't been performed by the Midwives?" she asked finally, buckling the straps of her overalls.

He picked up his jeans and began unhurriedly dressing while still sitting on the floor, like a kid putting on his snow pants. Clearly, he'd overstayed his welcome. He needed to extricate himself as delicately as possible. It seemed like a switch had been turned. She'd gone from flirty to crazy in sixty seconds. He zipped up his jeans.

"I should go. It seems like you've got a lot to do..."

She looked down at him with full-blown paranoia in her eyes. "Don't you remember them, Martin? The old ladies with their knitting needles and disapproving glares? Their clucking tongues. Weren't they old when we were kids? Don't you think that's *strange*?"

"Betty White and Sean Connery have looked the same for forty years," he said, putting on his shoes.

This seemed to derail her. She blinked at him several times. Then she let out a dry laugh. "You don't know. You haven't lived here. Under their shadow. The way people act around them. The way they *talk*."

He flashed on the night of the fire, the smiling old woman Aunt Norma had chased into the dark, their shadows thrown long and wavering from the blaze.

Was that who she meant?

He opened his mouth to ask. Shut it again and tugged his shirt over his head, refusing to fall into her paranoid trap. Evil old ladies? The entire concept was preposterous.

"Do you know where the word *glamour* comes from, Marty?" She crossed to the door. "It's a Scottish term for a magical enchantment. Making things appear different than they are. Like the emperor's new clothes. A trick played on the eyes of the beholder. Synonyms for glamour include enchantment, charm, *bewitch*."

He followed her, anxious now, holding his shoes in a clenched fist. She was starting to sound a lot like James Barclay. He'd already gotten a lifetime's supply of that brand of crazy in the past few days.

"Look around you, Marty. Doesn't this town seem strange to you? Doesn't it feel *not right*?"

She pulled back the door shade enough to peer out, eyes narrowed.

"Nadine, what are you saying to me? You're scared of a bunch of little old ladies?"

"You have no idea, Marty. She's *blinded* you to it. She used a glamour on you so you can't see her as she really is. She's blinded *this whole town*."

"She? She *who*?"

When Nadine turned back from the windows, all the menace and fear had left her eyes. They held only pity.

"The wickedest witch of them all, Marty. Your mommie dearest: Miss Ruby Savage."

# CHAPTER 9

## SUSPICIOUS MINDS

"I'M LEAVING THIS shithole town on the last ferry out," Nadine said, rushing Martin out the door with his belt unbuckled and one shoe still in his hand. "If you're smart, you'll do the same."

Then she pushed the door closed and pulled the shade back down.

He stepped into his shoe and walked back to the house with one damp sock. The after-sex high and slight buzz from the weed did nothing to stop the paranoid thoughts of what she'd said to him from circling his brain like vultures over a corpse.

She was clearly deeply disturbed. How likely was it that everyone in town was out to get her at the behest of his mother and her friends? It was madness.

*Witches. Glamours.*

She had to be out of her mind.

And though he couldn't deny a creeping suspicion that something was rotten in Barrows Bay—had possibly *always been* rotten—he wasn't about to buy into her paranoid fantasies wholesale.

The pink Cadillac outside the store. The hole smashed through her front door. Maybe someone was messing with her. Gaslighting her. Trying to drive her crazy. Run her out of town for God knew what.

Or was there something about this place that bred these wild suspicions? A symptom of island life, lived both in isolation from the rest of the world yet never truly alone in such a confined space? Was it the harsh Atlantic winters? The weight of shared secrets kept from outsiders?

He didn't know. But as he walked across town, he felt judgmental stares from behind lacy curtains and crooked blinds. From strangers he passed in the street.

*It's Aunt Norma's Them. Sweet-looking old ladies with sharp needles and murder in their eyes. The Barrows Bay Knitting Circle and Murder Syndicate. Knit one, kill one.*

Martin laughed aloud, startling an old man trimming hedges, a wide-brimmed straw hat casting his face in shadow like the old lady across the street the night of the fire.

The man seemed to recognize him. Almost said something, then reconsidered it.

His shears went *snick!* and another branch fell, and in the same instant a fat black spider of terror crawled out from Martin's subconscious, causing him to break into a full run, glancing back at the startled old man, running until he was safely around the corner, behind the hedge, wondering what the hell just happened and why he started running in the first place.

Something about that sound—*the terrible sound*—had triggered a panic attack. Fight or flight. Run, Marty, run.

He couldn't remember the last time he'd had one so sudden. So severe.

Did the hedge clippers set him off? Remembering something about what Barclay had done to Tish? Or had he known the old man from childhood? What kind of maniac clipped their hedges in March, anyway?

He gave himself a moment to recover, getting his breathing under control in the shade of a large red maple. Thinking back to what Nadine said about living under the shadow of his mother and her friends.

She called them midwives. Not just midwives—*the* Midwives. With a capital M.

She seemed to be implying Ruby wasn't his mother, just a woman who'd delivered him. That—what?—she'd taken him from his birth mother? A stolen child, like the Yeats poem about faeries stealing children on a leafy island in Sleuth Wood? *Come away! O human child.*

He felt sudden pity for her. But what could he do? She was leaving the island on the last ferry out. His knowledge of psychology was limited, just enough to serve his literary career and help get him laid. Sheila was infinitely more qualified to help.

But no. That wouldn't fly. He would have to tell her about his encounter, and she'd figure him out right away. She'd probably smell it on him the second he walked in the door, the sex and patchouli. As good a liar as he was, he'd never been able to keep things from her. Just like his mother, in that sense. Sheila could always tell when he'd been with someone. It drove the final wedge in their brief relationship.

She hadn't even been angry. Almost as if she'd always expected it to happen, eventually. As if she'd known he couldn't keep his dick in his pants longer than it took to zip them up.

The onus was entirely on him. She'd never been jealous. Wasn't needy. She hadn't pushed to move in together or get serious. He simply lacked the gene for monogamy. Relationships would last a few months, maybe a year before his attention would start to wander.

Sheila said he suffered from abandonment issues during their last argument, the one that finally broke them. That he might harbor some hidden trauma causing him to substitute sex for love.

Maybe that was true. Whatever his problem was, he'd sure fucked things up royally with Sheila. At times he could convince himself it had been for the best. But even though she'd forgiven him—or maybe because she'd gotten over it so eagerly—the way they'd left things was always something that bothered him.

*Fuck the pain away. That's what she said, wasn't it? And when the going gets tough, Smartypants Marty gets going. I run away, just like I always have.*

*Escaped from Barrows Bay. Escaped Stratford and left poor Norma to look after Ruby all on her own. Send money at Christmas, but never write back when Norma sends her letters.*

*And when the boogieman comes chasing after me, what do I do? Run again, right back home to Mommy. Home again, home again, jiggety-jig.*

*Killer? Nah, not this guy. Fucking coward, that's what I am. Fucking coward with a trail of blood behind me.*

---

He smelled the pie baking the moment he stepped into the gingerbread house, slipping off his coat and shoes. Tangy, sweet, flaky and buttery.

"I'm home!" he called out.

He meant it to be ironic but it suddenly struck him that it had never felt so true. Likely just the smell of home baking and the memories of the house making him nostalgic. He suddenly wanted to slide down the carpeted stairs on his butt like he did when he was small. *Thump thump thump* all the way down to the bottom.

"'Bout darn time," Norma said. She and Sheila were in the kitchen, sitting at the table.

"The pie smells amazing." He kissed the soft white hair on Norma's crown. "Where's Ma?"

"I drew her a bath. Sheila here's been filling me in on your exploits with the ladies in the meantime." She gave him a disapproving glower. "Sounds like we're gonna have to spike your morning coffee with saltpeter."

Sheila laughed. "Looks like you had fun with Barrows Bay's answer to Annie Wilkes." She nodded toward his groin. He saw the tail of his shirt peeking out of his zipper. Made a quick adjustment before zipping up.

"We caught up over a coffee and I used the little boy's room. Guess I forgot to zip up."

Aunt Norma clucked her tongue. "Mm-hmm, I'll bet. Same old Marty. Ladykiller in his teens, too. I tried to teach him respect for women, but it was like trying to teach a rich kid the value of money."

He favored them with a sarcastic glare. "Well, if you two hens are gonna cluck all night, I guess I'll go to check out my old room."

"Don't think I don't know what you're doing up there with the door locked," Norma said. He left to the sound of their laughter.

As he ascended the stairs, a creak came from above. He

froze, momentarily anxious. *Mom's in the bath, Smartypants,* he reminded himself. Nadine's paranoia had him jumping at shadows. In his own house, this time.

The bathroom door was open a crack. Water sloshed from within, a thin trickle of steam escaping through the doorway. He ignored the urge to check on Ruby and continued to his old bedroom.

Cardboard boxes had been stacked around his small single bed, which stood in the alcove between two sloped walls surrounding the single window. He raised the flap on one of the boxes and peered inside at a jumble of dusty framed photographs, trophies, old newspapers and other things he didn't recognize or recall. All he knew was that they didn't belong to him. Maybe they belonged to Norma's family or his mother.

The walls were bare, flocked wallpaper like the rest of the house. He'd been too young for posters and Ruby probably wouldn't have allowed them anyhow. He hadn't started putting things on his wall until he was a little older, maybe nine or ten, when he'd cut out photos from magazines.

He closed the door. It opened again easily, didn't jam or lock on its own. The keyhole was still scratched on the outside where Norma had tried to jimmy it during the fire.

He remembered pulling on the handle in terror, the smell of smoke already heavy in the air. Norma carrying him down the stairs in her arms. The heat of the fire like a bad sunburn as they rushed to the front door.

He looked at the scar on his hand. The door handle was glass and he remembered it had been cool, like it was now, so it couldn't have burned him. The memory of having burned it on a woodstove wasn't possible either, according to Norma. But he already had the injury by the time they moved to Stratford.

Something had to have caused it. He supposed it didn't matter. It was just weird that he couldn't remember.

Could that be the hidden trauma Sheila hypothesized? The one that made it difficult to share his life with someone else? The one that made him impossible to love?

He sat on the foot of the old bed. It was small but better than the sofa. Sheila would get the guest bedroom, which had a double bed, since she was technically the only guest.

He lay back on the small pillow. Shadows of the tree outside played on the stucco ceiling. He tried to imagine having slept in this bed when he was little but it felt foreign. Like someone else's life.

"Norma?"

Ruby's voice was so weak he barely heard her. She called again a moment later, not much louder. Worry in her voice. He pushed up from the bed and stepped out into the hall.

"Ma?" He approached the bathroom door, hearing the squeak of wet skin on porcelain. "You okay in there?"

"Martin, get Norma, dear. I'm shriveled up like an old prune."

He leaned over the stairwell. Sheila and Norma were talking loudly to hear each other over the oven exhaust fan and clanging pots. He'd have to go down to the kitchen to get her and she would probably castigate him for bothering her while she prepped dinner when he could easily help the old woman himself.

"I can help you, Ma," he said, resigning himself to having to glimpse his mother's withered, naked body.

"Don't trouble yourself," she said brusquely. "Norma is perfectly capable."

"She's busy with dinner, Ma." And though it was the last thing he wanted to do, he added, "Let me help you."

"I don't have my face on."

"It's just me, Ma. You don't need makeup."

She sighed heavily, resigned herself. "My towel's on the door."

He opened it cautiously and reached for the towel. Her back was facing him but he caught a flash of her in the foggy mirror, hunched over herself like a wizened crone with her chin jutting out and a dour expression. The sharp ridges of her spine poked through waves of loose, damp gray hair. Her body riddled with dark Rorschach splotches he supposed were a combination of collapsed veins and liver spots. The old white scar on her right wrist was still visible after all these years, just like his own on his left palm.

*The White Place*, he thought. It was the name he'd given to Saints of Mercy Sanitarium when he was little. Because of the white walls, the white furniture, the white bedspreads and covers and uniforms and gowns.

He'd forgotten all about that name until now.

He held the towel in front of her and grasped her upper arm. She sucked in a hissed breath.

"Be gentle, for Pete's sake! I brought you into this world, I can just as easily take you out."

"Sorry." He loosened his grip. "Better?"

She scowled up at him. "Do you always require constant affirmation? Yes, it is much better, thank you. Now help me out."

He slipped a hand around her, feeling her ribs as if there was no muscle beneath her skin. She stepped out cautiously and he wrapped the towel around her, careful not to look in the mirror. She stood there huddled in it, holding her walker with one hand while she shivered and scowled at him.

The thought that he'd have to help her get dressed made him shudder internally.

"You don't need help, uh...?"

She clucked her tongue. "Don't be a prude, Martin. And no, I won't need your help toweling myself or dressing myself. I'm a grown woman and woe betide you for suggesting otherwise."

He grinned. Same old Ruby, fiercely independent despite the limitations of her age and body. It almost made him laugh to think of how Nadine had described her, as some all-powerful magic woman.

"All right then. I'll let you get to it."

Ruby began singing what sounded like an old folk tune as he stepped out and closed the door most of the way. "*The shamrock is by law forbid to grow on Irish ground.*" Her voice was surprisingly musical, despite its frailty.

Returning to the stairs, he slipped in a small puddle on the hardwood floor. He bent down and spotted another small puddle at the top of the stairs. On the carpeted risers it was easy to see the wet spots for what they were.

Footprints.

He followed them halfway down the steps, until they were no longer visible. The carpet was dampest here, spattered with multiple drops. As if someone had been there, not sitting on the stair lift—he would have heard its motorized buzz from the kitchen, anyhow—but standing on the stairs dripping wet.

*"For they're hanging men and women for the wearing of the green,"* came his mother's voice from above.

He caught a glimpse of Ruby just as she left the bathroom and in the brief glimpse it looked like she was doing the Charleston down the hall.

When he rose two steps to get a better look, she was already in her bedroom. Her door slammed, and he was suddenly stricken by an inexplicable panic.

He ran all the way down the stairs before the embarrassment of running away from a little old lady who wouldn't harm a hair on his head settled in, and he laughed at himself.

"What's so funny?" Sheila asked, stepping in from the living room.

"Nothing. I just, uh, it's weird to be back here is all."

"Weird is one way to put it. Norma said to get you for dinner," she added, heading toward the delicious smell in the kitchen.

DINNER TASTED as delicious as it smelled.

They had roast beef and mashed potatoes in a thick gravy and onions and cooked baby carrots, the four of them sitting around the dining room table. Norma had buzzed Ruby's meal a few times in the food processor to make it easier for the old woman to chew without her dentures. Martin tried not to spend the entire time watching in horrified fascination as she gummed the brown, pureed food paste to death.

Ruby abstained from drinking the bottle of white wine Sheila picked up at Sinjin's grocery store, choosing prune juice instead. The two guests and Norma enjoyed it—although it wasn't exactly up to par with what Martin usually drank, when he did drink wine—and got caught up in amiable conversation about their lives in New York and on the island.

Norma and Ruby had returned to Barrows Bay ten years prior. They didn't go into detail about their return, but he remembered in a long-ago letter from Norma that patients had been released from the institution into other hospitals due to cuts in funding, and it was just around the time she was starting to tire of her own job, wanting something a little more stable in hours, with more of a personal touch than the old folks' home where she'd worked part time for over a decade.

Rather than let Ruby waste away in another hospital, Norma became the old woman's legal guardian.

Life in Barrows Bay quickly went back to normal. Ruby resumed her bridge club evenings and spent several nights a week with the "old biddies," as Norma called them, while Norma kept the house in good shape.

Neither woman seemed in need of a job, and Martin supposed his mother must have been well-off or Norma had come into an inheritance. The money he sent at Christmas couldn't have supported them all these years. However it was they got by, Ruby would consider it rude to ask and "woe betide him" for even considering such a transgression.

"I suppose it's high time to discuss the elephant in the room," Ruby said once she'd finished her meat paste and returned her dentures to her mouth. "The two of you are on the run from a dangerous psychopath, and by returning home you may have put the people of this island in danger. Our nearest constables are across the sound, I'm afraid, and also quite incompetent. So it behooves me to ask if either of you are armed."

Sheila and Martin shared a look. The two of them broke into laughter.

Ruby glowered at them until they stopped.

"I don't like guns, Ruby," Sheila said.

"And I left mine in my footlocker," Martin joked.

"Good then," Ruby said with a nod. "I'll not have a gun under my roof, thank you very much."

Truthfully, Lumsden pretended he hadn't seen the Glock and Martin tucked it into his bag with an armful of loose clothing. The bag was in the trunk. He'd have to remember to tuck it into the glove compartment before bringing his stuff inside. If Norma went snooping, as she had when he was a teen, she'd give him fresh hell for lying. But he couldn't give up his only source of protection if Barclay somehow figured out where they were hiding.

Better to keep it safely locked inside the car.

*So long as no one steals the Lexus. Should probably park her in the garage after dinner.*

"Who's ready for dessert?" Norma asked, easing out of her chair.

They each ate a huge helping of strawberry-rhubarb pie, all except Ruby who abstained. Sweets and spirits were too "decadent," although she always enjoyed baking.

It was as good as he remembered, the crust flaky and rich and the filling both sweet and tart. A time capsule on a plate. He could almost remember a time when he was happy here.

"This is delicious, Ma."

"Don't speak with your mouth full, Martin."

"Everything was great," Sheila said, clearly trying not to laugh at his scolding.

"I'm glad you both like it. I may no longer be in control of all my faculties but it seems I can still bake a mean pie."

"You said it," Norma said, standing with her plate. She picked up Ruby's bowl. "I'll wash up."

Sheila leaped to her feet with her own plate and grabbed Martin's. "I'll help you."

Martin sat at the end of the table, realizing he was currently in a quandary. Ruby watched him like a hawk. He knew Norma would protest if he helped clear the table—she always had when he was a teen. But he couldn't sit here with Sheila giving him the stink eye every time she came in from the kitchen.

He got up, grabbed the serving plate and gravy boat. His mother reacted as if she'd been slapped.

"You put those down! That's woman's work."

He dreaded Sheila's response—but he dreaded his mother's disapproval more, and he was just about to lay them back on the tablecloth when Sheila stepped in holding a ratty dish towel.

"*Woman's work?*"

"That's right," Ruby said. "Man may work from sun to sun, but woman's work is never done."

Sheila scoffed. "Well, in case you haven't noticed, Ruby, Martin *hasn't* been working all day. He's been off fornicating with local bookshop owners."

He stood there holding the meat, feeling ridiculous, caught between incompatible generations and ideologies.

"And who would you say is to blame for that?" Ruby shot back. "Loose women and their modern feminism, that's who. Men are weak-willed as dogs. It's our job to keep the supper dish tucked away in the cupboard until it's time to eat."

Sheila threw the towel on the table. Her face was red. The raised vein that he'd often joked looked like the Missouri river zig-zagged across her forehead. Norma loaded the dishwasher, pretending not to be listening.

"I'm trying really hard to be respectful because we're in your house. But your antiquated values are the same ones that held women down for centuries."

"Tosh!" Ruby folded her arms across her chest, looking away with a scowl. "It's what we do, girl. I've never felt oppressed."

"That's because Norma does everything but wipe your ass!"

Ruby snapped back to face Sheila, her withered jaw dropped. Expecting her full fury, Martin took a step back from the table. Sheila stood frozen, obviously mortified by her own anger.

Ruby surprised them all by belting out laughter.

"Oh, thank you, dear!" she said, still laughing. "I haven't had a row like that in years." She wiped tears from her eyes with her napkin. "It's quite invigorating, truth be told. The ladies will think I've stumbled upon the fountain of youth."

"Well, I suppose I'm glad to have added a few years to your life," Sheila muttered, picking up the dish towel with a look of confusion.

"Oh, for Pete's sake, Martin!" Ruby tossed her napkin on the table. "Take the bloody dishes to the kitchen. Lord knows you want to."

Ever the good son, Martin did as he was told.

---

AFTER DINNER, Sheila, Martin and Norma sat in the living room with the TV on mute and Norma's Elvis albums on the record player. Ruby had gone off to bridge in the pink Cadillac Sheila had seen earlier in the day. Sheila, meanwhile, tried to formulate an opinion about the old woman. Tried to analyze her as she would have in her former practice.

Ruby's entire personality seemed at odds with her world view. A woman like her could have been burned at the stake in the era she seemed to prefer. Especially in this Boston marriage she and Norma appeared to be living in.

She chuckled. Had Martin been so clueless his whole life

that he hadn't seen the signs? Their devotion to each other was clear. They even had the witty back-and-forth repartee of an old married couple. And though Sheila couldn't fathom either woman engaging in sexual congress, she felt the same about most elderly people. She supposed she'd change her tune when her own time drew near. It wasn't likely she would give up sex the day after sixty-nine.

She looked at Norma. The woman sat in the Lazy-boy recliner with her arms on the rests as if to secure herself, watching the local news with the captioning on. They were covering the upcoming election—*Weren't they always?*—and Norma chuckled every so often. Every time Sheila looked up to see what she was laughing at the captioning had already moved on.

While Elvis began to mourn about how he and his lover were caught in a trap, she turned to Martin. He sat cross-legged on the floor in front of a bookshelf, sifting through old yearbooks. She'd sat with him for a while, laughing at pictures of him during his formative years. Once they'd reached high school he started to moan about his lost youth and Sheila had no interest in following him down the rabbit hole.

*You can't spell "martyr" without Marty*, she thought.

She picked a book from the shelf—a Hitchcock mystery anthology—and read it in intermittent bursts of concentration while Norma chuckled at the talking heads on the news and Martin waxed nostalgic.

The book was a time capsule of an era Ruby likely appreciated. Every other story seemed to be about some hen-pecked husband deciding to murder his wife in some vaguely creative way. Really tedious, openly misogynistic stuff. She set it aside and got up from the sofa.

"I'll be right back."

Martin glanced up as she passed. "Where ya going?"

"I'm just gonna take a walk down the street, I think."

He closed the yearbook and stood. "I'll come with you."

"You don't have to."

"I could use the exercise. Unless you'd rather be alone?"

"Why would I rather be alone?"

Norma glanced back over her shoulder. "Would you two get a room already? *Sheesh.*"

He laughed. Sheila shook her head. "Come on then," she said. "Before Norma breaks out the violin and roses."

The air was brisk out on the porch. The wind chimes tinkled. She zipped up as Martin headed down to the walk. She looked out at the darkened, empty street. The closest sound was the distant crash of waves against the shore.

"Do you think we're safe here, Martin?"

He seemed to consider it. "I think we're as safe as we'll ever be." He swept a hand toward the ocean, black against the starless sky. "We're surrounded by miles and miles of water. The ferry workers and the local cops all have a description of Barclay. Unless he swims across the bay or drastically changes his appearance, there's no way he's getting on this island."

She nodded. She was still a bit buzzed from dinner, and the argument she'd had with Ruby followed by reading the murder book had probably put her more on edge than she would've been otherwise. "You're right. We're safe. This is fine."

He gave her an odd look and opened his mouth as if he was about to say something. Then he started toward the sidewalk.

She hurried to catch up. They walked to the corner. Every house had lights on but there wasn't another person in sight.

"Any idea where you wanted to go, or are we just wandering?"

"Just wandering," she said.

They crossed the street. Somewhere out on the ocean a ferry horn sounded. Martin glanced at his watch. "Must be the last ferry out," he said.

It seemed to mean something to him but she didn't ask.

They walked a few paces in silence. He peered into brightened windows. She looked at her feet, careful not to break her mother's back.

They passed a newish bungalow at the end of his old street, still decorated from Christmas. In the window a mother and father and two children played a board game over the dining room table, laughing as the smallest child moved her piece across the board. It felt like a relic of a simpler time: a family enjoying each other's company with no cell phones, computers or big screen televisions to distract them.

They both wondered how nice it would have been to grow up in a normal household with a loving family.

"Ruby's quite a formidable woman," Sheila said, breaking the silence, if only to stop thinking about her own mother.

"That's one way of putting it."

"Was she like that in the hospital?"

"No. She wasn't lucid most of the time. I don't think she even knew who we were when Norma and I visited. She'd say all kinds of weird stuff. One time she attacked me."

"Oh?"

"Yeah. I guess she thought I was this guy named Ledbetter, because she kept calling me that. Sounds like a lawyer or something. She said I was the one that did it, only she said 'the one *what* did it,' in that thick Irish brogue she gets when she's upset. 'He's the one what did it,' she kept shouting, pointing at me when the orderlies came in to restrain her. 'He's the one what dashed poor Violet's crown upon the rocks.'"

"Who's Violet?"

"No idea. Maybe a distant relative?"

Sheila considered it. "That's not so odd, under the circumstances. People say all kinds of peculiar stuff when they're having an episode. The wires get crossed. It's—"

Martin's phone rang, interrupting her. He reached into his jacket and pulled it out. "Savage," he said. That obnoxious, self-important greeting that always annoyed her.

His features went slack. She couldn't hear what was being said on the other end but it was obviously a shock. He nodded, said, "Uh-huh," and "You're sure?" Then he shook his head somberly. "Okay. Thank you, Detective Lumsden."

He hung up. Tucked the phone into his coat pocket.

"What happened?"

He looked like he might be on the verge of tears or a breakdown or both. "God, Sheila—he said Pennsylvania P.D. went to Tish's apartment and practically found a *shrine* to Barclay. Clippings, photos, all kinds of books about witches and my book about him crammed with sticky notes and underlined in red pen. The two of them had been *writing letters* to each other."

Sheila wished she could say it surprised her.

"Jesus, Martin, I'm so sorry."

"How could I have been so stupid? How could I not see the signs?"

"How would you have known?"

"The Bible. Her obsession with serial killers. How she

glommed on to me the way she did. And the thing with the mirror mask."

"What thing?" Sheila asked, but he was still talking, still working out what happened out loud.

"He must have put her up to it. Convinced her to get close to me, planning the whole time to kill her while I watched. Did she know what he would do to her? Did she *sacrifice* herself for him?"

"Martin, this wasn't your fault. You've dealt with border-line-obsessed fans before. Maybe you should've been more careful, but how could you possibly know something like this would happen? How would *anyone* know?"

He nodded, looking off at the flashing red light hung over a distant intersection, intermittently casting its eerie glow over the surrounding conifers.

Finally, he spoke again. "Detective Lumsden said she was pregnant."

Sheila didn't know what to say to that. She just blinked at him in the intermittent red light.

"We used protection," he said, looking down at the sidewalk. His eyes rose to meet her gaze. He held it decisively, as if to sell what for all she knew could be a lie.

"But the coroner pinpointed the date of conception to the past few days. I mean, it's possible... they're not one-hundred percent effective... maybe she poked holes in them. Maybe *he* did. He was *in my house*, Sheila. I had sex with—with his *groupie*."

*As opposed to one of your own*, Sheila thought. She hesitated in reaching out, wanting to console him but feeling somewhat repulsed by everything he just revealed. "It's not your fault, Martin," she said, in lieu of physical comfort.

*It's never his fault. He stumbles through life, constantly tripping over his own dick and this is what happens when you stick it in every piece of ass that shows you the least bit of interest, Martin. This right here is what happens.*

She felt guilty for thinking it, but there it was. The truth laid bare.

He stepped toward her, holding out his arms like a sad little boy needing his mother. She pulled him into an embrace, even though what she really wanted to do was walk away from Martin Savage and hop on the next ferry out of town.

But doing that would be a death sentence for both of them. Barclay would find her. It wouldn't be long before he'd torture her into revealing Martin's whereabouts. Then he'd either kill her or use her as bait to lure Martin out of hiding. Might even kill Ruby and Norma just for fun.

The safest place was right here. Together. Whether they wanted to be here or not.

*We're caught in a trap,* she thought, absently patting his back.

## CHAPTER 10

**GLAMMERS**

MARTIN SAT ON the oval rug in his old bedroom and pulled down one of the musty old cardboard boxes he'd pushed up against the wall earlier in the day. After the call from Lumsden he was feeling maudlin. As an eligible male on the Manhattan dating scene with a reputation for promiscuity, he'd had several brushes with pregnancy. Broken condoms. Drunken sex without them. Close calls and dodged bullets.

This time was different.

This time he was the direct cause of the termination of a child in utero. He supposed Tish might have gone to prison for her involvement in Barclay's escape, whatever it was. She was a nurse, though he supposed Lumsden and the investigators would know by now if she'd worked at the psychiatric facility in Marcy—if she'd been the one to let him free.

She might have been allowed to carry the child to term in prison, and he supposed he might have been allowed certain rights to it, even if she didn't want him to. For all he knew, Barclay himself was the father, though he suspected the killer wouldn't have been so cavalier about it if it had been his. The man was a lunatic but Martin doubted he would have nailed his own unborn child to the wall—however recently conceived— just to serve as a threat. He had a code of ethics, however warped. He'd proudly proclaimed his virginity during the trial and would definitely have abstained from sex with Tish.

His "mission from God" was to murder the Devil's spawn, according to Sheila. Aborting his own seed would have been outside of his M.O.

*Shows how much he thinks of me*, Martin thought. *The Devil's spawn. Fucking psycho.*

He opened the flaps of the box he'd pulled down. It was filled with framed photos, stacks of paper twenty years old or more. Some appeared to be his stuff, report cards, awards and drawings, and some belonged to Aunt Norma and Ruby.

He lifted the box off the stack—slightly heavy, the weight lopsided, its contents rattling, making him wince at the thought of waking his mother, woe betide him—and he sat down cross-legged on the rug with it.

The first thing that piqued his interest was a photo of Ruby's bowling club. The fact that she'd been a bowler and had won at least one tournament was surprising in itself. Seeing her and her friends all decked out in their matching team shirts was another thing entirely.

One woman wore her hair in a beehive, another had a kerchief covering her head, a third wore white gloves, the fourth had sunglasses and a cane. And there in the middle stood his dear mother, smiling to beat the band.

The woman with the sunglasses stood with her back to the photographer, her face turned slightly toward the camera. *Would they even let a blind woman bowl back then?* he wondered, then he considered she might have been there for moral support, their mascot. The team name was emblazoned in pink letters on her black bowling shirt, in the same font as the girl gang from *Grease*. Only these letters spelled out THE BABY SPLITS.

The women all looked to be in their late-50s or early-60s. His mother seemed to be the oldest, the Sophia to the rest of their Golden Girls. According to the trophy Ruby held up along with the gloved woman and the woman with the kerchief, the tournament had occurred in 1980, just a few years after he was born.

He chuckled quietly to himself and slipped the framed photo back into the box. Through the closed door, he heard

Sheila climb the stairs and begin washing up. He couldn't help but think *warsh* and was struck by a moment of sadness and anger, thinking of Tish and what she'd gone through, what she'd put him through.

The toilet flushed and a few minutes later Sheila's footsteps creaked softly down the hall. Her door closed with a slight squeak and click.

A good half hour later, sifting through the assorted junk of his childhood, he came across a book he hadn't seen since he was maybe ten years old. It was his favorite when he was very little, but he'd forgotten all about it until he pulled it out of the box.

*The Big Book of Fairy Tales.*

He flicked through its pages, crinkled and warped from water damage and age, looking over the illustrations.

There was Perrault's Bluebeard, handing a set of keys to his new bride with a murderer's gaze. The stepmother and evil stepsisters from Hans Christian Anderson's "Cinderella." The Brothers Grimm's Pied Piper leading the children of Hamelin into a cave in the mountains. The troll lurking under a bridge as the Three Billy Goats Gruff stood at its edge, preparing to cross.

*No wonder I'm so obsessed with the macabre. Look at these things. Other kids had Walt Disney and Judy Blume and I had this. They sure don't make them like this anymore.*

The two following pages were stuck together. He had to peel them apart, tearing the edges.

What he saw caused his hands to tremble, the page fluttering audibly.

He must have scrawled the word in red crayon on the page himself when he was very little judging by the jitteriness of the handwriting, but he didn't remember it at all. He knew it was him because he'd used the same crayon to scribble in another of the books he'd already found. The well-worn nubs lay at the bottom of the box, rattling when he'd brought it down from the stack.

The illustration from the Grimm Brothers' "Hansel and Gretel" was of the children nibbling on the gingerbread house, while the evil old woman lay in wait, her fingers curled around the wall, a hungry grin displaying her sharp teeth.

Young Martin had scrawled a single word in red crayon, circled several times for emphasis, a squiggly arrow pointing toward the witch.

The word was MOMMY.

———

NADINE HINKLEY HAD NEVER FELT at home in Barrows Bay, despite having been born and raised here. Now that she had everything packed up and ready to ship to her new apartment in Providence, she wondered why she'd waited so long to leave.

Living here had always felt like staying in an abusive relationship. From being bullied during her early years to the constant surveillance and harassment by the old ladies and their minions since she'd first blossomed into adulthood, she'd only been making excuses for herself to stay.

She'd needed to take care of her ailing father from her late-teens. But he passed away from prostate cancer nearly fifteen years ago now, leaving her with absolutely zero emotional ties to the island. By then she'd argued that she couldn't leave the store. In recent years it wasn't doing the business it once had, almost as if tourists had been cautioned to stay away.

The only thing preventing her from leaving now was spite.

Because more than anything she didn't want the old witch and her cronies thinking they beaten her. That they'd worn her down.

Except now they truly had. The brick lobbed through her window had been the last straw, but the campaign to run her out of town started months before that, when the landlord decided, after fifteen years of minimal increases, to jack up the rent by a thousand dollars a month.

It was far more than Nadine could afford with the few customers she got and she was certain the old bitch Midwives were behind the decision. Left with no other option but to close the store, she only hoped she could liquidate the remaining assets at auction in a few weeks' time. Even though she wanted to walk away from this godforsaken place and never return, it would have cost too much to ship everything in the bookstore to Providence along with her personal belongings.

After closing up shop for the final time, she biked to the

ferry with a large camping pack stuffed full with pairs of everything, some toiletries and a few things to eat on the bus from the ferry dock in Point Judith.

It was dark on the backroads but there wasn't ever much traffic to worry about this close to the last ferry. Most tourists took the main road. Besides, her bike was decked-out with flashing reflectors and an LED spotlight. She'd added strips of reflective tape to her backpack when she biked down into the Adirondacks two springs ago.

She rode the dark, winding road, the white spotlight shining her way through the black swath of trees, Queens of the Stone Age's "Feel Good Hit of the Summer" blasting on her headphones.

*And of course—offuckingcourse!—Smartypants Marty comes back just as I'm on my way off the island for good, like the old cunt was just rubbing it in my face.*

*I bet she* begged *him to come, just to fucking see me off. Well I rubbed it all over* his *face, you bitch. And he begged* me *to come.*

"You old bitch," she muttered aloud.

Not far from the ferry dock now. She slowed as she approached the intersection of Kildare and Galway, where a car idled with its brights on, only its shiny grill visible beyond the trees.

"You gonna go or what?" she grunted.

Exhaust eddied within the glow of the headlights. Nadine pulled out her earbuds and slowed to a stop maybe twenty feet from the intersection, close enough to recognize the car's chugging, wheezing rumble.

It was that dotty old bitch Mavis. Her Cadillac roared like a giant pink beast as she revved the engine in the dark.

Not another car in sight. The woods eerily silent, closing in around them.

"How the fuck did she know I'd be here?"

*Last ferry out, that's how. You always take the backroads, everyone in town knows that.*

"Well, fuck her. I'm not going around. What's she gonna do, run me over? She doesn't have the balls."

Nadine put her headphones back in, put both feet on the pedals and rolled toward the intersection.

Fifteen feet away, Mavis became visible in the interior dome light, her big Kentucky Derby hat casting her face in shadow.

At ten feet, Nadine could see someone else in the back seat, hunched over in silhouette.

She heard the engine rev, louder than the music in her ears. A ripple of fear traveled up her spine and settled at the base of her skull.

"Come at me, you Boomer bitch," she said to spite the fear. "I fucking dare you."

The shiny American-steel grille gleamed like the teeth of a predator as the headlights caught her, throwing her shadow long.

So close now, but neither the driver nor her passenger were visible any longer. The headlights were too bright and the miasma of exhaust too thick, swirling up around her like a toxic fog.

Nadine threw a middle finger toward the grumbling beast as she passed and steeled for the sound of peeling tires, the crushing impact of steel shattering her bones.

And then she was pedaling out of the bright, swirling exhaust.

The car hadn't made a move to strike her. Mavis and the woman in the backseat still sat idling at the stop sign, as if they'd merely come to watch her leave.

Nadine let out a triumphant laugh. She'd survived.

She turned back to the road ahead just as a large buck leaped out of the woods.

Too late to stop. Barely enough time to swerve.

The antlers caught in her back tire and she hurtled over the handlebars. Then she was floating in the wavering arc of the bicycle light.

She struck the ground, shoulder-first. Felt her clavicle snap like kindling. Her cheek and palms shredded on sharp gravel. Her knees grinded, her legs flinging up like a ragdoll's.

Her helmet cracked, sending a shockwave through her skull.

She saw stars. Not in the sky. In the road.

Lying there, the pain sharp, she spat out a mouthful of gravel dust. A thick wad of blood came with it. At least she was alive. Her headphones lay a foot from her face, the funky bassline of "The Lost Art of Keeping a Secret" playing a tinny soundtrack to her misery.

A mewling sound accompanied it, like a strange breakbeat backing track.

*Where the fuck did that deer come from?*

She blinked. Tried to raise her head. Agony shot up from her shoulder and stars flooded her vision again. She wouldn't be going anywhere for a while. She doubted Mavis and her passenger would bother to help her or even call for an ambulance. They'd be more likely to watch her die in the road like a wild dog.

The Caddie's engine rumbled. Gravel crunched under its whitewall tires and the headlights swept across the pines and tall black spruces toward her.

She saw the buck's antlers in shadow, its body writhing. Her mangled bike.

*They're gonna run me over*, she thought.

The car rolled forward until it was only a few feet from her and stopped, catching her in the headlights. Mavis ran the engine, waiting. Nadine couldn't turn her head to see.

"*You gonna just sit there?*" she screamed over her bleeding shoulder, her throat raw. "*Huh?*"

A rumble came from the woods. Branches swishing and snapping. Something was out there.

Something *big*, moving toward her.

"*What is that?*" she cried over the suddenly deafening, thundering sound.

A moment later they burst forth from the trees—a stampede. Bucks, does and fawns trundled up from the ditch and onto the road, kicking up gravel.

Before Nadine could even attempt to drag herself out of their path they were trampling her, hoofs pressing hard into her flesh, breaking her bones, kicking her teeth in, smashing her jaw, her ribs, her spine.

Then they stopped and gathered around her in a tight semicircle. Panting. Black eyes unblinking. Her blood on their hoofs and flanks and throats. Leaving her in agony, ragged and bloody.

All she could think was that they'd come to defend their fallen brother. But why wouldn't they attack the Cadillac? Why would they circle so tightly around it, from headlight to headlight, as if the vehicle was one of them?

As though Mavis was their alpha?

The largest buck bowed its head. Its black eyes regarded her and it snorted, clear phlegm spurting from its nostrils, bright in the headlights. Then it dashed at her.

She threw up her one able arm to defend herself. The antlers impaled it, shredding through her jacket and her skin. They penetrated her sternum, her throat, her ribs and stomach.

The buck raised its head, lifting her roughly into the air. Every movement was excruciating, her bones made of shattered glass. She hung loose over the animal's head. She smelled its hide. Her blood dripped down the smooth, tawny hairs on its cheeks and neck, blinked away from its pretty, girlish eyelashes.

The buck took two sudden, jarring steps forward. Drifting in and out of consciousness, Nadine heard the rumble of the car beneath her. Felt the heat of the engine baking her skin.

She knew then what was happening. The herd hadn't come for revenge. They'd been summoned by some kind of sympathetic magic. The animal was presenting her ravaged body to them, a gift to the old bitch Mavis and the woman in the backseat, to Ruby Savage and the Midwives.

She was their sacrifice. Just as she'd always suspected she might be.

Her blood-pink smile shone in the headlights. Vindication swelled within her, making her strong. No one had believed her. Her mangled body would be the proof she'd always hoped for. Her death would be a harbinger to the few people she trusted enough to confide in.

*The evil is real. I told you. I told you all.*

She laughed, pain wracking through every nerve of her body until her laughter ebbed away along with her life.

Then the big buck wrenched its head, flinging her ragged corpse into the woods.

---

DERRY'S ALL-NIGHT Car Wash stood silent and bright against the surrounding trees as Mavis Lynch pulled her pink Caddie into the lot.

The wash was automated and required no attendant. Since there was very little crime in Barrows Bay it had no security cameras. No one would see her wheel the Caddie into the tunnel and onto the track.

Mavis loved going through the car wash. It reminded her of her father, who used to let her sit in the back of the family Studebaker with her dolls while he washed it down with soapy water and a sponge and the garden hose. It was a pleasant memory of an innocent, long-gone time, before decadence and debauchery replaced respect, common courtesy, a hard day's work and the sanctity of family.

Though she wasn't a fan of most technological advances proceeding the television and microwave oven, the car wash was something she could see the value in. It wasn't like she was spry enough to wash the blessed thing by hand, and she sure as sugar wouldn't let the slouchy little Neanderthal neighbor boy get his mitts on it.

The Caddie lurched forward on the track and a gush of hot water pounded the chassis, blasting away Nadine Hinkley's blood from the hood and headlamps. That had been quite the *glammer*. Mavis was pleased to see her dark magic work without her sisters. She feared she may be required to use it against them someday, perhaps soon.

*Sooner by the moment*, she thought darkly.

It was wise to keep such thoughts to herself. To prevent them from rising to a conscious level, where the others might eavesdrop. Their minds were linked, like a telephone on a party line, where voices—*inner voices*—would drift in and out of clarity.

Geraldine MacKenna seemed to possess this sense the strongest, aside from the Mother. Geraldine was Mother's right-hand woman.

While water pounded on the rooftop and the spinning, foamy brushes slapped the chassis and windows, it seemed for a time the party line was vacant. Mavis heard her own thoughts and hers alone. She could think freely, without fear of someone overhearing. Particularly Mother.

Mavis had grown powerful while Mother had been "indisposed." While Mother weakened it behooved Mavis and the others to foster their own powers. Barrows Bay needed them. Without their influence, her people would suffer. The town itself would wither into chaos and decay.

The island was far more than it had ever been before Mother left. And did she ever thank them? Not likely.

Though Mother *had* trusted her enough to take care of the Hinkley woman on her own. She supposed that was something.

Nadine Hinkley had been a thorn in their sides since her early years as a tomboyish brat. Even back then some of the ladies believed she might have been a lesbian, but Mavis had seen her court many a hapless male victim, like the spider and the fly. Every one of them an out-of-towner. No self-respecting Bay man would be caught dead with a slut like her. She lured them up to the loft above her hippy bookstore. They'd leave a brief time later reeking of patchouli and vaginal secretions. Brief enough for Mavis to consider the woman might be running a side business as a whore.

Still, they might have let her go quietly. They might have been satisfied watching her take that last ferry out of town to never return. Banishment would have sufficed. If only she hadn't lured Martin Savage into her parlor. If she hadn't used her feminine wiles to get back at Mother.

And the bitch had laughed in those final moments. *Triumphant* laughter. As if she'd beaten them. As if she'd won.

No matter. The deed was done. The woman was dead. What difference did it make if she'd found something amusing about death? Perhaps she'd seen it as a mercy. Women of loose morals trended toward self-harm and suicidal impulses. Perhaps she'd even gotten her rocks off.

The Cadillac rolled out of the car wash a vision of gleaming pink and white and American steel.

*Beeeeep! Beeeeep! Beeeeep!*

The infernal machine at the window demanded payment. The barrier wouldn't rise without a credit card, and Mavis had never found much use for them. What was wrong with coins and bills? Money you could touch? Plastic—no thank you. She preferred to keep her money close at hand, where she could see it. Where she could *touch* it.

She peered into the rearview, adjusting the wide brim of her hat until it was just so. Her cheeks were ruddy, the flesh around her jowls saggy. But her gray eyes were fierce. By all accounts, she was still a formidable woman, especially for her age.

With minimal effort she pushed her mind into the machine.

These little tricks were simple. Machines weren't quite so complicated as animals, particularly not an entire herd. Simpler still than humans.

But even the simplest glammer required energy. She and the others would soon need to feed.

The screen flashed PAYMENT ACCEPTED, beeping incessantly as the barrier rose. She gripped the wide pink steering wheel and drove out of the lot.

Things were about to change. The boy had returned. He would have to be dealt with, whether Mother allowed it or not.

And this time, Mavis suspected Ruby might—she felt the old woman's power draining already, like a well bucket with a hole, as it had when the boy was under her roof the first time.

But Mavis left these dark thoughts in the car wash.

Her mind, like the car, was squeaky clean.

# CHAPTER 11

## A Woman's Work

MARTIN SAT UP abruptly in the dead of night. Something had woken him. A sound, though he couldn't tell if it had been in his dream or in the room with him.

He drew his knees up in a panic, the sort of thing he would have done as a little kid, terrified of the monster under the bed. What better setting for it than his childhood bedroom?

Only the monster wasn't under the bed this time. Barclay was miles behind them, hiding in some abandoned building or rain-choked grotto, biding his time for the manhunt to die down to begin a hunt of his own.

*We're safe here*, he thought. *Sheila wouldn't have said it if she didn't believe it. We're safe.*

A floorboard creaked, startling him. The same sound that woke him. He peered into the semi-dark.

Stacked boxes. The closet door open, dark and full of old shoes and clothes on hangers. Was it open when he drifted off to sleep? No clue. It was open now and he couldn't see a damn thing in all that dark.

He took a deep breath. Old houses made noises all the time. Random creaks, snaps and groans. Like an elderly person without the gas.

Another creak. He rolled to his side, eyes wide in panic, heart thumping. Lying there in his boxers on the too-small bed with the Glock tucked away in the glove compartment of his Lexus he was entirely at the mercy of anyone who could have come creeping into the house in the dead of night.

*Aunt Norma's Them? The old woman from the night of the fire, come back to finish the job after all these years?*

The hall door stood open. He was sure he'd closed it.

The sound came from there.

He laughed at himself, mostly to bolster his own courage. Someone must have woke to use the bathroom. He waited for subsequent footsteps, heart pounding in his ears. The wind howled outside, rattling the windows. Otherwise, the house stood silent.

A dark shape in the corner of the room moved. He blinked furiously, praying for his eyes to adjust. Finally he saw her, hunched within her nightgown and ghostly pale. An apparition in the moonlight.

"Ma? What are you doing up? How did you get in here?"

The old woman said nothing. She shivered. He heard her hurried breath. Her teeth chattering.

He pulled off the covers. "Ma, are you okay?"

She ran at him, bare feet thumping, impossibly fast. Swinging out with one seemingly feeble arm, she cast aside boxes until she reached the foot of the bed.

He drew back and bumped his head hard against the wall, hard enough to see stars, to bite his tongue again and taste fresh blood. She leaped at him, gnashing her teeth, her withered fingers gnarled into claws.

He reached out instinctively with his right hand to hold her back, pressing his palms against her collarbones. Not wanting to hurt her. Only to protect himself.

*"They're hanging men and women for the wearing of the green,"* she snarled. Spittle flew from her lips like a rabid dog. Eyes wild. Feral.

He thought, *I won't be bad no more, Ma, I swear, please stop—*

And suddenly it clicked. She was having an episode. Like she did when he was little. Before they took her away.

Whatever it was, she was still dangerous. And much stronger than she looked. She thrashed against his hands. The wound on his palm tore open as she bore down on him, hard enough he thought her ribs might crack.

Her bony fingers with brittle nails like fragile talons swiped at him, her snarling lips nearing his face, stained dentures clacking. A low, guttural growl rising from her sallow chest—

"*Ma!*" he cried, the purest childhood terror gripping his heart.

She vanished. He held nothing but chill night air. Heart pounding. Hand still hurting. He blinked, peering into the dark. Looking for any sign of her. But Ruby had never been there.

He must have dreamed the whole thing. Hallucinated it. *Something.*

He sighed, but the fear didn't go away so easily. He could still feel her crepe-paper flesh on his hands. Blood had seeped through the bandage. Must have happened while he was sleeping. Must have caused the nightmare.

*Or whatever it was*, he thought.

One thing he knew for sure, Ruby was stronger than she looked. He suspected it when she left the bath last night. Dancing down the hall to her room, singing that strange song. The wet footprints on the steps meant she'd crept down the stairs while the three of them had been talking in the kitchen, without using the stair lift. She'd gotten in and out of the tub on her own, yet she claimed to need his help moments later. Even allowed herself a rare moment of vulnerability, standing naked in front of him. And she still needed the walker and a stair lift just to get around.

Was she faking it? Was her weakness a way of exerting power over Norma? How could he find out for sure? Pull away her walker while she stood? Challenge her to a fucking arm wrestle?

He let out a dry chuckle. *Yeah, that's a great idea, Martin. Abuse an old woman in her home. Good way to get yourself locked up. Local Writer Attacks Mother. Breaking news, story at eleven. Bet I get a visit the very next morning from my best friend and yours, the Witch Hunter himself, Mr. James Barclay.*

He'd have to keep an eye on her. Not that he was afraid of her, not like he'd been when he was a kid. The nightmare—that was clearly what it was, just a nightmare, an undigested bit of beef, the ghosts have done it all in one night—likely had a more

Jungian meaning than literal. Still, he would need to be more careful dealing with her from now on.

She was old but she was just as formidable as he remembered. Sharp as—*claws*—nails. She might not be able to physically harm him but she could do worse damage with a swift jab to the psyche, an uppercut to the ego. She could cut him down to the size of a weeping child.

If he wasn't careful, he might end up falling for her wounded puppy act. Then he'd be stuck in Barrows Bay forever, living at his mother's beck and call just like Norma. Like he almost did when as a teenager, when guilt over her condition nearly prevented him from leaving Stratford for the MFA program at NYU.

Even though he had nothing to feel guilty about.

Ruby tried to kill herself. Slit her wrist with a pair of scissors and held it out for him to see. As if to say, *You did this, Martin. You killed me*. He remembered the blood—so much blood. Gleaming bright red under the bare lightbulb, oozing through her fingers and spattering on the—*concrete*—floor.

Only five years old at the time. Much too young to shoulder any of the blame.

Nadine was wrong. He *had* lived under his mother's shadow. His whole damned life he'd cowered there. His childhood fear of her—along with whoever had tried to burn him and Norma alive in their own home—had twisted into a career writing about real-life monsters.

Let Nadine run if she wanted to. He'd be damned if he was going to spend the rest of his life cowering in fear.

*No more*, he thought. *Not this time*.

First thing tomorrow, he was going back to the city.

---

Norma woke to hushed voices, sibilant in the dark, prickling the hairs on the back of her neck.

She drew the covers up to her chin, fear crawling in her belly, and the voices stopped abruptly, as if they'd merely followed her out of sleep. Just the remnants of a bad dream. She sighed.

*Or They know I'm awake*, she thought. The fear redoubled,

her heartbeat quickening, worrying her. The blood thinners she took should prevent an incident, but it was best to try and keep herself calm.

*Easier said than done, Missy.*

She couldn't remember the last time she'd woken to voices in the night. Long enough ago that she assumed they must've been a figment of her imagination, a recurring nightmare confused with waking memories. Was it possible they'd been with her all along, waiting for the right time to let themselves be heard again?

*Gosh, how long has it been?*

*You know exactly how long. And you know why they've come back.*

She did. But this thought hadn't seemed like her own. She loved Marty. She'd missed him and wished he would have visited sooner. She also understood why he hadn't. This town was full of bad memories for him. For the both of them. But the Bad Times were in the past. Long ago and far away.

*Are they, Love?*

*Do you think so, Dear?*

Not her thoughts. Other voices. Women's voices. Toneless and unrecognizable, yet somehow coming from inside her own head, like listening to the radio, half-tuned to multiple stations at once. Or like those old party-line phones, the kind they had on the island before they modernized with satellite signals and internet tubes. Where you could hear snippets of other conversations while trying to have your own.

The last time she heard them they tried to make her do things.

Terrible things. They wanted her to hurt Martin. To smother him while he slept. To drown him in the bath. To burn the house down. To push him into the furn—

*Cripes!*

He'd just about remembered what happened to him that morning. What they'd gone through. What he'd done and what Ruby had done. The old white scar on his palm and the white slash on Ruby's, a half-forgotten nightmare. A buried memory.

She remembered him, covered in Ruby's blood. The silver sewing shears, rinsing them off in the sink.

The hurried phone call in the kitchen.

Ruby bleeding like a stuck pig on the sofa and poor little Marty with his hand wrapped in gauze, the bubbling wound oozing puss and blood.

She hoped he would never remember what had truly happened that day. Why his mother had to be sent away for a very long time. Be kept as far away from her son as possible.

He'd been so quick to forget it. *When is Mommy coming home? Why does Mommy have to stay in the White Place?* And she would tell him it was for his mother's own safety. Not for his. Ruby had to stay in the White Place because she was sick. Because she hurt herself. But not like how he hurt his hand. His mother had cut herself *on purpose.*

Only that wasn't the truth of it.

He'd asked about the woodstove this morning and she'd momentarily forgotten all about her cover story. So long since she last had to use it. That he burned himself on the woodstove, trying to climb up and sneak a taste of Ruby's strawberry-rhubarb pie.

She repeated it so often he eventually believed it, even though they never had a woodstove. She'd almost believed it herself. Why she'd said woodstove when she could just have said stove—*the smoke, the black smoke*—was anybody's guess. Now he'd be second-guessing himself. He'd wonder, if we never had a woodstove, where did I get the burn?

*He'll go down the basement, Love.*

Norma pushed the duvet aside and shot out of bed. She stepped into her fuzzy pink-bunny slippers, drew on her nightgown—*ah, warmth*—and treaded carefully to the bedroom door.

Having lived with Ruby for so long, not wanting to wake the old broad in the night, she knew every joint that creaked, every board that groaned. She reached the door with barely a sound, just the whispers of her slippers on hardwood.

The hinges squeaked as she opened the door. Not loud enough to alert anyone who wasn't already awake. The house was silent but for the wind rattling the windows.

*Howling like banshees out there.*

*What an unpleasant turn of phrase, my dear.*

She crept past Ruby's room to the stairs, holding the railing. She knew exactly how many steps to reach the bannister, how many more to the bathroom. A misstep in the night could be deadly. The last thing she needed was to fall down the stairs and break a hip.

She thumped into Ruby's stair lift chair, barking her shin against the armrest. Instinct kept her from crying out. She sucked in a winced breath and stood a moment rubbing the spot.

It would bruise tomorrow. She bruised so easily these days.

*Least it didn't break the skin. Thank God for small favors.*

Placing her footsteps close to the wall, she descended the stairs, holding the railing to steady herself. Less creaky that way. When she reached the bottom she startled, certain for a moment that someone was standing by the door.

*Breathe, woman. Don't lose your head.*

Her eyes adjusted. It was only Sheila and Marty's heavy winter coats on the rack.

Spring would soon be here, thank the Lord. Winter was filled with back-breaking work: snow shoveling, constantly mopping the foyer floor, repairing windows broken by heavy island storms. Spring was a blessing of gardening, sunshine and warm rain. She smiled at the thought of it, her rabbiting heartbeat slowing.

The closet under the stairs was where she kept many of her cleaning supplies, the mop, the broom and dustpan and sundry household items: spare lightbulbs, batteries, paper towels and the like. It also led to the basement.

Norma knew of only three houses with basements in Barrows Bay. The parish had one, as did the old schoolhouse, which had burned many years ago. And this house, often called the Gingerbread House by folks in town, particularly those on the Historical Society.

The door was locked, just as she knew it would be. She took the skeleton key out of the front pocket of her nightgown. It was finicky—*not half as finicky as the night of the fire*, she thought—but she finally managed to turn the lock and twist the knob, opening the door on the smell of must and decay, of damp concrete and dirt.

*Of ancient history*, she thought. *Long-forgotten nightmares, at least for Marty. Not me. No, I've had to live with them my whole life. Cursed to hold back the—*

*smoke, black smoke*
*—the flood. Too bad so sad and sucks to be me.*
*Hush, you ninny,* came another voice, as familiar as a name on the tip of her tongue. It seemed to come from the house itself rather than inside her head.
*You haven't been cursed. You've been chosen.*
"Chosen," she said with caustic bitterness.

Her voice in the darkened stairwell made her jump. She flicked the light on hastily, only to assure herself there was no one here with her, listening as she talked to herself like a crazy loon.

She was alone. The furnace in the darkness below ticked but otherwise the basement was quiet as the grave.

Eager to get this over with as quickly as possible, Norma descended the stairs. There was a big canvas drop cloth on the table at the foot of them. She draped it open, raising a cloud of dust. She thought it would just about fit.

The cellar ceiling was too low for her to walk without hunching. Norma had been tall since the eighth grade. The other kids had called her hurtful names. Many were dead now, their names and faces long forgotten. She held no ill will toward them, felt no joy in their passing. But the insults remained, tattooed on her heart.

*Get it together, woman. You've got a job to do.*
She was far too old and in too much pain to let the names bother her now. It hurt to stand with her back bowed for too long so she crossed the room hurriedly, her slippers scuffing on the rough, dirty concrete.

The gas furnace ticked and hummed pleasantly. Beyond it, in a darkened, cement-walled chamber covered in cobwebs from floor to ceiling, stood the old wood furnace.

It looked like a squat black monster on clawfoot legs. The boys from HVAC had removed the thick black stovepipe from the top when they put in the new furnace. The joists above were still charred from the fire in '83.

She remembered dragging Marty away from it. His palm red and angry, oozing puss and blood as she carried him hurriedly across the room. She'd torn off the hem of her sundress and wrapped it hastily around the slash on Ruby's wrist as—*smoke, it was smoke, wasn't it?*—blood poured out like a leaky faucet.

The scissors at Ruby's feet, in a pool of her blood, bright crimson under the bare lightbulb. More blood on Martin's face, on his *lips*—

*Don't you think about that, Missy.*

Norma regarded the place where she'd found them. God only knew how Marty had come across Ruby's special shears. It wasn't like she ever used them herself. They were a family heirloom, she said. *Precious.* Not so much in their monetary value as sentimental.

*Where are they now?* Norma wondered. Tucked away in her sewing chest? She hadn't thought of them in—gosh, at least twenty years.

She flapped out the drop cloth and let it settle over top of the furnace. With the door to the basement locked, Marty wasn't likely to come down here. Still, it was best to be sure. He'd always been crafty. If he wanted to get down here badly enough, he would find a way.

With any luck, he wouldn't bother with the thing under the tarp.

And the thing under the tarp would have no business with him.

*Best that he not remember, Love,* the voice said. *For all of our sake's.*

Norma still didn't recognize the voice but she couldn't help but agree.

She left the basement, locked the door behind her, and returned to her bedroom.

The duvet was warm and inviting. Come the next morning, she would forget having gone down to the basement at all. She would look at the bruise on her shin and the dirt on her pink bunny slippers while perched on the porcelain throne and wonder what in the heck she'd gotten up to in the night.

And the creatures eavesdropping on her thoughts would be just fine with that.

---

Ruby slept fitfully.

Bridge hadn't gone well that night. Typically, she and Geraldine were a pair to be reckoned with—as a team, the others had nothing on them. Tonight she'd been focused more on the nasty business Mavis had been involved in than the cards in Geraldine's silk-gloved hands and her own. As a consequence, Helen and Ethel had taken every single trick.

They would be first to feast when the time came.

The business with the Hinkley woman was messy but unavoidable. First and foremost, the woman was a magpie, particularly whilst in her cups. Constantly attempting to sow seeds of discord among the people, chattering to anyone who'd give her a moment's pause.

Secondly, she was a slut—a sin perhaps less forgivable than the first. Tempting Martin with her wickedness had driven the final nail in her coffin.

Even worse than this was the fact that she had begun to *see*. She had spotted the cracks in the façade, the spackle over the grit and grime of reality.

Geraldine had been first to see the Hinkley woman had noticed things were not quite what they appeared to be. That Barrows Bay was not all cheers and charity, love thy neighbor, smiles and sunshine.

Somehow, Nadine Hinkley had seen beyond the glammer. Though no one in their right mind would ever have believed her, it was not an ideal situation for Ruby and the others.

When a blemish was pointed out it would soon become all a person could see. They would seek out more imperfections. Eventually, they might realize the whole thing was rotten right to its very core.

The woman couldn't be allowed to live. Not here or anywhere.

Mavis had been more than eager to handle the job. She'd always been a vengeful creature. Ruby knew what her sister had done all those years ago, while she'd been incapacitated, locked up in that endless hell of lily-white walls.

The not-so-secret deed lay between them now, festering like an open wound.

Neither woman dared speak of it. Ruby, humiliated by her own unforgivable indiscretion. Mavis, ashamed she hadn't finished the job.

Killing the Hinkley woman redeemed her.

Still, Ruby had overseen the assignment. While she and the

others played their tricks, Ruby—with Ethel's assistance—projected her *fetch* into the backseat of Mavis's car. They had done it without Mavis's permission, projecting only a hint of the fetch so as not to be detected.

Both women knew Mavis Lynch didn't appreciate being spied on. She was an intensely private creature, her mind walled off to the others as often as she could manage. If she'd known Ruby had been with her, she would have overreacted.

As it turned out, Mavis hadn't required supervision. She'd performed quite impressively on her own. The deer had been Ethel's idea. Helen Birch suggested Mavis run the woman down with her Cadillac. Mavis balked at the thought. She treated the pink monster—which she called "Princess"—as if it were her only child.

Ruby wouldn't have allowed it, anyhow. She'd seen enough of Norma's crime shows to know better. It was all too easy these days to link vehicles with murders, particularly if the vehicle in question had been in a recent accident.

Employing the use of the animals was a masterstroke of Ethel's incredible gift for foresight. Mavis had always been better able to communicate with animals than people. Her many overfed, over-loved cats would attest to it, could they utter anything but mewls.

Tonight's performance had been a true test of her skills. Surely, one for the books.

The Hinkley woman's body would be found in the morning, trampled and mauled by deer. Some might wonder how or why such a thing would happen but no one would come close to gleaning the truth. They were as blind as Ethel—more so, since Ethel Kelly could see further with her mind's eye than most could see with the globs of fluid and anatomy made strictly for the purpose housed within the sockets of their skull.

No one would tie the slut's death to the Barrows Bay Bridge Club, known to most as the Midwives.

But it wasn't these thoughts that troubled Ruby, interfering with her sleep.

It was Martin's return that vexed her. He'd come home after all these years away, and all of the bad blood between Ruby and the others came bubbling back up, like bile after bad chowder. She could sense it, simmering just below the surface.

The uneasy peace she held with them had begun to show cracks.

She would have to do something about it soon.

*A place for everything and everything in its place.* Neat-freak Helen often said this. Her home was as spotless as the reverend's bedsheets.

*Everything in its place.*

Martin's place was far from Barrows Bay.

Just him being under the same roof, she could feel her strength sapping away by the minute.

Ruby tossed and turned as the wind howled outside her window, fully aware she wouldn't be able to protect him for long.

From Mavis. From the others. From *herself.*

And worse, she feared she might not care to spare him at all.

This was why, while the rest of the house slept, Ruby Savage tossed and turned, moaning softly in her restless slumber.

A woman's work was never done.

# Chapter 12

## Barrows Bay Tradition

RUBY DIDN'T COME down for breakfast. Norma said it was the first time the old bat slept late in as long as she could remember. "Must be knowing you're home," she said. "Made her relaxed. She worries about you, Marty. She worries a lot."

Martin didn't believe it, but it seemed to comfort Norma so he let the comment slide.

His nightmare had faded in the morning light, leaving him with only a vaguely uneasy feeling about Ruby, a sense that something wasn't right about her, that maybe they'd been too hasty letting her out of the mental hospital.

He felt like she was wound up by a tight, thin thread that could snap at any moment. Just the thought of her entering the room made the scar on his palm throb like a migraine. It was taking its sweet time healing, too—tearing open afresh anytime he moved his hand the wrong way, oozing blood into yet another bandage.

After breakfast they helped Norma clean up. Then they all sat in the living room, talking about trivial things: when the weather would swing toward spring, how much the town had changed since they used to live here, their pastimes. Ruby's bridge games. Norma's cross-stitching, the products of which were relegated to her bedroom, where portraits of terriers and floral patterns took up much of the wall space not crowded by photos of relatives from all over the east coast, even up into Canada. Sheila's interest in learning new languages (she'd forgotten the English to Japanese book she'd been reading in preparation for a trip she hoped to book next year). Martin's childhood obsession with silhouette portraits cut out of black construction paper.

"I forgot about those," he said.

"Had them tacked up all over his walls. Strangest thing. After a year or so he had a portrait of just about everyone in the neighborhood and every one of his teachers and friends. Then one day he packed them all up and put them in a box. Said he was done with them."

"Why silhouette portraits?" Sheila asked, grinning at this peculiar glimpse into his past.

"I dunno." He shrugged, slightly embarrassed. "I guess I just liked them."

Sheila watched him for a long moment, hoping to glean something from his mannerisms, whether he really didn't remember or he was a vault. Either way, she gave up.

Talk eventually drifted around to the future, none of them eager to discuss the elephant in the room. Norma asked what Martin was working on—he lied and told her he'd started research for his latest book about Jim Allen Biggs, a Miami serial killer—and if Sheila was eager to get back to "headshrinking." Sheila skirted the unintended offense by politely replying that she was eager to get back to it but she was glad for the break, and to finally meet Norma and Ruby.

Martin didn't mention he planned to leave shortly after his mother came down from her room. He hadn't discussed it with Sheila, certain she would try to convince him otherwise. But he'd made up his mind. He wasn't going to let James Barclay keep him from his city, his work, his home.

The buzz of Ruby's chairlift announced her arrival at quarter to twelve. After considerable grunts and groans she stood in the living room doorway, hunched over her walker. "I'm famished," she said. "What's for breakfast?"

"More like lunch," Norma said. She pushed herself out of the recliner with a grunt of her own. "I'll whip something up."

Sheila rose from the sofa. "Let me help."

"Nonsense. You're guests. You've done more than enough already." Moving past Ruby, she muttered, "You slept like the dead, woman."

Ruby tutted. "Must have been all the excitement yesterday."

For lunch Norma made chicken soup and tuna salad sandwiches with the crusts cut off, the way Martin had enjoyed them as a kid.

"At least now we know why he acts so entitled," Sheila said, observing the leftover crusts on the cutting board. Norma clucked her tongue disapprovingly, but Martin couldn't help notice the ghost of a smile on her face as she turned to swipe the crusts into the trash.

They ate in silence, Ruby gumming her food to death, spoons scraping the insides of bowls. Martin struggled with how to broach the subject of leaving. Several times he caught Sheila watching him eat, until he frowned at her and she began studying her soup bowl as if looking for signs and patterns among the noodles.

He opened his mouth, just about to announce his intentions when the telephone rang. The jarring old-fashioned *br-rrrrrrrinngggg!* startled everyone at the table.

"I'll get it," Norma said, standing abruptly. She grabbed the receiver off the wall and for an instant Martin saw blood on her hands, smearing on the cream-colored plastic, just like that morning. "Hullo?" She paused a moment, scowling, then held out the receiver. "It's for you, Marty," she said with a quizzical tone.

He got up, wondering who the hell would be calling him on his old home phone. He hadn't given the number to the detectives, nor to Qurban.

He hesitated a moment. What if it was Barclay? What if he'd somehow figured out where they were hiding? It wasn't likely, but he'd been surprised far too many times this past week to allow Barclay the upper hand now.

The women at the table watched him. He tried to make his voice sound as unafraid as possible.

"Hello," he said.

"Smartypants!" came the baritone voice on the tinny receiver.

"Who is this?"

"It's your old pal," the guy said, and Martin placed the voice with the name.

"Sinjin?"

"You got it, buddy. Man, all these years later I still remember your phone number. Isn't that a thing? It's like when you haven't heard a song in thirty years and you start singing along like it was just on the radio the other day."

"Yeah, that is weird."

Sheila gave him a quizzical look. He shrugged.

"So what's up, Sinjin?"

"Ah, well remember youse said yesterday you'd love to come over, meet the wife? I figured today was as good as any for a lobster and clambake. It's a Barrows Bay tradition, the way we welcome back old friends and new friends to the island." He paused, let the offer hang a moment. "Unless you're too busy to hang out with an old pal, that is."

The thought of spending the afternoon with Sinjin and his wife, reminiscing about things the two of them might have done when they were four-year-olds, sounded like his idea of hell. But as much as he didn't want to stick around Barrows Bay any longer than necessary, news of passing on a lobster and clambake—especially if it was a *tradition*—would spread like wildfire on the island. Soon he'd be recognized not for being a local celebrity but as someone who'd lived too long in the big city. Gotten too big for his britches. Thought he was too good for a New England clambake.

He lowered his voice and turned from the watchful eyes at the table. "Nadine won't be there, will she?"

His mother tutted. Sheila snickered.

"Nadine?" Sinjin sighed. "Christ, I thought you mighta heard. I guess, why would you? Doubt even anyone knows you're here but me and the wife."

"Heard what, Sinjin?"

"Nadine died last night, Marty."

---

"COPS SAID she got trampled by deer, you believe that?" Sinjin said, exhaling a cinnamon bun-scented cloud.

They stood on the back deck of the St. Johns' house, the

covered barbeque and patio set like ghosts of summer under cream-colored tarps. Patches of snow lay on the brown lawn, where Sinjin had piled everything he'd shoveled off the deck throughout the winter.

"Old Joe Neely found her bike all mangled-up in this big buck's antlers, swears it was a twenty-pointer if it was anything. Cops took the damn thing, anyhow. Bet you anything they're having venison tonight down at the cop shop." He took another thoughtful pull on the vape. "Weirdest thing I ever heard of, though," he said on exhale. "You ever hear something like that happening? Such a shame, too. She had a rough life, Marty. Her mom dying when we were in high school, then her dad a while back with the cancer. I think she musta had bi-polar or something, the way she talked sometimes. Anyways, Laura and me feel really awful about it, you know? But what can you do? Circle of life, right?"

"I guess so," Martin said. He was still in a daze. The whirlwind he and Sheila had entered while being welcomed into Sinjin's home hadn't helped. The house was filled with Bay people, mostly couples and children. Some pretended to remember Martin. Others didn't bother, nodding their heads politely when Sinjin introduced him as "a famous Big City writer born and raised here in the Bay."

The women seemed keenly interested in Sheila right away and dragged her off to a raucous conversation in the kitchen while Sinjin and a few of the men talked shop in the living room with a basketball game on the big screen TV.

"Laura's got this funny idea we're all connected here on the island," Sinjin said thoughtfully, watching a vape cloud vanish into the air. "God closes a door, He opens a window. He blesses me and Laura with a child, so He has to take something away, you know? Tit for tat."

"Sure. Tit for tat." Martin thought about the last time he saw Nadine, pushing him out the door to her shop and into the street. She'd been so troubled, ranting about his mother, this town. And midwifery, of all things. "Are you and Laura planning a homebirth?"

Sinjin coughed out a lungful of vapor. Once he'd gotten his coughing under control, he said, "Is there any other way in the Bay?"

"I wouldn't know."

"I honestly can't remember the last time somebody had a hospital birth. We've always just done it this way."

Just like Nadine said. "Your mother did?"

Sinjin nodded. "Yours, too. Barrows Bay tradition." He shrugged. "Musta been strange for your ma though, being one of them and all."

"One of what?"

"A midwife. But I guess even garbagemen have to put out the trash for somebody else to collect." He gave Martin a self-conscious look. "I wasn't calling you garbage. It was just a... what do you call it?"

"A metaphor."

"Exactly. And that's what brought you back. A piece of you was always here on the island. Sooner or later, it pulls you back."

"Is that another metaphor?"

"No, I mean literally. When the Midwives tie off the umbilical cord, they let a piece of it dry out so it falls off on its own. Once it does, they bury it down on the beach in the sand, where the original graves used to be, the barrows. You, me, Nadine, nearly everyone here tonight," he said, nodding back toward the bustling house. "A piece of us is always in the Bay, no matter where we go."

Sheila interrupted with a knock on the window. She'd stayed in the kitchen making awkward small talk with Sinjin's immensely pregnant wife and a small group of housewives. She looked annoyed, probably having to field questions about her reproductive plans—or lack of—and whether or not she and Martin were a hot-ticket item.

*Oh, to be a fly on the wall for that conversation.*

"I guess we're needed in the kitchen." Sinjin tucked the vape into his coat pocket and opened the door. The pungent smell of cooking seafood wafted out. "They should make clambake flavor e-juice. I would definitely vape that."

"Something tells me it wouldn't be a big seller outside of the Eastern seaboard."

Sinjin laughed. "Yeah, good point. Still though."

They stepped into the kitchen, the ladies all cheering their return. The party was in full swing, '80s pop music thumping from the living room speakers. Sinjin slipped an arm around his wife's waist and hugged her to him.

"Suppa's almost ready," Laura said. She wore a striped dress that accentuated her pregnant belly rather than lessened it, her brown curls springy on her shoulders.

"It smells amazing, hon. I was just saying to Marty," Sinjin added, addressing crowd. "They should sell a clambake flavored e-juice."

Everyone seemed to think this was the greatest idea since the first boiled clam. While they laughed and clapped his back and a guy with a Just For Men-black goatee and plaid fedora said he'd "run it up the flagpole" with his superiors, Sheila and Martin gave each other a look signaling their plan to leave at the earliest chance.

Less than fifteen minutes later they were all gathered in the dining room, the table piled high with seafood, corn, sausages, cheeses, breads and greens.

The St. John house was cozy but still had the square footage of a place a dozen times its worth anywhere in New York City. Everyone fit snugly around the table while they served themselves and their children. But eating would have to be done throughout the house, on laps and end tables, chairs and stairs and cross-legged on the floor.

Sinjin tapped on his glass of local craft beer with a fork. "Hey, folks, can I get your attention?" Once everyone had quieted down, he continued: "Laura and I would like to thank you all for coming, especially those of you who couldn't manage to get a sitter and came anyway, bringing your wonderful children into our home. As you all know, we're about to be blessed with a child of our own. A girl, they say—"

Martin turned to Sheila and whispered, "They know the sex?"

Sheila shrugged.

"—so that means all you little ones, and not-so-little ones— Angus, I'm looking at you, big guy, Barrows Bay Bumblebees is looking for a new quarterback—"

A large, pasty-faced red-haired boy in a sweater two sizes too small blushed.

"—well, you'll all have someone new to play with soon." Sinjin hugged Laura at his side. She beamed up at him and pouted as he started to tear up. "Anyways, I just wanna say, we love you all."

A woman directly behind Martin let out a prolonged, "*Awwww.*" The guy with the plaid fedora—who'd introduced himself as Mike or Mark—cheered, "We love you too, buddy!"

Sinjin's already rosy cheeks reddened further. He swiped at his tears and raised his glass in a toast. Others followed his example. Even some of the children raised their juice and pop cups, mimicking their elders.

"To the Bay," he said. "The best little island in the world!"

Everyone returned the cheer: "*To the Bay!*" They drank up.

"All right, folks," Laura said. "Let's tuck in, huh?"

THE HOUSE FILLED with laughter and song, the thud of children's feet as they chased each other room to room, the clink of cutlery on tableware and pockets of idle chatter.

Sinjin's voice was loudest of all, commanding the attention of anyone within shouting distance, his funny-sounding laughs causing others to laugh along with him. He was the life of the party. Martin found it difficult not to warm up to him. He was just so full of joy that it spread to everyone around him.

His wife was full of love, enough to go around. She'd hugged and kissed everyone as they arrived, friends and strangers alike, despite the girth of her pregnant belly. She welcomed them into her home, shoes on, shoes off, offered drinks, something to snack on. She was extremely organized and yet slightly scatterbrained during conversations, often half-attentive to the gigantic meal she'd been preparing in the kitchen.

Now that she could let her hair down, she ate for two or more, fawned over someone's crying baby, and spent a few minutes sitting down with each couple, making sure they were comfortable, that they had enough to eat, if they had a designated driver, etcetera.

Martin and Sheila sat on the stairs, not talking much except to comment on the quality of food, looking in at these people through the living room doorway. It was so unlike anything they were used to in the city it was almost like watching the occupants of a strange new planet through a dimensional portal.

No pretentions. No cattiness. No politics. Just friends enjoying the company of one another, the alcohol, the food.

*My God, the food*, he thought. If this was what it meant to feast in the Bay, he could easily see a return visit in his future.

"You know, I almost said no to this," he said, turning to Sheila. He licked salted butter and a corn kernel off his palm.

"God forbid." Sheila sucked on the end of a crab leg. "We never did get to talk about your friend."

"What friend?"

She blinked at him. "The woman from the bookstore. The one who died last night?"

He scowled, glancing around to see if anyone had heard. Those who might be in earshot were entangled in rapturous conversation and good cheer. "Later, huh? On the way back."

Sheila eyed him. He could tell she knew he was trying to put it off. But now really wasn't the time. She knew that too. They ate in silence for a moment, until a small voice from above shook them from their thoughts.

"Excuse me."

A little girl of about six or seven with long blonde curls and a smile almost too big for her face stood halfway down the steps. They scooched to either side of the stairwell to let her through, and the girl trundled down the last few steps and ran into the living room to grip the hand of her mother.

It was weird, seeing all these kids sitting quietly with their parents or playing games with other children. Not a single one of them had a cell phone or tablet to fiddle with. No one wore T-shirts featuring WWE or "ironic" rock bands or some stupid, funny-for-half-a-minute meme. No swearing or whining or bitching at their parents. Almost as if these kids were blissfully unaware the possibilities existed.

"I used to have curls just like that," Sheila said.

"Oh yeah? I wish I knew you back then."

She turned to him with slight surprise. Then she smiled. "You wouldn't have liked me. I was a bit of a know-it-all."

"Kids called me Smartypants Marty at that age. Sounds like we would've been peas in a pod."

"I wonder how our lives would have turned out, if we'd met each other when we were kids instead of through *him*?"

The name didn't need to be said. They both knew exactly who she was talking about.

"We wouldn't be sitting here. Eating this terrific meal."

"Likely not."

They sat in silence a moment, until Sheila broke it. From the hasty way the words spilled out it seemed like she'd been thinking about it for some time.

"Do you ever wish you could go back, change the way we ended things?"

This time Martin was caught by surprise. "I wish I could take back what I did. Of course, I do, Sheila. But would it have changed at all? If anything, it probably would've just taken us longer to self-destruct."

She nodded, thoughtful. "You're probably right."

He grinned. "That's a lot of probablys."

"Isn't that what life is? Probablys? Maybes? I don't know about you, but I haven't seen a lot of definitelys lately."

He grinned. "You're definitely a little drunk."

"Yeah, that is a definite." She handed him her empty wine glass and set her plate down on the step behind her. "Keep an eye on this, huh? I'm gonna go use the little girls' room."

She got to her feet a little wobbly, her face so close to his for a moment he thought she might try to kiss him. But she stood before he could—*reciprocate? initiate?*—and sashayed drunkenly up the stairs.

He watched her until he realized people might be watching him watch her, then he turned away, pretended to be looking at the family photos on the stairwell wall.

From the living room, Sinjin caught his eye and mouthed, *You okay?*

Martin raised his beer and gave the man a thumbs up. Sinjin nodded in reply, but he looked troubled. A moment later, Martin discovered why.

Once again, Sinjin tapped his glass until everyone quieted down. "Folks, I know we're all here for a celebration, but something's been on my mind and I just have to say it."

Laura looked back at him, in the midst of a hushed group conversation, a slight scowl flashing over her rosy features.

"As many of you may already know, one of our own passed away last night," he continued, despite his wife's disapproval. "Her name was Nadine Hinkley."

The looks of cheer vanished, making it obvious the kind of woman they all thought she was—or had been. Like a shout of "fuck the Irish" at the St. Patrick's Day parade, the mood suddenly swung from cheerful to borderline hostile.

"Come on, Singe," Mike or Mark said, the plaid fedora currently in his lap.

"No, this has to be said. She may not have wanted to be one of us, and heck, maybe some of that's on us. But she was born here, just like the rest of us. And her passing deserves to be mourned in our way."

Martin sensed the importance of those words: *Our Way*. As if "their way" was somehow different from the people who mourned elsewhere, outside of this small island.

"Hon?" Laura said, concern in her voice.

Everyone turned to her. The problem was immediately apparent. The crotch of her dress was soaked through.

Sinjin put his glass hurriedly on the mantle above the fireplace and pushed through the crowd to get to her side. He knelt in front of her, taking her hands. "Is it now? Should we call them?"

Laura nodded cautiously, as if to prevent further slippage. Sinjin looked up at the gathered crowd.

"Somebody call the Midwives," he said, his big hands on Laura's belly as she breathed through the pain. "I'm gonna be a dad!"

Before anyone could congratulate him, cheer or react in any fashion, the glass slipped off the mantle and shattered on the floor.

"What did I miss?" Sheila said, standing halfway down the steps.

# CHAPTER 13

## THE CIRCLE

WHEN LAURA ASKED her to stay, Sheila was so astonished all she could manage was a feeble nod. By then it was too late to say no. She cleared her throat, summoning sobriety, and said, "I'd be honored."

She had no idea why Laura St. John would want her around for what was possibly the most intimate moment of her life. Particularly when the other guests were asked politely to leave, and all the men specifically sent away, leaving Sheila alone with a handful of mothers, young and old.

It reminded her of black-and-white TV shows where the men all stood outside the hospital room smoking cigars. All the gender-roleplay seemed peculiar and archaic.

The midwives arrived one by one. First came a fragile-looking elderly woman with white silk gloves and a powdered face. She wore a thick sweater with the face of an owl on it and spoke so softly Sheila couldn't hear a word as she greeted Laura and instructed the others to fill the blow-up wading pool Sinjin had dragged in from the shed before he left with the men.

"Warm water, please," she said, her voice barely rising above a whisper, as if she couldn't speak any louder. While the remaining women went to the kitchen, she comforted Laura, asked about her contractions, told her to remember her breathing.

"That's Geraldine," the woman at Sheila's side said as they entered the kitchen. Her husband had introduced her as Pauline. She wore too much makeup and smelled like violets. "She's the one who delivered me. My three boys, too."

Sheila stopped in the doorway, struck by the comment. Another agonized groan from the living room got her moving again, reminding her why she was here.

Pauline ran the sink until the water was warm, turned it off, then asked for Sheila's help to connect the hose Sinjin had hauled in. It was still cold from being out in the shed. They unspooled it carefully, streaking their hands with cold mud.

Pauline told Sheila to wait there, then dragged the hose through the dining room into the living room, leaving clods of mud and pine needles in her wake, all the furniture moved by the men to make room for the pool.

"All right, youse can turn the water back on now, hon!"

Sheila did. Water dribbled out from around the connection so she tightened it until it stopped. Then she returned to the living room, where everyone stood wearing looks of nervous expectation, watching the pool fill agonizingly slowly.

While they waited for the other midwives to arrive, Geraldine held Laura's hands and offered whispers of encouragement. She looked to be in her late-seventies, maybe older. Sheila wondered who else among these women had been delivered by her. Besides Laura and Pauline there were two other women, Darla and Dianne. They'd been calling themselves Double-D all night. Sheila assumed it was meant to be ironic, since neither of the bottle-blondes looked to be above a B-cup. Like calling a fat guy "slim." Darla was the mother of the little blonde girl from the stairs.

The doorbell rang. Double-D Dianne hurried to get it.

"It's colder than a witch's tit out there," came a gruff woman's voice. She stepped into the living room doorway, removing her coat. Dianne took it obsequiously, practically bowing as she slipped away and hung it on the coatrack with the others.

This woman's hair was done up in a perfect silver beehive. Her cheeks were rosy and quite chubby, though she appeared slim, as if she'd lost a fair amount of weight and her face hadn't gotten the memo.

She went straight to Geraldine's side, though she remained standing while the other woman sat. "How far apart?" she grunted.

Geraldine said something Sheila couldn't hear and the woman with the beehive nodded. "Good, good." She turned to dip a finger in the pool and slosh it around. "Let's get you in that pool, lady."

Pauline and the woman with the beehive helped Laura to her feet and raised her top over her head. Below her heavy, freckled breasts straining within the confines of her black bra, her belly was pale and round. A dark pregnancy line rose from below the waistband of her stretchy, flower-print pants to her distended belly button.

They slipped down her pants—she wore a pair of loose granny panties underneath—and walked her to the pool while she breathed through her teeth, as if the baby might burst out of her like some alien parasite at any moment.

"That's Helen Birch," Pauline whispered, nodding toward the second midwife. "She used to run the hair salon downtown when my mom was just a girl."

Headlights shone through the blinds. It had grown dark in the course of an hour since everyone left the house. A horn honked in the driveway, loud as a train. Sheila peered through the slats at the classic pink Cadillac she'd seen the other day.

When the driver door opened, the interior light illuminated two women in the front seats. The driver wore a large hat. The passenger had a short dark bowl cut and wore overlarge sunglasses.

The passenger said something which made the driver pause in stepping out of the car. They conversed for a moment. The driver nodded. She stepped out and went around the front of the car to open the passenger door. Helped the other woman out. When they made their way to the front door, Sheila saw the woman with the sunglasses held a long white cane.

"The blind woman's Ethel Kelly," Pauline said, having appeared beside Sheila without a sound. "The one with the hat? That's Mavis Lynch."

Sheila noticed a trace of ominousness in Pauline's voice, as if she feared this woman.

The front door opened without a knock and Mavis stepped

in with Ethel in tow, the soft round tip of the cane thumping on the floorboards.

"The party can start now," Mavis said. "We're here."

"Is Mother with you?" Helen asked, helping Geraldine ease Laura into the pool.

"What do you think?" Mavis snarked.

She removed her hat, revealing a sparse head of white hair and a ridged terrain of pink scar tissue. Dianne took the hat and hung it on the coatrack. As Mavis strode into the living room, tossing her long, forest-green peacoat on the accent chair in the corner, Dianne helped Ethel out of her colorful striped coat.

"Thank you, Dianne," the blind woman said, though Dianne hadn't said a word since the two new midwives entered. It was as though Ethel could tell the woman from her scent. "How are you, my dear?"

"Fine, Ethel. Just fine. How are you?"

Sheila eavesdropped on their hushed conversation while Mavis crossed to the pool to supervise the other two ladies.

"Aside from the rheumatism, I'm keeping well."

"That's good to hear, Ethel." Dianne spoke delicately, like she was talking to a child. Or to someone she revered.

"And your girl? Jaden. How is she, my dear?"

"She's great. Won first place in track and field last fall, just like you said she would."

Ethel smiled lightly, clutching her cane to her sternum. "I could tell the moment she popped out of you she'd be a fast one. Those big lungs of hers. Either a swimmer or a runner, just as I said."

"Just like you said, Ethel. Thank you."

On her hands and knees in the pool, Laura groaned.

"It's time," Mavis said. "Towels?"

As if on cue, Double-D Darla came down the stairs holding a stack of fresh white towels. "Right here, Mavis."

"Good. Bring them over, girl."

Darla did as she was told, slipping between Sheila and Pauline.

"Okay, now push, girl," Mavis said.

Darla knelt and laid the towels at the foot of the pool.

Helen smoothed Laura's damp hair.

Geraldine clasped Laura's left hand in both of hers.

Laura's tormented wail rattled the plates on the mantle. Her teeth gritted. Sweat pooled on her knitted brow.

*The miracle of childbirth*, Sheila thought. *Count me out.*

"Push, mama!" Mavis cried.

"You can do it, Laura," Darla said.

Mavis flashed her a look so malevolent Darla's whole body rocked from the sting of it. She backed away until her calves bumped into the accent chair, where she stood clasping her hands against her breasts, her brown eyes wide with muted terror.

Laura screamed as if her entire body was splitting in two. Helen kept smoothing her hair but Sheila caught the look she shot at Geraldine, whose gloved hands were squeezed so tightly it made the tendons visible in her neck. The look was brief but anxious.

"The baby is breeched," Ethel said.

She stood several feet from the pool and couldn't possibly have known unless she somehow recognized something in the new mother's cry.

"She's right," Helen said gruffly. "I see her little bum presenting."

*She said presenting, not crowning*, Sheila thought, anxiety tightening her stomach.

Delivering a breeched baby could be incredibly dangerous —to the baby and the mother. Any doctor worth their salt would recommend a cesarean birth. She knew that from four years of med school prior to her masters in forensic psychology.

"Let's get her out of there," Mavis said. "Quickly, ladies."

"No," Laura moaned. "No, no, no, no...."

"Hush, girl. Just breathe. You're doing fine. Breathe and push."

"I think we should call a doctor," Sheila said.

Laura's tear-filled eyes looked in her direction. She nodded vehemently. "Yes! I need a doctor! I need an epidural!"

"It's too late for that, sweetie," Helen grunted.

Mavis turned a cold glare on Sheila. "Just who do you think you are, sister? Do you have any idea how long we've been delivering children?"

"I have medical training—"

"Well, la-di-freaking-dah. Why don't you make yourself useful? Brew up some strong chamomile."

"*Tea?* She needs to go to the hospital—"

"*Get her out of here,*" Mavis snarled at Darla and Dianne. Double-D snapped to attention and took Sheila by the arms. She didn't fight. It would have only further enraged Mavis, and now more than ever she wanted to be here, to see this through.

Did any of these women have medical training? The young mothers, Darla and Dianne, were both housewives, though they called themselves "homemakers." Sheila let them drag her past the pool toward the kitchen, Darla giving her an apologetic look with her pageant-blonde curls bouncing on her shoulders as they hustled Sheila along.

Feeling like the outsider she was, an interloper ousted to the sidelines, Sheila watched the rest of the proceedings from the kitchen, wondering why Laura had invited her to stay in the first place.

Before dinner the women had been asking all sorts of personal questions about her and Martin. How long had they been together? Had they ever talked about having children? Had she ever considered it? Martin had *such good genes*. He was *so good-looking*. And *smart*. Imagine the superbabies the two of them could have.

When she told them she didn't want children, Pauline said, "You'll change your mind." The other mothers had nodded knowingly, like members of a secret club.

*Is that why they invited me? To convince me* this *is what I really want?*

She wondered how they would have reacted if she told them about her abortion. They probably would have kicked her out of the house. Definitely wouldn't have invited her to stay for the birthing.

Double-D stood by the pool and helped out whenever Mavis barked an order at them. As Laura's best friend, Pauline stood as close to her as the midwives would allow, hands clasped in prayer, whispering words of encouragement.

"Push, Mama!" Mavis shouted.

"*Push!*" the others echoed.

"You can do it, Lala," Pauline said.

With an enormous cry of animal rage, Laura bore down once more.

"She's out!" Helen cried, her thick arms in the water up to her elbows.

Everyone breathed a sigh of relief, including Sheila. Her guts unknotted and she let her hands relax. She must have been clenching her fists ever since she'd been relegated to the kitchen. Her knuckles went from bone-white to red as the blood returned.

Laura gasped and slumped over the springy edge of the pool as Helen pulled the baby from the water.

Geraldine swaddled the wrinkled, purple thing, its limbs hanging limply, its head lolling. The umbilical cord looping down into the pool made Sheila think of power cords. The little baby was still running on Mommy power. Geraldine wiped the vernix caseosa from the baby's scalp and face but still the child made no movements of her own, no plaintive wail. She needed to be able to run on her own but her battery didn't appear to have a charge.

Then she cried.

Sheila didn't *see* it. Somehow the visual didn't match the auditory. But she would swear in court she'd heard her cry. No one else reacted. The faces were wooden, waxy, as if they were all still holding their breath. Waiting for word.

*Why do they all look so glum?*

Geraldine turned to the other midwives, who each nodded ominously.

"I'm afraid she's gone, child," Ethel said.

*But I heard her cry*, Sheila thought. *I heard it.*

"No!" Laura wailed, reaching out for her baby. "No, I could feel it! I could feel her heartbeat inside me!"

"See for yourself, sweetie," Helen said.

"Yes," Laura said, holding out her hands. "Give her to me. Give me my baby!"

Dutifully, Geraldine handed over the baby in its swaddling. Laura held the child to her bosom and only after she'd looked down at it for what felt like an eternity, rocking in the sloshing water, only then did her face finally crumple and she began to weep.

"No. No, it's not fair. It's not *fair*!"

"Late-thirties pregnancy," Mavis said, taking a step toward

the pool. Something metallic glinted in her hand. "We warned you of the risks."

Laura pulled away from the midwives, protecting a child who no longer needed protection. "Stay away from me, you witch!"

"You hold her as long as you want," Helen said as soothingly as her gruff voice would allow. She gave Mavis a stern glare. "But we need to cut the cord."

Mavis held out a pair of silver shears. The others eyed them reverentially, as if they'd all seen them before. As if they'd cut the cords of their children and their own. She opened the blades and snapped them shut—*snick!*—and each of the younger women flinched.

All except Laura, whose attention was focused solely on the dead child at her breast.

But she *had* cried. Sheila was certain of it.

*You heard what you wanted to hear*, she thought. *Wishful thinking, that's all.*

Maybe it had been. Maybe she was still a little drunk. Her mind overtaxed. Wound up by the altercation and anger and Barclay and all kinds of swirling emotions she couldn't quite hold on to long enough to decode.

An auditory hallucination. That was what she would've said if someone told her about it. If she hadn't experienced it herself. Not the worst thing to befall her. Under the circumstances, probably even justified.

Helen took the umbilical cord in both hands and held it for Mavis to cut.

Laura cradled her baby and let them, all the fight worn out of her.

Mavis eyed her cautiously as the blades cut through the meaty tissue and came together audibly. Dark fluid oozed from both ends as the fleshy material slipped back into the pool.

It happened so fast Sheila couldn't be sure, when she looked back on it after the confusion of the evening, that she hadn't been mistaken. That she hadn't maybe hallucinated it, like the dead baby's cry.

When it happened, a cold hand of terror clutched her spine.

It could have been from concentration, general dryness or an unconscious tic—but for one fleeting moment as Mavis

Lynch's tongue flicked out and moistened her lower lip, Sheila was sure she saw anticipation in the old woman's eyes.

She puzzled over that look for several minutes.

The only sound in the St. John house during that time was Laura's weeping as the other women circled around her to mourn.

<hr>

MARTIN GAZED up at the stars and marveled, still slightly drunk from the Legion bar. He hadn't seen so many stars since he left Stratford for the city. Even on vacation it seemed like there was less visible in the sky than here and now. The kind of night to contemplate your place in the grand scheme of things. The kind that made your own problems feel insignificant, no matter how insurmountable they might seem.

It had become that kind of night long before he stood in the middle of a deserted island road in the woods—County Road 8, according to the sign—the streetlamps on either side burned out, the ocean beating against the shore the only sound for miles. What happened at the St. Johns' house had cut the festivities tragically short.

Sinjin and four of his closest buddies were at the Legion bar when the call came just after nine. He said he'd only be a minute, would return with good news and another round to sneak in before they could all head back to the house drunk and happy.

When he finally returned to the table, it was with glassy, red-rimmed eyes, not the cheery face of a man bringing good news. His pallor as white as soap. His empty hands hung slack at his hips.

While the Rolling Stones hooted their sympathy for the devil over the old bar speakers, the boys cheered Sinjin's return, clapping him on the back, calling him the "man of the hour," handing over a sloshing shot glass full of piss-colored booze.

Sinjin set the shot glass down soberly on the rickety card table covered in peanut shells and glass-sized circles of condensation, and locked eyes with Martin. As drunk as Martin was, the look got through to him. Something had happened. Something terrible.

His head swam from one too many celebratory tequila shots, stomach churning as he tried to formulate a tactful way of asking if there were complications. It wasn't like he knew the guy. But someone had to say *something*. The others seemed completely oblivious to their friend's pain.

"She's dead," Sinjin said, his voice barely rising above a whisper, smothered by Mick Jagger's howls.

"What?" Martin shouted back.

"She's dead! Ruby's dead!"

For one awful instant Martin felt relief.

His mother was dead. No more worries about her health, about her feelings toward him, about when she might decide she'd had enough of him and send him packing back to New York, into the clutches of a sadistic serial murderer.

Guilt rushed in on the heels of relief.

He was a bad son, a terrible son, wishing his mother dead to spare himself inconvenience. He'd always been a terrible son, ever since they sent her to the White Place and he wished, he'd *prayed*, that she would die soon so he'd never have to go back to that awful, depressing place again, where glazed-eyed patients in lime-green pajamas drooled and screamed and blew snot bubbles and stared at him accusingly, as if they might kill him just to switch places, to see what life was like beyond those plain white walls.

Then he wondered, *Why would they call Sinjin and not me?*

Drunkenly, it all clicked into place. Ruby was the baby. They planned to name her Ruby—for God knew what reason, probably after the boat and not *his* Ruby—and it was the little girl who died, not his mother.

How could he comfort this man he barely knew? And why would Sinjin look to him for consolation, of everyone here? Why was he invited to this celebration at all? He felt so out of place among them he'd spent the whole night getting hammered just to cover up the fact he had nothing to add to their childhood reminiscing.

"Jesus, man, that's terrible," was all he could think to say.

"No! No!" Mike or Mark cried out, finally clueing in. He took off his fedora and held it somberly over his heart like the national anthem was playing instead of the Stones. "That's not right, man! That's not friggin *right*!"

He grabbed Sinjin in a bearhug. The other guys circled around their friend in an embrace and Sinjin began to weep, big tears rolling down his reddened cheeks and splashing on his T-shirt, while Martin sat awkwardly to the side, feeling more like an outsider than he ever had in his life.

Sheila had already left the St. Johns' house by the time the men returned. Upon seeing the state of his wife, Sinjin sent the rest of them packing. Now Martin stood in the middle of the road, bundled up against the sobering chill of a cloudless island night, staring up at countless stars and planets and the occasional satellite.

Thoughts of his own insignificant life came swirling back to him and he found his place in the universe again, his feet planted steadfastly on the hard macadam. He began to contemplate the choices in life that led him to the place he stood, in the town where he was born, alone and afraid, staring up at the sky.

He wondered what the fuck he was going to do with himself if they had to stay in Barrows Bay much longer. Work at the grocery store? Sell fresh produce at the local outdoor market? Try to get the Constant Reader back up and running, if Nadine's estate hadn't already sold off her inventory?

*You could start writing a new book.*

That was always an option. The inspiration just wasn't there. The only murderer he had any particular interest in at the moment was James Barclay. He'd promised Qurban a sequel but right now there wasn't even enough to fill a couple of chapters. Barclay was still at large and so far as anyone knew he hadn't crawled out from whatever rock he'd hidden under to kill again.

A snapped branch perked his ears. He froze, scanning the pitch-black woods on either side of the road. He was pretty sure there were no bears on the island. Wouldn't be much for them to eat but trash if there were.

*What if it's him? Speak of the devil and he shall appear.*

"Hello?" he called out warily.

No answer but the swish of trees against the chill wind.

He kept walking, a little faster now, nerves as tight as guitar strings. A bit further up the road he thought he saw glimpses of bright white flashing in the trees, there for a moment and then gone.

He stopped at the edge of the ditch and stared into the black expanse. Another flash of white deep within the woods and gone again.

*Kids*, he thought. *Out drinking after dark.*

Not exactly the right season for a bush party, though. But even though the kids at the party seemed well-behaved almost to the point of suspicion, it didn't mean they wouldn't rebel when they got older. Kids were kids everywhere you went.

Martin smiled a bit wistfully, thinking back to his high school years. *Take a trip down memory lane, Marty, old pal—watch out, don't fall now, ha ha. Man, those were the days though. All-night parties. Freedom. No schedule to worry about. No bills to pay, no demands.*

*Just school. Oh yeah, forgot about school. Stay in school, kiddies. School is cool ha ha.*

A dark shape broke through the trees up ahead with a commotion of snapped twigs and swishing brush.

He stopped in his tracks, on the verge of terror.

The large shadow rose, black wings spreading. It stood on four legs—a bird with four legs and wings on its head. Some kind of folk horror terror, a beast from a fairy tale.

His alcohol-addled mind struggled to comprehend the shape before him.

The bone-white moon shivered out from behind a shawl of cloud, illuminating the creature. Its black eyes stared at him. The beast snorted, hot breath pluming out from its wet black nose.

Martin laughed at his own fear. It was a massive stag, not a monster or a bird. It could easily kill him if it charged, but it was only a deer.

*The same deer that trampled Nadine Hinkley?* he wondered suddenly. A freak accident like that was surely a once in a lifetime occurrence. Literally, in Nadine's case.

The stag held him in its gaze, seeming to regard him. To size him up. Cocked its head to the side and blinked its frilly, girlish lashes.

Were deer supposed to look away when you stared at them, deferring like dogs? He didn't know. This one made no attempt to shy away from his gaze. It stood with its head lowered, staring him down. As if challenging him to move first or blink.

His eyes began to water from the cold. They stung. He didn't want to give in, to let the stupid animal win. No use. He blinked.

The animal snorted, a cloud of vapor rising from its nostrils. The black lips seemed to curl up in a smile, revealing brown, jagged back teeth. Then it turned and dashed away down the road, its hoofs clopping into the distance until the animal vanished in the darkness.

*Close call*, he thought, catching his breath. *Next time I'm out after dark I'll take the gun with me. Just in case.*

*It's not paranoia if someone's literally out to get me.*

When he got back to the house only the porch and kitchen lights were on. Norma and Sheila sat at the kitchen table, steaming mugs of hot cocoa between them. Sheila's eyes were raw from crying.

They both turned as he entered, identical expressions of disappointment on their faces. It made him think of the times he'd come home drunk or high to find Aunt Norma waiting for him in the kitchenette. The look had always sobered him up in a hurry. If he hadn't already lost his buzz on the walk home, he was stone sober now.

He put a hand on Sheila's shoulder and she nuzzled her head into it for a moment.

"It's awful, what happened," he said. "I'm so sorry you had to be there to see it."

She smiled wanly up at him. "In a way I'm glad I was there."

"Oh?"

"Yeah. I'll tell you later, 'kay?"

Norma tutted. "Care to share with the rest of the class?"

Sheila patted the old woman's hands, offering her a conciliatory smile. "Not just yet, Aunt Norma."

Norma returned the smile, nodding. "Uh-huh, kids only. I get it. Never let it be said I can't see when I'm not wanted." She pushed up from the table. "All right, you two. I'm heading up."

"Mom gone to bed?"

Norma nodded, dumping her cocoa down the sink and setting the mug beside the dish rack. "Said she was feeling under the weather. Breakfast bright and early?" She winked. It was what she used to ask when she knew he'd been up late partying.

"At the crack of eight," he said.

She grinned. "All right then. Nighty-night."

"G'night," Sheila said.

"Night, Aunt Norma."

Once the creaks of her footfalls reached the top of the stairs and moved above their heads, he sat beside Sheila at the table.

"You okay?"

"I'll live." She sniffled, wiped her nose absently on the back of her hand. "It was just so *weird*, Martin. The whole thing was weird. Those old ladies, they—"

She stopped suddenly, peering through the doorway into the dark hall as if she was afraid Norma was still out there, listening in.

"What?"

"Not just yet," she said, her voice a little quieter. "I'm still working it all out in my head."

He nodded. No sense in pressuring her. Whatever she had to say she would tell him on her own time.

"Let's go to bed, huh?" he said. "It's been a long day."

"The longest. I'm exhausted. But I think I'll stay up just a little while longer. I've got a lot to think about."

He got up from the table.

"Aunt Norma's a good woman, Martin. You were lucky to have her."

He smiled. "I know. See you in the morning?"

Smiling back, she mimicked Aunt Norma: "Bright and early."

He left her sitting there, wondering what she had to tell him that could be worse than what he already knew. He was curious about the birthing ceremony, the ritual, whatever they called it. If not for the death of the child, he almost wished he could have been there himself.

*I could write a book about this town*, he thought.

He'd meant it as a joke but as he crept up the stairs so as not to wake his mother, the idea started to take hold. It felt like something that would hold his interest. A semi-autobiographical book, starting with the house fire.

He would need to do a ton of research. Hit the town hall records, the library, the newspaper office and the old schoolhouse. As he reached the top of the stairs, the idea began to feel like it had legs. He could almost see it taking shape in his mind, like a tree growing from a seed in fast-motion, his writerly mind already making connections where there were none before, jumping from scene to scene, building a mystery.

A small moan came from the bathroom. For a moment he dismissed it as someone—Norma or Ruby—having trouble doing her business and felt a flicker of embarrassment. But the moan came again and this time he recognized it as his mother—and the fear in it, the pain, was more than just the sound of someone trying to pass something that wouldn't move.

"Ma? You okay in there?"

A swish of darkness interrupted the light under the closed door. Then the sound of fingernails, lightly scratching. A weak thud.

"Mmmuh," she said weakly. "Mmmuh."

Trying to call out his name? Was she having a stroke?

"Ma, I'm coming in."

He jiggled the handle. Locked.

Fortunately, the door opened outward. He wouldn't have to worry about hitting her if she was in the way when he tore the thing open.

"Something wrong?"

Sheila stood at the foot of the stairs.

"I think she's having a stroke or something."

Sheila dashed up the stairs. He yanked on the door handle. She pulled with him. The door wouldn't budge.

Norma's bedroom door opened and she leaned into the dim hallway. "What's the hubbub?"

"Ruby fell. The bathroom door's locked."

Norma hurried into the hall in her bunny slippers. She reached into the breast of her nightgown and out came the skeleton key on a string. "Move it or lose it."

They stepped back as she reached the door, twisted her key in the lock and drew the door open quickly.

Ruby lay sprawled on the cold tile floor. Her nightgown was hitched up around her hips and one of her slippers had fallen off and lay beneath the toilet. The lid was up. She must have been trying to use the toilet and fell. Her eyes were closed. Yellow light from above made her eye sockets look skeletal.

"Ma!" He knelt down before her. Plucked up her wrist with its long pale scar and felt for a pulse.

For a moment he felt nothing and glanced up fearfully at the others, who waited for word.

Then he felt it. A soft, almost dry movement like a hard-shelled bug skittering under her paper-thin flesh.

"She's alive," he said.

Norma let out a relieved sigh. "I'll get a damp cloth." She turned on the faucet in the bath, grabbed a cloth from the lip of the tub and ran it under the cold stream.

"Ma, can you hear me?"

Ruby moaned softly. Her eyelids fluttered.

"Are you hurt? Is anything broken?"

An almost imperceptible shake of her head.

"I think we should get her into bed."

He looked up at Sheila, the only one of them with practical medical experience.

She nodded. "If nothing's broken, we should be fine."

The two of them lifted her gently to her feet. When they got her back to bed, Martin saw her walker was collapsed at the door.

"Ma, why didn't you have your walker?"

The old woman stared blankly at him. It reminding him of how she'd looked in the White Place, and a cold shudder passed through him. He remembered once thinking she'd never leave there. That she would live the rest of her life wasting away in that awful, dead-end place. Now he worried she'd have to go back.

Norma placed the cold cloth on her forehead. Ruby blinked but didn't speak. The lamp on the nightstand made the pits of her eyes look like she was scowling. Her chest barely moved as she breathed.

"We should call a doctor," Sheila said, staring with suspicion at the walker herself.

---

WHILE MARTIN WALKED ALONE down County Road 8, the Midwives took the precarious switchback path down the side of the cliff to where the ocean beat against sand and rock and crushed clamshells, the sound like rattlesnakes as the water sifted through them, drawing back into the black expanse.

Their white cloaks stood against the ancient woods like wraiths, pallid in the patches of moonlight that shone through bare branches.

The switchback trail was dangerous this time of year. Most often they would time these treks to occur between late-spring and early-fall, when the ground was firmer and less likely to cause a spill. They were at an age where they worried a fall might cause a bad break, perhaps unrepairable, even after the effects of the ritual. They had watched many women pass this way over time, with an infection of the blood or the bone, succumbing to dementia, wasting away in a hospital bed.

The Midwives were no ordinary women—but it troubled them just the same.

*Soon*, though... soon they would not have to worry again for quite some time.

They drove to the cliffs on the east side of the island in Mavis's Cadillac. The Pink Princess purred through the darkened streets of Barrows Bay while most of the town slept, the child swaddled in Geraldine's lap in the passenger seat, not a single one of them speaking of the events that had transpired in the St. Johns' house.

"The new woman," Ethel said as they reached the county road, sitting behind Mavis with her cane in her hands. "Sheila Tanner. She heard the child cry."

Mavis looked at the woman in the rearview. Ethel's Jackie Kennedy sunglasses glinted momentarily as they passed under a streetlamp. "The bitch almost threw a wrench in the whole damn thing," Mavis agreed. "We shouldn't have let her stay."

"It was Mother's decision," Helen said beside Ethel, throwing Mavis a stern glare. "You know why."

Mavis grunted in reply. She wasn't about to voice her concerns with both Helen and Geraldine in the car, even if Ethel might be sympathetic. From her lips directly to Mother's ears.

As if to remind them of her presence, the baby cooed.

Geraldine shook her lightly on her knee and placed an index finger in her mouth. The girl sucked the silky fabric greedily, latching with ease as if to her mother's breast. Easy latching meant she would live a charmed life and love as easily, perhaps to have many children of her own.

Ethel couldn't hear the baby's thoughts, but could sense its contentment. If only the poor dear knew what awaited her at the edge of the ocean, within the circle of standing stones.

The women finally descended onto the beach and each breathed a sigh of relief at having made the trip once more without injury. If there had been any choice, they would have waited for a summer birth. Frannie O'Neill was due at the end of June, close to midsummer. But Mother's strength had waned with the arrival of her son, the same sort of psychic draining she'd experienced when he was a boy. It meant the others had to work double-time to keep up.

For the sake of Barrows Bay and all she represented, this baby, who would have lived a long and blessed life, must be sacrificed.

Sheila Tanner may have thrown a wrench in the works, as Mavis complained, but her presence there would serve two purposes.

First, she would shoulder a good portion of the blame for the death of the child. An outsider at a birthing would be seen as a bad omen. Despite wanting to do what she thought was the right thing, her interference would be remembered by those in attendance. It would be spoken about. The young mother who'd suggested Sheila should stay in the first place—though the decision hadn't been her own, even if she might have thought so—in time would come to believe it herself.

The other reason was best not thought of. It had been Mother's decision. A penance, for the unforgiveable crime she'd committed some forty years ago. Mavis didn't like the idea, nor did she condone it. If it were up to her, she would drown Martin and his whore in the sound and be done with all of this sordid business.

The stones stood black against the moon-dappled water, reminding Mavis of her place.

The Midwives entered and formed an inner circle around the sacrificial stone at its center. Geraldine laid the baby on its cold surface and stepped back into the circle.

The women each removed their hoods, baring their true faces to the sky, the water, the trees. Faces of depthless black smoke, churning like the ocean.

Helen produced the *skean* from the folds of her cloak, the

emerald glinting in its haft. She held it aloft as the Midwives began to speak the incantation, invoking the Ancients.

On the flat stone, the baby let out a shrill cry. Her tiny limbs struggled against the tightly swaddled cloth. Ethel sensed no fear in her, only distress. She'd soiled herself, the fabric rubbing unpleasantly against her soft newborn skin.

The old blind woman took comfort in the fact that this pain would not trouble the child very much longer.

With the words spoken, Helen twirled the *skean* in her hands until the snaking blade faced downward. She seemed reluctant, Mavis thought. As though she hadn't performed this part of the ritual many times before.

As though they hadn't gorged themselves on this forbidden fruit many, many times.

The *skean* swished in a downward arc. Its blade reflected moonlight until it plunged through the cloth and into the baby's small heart, silencing her cries. The tiny body went limp, her head slowly rolling to the side. Blood soaked through the fabric, black in the moonlight.

Helen removed the blade, its rounded edges thudding hollowly against the child's slender ribcage, barely audible amid the waves.

She handed the blade to Geraldine and unswaddled the dead child. Its limbs fell to its sides and a gush of blood spurted from the wound. Helen pressed her thumb against it, stemming the flow.

"For the Mother," she said, holding the baby aloft.

"*For the Mother*," the others intoned in respectful reverence, moving in around Helen in a tight circle.

Helen removed her thumb and a geyser of blood sprayed their hungry faces.

They lapped it up until its hot, wet flow waned, and then they carved the small body into bite-sized pieces, gnashing their teeth on the chewy meat, gooey fat and stringy sinew. Gnawing the flesh off her fat little toes and fingers. Chewing the gristle off her bones.

The lion's share they saved for Mother.

Ever thoughtful, Helen brought along a Tupperware.

# Part Three

CRONES

# Chapter 14

## Women's Intuition

THE MIDWIVES ARRIVED at the Gingerbread House just before nine, a plump woman with a beehive hairdo and a delicate-looking woman wearing white silk gloves, holding a Tupperware container. Martin recognized them from the photographs in the box in his room. They were members of his mother's bowling league. What was it called? The Baby Splitters? The picture had looked pretty old but the women didn't appear to have aged a day.

Martin felt a vague sense of unease moments before he opened the door—Norma would have said someone must have walked over his grave—but he passed it off as an effect of the hangover. He hadn't gotten much sleep and his head still throbbed from too much drink at the Legion.

He held the door open but the women remained on the porch, the morning chill fogging their breath.

"Come in," Martin said, wondering if they needed an engraved invitation.

They stepped across the threshold together.

"Can I take your coats?"

"No, thanks," the woman with the beehive said gruffly. She looked around the foyer. "Place sure has changed."

"I'm Martin, by the way." He stuck out a hand.

She nodded brusquely, ignoring the hand as she kicked off her boots. "We know who you are. We delivered you."

Slipping off her coat, the woman with the gloves nodded and smiled. Her teeth were very small and close together. The smile itself seemed to contain all of the secrets a woman her age might carry with her to the grave.

Martin took her coat and hung it on the rack. He turned to watch as they headed for the stairs.

Norma stood in the kitchen doorway, eyeing their uninvited guests suspiciously as she worked a hand towel in a wet mug.

"Norma," the beehive woman said. "How are you, dear?"

"Been better."

The bitterness between them was unmistakable. The woman with the white gloves ignored them, already softly ascending the steps with the Tupperware.

"Can I get either of you something to drink?" Martin asked, since it didn't seem like Norma was about to offer any hospitality.

"We're fine. Pretend we're not here."

As the two women rose the stairs, Martin gave Norma an inquisitive look. She shook her head and returned to the sink. Martin followed the other women up the stairs.

The gloved woman knocked lightly on Ruby's door.

"She's sleeping," he said. "The doctor said not to disturb her."

"Doctor?" the beehive woman grunted. "Mother doesn't need a doctor, she needs good old-fashioned home remedies."

"Mother?"

The woman blinked. "*Your* mother. Ruby."

The gloved woman smiled her secret smile.

"What's in the container?" he asked, nodding at the Tupperware.

"Cure-all," the woman with the beehive said. "Old family recipe."

It looked like mush to Martin, similar to the pureed roast beef and mash Norma served Ruby their first night home, though more like turkey giblets and neck skin, as there were little bits of rubbery-looking pink and gooey fat and small grayish-brown lumps. Looking at it too long made the queasiness return, and he excused himself to go to the bathroom.

He stood in front of the sink, splashed water on his face and toweled himself off. When he emerged his mother's door was open and the women were standing on either side of Ruby's bed.

Ruby looked like she'd been hit by a train. During the doctor's very brief visit—it hadn't seemed like he wanted to stay even as long as the next ferry—he'd suggested bed rest. She had bruises where she fell which would "get worse before they get better," he said. But from her mobility, which he tested by moving her limbs himself and asking her if she felt any pain, to which Ruby had muttered and shaken her head, it didn't appear she'd broken or fractured anything.

"We won't know for sure without an X-ray, but of course your mother doesn't want to be moved to a hospital, against my better judgment, so we'll just have to hope for the best. If she has trouble breathing, signs of fever or starts to act strangely, call me. It could be a sign of fat embolism syndrome."

Martin considered mentioning that acting strangely was Ruby's modus operandi, but told the doctor he would call.

Beehive raised Ruby to a seated position while White Gloves stacked pillows beneath her. Ruby didn't appear to be conscious.

"Be careful, please."

"We've been around some," Beehive said dismissively.

Martin watched from the door, feeling ineffectual. He could have used Sheila's take-no-bullshit attitude but she was out for a brisk jog around the island. She'd been gone for several hours now. Considering all that happened last night, he supposed she had a lot to think about.

"Ruby, dear," Beehive said. "Time to take your medicine."

White Gloves had removed the lid from the container. The smell of it struck him—a rich iron scent like liver and a coppery tang and sharp herbs and something vaguely rotten—and he had to cover his nose.

She spooned up some of the mush. It looked like wet dog food on the spoon as she brought it toward Ruby's mouth.

"Open up, dear," Beehive said. "Here comes the aeroplane."

Ruby's lips remained firmly closed. White Gloves pushed the spoon between them and virtually pried them open to shove the horrid mess into her mouth.

"Hey, hey, do you have to force feed her that crap? Can't I just give it to her when she wakes up?"

White Gloves said something only Beehive could hear. The other woman nodded. "If you want her to get better, this is how it's done."

He turned away as Beehive began working Ruby's jaw and massaging her throat to make her swallow. What could he do? Call the cops? They were Ruby's friends and they were just trying to take care of her.

The worst that could happen was Ruby could choke on their old-wives' remedy. He didn't want to have to give his mother CPR, especially knowing he'd be tasting that putrid mush and so close on the heels of having seen her naked coming out of the bath, but he supposed he'd do what was necessary. Their relationship was complex but he wouldn't let her choke to death to spare himself a few moments of awkwardness and disgust.

"There you go," Beehive said. "Num-num. Eat it all up."

White Gloves plunged in with another spoonful. Ruby's chapped lips were moist with brown lumps.

"Okay, I'm tapping out," Martin said. He went back downstairs. Norma was still busying herself in the kitchen, wiping the inside of the oven.

"Need help?"

"I'm fine," Norma said, scouring away a nasty stain.

"Hey, what's your deal with those two?"

"I'd rather not talk about it."

He'd never known Norma to be so closed down. There must have been a fair amount of bad blood between them. He decided not to push her—she'd tell him on her time, if she wanted to—and do a bit of thinking about his next book instead.

An hour passed while he sat in the living room with a legal pad, scrawling notes in handwriting only legible to himself. He'd been thinking a lot about the direction he might go with this one. Whether he'd delve deeply into the real-life history of Barrows Bay or use it as a springboard for a fictional town, the way Stephen King had written *IT*'s Derry as a stand-in for Martin's second childhood home of Stratford, Connecticut. Though they'd lived there decades apart, Martin had still felt the town in every page. All eleven hundred of them.

He'd already decided to use aspects of his own life within the story, though he wasn't sure how much of his past would make it into the final draft, and he wasn't so vain as to make himself the main character. Due to its subject, he thought the protagonist should be a young pregnant woman. An urban professional with a very liberal mindset, returned to her small-town home due to financial difficulties. A sort of folk-horror *Rosemary's Baby* for modern readers.

He thought that would make for an interesting twist, though he'd have to press Sheila for details about what happened last night and she didn't seem ready to talk about it yet. He wondered if she ever would.

He didn't suspect writing a book about mainly women and "women's issues" would be a problem, despite the trend toward what literary agents called "own voices" fiction. He'd written enough true crime from a female perspective and had received some praise for that approach. He'd also grown up mainly in the company of women and his early influences were maternal. Empathy and research would help with anything he might lack. It might even pass the Bechdel test.

Motivation would play a bigger role in whether or not he could pull it off. *Dead Weight* wasn't doing all that well, not like his True Crime books. At least this book would have the benefit of being his second novel. But when sales were little more than a trickle, it was difficult not to seriously consider sticking with what paid the bills.

He was filling up the notebook fast when the woman with the beehive clodded into the living room doorway.

"Your mother's asked for you."

"She talked?"

Standing behind her, the woman with the white gloves smiled her tiny-toothed smile.

He laid down the notebook and headed for the foyer, reconsidered and returned for his notebook, worried they might read it while he was upstairs with his mother.

Ruby was sitting up of her own volition, her back resting on the mound of pillows. She had some color in her cheeks and the pits of her eyes seemed less prominent, though it could have been a trick of the sunlight streaming in through the curtains. Whatever the old family recipe was, it had done more for her than the doctor's brief visit in little over an hour.

"You look better."

"I feel better." Her voice sounded strong. Back to normal. She patted the side of the bed. Her gnarled hand still trembled, and the bruises on her arm still looked awful. He came over obediently and sat beside her, setting the notebook on the table. The stench of the leftover mush prickled his nostrils

"Martin, I'm not terribly skillful at expressing it but I am glad you came home. I'm proud of what you've accomplished without me. Despite me. I want you to know that however you feel about me, it was never my intention to make you feel unwanted."

"Aw, jeez, Ma." He felt tears prickling his sinuses. "You don't have to—"

"I want to." She patted his hand. "You're a good son. You took care of me for as long as you could, and you should never feel guilty about leaving us. You deserved a life of your own. Norma feels the same. You're welcome to stay here as long as you like. You and Sheila both." She squeezed his hand softly. "I'm *inviting* you to stay."

"Mom... thank you." The tears stung his eyes but he held them back. He turned his back to her. Couldn't say what was needed to her face. "I was so scared of you for so long..."

Ruby tutted. "Scared of *me*?"

"You have no idea. Even before what happened the day they took you away—"

"You remember it?"

He nodded. A tear fell and he wiped it briskly away.

"Perhaps you do." She sighed softly, patting his thigh. "Perhaps."

"And after that, seeing you week after week in the White Pl —in the sanitarium. Watching you wither away. It was terrifying. There were times I..." Could he admit to it? He pushed on. "...times I wished you would just die so I could be free."

"I understand. You were afraid."

Her gnarled fingers squeezed into the meat of his thigh. The grip was strong, hard enough to paralyze him. He tried to turn but found he couldn't pivot at the waist and his legs wouldn't move. He couldn't turn his head.

"You were a weak boy, Martin. A weak, scared little boy. You've always *been* weak and scared. That weak, vain little boy grew to a bitter, loveless, unloved man with a Peter Pan complex and a booze addiction. A selfish, boorish beast. Afraid of aging for fear you'll lose the one advantage you have over your prey—those pretty young women who make you feel young, if only for a moment."

Her fingernails pierced the fabric of his jeans and tore into his skin. He felt blood trickle down his thigh but he couldn't tilt his head, couldn't even move his eyes to see if her hand had changed into a monster's claws the way it had in his childhood nightmares where she chased him through dark, winding tunnels.

*I was wrong about her. She's not the witch. She's Grandmother Wolf.*

"Death is what you truly fear," the old woman said. "It gnaws at you, like rats in the rafters. Like grave worms. But I'll tell you something, Martin. You shouldn't be afraid of dying. Embrace the immortal darkness within you. *Taste* life. Become the killer they say you are. The killer you *know* you are."

Her grip released him. He sucked in a gasped breath, only just realizing he hadn't breathed since she'd grabbed him, and turned to confront her. Not caring there were tears in his eyes. Not caring that he was still bleeding.

But Ruby was asleep. Breathing in and out peacefully through her nose. Blood throbbing steadily in her jugular, clearly visible under paper-thin flesh. Arms tucked neatly under the covers.

He stood abruptly, trying to comprehend what just happened. His leg wasn't bleeding. The jeans weren't torn. The injury itself was imagined.

Looking at her, the cold realization struck him that she couldn't have gripped his leg so hard with her weak, bony fingers, let alone forceful enough to paralyze his entire body. She wouldn't have the strength. The exertion would have quickened her breathing. Her pulse. And he would have heard her hands slipping back under the covers.

*I'm losing my mind*, he thought.

*Or maybe it was never there to begin with.*

He watched her sleep for a long moment, wondering what

was wrong with himself, then he crept out and quietly closed her door.

When he got back downstairs, he saw the Midwives had already let themselves out.

---

SHEILA RAN.

In the city, there were hard sidewalks and cramped streets to clear her mind of distractions, to focus her thoughts on whatever she needed to work out. A trial. A major life event. She usually ran from her apartment in Gramercy to the Central Park Loop and around the Reservoir in a loop-de-loop. When faced with a particularly difficult problem, she might run the Lower Manhattan Loop, with its various monuments.

In Barrows Bay, there were few distractions. This was her third run since they arrived, and she was sure by now she'd seen the entire island, from the sandy peninsula on the northernmost tip to the craggy bluffs and crunchy seashell beaches to the south. She'd run through forests and roads cut through granite. Past grassy fields and crumbled wooden shacks and farmland. Breathing in clean ocean air, spicy conifers, damp earth, diesel fuel from the ferry docks and pungent pig manure from a farm off the main road.

She seemed to be the only runner on the island. Plenty walked, rode bikes, drove ATVs, ramshackle trucks and farm equipment. Most people she passed looked at her as if she were an alien from another planet. Which in a way, she supposed she was—Manhattan was like Mars compared to island life.

Yesterday on her run she tried to work out what to do about the Midwives. Their negligence that caused the death of little Ruby St. John. The main distraction was Barclay. She'd been trying to run him out of her mind since the day she found out he escaped. Their last day in the city she'd arrived home from a run attempting just that when she found the ankh necklace he'd left for her, which had apparently belonged to Letitia May Cotton, his erstwhile accomplice.

It was no good. The killer was ever present in her mind, living rent-free in her amygdala, the fear center, the almond-shaped nuclei where nightmares live. He was next-door neighbors with spiders and creaky stairs and her mother's china dolls and all the other things that frightened her.

Today she ran with a secondary purpose. She was returning a Tupperware.

Geraldine MacKenna lived close to the ferry docks on the northwestern face of the island. Sheila wasn't looking forward to conversing with the old woman, particularly after what Martin said about the way they'd barged into the house yesterday and force fed his mother some kind of vile-smelling meat and herb concoction, neglecting the advice of the doctor to keep her off solid foods for several days.

This morning Ruby seemed fine. Someone who didn't know better might have considered the change miraculous. But Sheila knew medical "miracles" happened often. The human body had an incredible power to heal itself. Mind over matter worked, as evidenced by the placebo effect. Thoughts could affect health negatively or positively, depending on the severity of the illness.

Ruby was a strong-willed woman. She had simply willed herself well.

With every day spent under the Savage roof, Sheila understood more about Ruby and her son. She could see why Ruby would have terrified him as a child. She was quick to judge, opinionated, forceful, brusque, constantly challenging the two of them and always criticizing Norma and Martin. It was no wonder he gravitated toward meek women. Women who wouldn't push back.

*What does that say about me?* she wondered.

"You're the exception to the rule," she said aloud, almost a war cry, pumping her legs, pushing herself to run harder, faster, the Tupperware slapping against her thigh.

*Am I though?* From what he said about Tish, it sounded like she was a tough cookie. Aside from her apparent worship of a serial killer of women, which inevitably led to her own death.

Not to mention the bookseller, who'd apparently made many enemies in town with her pushback against the Midwives.

*Attraction-repulsion. Unconscious Oedipal urges lead him to seek out women who are very unlike his mother but also very much like his mother.*

"Thank you, Dr. Freud, for your thoroughly pedestrian analysis," she said, breathing heavily.

Geraldine's house wasn't much further. Sheila remembered passing it on her first run. It was Ruby who suggested she be the one to return the Tupperware. Martin said he'd run it over in the car but Ruby said Geraldine felt they had left things badly between them at the birthing and she wanted to "bury the hatchet."

Sheila had no intention of allowing Geraldine to butter her up or make her consider dropping the subject, but she did feel it was in her best interest to give the woman the benefit of the doubt. Particularly if they were going to be staying here much longer. With Martin working on a new book—apparently incorporating elements of this town and his own childhood, at least as far as the glimpse she'd gotten at his notepad had hinted—it was likely they'd be here until Barclay was caught again.

Or either him or the two of them were dead.

Making sure the Midwives believed she had no ill will toward them was a wise move, strategically.

She rounded a curve and spotted the mailbox on the right, shaped like a cartoon owl. She stopped at the side of the road and caught her breath, hands on her knees.

Geraldine's house was set back from the road, nestled in the shade of tall pines and a giant red oak tree. The last snowfall still hadn't fully melted and lay in white patches here and there, giving the place a distinct "sweet old lady's cottage" feel. The roof was steep and taller than the entire first story, the siding old, gray cedar shakes. A stone chimney rose from the side nearest the sound.

Sheila walked the gravel path lined with small wooden windmills that spun lazily and plastic and ceramic woodland creatures, from snowy owls to squirrels standing to nibble on plastic acorns. The door knocker was a barn owl.

The door opened just as she raised the knocker, prepared to strike. Geraldine must have seen her walking up the drive.

*Either that or she's psychic, ha ha.*

The old woman stood in the doorway dressed in jogging pants and a bulky knitted sweater. She held knitting needles in one silk-gloved hand. A half-formed pink baby's booty dangled from it, with loops of pink wool that made Sheila think of Mavis snipping the umbilical cord.

*Snick!*

She flinched.

"Hi, Miss MacKenna," she said, covering for her sudden fear. She held out the container. "I brought your Tupperware."

"Oh yes, thank you, dear," the old woman said, her voice soft and lilting, barely above a whisper. It was still the loudest Sheila had ever heard her speak. She made no move to accept the container. "Come inside, you'll catch your death out there in the chill."

She hadn't planned to stay, had hoped to get a quick apology and run back to the house along the beach. She glanced back anxiously at the road, thinking the old woman would take the hint.

"Thank you," she said finally, and followed Geraldine inside.

The interior was dim and utterly lifeless. Drab flocked wallpaper that looked older than time. Dark, dull wood furniture and an old grandfather clock. Everything smelled of dust.

There were no photos on the walls, no paintings. The only personal touch appeared to be owl figurines and stuffies of various sizes placed here and there throughout the small foyer, the sitting room and dining room.

"You like owls?"

"Not especially," Geraldine said, and showed her tiny teeth in a brief smile.

Sheila scowled slightly.

Geraldine directed her toward the sitting room with a gloved hand. "Please, come in. We have much to discuss."

"I really should get running—"

"Oh, please. It's no trouble."

Sheila nodded, though she thought it must have looked like she was partially shaking her head. She stepped across the threshold. A large owl was perched on the mantel, its wings spread wide. She flinched and did a double-take, thinking it was a pet, before realizing it was taxidermied. The sofa and chair were covered in clear plastic.

*I guess I won't have to worry about sweating all over her furniture.*

"Please, sit. I'll make tea."

"If I have tea, I'll be peeing in ten minutes."

"What's to stop you?" Geraldine placed the knitting needles

and half-formed booty on the coffee table and shuffled off to the kitchen, leaving her alone with the owl. Its eyes seemed to follow her as she sat on the sofa. The plastic grumbled under her weight.

"Ruby tells me the two of you play bridge," she called out. The woman either didn't hear or didn't care to raise her own voice to reply.

She fidgeted, feeling anxious, wanting to get back out on the road and run off her agitation.

She looked at the booty. Was there really any point finishing it now that the little girl was dead? But she supposed there would always be another. Wouldn't be much use for midwives without pregnant women.

Out in the hall, the grandfather clock chimed, startling her. It was ten. The chime echoed throughout the house. By the third chime she plugged her ears. The rest were muffled by the blood thumping beneath her fingers.

Geraldine returned with the tea in a blue Willow china set, cups and saucers, sugar dish and cream pitcher. She laid the tray on the table and sat on the grumbling plastic covering the chair, leaned over and poured two cups.

"Milk and sugar?"

"No. Thank you."

Sheila sipped hers dutifully. It tasted sweet without sugar and rich without milk, with a strong herb flavor she couldn't quite pick out. Anise, maybe. Or cinnamon. She knew the flavors were entirely unalike but the taste defied description. Each sip tasted entirely different. Before she knew it, she'd finished the entire cup.

"This is delicious. Where did you get it?"

"Helen Birch makes it. Her own concoction, from fresh herbs and sundry."

"Sundry?"

"This and that." The old woman glanced up at the owl on the mantel, sipping her tea thoughtfully. "This one... this one is quite menacing, isn't she? You know, many native Indian cultures believe owls are a symbol of death."

"Is that why you collect them?"

"Oh no. No, no, no." She set her teacup and saucer down. "Would you like some more?"

"I'm fine, thanks."

Geraldine nodded. She smoothed her jogging pants and re-garded the owl again. "The owls remind me to ask, *Who am I?*"

"Who are you."

Geraldine smiled. "Yes."

"And why is that important to you?" Sheila asked, uninten-tionally lapsing into psychologist-mode. "I'm sorry, that's too personal."

"Oh no, don't be. I believe it's important to hold a mirror up to ourselves, so to speak. To remember where and what we come from. It keeps us grounded. The Ancient Greeks have a saying, *Know thyself.* I believe it's fair to say your profession is built around this—knowing oneself. How well do you know yourself, Ms. Tanner?"

Sheila shrugged. "As well as anyone does, I guess."

Geraldine tutted. "I'd hazard you know a bit more than most."

"Like you said, introspection comes with the territory."

The old woman smiled, looking very pleased. *"Physician, heal thyself."*

"Luke 4:23."

"You know your Bible."

"I know the quote."

The old woman glanced at the unfinished booty. "Would you like to know yourself better, Ms. Tanner?"

"Sheila. Of course. Who wouldn't?"

"Oh, I'd imagine many would shy away from a light shining on every dark corner of themselves. We've all got things to hide, don't we? From ourselves as much as from others."

"Do you?"

Geraldine's smile returned. She didn't answer.

"Well, I really should get running—"

"Running, yes. Always running. But from what?"

Sheila squinted at her. It seemed like a challenge.

Geraldine removed her gloves, one by one. The flesh be-neath was pitted and black, like blood clots from disuse. She held them out, palms up, over the tea set. The palms had no lines.

Seeing this, Sheila felt a prickle of revulsion. She tried to reason it away, tried to convince herself there was some kind of heavy-duty hand cream in her gloves that would prevent her palms from creasing or they'd been worn away in some kind of accident like a chemical burn but she couldn't, and looking at them made her feel slightly ill.

"May I?"

"May you, what?"

"Read your palms, of course."

Sheila laughed. "You want to read my palms."

"Unless you're afraid—"

She shook her head. "Why would I be afraid?" But the thought of putting her hands anywhere near those baby-smooth palms repulsed her.

"I believe we've already gone over that," Geraldine said, not retracting her hands.

Sheila tugged up her sleeves and placed her hands, palms up, in Geraldine's.

The old woman's flesh was the exact same temperature as the room. If she couldn't feel the skin beneath hers, she would have thought Geraldine wasn't there.

"Turn them over, please. I need to touch them, palm to palm."

Despite not wanting to touch the old woman's hands with the more tactile parts of her own, Sheila did as she was told.

Geraldine's eyelids fluttered closed. "You have a complicated relationship with your parents."

That was easy. Most people had a complicated relationship with their parents. *Cold Reading for Dummies*. Parlor tricks. Impress your friends.

"Your parents themselves didn't get along. They fought terribly. *Viciously*. For about as long as you can remember. Possibly ever since you were born. Not with violence, mind. Only words. But often, words can sting more than fists, can't they? The wounds last longer."

It was true. She could hear them arguing through the floor vent. Arguing about her. Her face must have given her away. Geraldine was reading her expressions. She had to be more careful, make a concerted effort not to react.

"You were the apple of your father's eye. Daddy's little girl. But mother didn't want you, oh no. Not after the ordeal of your sister. And she made sure to remind you every chance she got."

Sheila withdrew her hands, standing abruptly. "Okay, game over." Her heart was thrumming. She felt sick to her stomach and slightly woozy, her face flushed.

"Oh, please," Geraldine said. "Things were just starting to get interesting."

"I really need to use your washroom."

The old woman sighed. The plastic grumbled as she sat back in the chair and pointed dismissively. "Last door on the left."

Sheila skirted around the table, heading for the hall.

"You didn't ask about the booty," Geraldine said, stopping Sheila in her tracks. "Don't you want to know who it's for?"

"Not really, no."

"Oh, but I think you do. And I think you know who it belongs to."

Sheila turned on her heels, annoyed and eager to get out of the woman's sight and collect herself. "Why would I know that?"

"Because it belongs to *you*, Sheila." Geraldine smiled, showing her small teeth. "I should think you'd want to *thank* me."

*Senile*, Sheila thought. *She's lost her mind.*

*Then how did she know those things about my me? About my sister. About Mom?*

She turned and hurried down the hall, passing a door, open a crack, on her way to the bathroom. The queasiness was almost unbearable, made worse by the smell wafting out of the doorway, like damp earth and rotting vegetation.

An owl clock ticked away on the wall directly across from the door, its eyes slowly closing and flicking open abruptly, as if trying to stay awake.

*Who am I?* she thought.

*Have I become my mother?*

She slipped into the bathroom and closed the door. With barely a moment to spare, she raised the fuzzy blue toilet lid and puked. Chunks of half-digested breakfast splattered up the sides of the bowl, the color of Helen Birch's tea.

*The old bitch poisoned me.*

She staggered to her feet and stood at the sink. There was no mirror, just the flat wood surface of a medicine chest.

The toilet gurgled as she turned on the tap. Splashing her face with water cooled the flush in her cheeks and neck. She still felt woozy and nauseous but it was more likely an allergic reaction than poison.

The toilet gurgled again, bubbling like a cauldron. She hesitated to peer into the bowl, not eager to see what she'd thrown up, let alone if sewage was sloshing up from below.

A splash in the bowl. A high-pitched mewl.

She stumbled back against the door, banging her head painfully on a towel hook.

The mewling grew louder, the splashing more frantic.

*There's a kitten in there. The crazy old bitch tried to flush a cat.*

She stepped closer, hesitantly peering over the lip of the bowl.

When she saw what lay in the putrid water, her mind course-corrected. It wasn't a kitten. It was a baby, a tiny purple thing trashing in the bottom of the toilet, the water pink with blood. A fetal girl, the umbilical cord trailing into the drain.

"That's not real," she said aloud, trying to convince herself. "She drugged me and I'm hallucinating."

The baby cried louder.

"Shh! Shh!"

The last thing she wanted was Geraldine checking up on her. Someone who would drug a person without their knowledge was liable to do just about anything.

But what could she do? The baby was crying and she couldn't just leave it in the toilet, couldn't just let it go on screaming like that, she had to make it stop or it would drive her crazy, make her hysterical just like her sister's crying made her mother—

She reached out and flushed.

Because it wasn't real. She knew it wasn't real. But she couldn't go on listening to it scream.

Only once the toilet gurgled and the tank had started refilling did she dare another look into the bowl. The water was clear. The bowl clean, aside from some streaks and flecks of vomit, which she quickly wiped away with a scrap of toilet paper, more out of embarrassment than conscientiousness.

She washed her hands hurriedly, dried them on a towel and stepped out into the hall, eager to leave. Paranoia made her anxious. If the woman was crazy enough to drug her, would she let her leave so easily?

The cracked door creaked open slowly.

Anxious, Sheila peered inside.

Geraldine lay in bed, her gloved hands folded across her chest. She appeared to be sleeping, her breath even, her eyelids fluttering. Near the bed stood a chest of drawers littered with owl figurines, owl stuffies, owl-shaped jewelry. More on the bedside table, on the floor, paintings and photographs of them hung haphazardly all over the walls.

"Flushed another one, did you?"

The old woman's voice came from very close, but her eyes were still closed and her lips hadn't moved.

Geraldine peeked out from behind the door, gripping it in her bare hands, her fingers almost entirely black, smiling with her tiny teeth.

On the edge of delirium, Sheila turned from the woman at the door to her doppelganger in the bed.

"You're just like her, aren't you?" Geraldine said at the door. "Your mother's daughter. She would have flushed you too, if dear old Daddy hadn't set her straight."

Sheila couldn't hold it back any longer. She screamed.

As the woman in the door and her twin on the bed began to laugh in tandem, Sheila turned and bolted down the hall, through the sitting room where a third Geraldine sat casually sipping tea, and out the front door, running from the cottage in the woods as fast as her legs would carry her.

# CHAPTER 15

## A Trail of Blood

I T WAS A somber Wednesday morning as everyone from the Savage house attended the funeral of Ruby St. John.

Martin sat beside his mother in the small church, shifting uncomfortably in the black suit he'd worn to prom, let out a size wider by Norma. Sheila wore one of his mother's black dresses that probably hadn't seen the light of day since the mid-1940s, with frills on the shoulders and sleeves, a pair of black stockings and Oxfords belonging to Norma, two sizes too big. All she missed to complete the outfit was a pair of black silk gloves.

He wasn't concerned about his ill-fitting suit or the fact that a woman he'd been intimate with was dressed in his mother's clothes. Three people had died within three days, each at least tangentially connected to him. A solipsistic part of him wondered if the child would have survived if he hadn't gone to Sinjin's that night.

Death and disaster followed him like a shadow. A trail of blood, just like Barclay had promised. Could it all be a coincidence? Or had he been touched by something beyond the realm of the known world? His encounter with the deer that night, followed by what he'd found in the old book of fairy tales, the death, the running, not to mention the frightening, almost definitely hallucinated encounters with some monstrous nightmare version of mother... all of it had taken a toll on his already troubled mind.

Sheila tried multiple times to get him to open up since the tragedy. But he couldn't speak to her about Nadine or Tish or Ruby St. John without bringing up the rest. He'd seen enough of the White Place to know he didn't want to end up there himself. And mental illness ran in families.

So he said nothing.

Sheila had her own struggle to deal with, wondering whether or not she should tell Martin what happened at Geraldine's house. Or what she thought had happened. Because she had to have hallucinated it. Helen's tea had a psychedelic effect on her. What would she tell him? That an innocent old woman drugged her and read her mind? If she told him that, she'd have to tell him about the baby booty and the fetus she thought she'd flushed down the toilet. She definitely wasn't ready to—*breech* —broach that subject, especially with Martin.

Knowing Ruby was friends with these women made it even more difficult. She wanted to talk about the night of the birthing but it seemed like the old woman was always within earshot whenever she tried to get Martin alone or get him out of the house to talk.

In the end she chose not to say anything, and they both wrestled with their respective secrets, parts of the same secret, without knowing it.

Dressed in an ankle-length black dress and veil, as if she were the grieving mother herself, Ruby Savage kept a secret of her own. Within an hour after wolfing down the giblets, the heart and a good portion of the child's placenta, all blended into a thick, gooey paste, the evidence of her many years began peeling away. She couldn't recall the last time she'd felt so vital, so *alive*.

The only worry was that her transformation had to be kept from Martin, Norma and Sheila. She could reveal it to them a bit at a time, like a man adding color to his graying beard, until the change would only be noticeable in a photograph. It would do no good for them to see her dancing the Charleston in the wake of such a tragedy. Nor for them to notice the wrinkles around her eyes and lips had diminished, like those advertisements Norma scoffed at on television.

Ruby applied plenty of powder to counter the effects of the

ritual and made sure to hunch over her walker, perhaps a touch melodramatically. She even mimicked the palsied tremors in her hands she'd suffered from only days before.

Oh yes, the little treat had done its trick. Her daughters' magic was strong and would only grow stronger in the following days and weeks leading toward spring and Midsummer, when the next feast would be had. It would be a glorious season of rebirth and abundance. She would see to it Barrows Bay thrived even more.

Reverend Atkins stood at the pulpit, reading words from the holy book he knew by rote. It seemed the entire town had shown up for the St. John girl's funeral. The little white church on Cavan Street was more packed than it had been in years. He spotted faces among the pews he would only ever see in passing. His subdued sense of elation was tempered by the unfavorable occasion, but not entirely absent.

It was such a tragedy when a little one passed. Not only for the parents but for the community at large. Many tragedies had befallen Barrows Bay during his appointment with God on this island, a calling which often felt like penance. But the good reverend knew the death of little Ruby St. John was part of His Divine Plan. And with a beatific smile he reminded those gathered in the pews of this, just as he would his ever-dwindling congregation during Sunday sermons.

Behind the little church stood a cemetery that had served as Barrows Bay's place of interment since its founding. The original barrows on the southern shore, near the standing stones, had been exhumed and reburied there.

The oldest headstones were crumbled, blackened from age and barely legible, marking the plots of those who had perished on the coffin ship, *Ruby*. Wildflowers and weeds grew rampant there, as if nourished by the dead moldering below. They needed to be cut back from smothering the graves weekly in the spring and summer months. Reverend Atkins paid Mavis Lynch's young neighbor, Charlie Watson, by the hour for the chore. Charlie worked like the dickens, his lean, muscular young body tanning and glistening with sweat under the hot summer sun.

Ruby St. John's tiny coffin was placed in the ground at just after eleven in the morning. The day was bright, sunnier than it had been since October, when winter had swept in from the north and smothered the island under its cold, harsh hand. Spring would soon be here, and though the townspeople had come to mourn, thoughts of rebirth and regrowth—and of the coming summer, long, lazy days spent on the beach and evenings at backyard barbeques and fireworks displays—weren't far from mind. God's plan and all.

The Midwives stood in funeral black to the left of the family, looking appropriately grieved beneath their veils, though inwardly they were quite pleased with themselves.

The county coroner didn't notice he'd performed his autopsy on a china doll stuffed with straw, removing giblets purchased from Sinjin's very own meat department. Nor was the funeral director aware of the embalming fluid oozing from tiny cracks in its porcelain fingers and toes, soaking the pale pink fabric of its belly and bum.

It had been a dreadfully successful glammer, all around. One for the books. Even the parents were none the wiser.

While Mother and the Midwives permitted the reverend to ramble on about his God and his God's only begotten bastard Son—this was after all an important part of the theatrics—Mavis studied Mother and her bastard son from the corner of her eye.

A new plan had been set into motion, of which Mavis Lynch wholeheartedly disapproved. It meant she would need to play her own hand sooner than she hoped. A bold move no one would see coming. A Hail Mary, so to speak.

For the sake of the others, for the sake of the *town*, Ruby Savage's boy had to die.

"'For God so loved the world, that he gave his only begotten Son,'" the reverend said, allowing his gaze to fall very briefly over the old ladies in black, attempting to gauge their reaction without alerting them. "'That whosoever believeth in Him should not perish, but have everlasting life.'"

*You keep on peddling that crap, Padre,* Mavis thought. *But who'll save your soul? With all that you know, and all you've kept secret?*

Hugging each other at the edge of the grave, Laura and Sinjin wept as the stainless-steel machine lowered their daughter into the ground. Separately, they had already decided this pregnancy would be their last attempt. Ruby's name had been chosen long before the poor soul had come and gone from this world, a fitting tribute to Barrows Bay and its history, a town that had provided for the St. Johns and been their home. The best little island in the world.

They could never have known how just fitting the name would be, that the ship which had brought so much death to these shores would have as its namesake a child who would perish without ever seeing the results of their ancestors' hardship.

They could never have known her death would give so much more life to the old woman who shared her name. The old woman who now stood with a ghost of a smile hidden beneath her veil, beside her caretaker, her son, and the big city bitch whose meddling had killed their child.

---

Though it was Barrows Bay tradition to hold a wake, the St. Johns declined. No one could blame them. Their child hadn't lived long enough for her life to be celebrated.

After the funeral service let out—everyone paying their respects to the bereaved, perfunctorily thanking the reverend for his thoughtful words and paying near reverential respect to Martin's mother, as if she'd performed the funeral services herself—nearly everyone went back to their respective homes to reflect on mortality with their spouses and relatives and friends.

Others moved on to the Legion for a stiff drink, while more immersed themselves in various forms of entertainment, unwilling to dwell on death and misery any longer. With this death falling just one day after that nutjob Nadine Hinkley's bizarre run-in with the deer, it was difficult for townsfolk not to wonder if a pall had fallen over Barrows Bay.

Any one of them could be next, at least according to some of the more wary types at the Legion, particularly veterans of the Vietnam War, who had reason to be distrustful.

Though there was no wake, no one could say the island of Barrows Bay didn't pull together during a tragedy. Norma made her famous marinated roast beef and Yorkshire pudding and Ruby baked another strawberry-rhubarb pie. Martin and Sheila left them both on the St. Johns' inner porch alongside dozens of Tupperware dishes, bowls and pans covered with tinfoil or plastic wrap and elastic bands, bottles of wine, vases brimming with flowers, cards with "love" and "condolences" and "deepest sympathies" scrawled hastily, printed neatly or written in cursive inside.

Sinjin stood in the dim light behind the screen door to offer brusque thanks but he didn't invite them in. The sound of Laura's crying issued from within: long, animalistic wails that sounded like they'd already torn her throat out hours earlier.

"This whole thing is just awful, Martin," Sheila said as they descended the steps. They headed somberly down the walkway between beds of last year's dead flowers.

"I can't even imagine what they must be going through right now," he said.

At the sidewalk, they turned left, heading toward the Savage house. They walked under a heavy silence for half a block, until Sheila, thinking of the unfinished booty, finally forced herself to —*breech*—broach the subject she'd needed to for the past several days.

"I told you I had an abortion, didn't I?" She looked at him askance, anxiously awaiting judgement.

"No," he said tonelessly. It didn't seem to faze him. She supposed he'd been through one or two himself, though it wasn't quite the same as her own experience. "When was this?"

"A few weeks after we split."

This got a small reaction from him, a slight look of shock. "You and me? Why didn't you tell me?"

She sighed and looked off at an old gray running shoe revealed by the thaw on somebody's lawn. "I thought you'd react badly. I thought you might tell me to reconsider."

He thought about it for a moment as they walked. "I couldn't have handled a kid. Imagine me as a dad. I can barely tie my own shoelaces."

"I think you'd do all right," she said, smiling in spite of herself. "I don't know about back then... Not that I want kids."

"Not with me, anyway."

"We never worked together. We had fun, but we'd kill each other if we lived under the same roof."

"We seem to be doing pretty okay now."

"With Aunt Norma and Ruby as referees."

He laughed. "Fair point."

She gathered her thoughts. She had a lot to say and wasn't sure quite how to start, despite having gone over it again and again in her mind. "Martin, I'm not sure why Laura wanted me there and I wish like hell I never agreed to stay. But I'm glad that I was there. The midwives, your mother's friends, they're responsible for that little girl's death."

"You think?"

"The baby came out breeched. I told them it was dangerous to deliver. They should have listened. They should have delayed the delivery and gotten her medical treatment as soon as possible. Any midwife worth her salt would have done that. For the safety of the mother as much as the child."

"But it's a small island," Martin said. "It would have taken hours to get her to the nearest hospital by ferry. Maybe less if they were able to get a helicopter—"

"There's a doctor *right here on the island*, Martin." Her face flushed with righteous fury. "A retired obstetrician. I found him on the internet yesterday. He owns a pig farm on the north end of the island."

"A pig farm?"

"Those dotty old bitches could've called him. Retired or not, he could have helped. He could have performed an emergency C-section. *Anything*. But they didn't. It was almost like they were *determined* to watch that baby die."

"That's a bit dramatic, don't you think?"

"Martin, I was *there*. It was bizarre. Like a pantomime. Like they'd done it a hundred times before."

"Haven't they? Sinjin said everyone born in Barrows Bay was delivered by those ladies. He was, his wife was—those two friends of my mom's who came over on Sunday said I was, too."

The comment derailed her. She tried to backtrack, tried to remember where she was headed with all of this. *The pigs*, she reminded herself. *Dr. Mulligan*. "I'm going to talk to him," she said.

"Who? Sinjin?"

"The doctor. He's been retired for over a decade. I'm gonna hear what he thinks about these midwives, and then I'll decide whether or not I push the St. Johns to file a civil suit against them."

"A lawsuit? Sheila, I don't think that's a good idea."

"Why not?"

"Well, for one, we're relying on the hospitality of these people for our own safety. Do you really want to go poking a hornet's nest right now? You saw how they treated my mother at the funeral. It was like that scene in *The Godfather*, everyone paying their respects to Don Corleone." He scratched his chin with the backs of his fingernails. "Bonasera, Bonasera."

"Now who's being dramatic?"

He shrugged. It was a bizarre scene, watching his mother accept their adulation and kind words, inquiries about her health and how she was getting along with Martin after so long apart. A few of them had even called her "Mother." All while the poor reverend stood gaping, his cheeks red from drink or embarrassment, as mourner after mourner shook, even *kissed* her hand.

Once again Martin found himself wondering who his mother was to these people. Was she just another midwife, the first face they'd seen in this world? Or was she more? Was Nadine right about her? What was it about these midwives, and Ruby Savage in particular, that held these people in apparent thrall?

"I think you're right," he said. "We should talk to this doctor. An obstetrician on the island and every childbirth goes through these midwives? It doesn't make sense. Tradition is one thing, but you'd think someone would buck tradition once in a while, you know?"

*Buck*, he thought grimly, remembering the deer that crashed out of the trees on his way home from the Legion. As though it had been following him.

*Nadine bucked tradition, and what did she get for it? A pair of goddamn antlers through the throat.*

"At the very least, he'll have some interesting stories to tell," Sheila said. "According to his website, he's also the town historian."

WHILE HIS FAVORITE fucking writer was attending a child's funeral in a small Rhode Island town a hundred and sixty miles to the northeast, Qurban Youssef stepped out of his Porsche at a parking meter half a block up from The Writing Room, a trendy bistro in Manhattan's Upper East Side.

Featured were shelves of books, a crackling fireplace, and photos of actors and authors from when it used to be known as Elaine's. Tom Wolfe, Norman Mailer, Mario Puzo and Joseph Heller had once been regulars here. Qurban's clients loved the atmosphere and the history but Qurban had disliked it even in the gregarious former proprietor Elaine Kaufman's day, when cigarette smoke still punctuated the smell of good food, booze and old books.

While his mother had instilled in him the art of making deals, his father had given him a love of literature. Qurban was a businessman, first and foremost. And though books and writers were his business, he was glad when the industry had begun its halfhearted shift from dusty old tomes toward electronic devices. Print was a dying beast, he believed, much too stupid to know it had been mortally wounded. E-books and audiobooks were the future.

Places like this were mausoleums. Monuments to a past that should be relegated to museums.

*Just try convincing my writers of that*, he thought bitterly, ducking back as a courier weaved by on the bike lane, almost hitting him. "You prick!" he called out.

The courier threw a middle finger back at him and carried on his merry way.

"I fucking love this city," Qurban said to himself, weaving between idling traffic to the other side of the street.

Despite the shift in consumer desires, his clients invariably wanted cheaply made trade paperbacks and leather-bound hardcovers with glossy dust jackets, perfect-bound covers with French folds and thick, rough pages with deckled edges made from eco-friendly recycled paper.

They all wanted to see their books in the gallery at Argosy and the window display at McNally Jackson. They looked down on digital marketplaces like Amazon and Kobo. The ebook was still the bastard stepchild of the industry.

*Or is it redheaded stepchild?* Qurban pictured his own children. Aadi was the apple of his eye but he would gladly trade Haaziq for a stepchild—redheaded or otherwise—who might be more respectful. Perhaps one who might follow in his father's footsteps rather than aspiring to be a hippity-hopper like Haaziq apparently wanted to be.

Qurban's client was "fashionably late" by twenty-five minutes, a young wallflower whose blog made headlines during the height of the #MeToo movement for its candid depiction of her own childhood sexual assault. He had no idea how much of it was true, but she was a competent writer and had a large and loyal following on social media, which she had the annoying habit of calling "soshe." She couldn't name a single writer from the photos on the walls, but she knew nearly every actor. Qurban thought she'd do very well in today's market.

He left the restaurant an hour later in a bit of a malaise. He was fifty-three years old, he drove a Porsche, owned a townhome in Murray Hill, had a decent 401K, a lovely wife who probably still loved him and two handsome male heirs. And yet he no longer felt fulfilled.

*It could always be worse*, he thought on his way back to the car, passing a homeless man sleeping on a splayed-open cardboard box with the jungle-thick hair in his ass crack exposed to passersby. *There but for the grace of Allah.*

The stinking mouth of an alley wafted out at Qurban like halitosis. He turned instinctively as if to marvel at whatever had made the smell.

It was surprisingly dark, just a narrow space between two buildings, bricks damp and dripping from a burst pipe high up. Empty aside from several trash bins near the far end and a single pigeon, which cooed and pecked at breadcrumbs on the wet concrete.

He shuffled by quickly, troubled for some reason. In the course of most days he walked by a dozen stinking alleys just like it, but something about this one—the look, the smell, the dripping pipe, even the way the pigeon had regarded him with its studious orange eyes—*something* gave him a cold chill. He pulled up the collar of his coat, walking hurriedly the rest of the way to the car.

He used his key and slipped in behind the steering wheel quickly, eager to get out of the neighborhood.

*Something has got my hackles up*, he thought. Not his favorite Americanism, but a fitting one. The hairs on the back of his neck felt like they were standing for *Ṣalāt al-Janāzah*, the funeral prayer.

The smell from the alley had followed him into the car. He couldn't seem to get it out of his nose: a mix of human sweat, raw sewage and a vaguely familiar musky scent.

He flicked on the air before starting the car, hoping to vanquish the smell from his nostrils, then pulled out into the street. Traffic was minimal for Manhattan. He thought of putting on the radio but the news just depressed him these days, all pot stirring and fear mongering. There was more than enough to fear in the world without the news constantly reaffirming it. Martin's books spoke to that.

A grumble of faux leather from the backseat made him jump. His shoulder jammed against the seatbelt.

The musky odor wafted from the back and he sensed rather than saw the man sitting up in the narrow backseats.

Instinctively his foot raised off the gas, jerking the car a few feet into the next lane. The SUV in his blind spot honked, and the man in the back laid a firm hand on his shoulder, snapping Qurban back to reality from his fear-induced stupor.

"Now just keep on drivin calmly and carefully an' I won't have to hurt ya."

Qurban recognized the voice and glanced at James Barclay in the rearview. The musky scent of his cologne, the accent, the dark, piercing eyes and the soiled cowboy shirt—even with several days' growth of salt-and-pepper scruff on his face a man like him stuck out like a sore thumb. He had an angry-looking slash across his right cheek and held a long kitchen knife in his left hand. The blade was rusty but still looked sharp enough to slice and dice Qurban if he didn't play by the killer's rules.

"How did you get in my car?"

"How does a fella do anything?" The killer grinned, his teeth crooked and yellowed. "I set mah mind to it. Now quit troublin yerseff with inconsequentialities and drive, my Middle Eastern friend."

"Please," Qurban said. "I have children."

"Then think 'bout your children an' play it smart." Barclay flicked his gaze ahead. "Why'ntcha go on an' take a left here?"

Qurban nodded. He flicked on the turning signal, checked his blind spot and slipped into the other lane.

He was moving on autopilot. All he could think about was the salmon tartare he'd had with lunch and how it would be found partially digested during his autopsy.

*Allah forbid. They'll find my body washed up in the East River, full of lobster brioche and champagne mimosas.*

He flinched as Barclay reached over his shoulder. The killer pinched the star and crescent ornament hanging from the rearview and studied it a moment. The smell coming off him was horrendous, barely masked by his cologne. He mustn't have washed since his escape.

"You a prayin man, Mr. Youssef?"

Barclay let the ornament go. Qurban watched it swing like Poe's pendulum for a moment, light from the late-winter sun glimmering off its gold surface.

"Not regularly, no," he admitted. He hadn't been to prayers since Ramadan. His brother had chastened him for breaking his fast by the third day.

The killer nodded. He sat with his elbows on the front chairs, knees near his chest. Taller than Qurban had pictured him. "Good," the killer said. "Never was a God-fearin man, myself. My mother, she had the fear a God somethin fierce. Made her pious. Vengeful. She murdered my daddy, did ya know that? Not that she didn't have reason to, y'understand. He was a real mean sumbitch when he got to drinkin, which I b'lieve he musta liked more'n breathin."

They were on 65th Street now, cutting across the south end of Central Park through the wooded, stone-walled transverse.

"What do you want from me, Mr. Barclay?"

"Oh, I 'magine you know that already."

"I don't know where Martin is." He wasn't lying. "The policeman said the less I know, the better."

"Well, that may be so but I don't reckon they were 'xactly right. See, I b'lieve you know a lot more about our mutual friend than ya think. An' I reckon if you were to put your mind to it, you might remember thangs you don't even know ya know. Ya know?"

The killer was watching him, his face—his animal *stink*—

uncomfortably close to Qurban's. Qurban kept his eyes on the road, not daring to look back.

Darkness descended upon them as the Porsche passed under a bridge. Light returned a moment later but there was a strange yellow tinge to it, as though they were passing under the eye of a hurricane.

"What kind of things?"

"Details," Barclay said. "The devil's in the details, so I'm told." The faux-leather grumbled as he sat back in the seat, placing his hands leisurely behind his head as if he might settle in for a nap.

"Where are we going?"

"Keep drivin. Take a left once we get to Columbus."

*Hell's Kitchen.* The office was there, but not much else that might interest Barclay.

They drove there in silence, traffic thickening as they reached Central Park West. Barclay didn't speak again. Qurban was glad not to have to listen to his Southern twang, but he worried about the killer's brooding silence. He suspected the man meant to torture him and might be devising the methods.

"Pull in here," Barclay said finally.

Qurban pulled in to the same alley where he met Martin last week, when he gave him the gun. As the tires crackled over crumbled bits of concrete and trash, his body began to tremble.

"Now now, no need to quiver. I ain't gon' kill ya, Qurban, just gon' rough y'up some."

Qurban nodded. He couldn't seem to catch his breath.

"Those kids a yours. They boys or girls?"

"B-boys." He wanted to cry.

"Good man. A family needs heirs, don't it? Someone to carry on the family name."

Qurban nodded. He agreed with the sentiment, but he would have nodded even if the killer had said Central Park East didn't smell like horse piss.

"Now you gave Marty a gun, dintcha?"

Again, Qurban nodded. Somehow the killer knew not just that but exactly where he'd handed it over. Barclay must have been following him for quite some time now. If so, it was likely he also knew where they lived.

Just the other day he'd jokingly suggested a sequel to *Witch*

*Hunter*. He had no intention of becoming a character himself, let alone his family. He'd even suggested Barclay might have been hiding in the back of Martin's Lexus, waiting to spring a trap.

*Be careful what you wish for, Qurban. It might come true.*

"Please," he said, his voice quavering. "I'll tell you everything I know—just don't hurt me. Don't hurt my family."

Barclay sat up, his stink following him. He gave Qurban a lopsided grin. "Well," he said, and exhaled languidly through his nose. "That all depends on if I like what you tell me, my Middle Eastern friend."

The grin chilled Qurban. He was a man of principles. A man of his word. A handshake still meant something. A promise made was a promise kept. Men like Barclay lived to push back against the rules. They were *wild cards*. A slightly crass Americanism, but the label fit.

A man could never be sure what a wild card would do.

He told the killer everything he knew.

---

OL' Gimme Jimmy let the agent's body slump over the console into the passenger seat. The guy didn't know Jack Shit, which was unfortunate for Jimmy but deadly for the agent.

After Jimmy roughed him up as promised, the agent blubbered and begged for his life to be spared and in his final moments he'd even prayed to his God. Jimmy slaughtered him *halal*, like his people would kill an animal meant for food, severing the jugular, carotid and windpipe with a single swipe of the rusty knife he found in a Dumpster stuck into the side of a hunk of stale bread like Excalibur in the stone.

He'd freed the knife only the day before, striking the stale bread against the brick wall until all that was left was crumbs. Looked like somebody spilled a bowl of croutons on the way to the salad. Like Hansel and Gretel's trail of breadcrumbs.

After he pierced the agent's heart to be satisfied the dead wouldn't return with thoughts of revenge in the afterlife, the blade came out much easier than it had from the bread, with a squeak against the ribs and a weak spurt of dark lifeblood.

Jimmy stepped out of the Porsche and wiped the blade on

his jeans. Once he'd choked poor, deluded Letitia May Cotton to death and removed her womanly workings to splay on the wall above Marty's bed, he'd run like the devil, knowing the cops wouldn't be far behind. He spent the past three days ducking in and out of alleys and underpasses, sleeping in the day, moving at night.

That first night he made the mistake of sleeping after the sun was down and woke up to some asshole tugging on his snakeskins. He put up a struggle and the thieving prick gave him a slash on his cheek for his troubles. The wound still throbbed, likely infected.

He hadn't had a thorough wash-up since the hospital and knew he must stink to high heaven. But the glory of his quest purified him, kept the ungodly stench from reaching his nostrils.

Jimmy Joe Barclay—same name as his daddy, Joseph James Barclay, only reversed—was on a spiritual quest. He had no fear of God, not like his momma, but he did possess a healthy, respectful fear of the Devil.

While God sat up on high, only intervening when it behooved Him, Beelzebub lived among men, poisoning their hearts and corrupting their minds. Why would the world be hip-deep in shit if it weren't true?

Marty Savage was a child of Satan himself. Ol' Jimmy had plenty of time in the loony bin to mull things over and he knew that as a certainty. Someone ought to have carved Marty whole and squirming from his mother's still-living womb and choked the life out of him with the umbilical cord.

Since they hadn't, that put the task to Gimme Jimmy, like the boys used to call him when he'd get to struttin. When God delivered Marty unto him the same as He had the Commandments unto Moses, Jimmy Barclay, Ol' Gimme Jimmy, he knew he'd been Chosen. And like Moses or Abraham, he would not hesitate to do what needed doing when the time came.

And that time was nigh on coming now. Jimmy could feel it in his bones. He just had to find the son of a bitch first. But Providence smiled on those who were diligent and no one could say Connie Barclay's boy wasn't that.

The cop was the key, this Detective Lumsden. He flipped the cop's business card over his knuckles from finger to finger, like the old coin trick he'd learned when he was a shy, lonely little Kentucky boy with no friends to give him nicknames, no purpose, no sense of the larger world around him, no *light of God* shining within.

He left the agent's body spilling blood on the faux-leather front seat with the passenger door wide. Eventually some hobo or punk kid would be brave and stupid enough to roll the corpse out the door and take it for a joyride, get picked up by the cops.

In the meantime, Ol' Gimme Jimmy had many miles ahead of him. The agent made it clear Marty was no longer in this stinking cesspool of a city. It was likely he'd gone back to Connecticut, to a town called Stratford, where according to the agent Marty still had kin.

Jimmy Barclay left the alley. The echo of his bootheels clocking on asphalt pleased him, as the first steps in a long journey always did.

"Tick-tock, Marty," he said, grinning to himself in the half dark. "Your time's just about up."

# CHAPTER 16

**SAVAGES**

WHEN THEY CAME across Dr. Ryland Mulligan, he was hunched over a fat sow in the barn, his tall boots streaked with mud, a concerned look furrowing his brow.

The barn reeked of pig manure, old wood and hay. Pigs grunted and squealed, accompanied by the squawking of chickens that rooted and tapped their beaks in the dirt.

Sheila knocked on the tall barn door, drawn open fully on its rail. Dr. Mulligan looked up at the sound and his expression softened. He smiled awkwardly and stood. "Got lost on your way to the ferry dock, did you?"

"It's Sheila Tanner, Doctor. We spoke over email the other day."

"That's right." He smiled, his teeth slightly yellow and unevenly spaced. "The forensic psychiatrist."

"Psychologist."

He chuckled softly. "I knew I'd get that wrong. It's not quite like the old joke about the fella who mistook the proctologist for a podiatrist, but it's a mistake I won't make more than once, either." As he approached them over the straw-littered ground, Martin stuck out a hand. "Never shake hands with a plumber or a man who's just been up to his elbows in the genital tract of a four-hundred-pound sow," Dr. Mulligan said. "If it's not already a cardinal rule it should be."

Martin hastily lowered his hand. "I'll keep that in mind, Doc."

"No need to stand on formalities. You can call me Ry."

Martin introduced himself.

The doctor's wispy gray eyebrows rose in recognition. "The crime writer?"

"Yessir. Be happy to sign a book for you, if you want."

Sheila rolled her eyes.

"Oh, I don't read true crime," the old man said. "I get enough of it in the news."

"You've heard of me, though. That still counts."

The doctor chuckled. "I suppose it does. Let's talk up the house."

In the pen, the enormous, hairy sow lying on its side with its many pink udders protruding began to grunt and squeal plaintively.

"When's she due?" Sheila asked, thinking how sad it was that the former obstetrician was reduced to birthing piglets.

"Oh, she's about to pop any day now. Sooner rather than later, I'd suspect."

Sheila pouted. "Poor thing. What's her name?"

The old man gave Martin an apologetic look as they left the barn. "Her name is Ruby. No offence to your mother."

---

"CAN I offer either of you a cold beverage?" Dr. Mulligan called from the kitchen.

From where he sat with Sheila in the dim living room, Martin could only see the old man's skinny rear sticking out from behind the fridge door.

"If you want beer, I only stock non-alcoholic, which is what I'm attempting to remain in my golden years."

"I'm fine, thanks," Sheila said.

"Just some water would be nice," Martin said. He always asked for water before an interview. Besides not wanting to get parched, people tended to be more open if you accepted their offers than if you refused them.

"Water it is."

The living room had what his mother's generation would

have called "a woman's touch." Aside from the tall bookcases stuffed full of books on early American history and Irish settlers, a large map of Rhode Island spread out on a table beside the cramped computer desk and a rifle hung over the fireplace, there were crystal dishes on lace doilies, patterned china and small glass animal figurines in a hutch, burnished silver candelabras on the mantlepiece, the candles melted down to nubs, and fine lace curtains—once white, now beige—draped over the windows. All of this was coated in a thick layer of dust that lumped up brown like eraser shavings when Sheila ran her finger across the lid of the upright piano as the doctor toddled into the kitchen.

He returned a moment later with a tall glass of water sloshing over the sides and a plate of cubed cheese and sliced meat. "Hope you don't mind. I missed lunch."

"Not at all," Sheila said, though now that she smelled the sharp cheddar and spicy sausage, she kind of wished she hadn't skipped lunch herself. Her stomach rolled. She took a sip of Martin's water, garnering a slight scowl from him, and placed it back on the ring of water it left on the glass tabletop.

The doctor plucked a piece of meat off his plate and began to chew, his chapped lips smacking lightly. "So," he said, still chewing, "you wanted to talk about my practice."

"Lack of practice, more so," Sheila said. "You said you've been retired—"

"Going on ten years now."

"And before you retired, you worked in Barrows Bay?"

"No, ma'am. I practiced out of Narragansett."

"Has there ever been a practicing obstetrician in town?" Martin asked.

Sheila gave him a look. She'd expected to be leading the interview and he'd taken the words from her mouth.

"Not to my knowledge, no." The doctor scarfed a chunk of cheese, breathing noisily through his whistling nostrils as he chewed. "Which is one of the reasons I got into the business in the first place. I've always found this town's fascination with those old dames a tad... well, cultish, frankly. The way people fawn over them. Talking about them in hushed, reverent voices in the grocery store, at the Legion Hall. Some of them even call her 'Mother,' as if she spat them out of her very own womb. It just curdles my blood."

Sheila frowned. "I read on your website you were born here, is that right? But you just said there was no obstetrician here before you got into it."

"If you mean to ask if I was delivered by a midwife, the answer is yes." He gave Martin a serious look, undercut by licking his fingers. "By Ruby Savage, in fact."

Martin blinked. "My mother?"

"No offence, but can I ask—" Sheila began.

"I'm seventy-three years old." He caught their looks of shock and chuckled lightly. "Oh, I know, I don't look a day over sixty. But there you have it. I'm seventy-three years old, and your mother was twice your age back then if she was a day. Impossible as it sounds, it's the gospel truth."

Sheila scooched to the edge of the sofa, trying to wrap her mind around it. If Dr. Mulligan was seventy-three and Ruby Savage was older than the two than two of them, it would make her over one-hundred and ten years old at the absolute youngest.

That would put her in the running for oldest person in the world, let alone America.

"And I tried," Dr. Mulligan said. "Believe me, I tried to wedge myself between these people and their false gods. Even tried to get the local religious man involved. But Reverend Atkins turned on me at the eleventh hour, the coward. I suspect they had something tawdry to pin on him, seeing as the only thing he's ever had to lose was that congregation of his, what little there is of it."

He glanced at the crucifix on the wall between the mantle and the rifle with a look of abandonment. As if to ask, *Why hast thou forsaken me?*

"And your mother's colleagues, Martin—this was while your mother was still Away, you understand. I don't suspect she would have stood for such dealings on her watch. Those harridans accosted me at my house in the middle of the night. Scared the living hell out of my wife. And so, with very little reluctance, I promised to stay out of their business if they would leave me to mine."

He flashed a bitter sneer. "Not a day goes by I don't regret not sticking to my guns. Oh, Barbara and I had eight more years together after that, some of them better than any we'd had before. Cancer took her in May of two-thousand. Ovarian. Doesn't that beat all? As if God were playing a sick joke on old Ry and Barbara Mulligan."

His eyes goggled behind the pair of bifocals strapped around his neck. "Wasn't a damn thing I could do about it, either. It'd already made a mess of Barbara's insides before we knew it'd burst through the door. I tell you, I felt just as impotent as the husbands of some of my former patients, if you'll pardon the somewhat clumsy metaphor."

Martin chuckled.

"There's a part of me, however small, who can't help but think what happened to my Barbara might have been a kind of revenge for sticking my snout where it didn't belong. I was born here, that much is true. But I didn't live here my whole life. I moved Away. Like you did. Some might say I *fled*, and I wouldn't argue that. We came back when my father passed on. Barbara knew nothing of this island nor my bitterness toward it. She'd fallen in love with the old farmhouse. Said we'd raise chickens when I finally opted to close up shop. I retired when I found out she was sick. *The very week*. It was barely six months 'til I had to bury her. I regret that, too. Not retiring sooner. Never raising those chickens with her."

"Looks like you've done a good job with them," Sheila said. "I'm sure she'd have been proud."

"Oh, likely. I suspect she might've grumbled some about the pigs. I've had Ruby going on nine years now. The name was meant as an insult. Thought I'd fatten her up and eat her by fall. Make a feast of it. A Bronx cheer—a middle finger, if you will— to the old gray mare herself. But she grew on me, much as I tried not to let her."

"I feel the same about my mother," Martin said.

The doctor laughed amiably. "She's a brood sow, if there ever was one. My Ruby, not yours. It would have been profane to eat her. And I learned a funny thing after she had her first litter the following spring." He paused to bend and place the empty plate on coffee table. "A sow will eat her own brood," he said, still hunched over the table, looking up at them over his glasses. "Did you know that?"

"Will eat—?" Sheila began. The thought of it sickened her, though in her many years on the court circuit she'd heard of worse behavior from humans. "Her own babies?"

Dr. Mulligan nodded with the look of a man who'd imparted a long-cherished secret and leaned back in the tatty armchair. "That's right. My Ruby gobbled up the sickest little male piglet I've ever seen. Nothing left but bones when I went to clean her pen the next morning."

"This little piggy went cannibal," Martin said.

The doctor laughed. "Indeed. And do you happen to know what it's called when a sow eats her own young? Martin, I know you'll get a kick out of this one."

"No idea," he said. Sheila shook her head.

"They call it *savaging*." The doctor gave them a sly grin. "My sweet Ruby *savaged* one of her sons. Now doesn't that beat all?"

DR. MULLIGAN TOOK down a spiral book with a laminated cover from the bookshelf, like a cheaply produced school yearbook. The pages photocopied rather than printed. The cover made from light blue Bristol board, laminated.

"I published this book in two-thousand and four. It's the only history on Barrows Bay that I know of."

He eased himself back into the armchair with a groan and settled the bifocals back up on the bridge of his nose.

"The year Barbara passed on, I took a deep dive into three things: working this farm, local color, and Narragansett Light. For that first year, I would have considered myself more a professional drinker than an amateur historian or hobby farmer. But the more I learned, the more I worked the farm, the less I found the need to rely on the beer to escort me through my time of grief."

He smiled briefly, his gaze falling over the photos of his wife in a small collage frame very near his armchair.

"Anyhow, long story short, I discovered a lot about this little island of ours that very few people know about. Things I didn't even feel comfortable putting in the book. Things that might have gotten me committed, had I included them. Or worse.

More in common with your material, Martin, than anything the blue-hairs on the Historical Society would like to read about in their history books."

"What do you mean?"

"Well, there are rumors the first settlers may have resorted to cannibalism."

Sheila choked on a gulp of water from his glass. She carefully placed it on the table, coughing behind a hand.

"You okay?" Dr. Mulligan asked.

She coughed a few more times, her eyes watering, her face slightly red. "I'll be fine. Go on."

"That would have been around the same time as the Donner Party," Martin said.

"1847, correct. I'd like to think that's a coincidence and not a trend."

"Most likely."

"From what I understand, the first few weeks after the *Ruby* sank off the southern shore had been difficult. Not many in the crew had survived, those who had were badly injured, and many were considerably weakened by the voyage, sick with cholera and typhus and the like. It was what they used to call in my day a 'heavy scene.' Conditions were certainly ripe, if you'll pardon the pun, for a Donner Party-type situation."

"Flee one island out of desperation only to starve on another," Martin said.

*Should've brought my notebook*, he thought. *The old coot's sitting on a gold mine of information here. Wonder if he'll let me come back, get a look at all these books.*

"Too true," the doctor said. "The Land of Opportunity must have looked quite inopportune at the time. If they'd capsized near the mainland, they might all have survived. Since they crashed here, out in the sound, they made due with what was obtainable. From my understanding there wasn't the abundant wildlife we see here now. No whitetail deer, for instance."

Martin winced at the image of Nadine's mangled body lying in the ditch. With the hundreds—*thousands*—of crime scene photos he'd seen in his lifetime he could picture it clear as day.

"No wild boar, like you might see on the mainland. The deer population boomed closer to the turn of the century, when some damned fool brought them across the sound two by two, like a latter-day Noah. Anywho, the point I'm rather clumsily trying to make is that food was in short supply with a high demand. Hence, or so the story goes, the strong set upon the weak, circle of life, Amen."

The doctor showed his teeth in a rueful smile. "And that story epitomizes the truth of this place, rumor or not. Barrows Bay was built upon the bones of its forebears. It's right there in the name. They weren't talking about garden tools."

"Do you believe it?" Martin said.

"Oh, I can't say either way. It doesn't seem unlikely, given the circumstances. Any recorded history of the time leaves a gap between the sinking of the *Ruby* and the prospective townsfolk coming together to establish a new life. Almost as though it's been deliberately omitted. If you'll allow me to read you a passage."

He shifted the glasses on his nose. "'In those first months, the inhabitants of this once-nameless island fashioned huts along the shore with broken planks and joists from the ship christened *Ruby*. They soon began moving inland, tilling the soil, hunting gophers and other small woodland creatures, and felling large white oaks and sugar maple to fashion what would soon become the town of Barrows Bay. While they toiled, they sang the songs of their homeland. *The Wearing of the Green* became somewhat of an anthem, an emblem of the first settlers' courage and perseverance—'"

"That's the song my mother was singing the other day." Martin thought of the single word—*MOMMY*—scrawled in red crayon in his book of fairy tales, and his mouth went dry. His hand trembled as he picked up the glass, water sloshing as he brought it to his lips and drank.

"It's our town song," the doctor said, lowering the glasses on his nose. "You don't hear it much these days, but it used to be played before town hall meetings, the fall harvest parade, military homecomings and the like. I wouldn't be surprised to learn old Mayor O'Donaghey plays it during his morning constitutional. Now it's a bit of forgotten Barrows Bay lore. Nobody cares for history these days. The memorial at the foot of King Street downtown will go next, mark my words."

He chuckled dryly, removing his glasses and closing the history book with an audible clap. "Some college kids drunk on

Sociology 101 will come home for Spring Break complaining about trivializing the plight of the Manissean Indians, and tear it down in the name of progress or dismantling patriarchal power structures, whatever the damn hell that means. We did it in my day, with the marches and the sit-ins, but by God it meant something then. Perhaps society will feel the same about the current run when the two of you are in your dotage, but I suspect—and excuse my cynicism, which likely comes from experience rather than age—but I suspect we'll look back on this current wave and chuckle at the sheer naivety of it all."

"Kids, huh?" Martin said, glancing at Sheila. She looked uncomfortable, shifting on the sofa.

"Oh, I know." The doctor smiled wanly. "I've overplayed my hand. Anyhow, the point I've been stumbling toward is that the history of Barrows Bay is violent and that violence never quit. Every town has its deaths, its tragedies. But I find quite a few of them here can be traced back to those women who deliver our children." He favored Martin with a dark look. "And in recent history, the cycle may have begun afresh with you, Martin."

"What do you mean?"

"Did you suppose your mother carried you in her womb, a woman her age? She may have fooled the rest of town but she never fooled me, no sir. See, I knew your grandfather."

"My grandfather?"

The doctor nodded. He eased himself out of the armchair with a groan and tucked his book back on the shelf. "Left town shortly after you were born, as a matter of fact." He swept a long, wizened index finger across the dusty spines, searching for something among the books. "That can be proven by the deed to his old house. It also happened to be shortly after the death of his own daughter, who was pregnant at the time."

Nadine's accusation from the old man's lips. "You're saying my mother isn't my mother."

Dr. Mulligan peered back over his shoulder, the lenses of his bifocals on the tip of his nose. "Based on the facts at hand, that would be my assertion, yes."

"But those aren't facts," Sheila said. "That's one man's word against his mother's. Against the whole town."

"That may be so." He'd gone back to searching, and spoke with a tired sigh. "Though I suppose you've spent enough time in the courtroom to know a thing or two about facts and how they can be malleable, should enough people choose to believe in them. American history certainly proves that. There is no doubt in my mind, Ms. Tanner, that those old psycho-biddies had the wherewithal to drum that man out of town. They tried to do it with Barbara and me. I made a devil's bargain, though I choose to believe I did it for love. As I said, I've come to regret that decision with Barbara gone. Which is why I agreed to speak with the two of you in the first place, when you emailed me."

Dr. Mulligan turned again, fixing each of them with an ominous look. The look of a man tired of bearing too many secrets, who'd gorged himself on the historical sins of an entire town and grown sick from it. Possibly even delirious, judging by what the doctor said next.

"I believe if you dig up that poor girl whose funeral you've just attended, you'll find an empty casket. Call me a fool, call me crazy, but that's what the facts lead me to believe—ah, there it is."

He pried something down from the top shelf, brought it over to the sofa, and placed it carefully between them on the coffee table.

It was a photograph, sepia-toned and worn at the edges, of a large gathering around a bandshell. Martin and Sheila bent to study it closer and nearly batted heads. He let her pick it up. She studied it a moment, then her breath caught.

"You see it?" Dr. Mulligan said. He was still standing over them, waiting for their reaction. Sheila nodded and passed it to Martin.

A summery photo, the crowd thick with people: children holding pinwheels on the shoulders of their fathers, dogs panting, ice cream cones melting in closed fists, several men in army fatigues and women in hippie dresses. The banner spanning the bandshell said MISS HARVEST FESTIVAL, 1969.

"What am I looking for?"

As Sheila reached over to point it out to him, he spotted the woman himself. It was only the side of her face in among the crowd, but he would swear in court it was the same woman.

Not just the same woman but the same woman at the exact same age.

Standing among the crowd of revelers at the 1969 Barrows

Bay Harvest Festival was the woman with the fancy hat. The woman named Mavis Lynch.

---

MARTIN AND SHEILA walked the dirt road back to the car from Dr. Mulligan's farm. Once they'd put it in the distance, with only the lingering smell of pigs to remind them of the doctor's strange and rambling story, Sheila finally spoke.

"You don't believe that, do you? What he said about cannibals...?"

She trailed off, remembering what Mavis Lynch had said about the placenta before the women left the house the night of the birthing. That even though the baby hadn't survived it was important for the mother to ingest a portion of the afterbirth. It would balance hormone production, raise the mood, prevent postpartum depression.

It was an old wives' tale. A superstition with no basis in science. But Helen Birch had packed the afterbirth away in a Tupperware nonetheless.

She couldn't be sure it was the same Tupperware container they had brought for Ruby—but it was likely.

After the drugged tea Geraldine had fed her, she didn't think it was wise to underestimate anything these women said or did.

"I'm not sure what I believe," Martin said, feeling conflicted. Should he tell her about the hallucinations? Could he tell her he thought Mavis Lynch was the same woman he'd seen standing under the streetlamp the night of the fire? Would she be more apt to believe him, after what Dr. Mulligan revealed? "Last week I was on the road selling murder books to yokels, thinking this small-town life is my literal idea of hell. Now I'm back home, I feel like I'm trapped in a theatrical production of *Peyton Place*. That or *The Hills Have Eyes*."

Sheila forced herself to laugh. She couldn't tell him. He hadn't seen the same things she had. He hadn't been at the birthing. Hadn't drank Helen's special tea, made from herbs and "sundry."

"He's obviously suffering from delusions," she said. "Maybe from a minor stroke or post-traumatic stress, still grieving over his dead wife. He couldn't really expect us to go digging up corpses based on a hunch, could he?"

"But that Mavis Lynch, the picture he showed us..." He had to tell her, couldn't keep it to himself any longer. "I'm almost certain she's the woman I saw the night of the fire, standing in the shadows. How is it possible she still looks the same as she did in the eighties, and again in 1969?"

Nadine had asked him the same thing, only she'd been referring to his mother. *Was she right? I laughed her off but what if she was telling the truth? What if she died for it?*

Sheila eyed him queerly as they walked, studying him. She would dismiss these thoughts as magical thinking. He knew that. Deer killed Nadine Hinkley. A tragic accident. In the wrong place at the wrong time.

*But if it wasn't? What then?*

"Maybe it's one of her distant relatives," Sheila said thoughtfully. "Someone who looks the same. My mother always told me I look like my great-aunt Dolores. She died when I was little, but the old pictures of her look almost exactly like me, aside from the hairstyle and clothes. My mother always hated her sister."

"I guess so," he said. "But the stuff about my mother, that she and the other midwives kidnapped me away from some dead teenager or however it happened—I need more than just one man's word and a grainy old photo to buy into that."

Sheila agreed with a nod. "We need to talk to this Michael Creemore. If he really is related to you, at the very least there's likely to be some family resemblance. He might even have some photos of his daughter. Maybe he can tell us why he left town so soon after her death."

"If he's lucid." Martin had interviewed several people in retirement homes and mental hospitals over the years. They rarely went as expected. He imagined having to question his mother when she was in the White Place—it would have been useless. She'd seemed to be living in some imagined distant past, like someone inventing past lives.

"Right. So we'll have to risk a trip off the island. We'll just have to hope Barclay's not staking out the other side, waiting to get the jump on us."

"You think he will be?"

"I doubt it."

"Me too. I don't think he'd risk getting IDed at the ferry docks even if he did somehow figure out where we are. But it is possible. He's been clever enough to evade the police this long."

"Cunning. And lucky."

"Luck o' the Irish," Martin said. "But if he is waiting on us, his luck's about to run out."

"What makes you say that?"

He gave her a sly smile. "Because of my little friend Tansy."

# CHAPTER 17

## SOMETHING ABOUT THE ISLAND

HELEN BIRCH STOOD at the door of the ferry dock terminal, a plate of freshly made chocolate fudge squares in hand.

"Oh, hey there, Helen," Loretta Jameson said as she held open the door, her eyes going from the sweet treats to the stout woman who brought them. "What's the occasion?"

"No occasion," Helen grunted. "The gals and I just figured you and the crew could use a sweet treat, being on your feet all the livelong day."

Loretta peered back at the chair she'd just been sitting in, her mystery book on the desk with a pen holding it open. "Yup, I s'pose we could." She took the plate off of Helen's hands. "Thank you muchly."

"You're very welcome."

Helen offered a queerly wide smile that made Loretta slightly unsettled, then turned and headed back the way she'd come.

Loretta didn't much care for Helen, who lived on the other side of Kildare Avenue from her, nor for the other ladies with whom she kept company. A Galilee gal born and raised, just about everyone on Barrows Bay seemed peculiar to her in their own way. Even the idea of living on an island, having to rely on the ferry to get you from point A to point B, struck her as odd.

But she supposed if they didn't live here, she'd be out of a job. Probably end up working at some temp agency or waitressing for lousy tips, having to grin and bear it every time a customer got frisky and decided to play a game of grab-tushy.

Already a few cars had gathered at the gate, mostly people she recognized by face if not by name. Island folk knew to arrive early if you wanted to get anywhere on time.

She watched old Helen Birch head back up the hill in that lumbering way of hers before returning to the desk. She set the squares down beside the radio, took two rigid steps back from the plate and gave it a forlorn look.

Much as she didn't want to break her diet, the salty-sweet smell was too much to resist.

*I'll just have a nibble*, she thought. She used a plastic knife from one of the desk drawers—the one the summer students had filled with take-out menus, packets of salt and pepper and ketchup, napkins and moist towelettes that smelled like synthetic lemon—to cut a small corner off one of the squares.

She nibbled at it while she finished a chapter, already pretty sure she knew whodunnit and there was still half the book left. Only vaguely listening to crosstalk on the radio.

Don Avalon, the ferry captain, was chattering to his crew. The National Weather Service reported storm clouds moving down the southern coast of Maine with winds at close to thirty knots. Captain Avalon wanted to be sure his people were ready should the storm follow west along the coast rather than blow off into the Atlantic.

*Could be whipping up for a Nor'easter*, Loretta thought, squinting out at the bright blue sky. *Hope to crap it doesn't snow.*

She set the book down again and cut another slice off the first piece of fudge. Nibbled it while watching Don Avalon turn the Hi-Speed ferry's rear end around and ease in to the dock, where it thudded against the large truck-tire marine bumpers.

Lois Permulter and Joey Dean hopped off and tied the moorings. There was some kind of skirmish as the walking passengers let off, a small dog she couldn't see yapping unpleasantly. After that, the unloading and boarding seemed to go by the numbers.

Loretta looked down at the plate. All that was left of the first piece was a wafer-thin sliver. She finished it eagerly, then grabbed two more and tucked them into a napkin in the cutlery drawer for later. Still plenty enough for Don and his crew.

By the time the ferry left for Block Island, Loretta had gobbled down all three squares of Helen Birch's special fudge.

Their intended effect didn't hit her until the ferry started veering off course, headed for the rocky bluffs on the southern shore.

By then she was in too deep a slumber to respond to their requests for assistance.

* * *

"SAVAGE," Martin said to the caller, tapping his fingers impatiently on the wheel. The ferry was already five minutes late when his cell rang. It wasn't possible to see its arrival through the trees from where he and Sheila were parked up the hill. The two of them were getting anxious.

"Martin, it's Detective Lumsden."

Lumsden's voice came over the speakers. The general bustling of a police station buzzed in the background, chatter and telephones ringing and shouts and raucous laughter. "I hope you're sitting down. I'm afraid I've got some bad news."

*What is it now?* Martin thought. *Did Barclay go through my contacts and carve up one of my exes?*

"Are you there?"

"Yeah, I'm here," he said, vaguely annoyed. Sheila watched him with concern. "What's the news, Detective?"

"Foot patrol found your agent's burned-out Porsche under the Williamsburg Bridge late last night—"

He gripped the wheel firmly, as if to keep himself from falling. It felt as though the seat had dropped out from under him, like a death-defying carnival ride.

"Not Qurban."

Sheila's concern deepened. She put a hand on his, still gripping the wheel, and squeezed.

"Afraid it's looking likely. Remains were found in the trunk. The coroner is still trying to get a DNA match but Mr. Youssef's wife reported him missing the other day. It's likely the remains were his. Which means Barclay is still very much alive and at large. Mr. Youssef wasn't informed of your whereabouts, so that's a plus."

Martin swallowed hard. "Yeah, I guess there's that." His favorite fucking agent, dead. The family would be devastated. He needed to send flowers, condolences. He couldn't attend the funeral, not unless they managed to catch Barclay before then.

*God, Qurban... but how?*

*A trail of blood between us, Marty.*

Helen Birch lumbered past on the passenger side and he watched her until she disappeared from sight in the rearview mirror, feeling vaguely uneasy, hoping the old woman hadn't seen him.

"Fortunately, he didn't approach Mr. Youssef at his home," Lumsden said. "This is a tragedy, Martin, no doubt of that. But it could have been a lot messier if Barclay had gotten the family involved."

"Thank you, Detective. I hope you're keeping an eye on them better than you did me."

The audio in the background muffled as though Lumsden had put his hand over the phone. Probably to curse Martin out to his partner.

"You can count on it, Martin," the detective said with a slight edge of aggravation. "We've had an officer watching them since the car was linked to Mr. Youssef."

"That's good to hear."

"And Martin, if he somehow finds you, don't be a goddamn hero. All right? Call me ASAP. The last thing we need is another dead body on our hands. His or yours."

Martin thought about the weapon in the glovebox, the one Lumsden had allowed him to keep, either intentionally or not, despite the fact that he didn't have a license for it.

The trail of blood was edging closer. How much longer until it led Barclay right to Ruby Savage's door?

"If I see him, you'll be first to know."

"Good. Stay put, stay cool and stay safe, you hear?"

"You too."

Lumsden chuckled. "Me? I'm cool as coconut water. Hopefully I'll have some good news for you soon. Is Ms. Tanner there with you?"

"I'm here," Sheila said. She reminded him yet again to call her Sheila.

"You take care, Sheila. And take care of your man."

She popped her eyes at Martin. "Thank you, Detective. I will."

Lumsden hung up.

"*Your man?*"

He shrugged. "I don't know what that was about."

"Probably nothing. I'm sorry about your friend, Martin."

He was surprised to feel tears threatening. "Thanks." He swallowed hard. "Qurban was a good man. A great agent. I don't know where I'd be today without him. He sold my first book, slapped a check for twenty grand right in my hand. You know what that kind of money looks like to a twenty-five-year-old kid, busting his hump for minimum wage, trying to pay off student loans? He got a bidding war going for *Witch Hunter*, you know that? It was a hot property, Sheila. New-York-real-estate hot. I might have had a career without him, but not like I have. And I'm glad his family's safe. They've had me over for dinner more times than I can count."

He shook his head, and a tear did fall. He swiped it away quickly. "It hurts like hell to know I won't ever hear him call me his favorite fucking writer again. I know that sounds egotistical, but it's not like that at all. He probably said it to all his clients."

"Oh, I don't know about that." Sheila squeezed his hand harder, genuine sympathy in her eyes. "You grow on people, Martin."

He chuckled softly. "Like Doc Mulligan's sow."

Just then the ferry emerged from behind the tree cover and started its wide turn to back into the dock.

He nodded toward it. Wiped his eyes again. "About fucking time."

The ferry slipped into the dock and the crew hopped out, mooring quickly and efficiently. A moment later the walk-ons filed out, passengers rolling their bicycles, some with large backpacks on their shoulders, others dressed well, likely returning from work.

The Lexus was five cars from the dock and neither of them could see what was happening when the dog began yapping excitedly. Voices rose to match it. Then a vicious snarl, the sound a dog made when it reached the end of its patience. A woman cried out in pain.

"What the hell's going on down there?" Sheila asked.

"Dunno. I guess we'll find out."

Finally, the vehicles started rolling up the hill and within a few minutes Martin put the Lexus in park near the deck doors in the middle of the ferry. They got out and headed up to the top deck, neither of them wanting to spend another moment in the hot car.

A silver-haired, deeply tanned man dressed in a pristine white captain's uniform stood over a young woman cradling her little gray poodle in her lap. The dog was shivering, its eyes bugged out in unresolved terror. The captain wrapped some gauze around the woman's bleeding hand, where her dog had apparently bit her.

She thanked the captain. As he passed Martin and Sheila, he flashed them a quick raise of his eyebrows. A female crewmember met him with a plate of what looked like choco-late brownies. He took one and bit into it as he rose the steps to the wheelhouse.

Sheila approached the woman with the dog. "Are you okay?"

"I'm okay." The woman's voice was jittery, badly shaken. "I just feel so bad for Duchess." The dog looked up balefully at the sound of its name. "She's never acted like that before. I don't know what got into her but she did *not* want to leave the boat. Did you, baby?"

She lowered her head to kiss the dog. It shied away from her until it was no longer able to prevent the unwanted affection.

"That's strange," Sheila said.

"The captain said it happens a lot on this route. People usu-ally crate their animals if they have to take them back and forth." She shrugged. "Something about the island. Animals can sense things like that, I think."

Less than a week ago, he would have scoffed at a comment like that. Now Martin wondered if maybe animals didn't have some sort of low-level telepathy. A vague psychic twinkle that humans had lost over time. Animals in the wild seemed to pos-sess a sense of impending danger to prevent them from be-coming food for larger predators. When it effected domestic animals, their seemingly aberrant behavior became the subject of viral videos.

Sheila gave Martin a peculiar look before they headed for the front of the ship. "That was weird, wasn't it?"

"'Something about the island,'" he repeated. "I'd love to have a chat with the captain. This sort of thing would be great for my book."

He was hoping she'd bite, ask him more about it. But she didn't seem interested, looking off toward the choppy waters of the sound. He dropped the subject unhappily.

The engines started and the horn blasted across the sound. Less than a minute later, the ferry began cutting a swath through the chop toward Block Island.

Sheila smiled into the sun, the wind whipping strands of hair from her ponytail. Across the sound the mainland was only half visible through a haze as the ferry began its westerly turn toward the bigger island.

Only one ferry serviced Barrows Bay, a smaller boat that ran three times daily. The others went back and forth from the fishing hamlet of Galilee in Point Judith to Block Island every two hours.

In a few minutes the island came into view in the distance, a bolt of green against the blue. Block Island was mostly flat with small hills, compared to the craggy island of Barrow Bay. In the deep water off the southeast shore several wind turbines spun. Whitecaps lapped against their tall white poles.

The ferry continued its slow turn until Block Island and the wind farm were on the starboard side. The female crewmember they saw earlier dashed out of the stairwell, calling the name "Don" frantically. She staggered, running toward the wheelhouse. Her eyes had a semi-dazed look, like she'd been up since yesterday.

She called out "Captain!" and tore open the door, slumping into it before she managed to step through.

"What the hell was that about?"

"I don't know," Sheila said, concern furrowing her brow. "She didn't look right, did she?"

"No." He stared at the closed wheelhouse door. "I think we're going off course."

"You think so?"

"That's Block Island back there with the wind turbines." He pointed toward them, at five o'clock from the bow and moving further toward the stern. "We should be heading toward it. I think we're heading south."

The concern in Sheila's brow deepened. "Barclay?" Her voice was barely audible above the engine, the sound of the waves crashing against the hull.

"I don't know. I think we should get down to the lower deck. Get life jackets."

She nodded. They headed for the stairs. The woman with the dog said, "What's happening?"

"Something's wrong," Martin told her. "We need to get down below."

The woman stood with her dog shivering in her arms and followed them to the stairs. Sheila opened the door, let the woman go through first. The upper deck was otherwise empty.

Martin headed for the stairs leading to the wheelhouse.

"Where are you going?"

"Meet you down there. I'm gonna try to find out what's happening. See if there's something I can do."

"Martin, they're trained for this."

"You said it yourself, she didn't look right. What if the same thing's happened to the captain?"

Sheila nodded again. "Five minutes. Then I'm coming back for you."

She slipped through the door. It closed behind her.

Martin headed for the stairs.

He bounded up them two at a time, soles clanging on the metal steps. The door was closed. The view inside was obscured by the scuffed and grimy glass.

A raised voice. The female crewmember radioing the terminal.

Her voice cut short.

Martin knocked.

No one answered.

The southern edge of Barrows Bay crept into view around the front of the wheelhouse—a long peninsula rising toward rocky bluffs on the southwest side.

The door handle wouldn't budge. Locked from the inside.

He beat a fist against it. The crew ignored his cries.

Left without a choice, he climbed precariously onto the metal railing to look in through the front-facing windows. The upper deck fifteen feet below, he reeled as the ferry continued its errant course.

He could only see the left half the bridge. Vertigo kept him from climbing further over the edge. The captain was sprawled over the wheel, the hat missing from his head. The other crewmembers weren't visible.

Were they drugged?

Some kind of poison or nerve gas?

No idea. All he knew was the captain appeared to be unconscious and the other crewmembers likely were too. The only smell was diesel fuel. The only sound the loud hum of the engine far below.

He considered smashing the glass, trying to get the boat under control. But what if it *was* some kind of gas that knocked them out? He couldn't risk it.

Even if it wasn't, he had no idea how to steer the thing, let alone stop it.

Reluctantly, he headed back down the stairs to meet Sheila.

Several passengers huddled in orange life jackets at the front of the boat on the lower deck. Barrows Bay loomed behind them, quickly closing the distance. Sheila stood by a large white pickup truck, wearing a life vest, holding another out to the driver.

"I ain't leaving my truck," the driver said. "This is a goddamn hemi, you know what that is? I still got six payments on this sumbitch."

"Fine. Sink with it, for all I care. At least put on the fucking life jacket."

Grudgingly, the driver took it and began to pull it on.

She caught Martin's eye and hurried over. "One of the crew was passed out in the lounge," she said. "Did you find out what's going on?"

He shook his head. "The rest of the crew's out cold."

"What the hell happened here, Martin?"

"I don't know. But if we don't crash into the island we're just gonna keep circling until we run out of fuel. Eventually the coast guard will come for us."

"We can't wait on that."

"No." He turned to face the bow. The island so close he could make out individual seagulls on the stony shore. "And I don't think we'll get the chance."

She followed his gaze. The rocky bluffs rolled into view. "Should we jump?"

"When it's time. If we have to. The water's gonna be freezing."

She nodded toward the others. "Let's get them ready."

As they approached the other passengers, the bluffs blotted out the sky.

"It looks like the whole crew is incapacitated," Sheila told them, taking charge. "We may need to jump but it's going to be very cold."

The passengers gave each other fearful looks, whispered prayers and curses. An older gentleman tucked his cane between his legs to fasten his life jacket. The dog owner kissed her poodle. Beside her a young mother tightened the straps on a little boy's life vest. His dark eyes were wide with fear.

"You need to start swimming for shore the second you hit the water. That should keep your limbs from going numb—"

As she said it the ferry lurched drastically to the left. Something boomed on the starboard side and screeched along the hull.

The passengers cried out, grabbing the railings, reaching out for one another.

Sheila and Martin shared a nervous look.

She took his hand. They headed for the starboard side of the bow.

The others followed. The screech of metal subsided, leaving nothing but the hum of the engine, the cry of nearby gulls.

The ferry chugged onward, fifty feet from where the waves, each at least five feet high, beat against the rocky shore.

Sheila climbed over the railing.

Martin followed her over. They leaned side by side over the edge in the shadow of the bluffs, gripping the cold, wet rails, preparing to jump.

Ry Mulligan rolled an udder between thumb and forefinger, squeezing down to the tip to find it dry, then the next. Translucent white fluid eked out from twelve of her sixteen teats. She would farrow any day now. By the look of her distended belly it would be the biggest litter of her life.

"There, there," he said as Ruby grunted, her wet snout wriggling. He fed her a handful of bran she ate greedily, slicking his palm with saliva.

Ry returned to the house. He washed his hands under the kitchen sink and began to prepare supper, scoring two fat potatoes from the bag under the sink—a few were starting to sprout, growing multiple eyes like hideous eldritch monsters in the damp dark beneath the counter—and dropping them on a greased dish to bake, one to eat tonight and the other he would save for tomorrow. When Barbara had still been with him, she would cook four. Though he'd never cared for leftovers he kept up the tradition in her absence.

It had been many years since the Mulligan house had any extra mouths to feed, outside of the occasional dinner guest. Barbara hadn't cared for children—her six nieces and nephews had been enough for her—and with all the pregnant women waddling in and out of his office, Ry hadn't ever felt the urge to push for a similar scene at home.

He figured much of his ambivalence toward having children of his own stemmed from growing up in Barrows Bay. The old midwives had terrified him when he was a boy. On Sundays his mother would schlep him round to their homes to "pay their respects," until his father put a stop to the practice once he was old enough to help out in the field and the barn.

Mavis Lynch had frightened him most, with her shrewd gray eyes and the ridged terrain of pale scars on her balding head and nape as if from some long-ago fire. He suspected it was why she'd been the one to call up to their bedroom window that night when Barbara was dressed in her nightgown and he in his skivvies, the moon high and bright and cold in the black autumn sky.

The memory of looking out the window at that awful old maid's pale moonface gave him a cold chill. He twisted the dial on the oven and the gas came on with a hiss and a dull thump. He went at a frozen clump of chicken breasts with a steak knife

—something Barbara would have paled at—prying them apart until one snapped free, clattering on the glass dish.

Barbara's pale-yellow curtains hung limply at the kitchen window. Beyond, the sky had already begun to darken.

Ry looked out at the barn. His joints ached thinking about the work he'd have to do tomorrow to get Ruby's pen clean enough for her to farrow within the next few days.

Barbara had always gone by the adage *Don't put off until tomorrow what you could do today*. Ry never cared for it. He was a procrastinator at heart. Her absence made him acutely aware of it. He'd often wondered if he ever would've made it through med school if he hadn't met her midway through that first semester of junior year.

She was Barbara Claire then, a slightly prissy seventeen-year-old with a blonde bob haircut, white bobby socks and penny loafers. Handing out tracts for some nascent libbers meeting and he'd just about stumbled over himself to get his hands on one, not caring a lick what it was for, only needing an excuse to get close to her.

He showed up to find the lecture hall brimming with estrogen and felt as out of place as an eighteen-year-old farm boy could, having grown up on a small island where "women's liberation" meant Mom could take off her heels and apron after the supper dishes were done and Pop would rub her feet while the three of them sat around the old black-and-white boob tube watching *Gunsmoke* or Ed Sullivan's "really big shew."

The oven beeped. He'd been standing there ruminating, looking out at the barn as the sky got darker, and completely forgot he was in the middle of making supper. He slid the two roasting pans into the oven and set the timer, then nestled into his armchair in front of the television. *Jeopardy!* was on. Ancient History was one of the categories. He settled in, ready to clean up.

Something clanged outside. Sounded like one of the trash cans.

"Who is Queen Gorgo of Sparta?" he said, responding to Alex's answer.

One of the contestants ringed in and said Helen of Troy. Ry chuckled derisively.

Outside the noise came again. His gaze fixed on the rifle above the mantle and crucifix.

"Goddamn raccoons," he groaned, easing out of the chair.

A moment later he booted the screen door open and stepped out onto the porch with the rifle in both hands. Barbara hadn't allowed guns in the house. He'd bought the Winchester .30-30 after she passed. It was the perfect tool for keeping deer away from his carrots and foxes out of the henhouse.

A rickety, squalling sound he recognized drew his attention to the barn. The door had just been dragged open, squeaking on the rail.

"That's no raccoon," he muttered, shuffling down the porch steps on stiff legs.

He trundled over crunchy dead grass to the barn, not particularly worried. Likely just local boys playing pranks, stealing eggs or riding his pigs or something equally stupid boys might get into.

He stopped in the doorway. High-pitched squeals and chicken squawks came from the gloom within. The sweet smell of hay and dung prickled his nostrils, a smell he'd always associated with childhood. Pleasant memories for the most part, of working under the hot sun, his mother's lemonade, his father's faint praise.

Someone stood in the middle of the pens. A silhouette cast in the moonlight seeping in through cracks in the barn beams.

He recognized the old woman by her hat.

"Miss Lynch," he said, unable to keep the fear from his voice. "To what do I owe the pleasure?"

He didn't lower the rifle.

Mavis stepped into a beam of moonlight streaming down from the rafters. The younger pigs, Ruby's previous broods, stepped back from their pens as she neared. A chicken—he thought it might be Lucille, the pure white one—skittered out of her path.

"The Savage boy and his floozy." Her voice was calm. The brim of her hat kept her face from view. "What did you tell them, Ryland?"

"Oh, I think you have a pretty good idea," he said, and was pleased to note the fear didn't show this time.

But he was scared. More scared than he'd been the first time she came out here, when he had much more to lose.

"We made a deal," the woman said.

"And you welshed," he spat back. "I know you and your weird sisters took my Barbara from me. I don't know how you managed it—poison in her food or some kind of black magic—but I've known for quite some time. After what happened to the Hinkley woman, I guess I made up my mind."

Mavis cackled. "And you told them everything."

"That's right." The joints in his fingers felt suddenly numb, as if they might come loose of their own volition and drop the rifle at his feet. He gripped it tighter. "Everything I know about you and your Mother. I suppose you didn't want that, did you?"

The moonglow brightened her smile within the shadow of her face. "Quite the opposite. You did exactly what we hoped you'd do, Doctor."

Ry didn't quite comprehend this. It was the Tanner woman who'd contacted him, not the other way around. Mavis and the others couldn't have planned for them to meet.

*She's lying*, he thought. But he couldn't bring himself to believe it.

"Still," Mavis said, "it won't do for us to have you around, spreading your lies."

He sneered. "Lies? You know as well as I do, it's the gospel truth."

The rifle juddered suddenly in his hands, as if something had gotten hold of it, something he couldn't see.

He cocked the lever without meaning to and looked down in abject terror as his own calloused hands jerked the barrel upward, moving of their own volition—or more correctly, of Mavis Lynch's.

The pigs squealed in their pens. Something upset them. He heard their hoofbeats in the dirt as they scurried anxiously.

Could they feel it? Could they sense the *wrongness* of this woman?

Hot liquid filled his briefs. For a moment the shame of having soiled himself surpassed his fear. Then the barrel slipped under his jaw, cold black steel scratching the snow-white bristles on his jowls, angling his chin toward the rafters.

*I'm ancient history, Barbara*, he thought. *I'm just too old and too damn pooped to fight anymore.*

In the moonlight, Mavis Lynch smiled.

The squeals were joined by heavy thuds, metallic rattles. By God, the hogs were throwing themselves at the gates of their pens.

"I'm coming home, Bar—"

His index finger curled suddenly, squeezing the trigger.

The gunshot cut his wife's name short and cleaved his jaw in two. Torn flesh flayed outward. Skull fragments, burnt flesh, shattered teeth, chunks of brain and blood painted the old gray barn beams.

His body collapsed rigidly like a felled tree, thumping down on loose hay and trampled dung.

For a long moment, Mavis stood looking down in mild distaste at the doctor's twitching corpse. The right eyeball hung from its shattered socket. The left eye had rolled inward, giving him the appearance of trying to look at the raw meat where his nose had been.

She chuckled softly. "What did you call it, Ryland? Savaging?"

As if on her command, the gates battered open with rusty squeals.

Snorting and squealing, the animals trundled out of their pens.

Dr. Mulligan's trigger finger was still twitching when the pigs set upon him.

# CHAPTER 18

SHIPWRECK

THE WATER WAS so cold Sheila thought it might literally stop her heart. She gasped, sucking in a mouthful of salt water as a wave slapped her in the face.

The undertow sucked her back toward the ocean. She kicked and paddled against it and another swell launched her forward, toward the rocks rising from the churning surf.

Already her hands and feet were chilled to the bones.

She couldn't see the others. Only heard their screams.

A terrible groan rose above the screams. An echoing boom. The ferry had hit the rocks but she didn't dare twist around to look. The surf would pull her away if she did. She had to keep swimming forward, keep fighting against the undertow.

The second she turned back it would be over.

Gasping, plunging forward, she called out Martin's name. He didn't call back.

The dog swam by easily on a swell, looking like a drowned rat. Its owner cried "*Duchess!*" from somewhere behind her.

Sheila tried to reply but a wave rolled over her and salt water filled her mouth and nose. She choked, coughing madly. Her arms were frozen, exhausted. She had to keep moving but the urge to give up nearly overcame her.

In the next instant a wave threw her onto a rocky outcropping, slick with algae. A seagull perched there stepped back from her and regarded her curiously with its yellow eyes. Then it flew off, shrieking, into the sky.

She caught her breath, hugging the wet, freezing rock. All around her passengers fought the current, their life jackets bright orange blobs bobbing against dark blue.

Impossible to tell which if any of them were Martin.

She looked back at the island. The beach, the trees, the bluffs, all fuzzy and indistinct, shimmering with sparkles of sunshine. For a moment, the scene seemed utterly unreal. As if she were hallucinating it. A mirage.

*Look, Daddy! The island sparkles!*

The little boy on the ferry had seen it. Sheila and Martin and the boy's father had looked at each other, mystified.

She saw it now. Even after she blinked to clear her vision of salt water. Like every molecule was dancing, every object still deciding what it could be. Like she was looking at the world without its clothes on.

*Maybe I hit my head*, she thought.

Duchess the dog splashed onto the beach and the shimmer vanished instantly, everything around the animal swimming into clear focus. Solid rock. Clamshell-littered gray sand. Long strands of seaweed. Grungy seafoam.

Another wave splashed over her, slapping her back to reality. The fear for her life, for the others. The damp chill in her bones.

Rolling to her left, she saw the ferry had slammed into the jagged rocks and tipped over. Several long gashes on its hull took on more water each time the waves withdrew.

A rusted-speckled red sedan hung half out the back. The boat rocked as another wave struck and the old Volvo rolled off the deck, splashing heavily into the ocean.

Once she'd hit the water she briefly doubted abandoning ship was the right decision. Those doubts vanished now.

Shivering, teeth chattering, she called Martin's name.

Another surge washed a body onto the shore. A man with short, dark hair. Face down on the beach.

She called again. With the surf pounding into a nearby alcove it was hard to hear anything over it.

A woman rolled up beside the man and began racking with coughs. The young mother. The moment she realized her son wasn't with her she screamed his name. "Ryannnnnnn! *Ry-yannnnnn!*"

Out among the waves the dog owner splashed her arms like a child in a mud puddle. The surf threw her into shore then pulled her back, hungry for a victim.

The old man was near the ferry, dangerously close to a giant gash in its hull. He pushed against it with his cane, crying out in fear as the water rolled in. The next swell sucked him away from danger, toward the shore.

Half a dozen heads bobbed in the water. Orange lifejackets. She still couldn't tell if Martin was among them. If he was the unconscious man on the beach. In all the commotion, she'd forgotten what he'd been wearing.

She wondered again if they made a mistake.

As if in reply, the ferry rose further onto the rocks. The hull juddered as it peeled open. A weathered aluminum camper rolled off the deck into the water, dragging a jam-packed station wagon along with it.

As they crashed into the surf a car horn blared. At first she thought it was an alarm but it was too intermittent, too frantic.

The ferry groaned again, lurching further onto the rocks, tipping further on its side. The back of the white pickup rolled out and its undercarriage slammed against the deck, the back wheels spinning uselessly.

She couldn't see the driver but he was obviously still inside, beating on the horn as if it would do him any good.

With the next surge, the ferry tipped at a forty-five-degree angle and the truck flipped onto the driver's side. The honking stopped.

The little boy washed ashore. His mother crawled toward him, still choking, calling his name. When she reached him, the boy grabbed her so tight around the neck she yelped.

The unconscious man still lay face-down in the wet sand and shells.

It was time to get off this rock.

The water churned in front of her, seaweed swirling. A virtual whirlpool. Fifteen feet between her and the shore, maybe less.

She got to her feet, standing precariously on the slick rock.

More passengers reached the shore, gasping for breath,

pealing triumphant laughter. A woman cradled her arm, crying out in pain. The old man with the cane rolled the unconscious man over.

It wasn't Martin. Whoever he was had a goatee.

Sheila looked down into the swirling abyss.

The water was so cold, but she couldn't stay on this rock forever. The tide would make the choice for her sooner or later.

She couldn't remember the last time she'd crossed herself. Probably back in middle school. She did so now.

Then she jumped.

The water sucked her under immediately. Seaweed slapped her bare arms and face, tangling around her legs. She kicked madly. The undertow spun her around and around until she couldn't tell which way she was swimming. Toward the shore? Back to the rock? Out to sea? She felt herself being dragged along, moving swiftly on the underwater current.

Was she anywhere near shore anymore?

Her knee struck something hard and jagged. A bright streak of red rose from the tear in her pants. She fought to reach the surface in a blind panic, no longer concerned about the cold. She was already close to losing her breath. If she didn't reach the surface soon she'd inhale water and then it would all be over.

In the deep below her she caught a glimpse of something shiny. Glimmering silver. She realized what it was but couldn't comprehend how it was possible.

She was looking at the camper on the sandy floor of the sound. The station wagon lay beside it, sodden laundry streaming out of its windows.

Suddenly something grabbed her by the hair. The pain in her scalp tore her away from the strange scene, like waking from a dream.

She reached up, grabbing back. Trying to tear herself free.

The last of her breath exploded from her lungs, bubbling up until it was lost in the churning water above her.

Her numbed fingers touched cold flesh, curled around what felt like a forearm. A second hand, this one wrapped in wet, gauzy material, grabbed her arm and pulled.

*Martin*, she thought. *He's alive.*

For the second time she felt as though her heart might stop.

She sucked in a huge breath the moment the chill wind touched her face.

Water caught in her windpipe and her whole body spasmed. The tendons in her neck pulled taut. Her face flushed, hot blood pumping beneath her frozen skin.

"*Are you all right?*" Martin shouted in her ear, to be heard over the crashing waves.

She coughed, dislodging the water from her throat. She spat it back at the sound. Her eyes stung from the salt water, from tears of terror—and now, from relief.

"I'm okay," she breathed. She laughed raggedly. "I'm okay!"

---

MARTIN HELD her in his lap until she stopped shivering. They sat on a rocky outcropping on the port side of the ferry. Somehow the current had beached him here. He couldn't remember anything after his head struck something in the water.

Saltwater stung the gash on his forehead. The vision in his right eye went pink again. He blinked away more blood.

The ferry loomed high above them, canted on a steep angle, both on its side and its stern. Rocking with the waves, gently now, its final resting place decided.

He could see through the bridge windows from here, though it wasn't apparent if any of the crew had survived. No way to tell how many passengers had made it either, if any. If there were any, they weren't on this side of the crash.

When he first washed up here he worried they might have all been safer on the boat. Then the pickup truck plunged into the ocean, the driver likely unconscious inside. The survivors would have been thrown back and forth between their vehicles like pinballs, incapacitated before they hit the water.

"I th-think we did the r-right thing," Sheila said, her teeth still chattering.

"I hope so. Did you see anyone else?"

Her felt her nod against his chest. "M-most of them made it to... the sh-shore."

"Good. That's good. Think you can stand?"

She nodded. Removed his arms from around her and staggered to her feet.

He stood beside her, the wet rock firm beneath his feet. No

algae slicked its surface. The injury to his head made him woozy, but he thought he could stand.

"M-Martin. *Look*."

Her face was pale as soap, her eyes wide. She pointed toward the beach.

He saw the stones standing in a circle in the sand and wondered how he hadn't noticed them before. He'd definitely looked in their direction to get his bearings when he washed up here. He must have overlooked them. Dismissed them for large tree stumps or irregular rocks. The crumbled foundation of an old dry dock.

Impossible to dismiss them now. They were standing stones, all right. How long they'd been here, he could only guess.

"This is where the *Ruby* sh-shipwrecked."

"You think so?"

She nodded. No way for her to be certain, but she seemed to be regardless.

Had the stones been here when the coffin ship crashed on the island in 1847? He had no way to know himself but he thought they had been. He suspected they might have been here much, much longer.

"I think you're right," he said.

Sheila began loping toward shore, favoring her injured leg. Her pants were torn. The gash beneath looked nasty. He took up behind her, brushing wet hair from the wound on his forehead.

The beach was sandy. He'd caught a glimpse of the shore on the other side of where the ferry had crashed before they jumped. All granite and jagged, crushed clam shells. The sand here was soft, leaving wet shoeprints behind them. Small flat rocks scattered everywhere, what they would have called "skippers" when he was a kid. A few ancient logs, gray and hollowed out. Beyond, the bluffs were covered in dense trees and underbrush. Late-winter pines rose like golden-tinged green spires against the lowering sun.

The sand within the standing stones was bare, devoid of rocks or ocean debris, as if someone had kept it that way, though it was flat and undisturbed until Sheila stepped into the circle, peering up at the tall stones, their strangely smooth surfaces black as if charred many, many years ago.

Martin stood back from them, wary for some reason he couldn't interpret. An almost primitive distrust. He thought the first settlers must have felt the same.

Nothing like this existed here, as far as he knew. Formations like these were found mainly in Western Europe, with some in Asia and Africa. The few standing stones left by Native American tribes were smaller, never this smooth or deliberately formed. And never left in circular henges.

These stones did not belong here.

He tried to picture crossing thousands of miles of open sea, surviving raging storms, cholera, dysentery, typhus and finally drowning, only to come to rest on this faraway shore and discover these pagan enigmas, these black idols to pre-Christian deities on a shore they did not belong.

What would the survivors have thought of them? What would they have asked of their God?

"Sheila..." he began. He wanted to warn her. Of what, he had no clue.

"They look so *smooth*," she said, reaching out to touch one with her fingertips. Flattening her palm against it.

A massive wave thundered against the ferry. He startled but Sheila didn't even flinch. She was staring at the stone. Enraptured. With her other hand she traced its contours. Gently, like a lover's warm, yielding touch.

"You need to feel this, Martin."

She didn't take her eyes off the stone.

A prickle ran up his spine at the thought of touching them. "I'm okay here, thanks."

Sheila closed her eyes, both hands flat against the stone. Her hips began to sway, as if to music.

"What are you doing?"

She ignored him, tossing her wet hair over her shoulder, come loose from its ribbon. Her hips snapped left to right, left to right.

Martin turned away from her. She was trying to entice him, to draw him into the stones. Using her sexuality, their shared history, as bait.

He thought of the last time he tried to initiate sex, how she callously rejected his advances. He was drunk and she'd been stone sober. He'd shown up at her door uninvited. No idea how he managed to weasel his way into her apartment but he remembered her consoling him.

He was crying—he couldn't even remember what he was crying over. Sheila soothed him, smoothing his hair, making soft shushing noises that jostled his head against her breasts. He leaned up and kissed her. Love was always his distraction of choice—she knew that as well as he did. From pain. From sadness, loneliness and fear. Childhood trauma. Abandonment. She kissed back.

Then the sudden slap. The sharp sting in his cheekbone sobered him like a bucket of ice water. He slinked off, hurt and embarrassed. Sheila apologizing, anger still bright in her eyes.

He had a black eye for a week after that. Told Qurban he'd gotten in a drunken fistfight. What could he say? That he'd looked for solace from an ex-girlfriend and she beat him up?

Her body twisted like a snake within the circle, palms still pressed flat against the tallest stone, eyes half-closed as if in ecstasy. He looked beyond her, to the trees at the edge of the beach where a narrow, uncultivated trail seemed to cut through the underbrush. Likely a deer path.

He thought of the stag. Imagining Nadine lying dead in the road, her bicycle twisted, one tire still rolling, bloody punctures all over her body.

He saw Tish's reproductive organs tacked to the wall, her face gray, the bow still taut around her throat.

Saw a baby in a coffin—little Ruby St. John—frail and purple in a tiny white lace gown.

Sheila would suffer a similar fate if she stayed with him. It made him want to run and leave her behind. But the trail of blood would eventually catch up with her, whether he stayed or ran.

Sooner or later she would die like the others, for the simple fact of being someone he cared about.

He stepped into the circle, feeling their power the moment he entered. A dull vibration in his fillings. A high, almost imperceptible whine in his ears. A softly ticking throb in his groin.

And something else—something he couldn't describe. For a moment it felt like he was seeing through two sets of eyes at once. His vision doubled. Five stones became ten, closing them in. A confusion of vague thoughts and images and emotions washed over him like a flash flood, so fast he barely had time to register them before they were gone.

Something had entered him, he sensed that much. A living thing—no, *multiple* beings. A *community*. He felt their presence, sensed their memories... and then they were gone, leaving an abscess, a vast black hole in their wake.

Sheila's eyelids fluttered. She craned her head back. "Can you *feel* it, Martin?"

He said that he could.

"Come," she said, still swaying. Her hands never left the stones.

Reluctantly, he came to her side, feeling the magnetic pull of the stone she held. It seemed to pulse between her fingers, like a living thing. The black heart of the island.

He put his hand on hers, right on right. Her fingers entwined with his. He felt high. Like he'd just taken a massive hit of the best shit on earth.

Before he could react, Sheila jerked his body around her and pushed him roughly up against the stone. Her eyes snapped open, locking on his. Irises impossibly wide, his reflection swirling in them, cauldrons as black as the rock. The stone was oddly warm. She pinned him there with her hips.

"Sheila—"

She pressed a finger against his lips, shushing him like she had that night nearly six years ago. This time, she kissed him first.

He stopped resisting, leaning in to her. The throb became an ache as she ground her hips against him. She reached down, slipping a hand between their bodies. Worked open his belt and unzipped his fly without taking her eyes away from his.

Her cold fingers grasped him by the root and tugged. She nestled herself against his thigh, squirming against him. He felt her heat through the fabric. He wanted nothing more than to come, to shoot gobs and gobs of his seed inside of her.

The phrase *Make her full of child* came to mind, though the words didn't seem to be his own.

When he opened his eyes again it was no longer just stones surrounding them. Five people in white cloaks stood between each stone, arms across their chests and hands tucked into their sleeves like monks. He couldn't see their faces, hidden within the deep shadows of their hoods. But he knew they were watching.

"Wait—" he said, pulling his lips only partway from hers.

With her free hand Sheila took his and slipped it down the front of her pants. He felt pubic hair stubble, then wet heat. He parted the labia, unable to stop himself. She moaned into his kiss as he found her clit with his middle finger and rubbed.

His defenses entirely broken, he unbuttoned her pants and peeled them down over her hips, pulling the panties down with them. He slipped a finger inside of her. She bucked against his palm, licking a trail of salt water up his neck.

Hot breath in his ear now, panting. She grabbed his jeans and jerked them down, guided him into her. Scalding in contrast to her ice-cold hands. She wrapped her arms around his neck.

The cloaked beings watched them. Their silent, eyeless gaze disturbing, a distraction from the business at hand. He focused on the black stone directly ahead of him, seemingly pulsing in time with the rhythm of their hips.

In a moment he forgot all about the watchful entities—not *humans*, he sensed that much—and threw himself fully into his work. Their grunts and cries of pleasure, the slap of flesh on flesh barely audible above the steady crash of waves against the shore.

A sudden jolt of pain in his right hand drew his gaze from the pulsating stone. Sheila had torn the bandage off. She brought his palm to her mouth and her tongue flicked out, tasting the wound. She raised his hand to his lips and the coppery tang of blood filled his mouth.

He thrust harder, countering his pain with hers.

Her moans intensified. She bit her lip. He couldn't hold back any longer. Didn't want to. His whole body shuddered as he came inside of her. She bucked against his hips until she was coming along with him.

Finally the spell was broken. They fell against the rock, half-naked and sweaty, breathing raggedly, sticky with each other's fluids.

Only the five stones circled them. The cloaked figures were gone.

They were alone again. Free.

Sheila backstepped away from him suddenly and stumbled, her pants bunched around her ankles. She hiked them back up over her hips, fear and confusion in her eyes. He tucked himself into his boxers and zipped the fly of his jeans.

"We shouldn't have done that," she said, not meeting his gaze.

"No. We probably shouldn't have."

"I don't know what came over me." She was still catching her breath. "It's like I was looking out through someone else's eyes."

He remembered the rush of blurred images. The doubled stones, the silent beings in white cloaks. He wondered if she'd seen the same, but his ego demanded answers first.

"Are you *blaming* me?"

"I'm not blaming you for anything, Martin. It just happened. We can't take it back."

"Do you want to?"

She met his eyes. "It shouldn't have happened," she said again.

He nodded. The throb in his groin subsided. A cold trail of semen oozed uncomfortably down his thigh. They both looked up at the stones and stepped out of the circle anxiously.

"These stones," she said. "There's something strange about them."

"Gee, you think?"

She glowered. "I've been down here before, Martin. I've jogged the whole island. These stones weren't here before."

Martin said nothing. He didn't know what to say.

"You don't believe me?"

"I believe you. None of this makes any sense, Sheila. Unless the survivors of the *Ruby* made this circle, these stones shouldn't be here. They're anachronistic. Out of place."

"No," she said. "They were here when the boat washed up. I *felt* it. When I touched them."

"I did too."

"Like someone was waiting for them. Or some*thing*."

"Something," Martin agreed. "*Things*. There were others, I—"

He turned to look at the wooded path. Sheila followed his gaze. She seemed to see something in the trees, narrowing her eyes to make it out.

"They watched from the forest when the survivors of the *Ruby* washed up on the shore," she said. It wasn't what Martin expected to hear. But he knew she was right. They'd shared the same vision. "They waited until the men fell asleep. Men with shiny clubs made of wood and iron—*rifles*. Then they took the children. A girl with red hair and a baby. Her little sister. Their mother died of cholera on the ship."

"The survivors searched the whole island," he said, sharing her memory of an event neither of them could possibly have had any knowledge of. "They came back to the beach at night to wait for them, sitting around a bonfire. They were so hungry. After three days and nights, the girls finally returned."

"Only something was different about the baby," she said. "The captain saw it right away. He called her a 'changeling.' The child of fairies, disguised as human."

"They smashed poor little Violet's head on the rocks," Martin said. "The captain did it. A man named Ledbetter. They argued for a while about what to do with her body, but they were all so hungry. Three days without food, who knew how long they went without proper sustenance on the ship. It didn't take much persuasion for Ledbetter to convince the others it was only right to eat her. So her precious little body wouldn't go to waste."

Tears spilled down Sheila's cheeks. "They ate her while her sister watched. She was *screaming* at them. I felt her pain."

"Me too," Martin said. For an instant, when he first entered the circle, it felt as though his heart had been torn right out of his chest. "She ran from them in the middle of the night. Ran into the forest and hid. She lived there while the others built their houses from the same trees the original inhabitants had made their home. The survivors of the *Ruby* called them the *Chadrach*. They were the first beings to inhabit this land, long before humans."

Sheila nodded. "And when the survivors of the *Ruby* grew fat and healthy, grew *complacent*, she took her revenge. She came to Ledbetter—he'd made himself mayor by then—she came like a wraith in the night and slaughtered his first-born son in front of him. She drank his blood. She *bathed* in it. And it kept her young."

The two of them stood watching each other, waiting for the other to add to the story. But it seemed the fairy tale had reached its end.

"How could we know all this?" Martin said finally.

"The stones told us. And not just that. Martin, I know who your mother is. It's not Ruby Savage. Her name was Rosalee. And your name was Stephen."

He tried the name on. It didn't fit.

"Your mother, the woman you call your mother—she's much older than any of us could imagine. Older than Dr. Mulligan thought. Older than the barrows. *Older than Ireland.* They held the thing—this *demon* in the body of a green-eyed, redhaired Irish girl—they held her down while they smashed her little sister's head on a rock. She couldn't do a thing to stop them. There were too many. But she bided her time. She waited *years.* Until that first child was born. And after she killed them all, when she stood among the ashes of their community, bathed in the blood of their first-born child, she named herself Ruby to *spite* them."

Sheila peered up at the stones, eyeing them cautiously. It seemed as if the stones were looking back.

"Ruby Savage is an ancient demon, an eater of children," she said. "But she's not your mother. Someone put these stones here to worship her, long before the *Ruby* washed up here. The thing that she was. The thing still inside of her. The Midwives are her daughters. Five stones for five demons."

If Martin hadn't experienced it all when he'd entered the circle, he wouldn't have believed a word of it. But everything he'd seen and heard since they arrived in Barrows Bay pointed in one direction—the woman he'd called his mother was some kind of demon.

A monster from a fairy tale.

This *Chadrach*, whatever that was.

"So what does all that make me?

Sheila turned from the stones, fear in her eyes. "I think it makes you a very big problem."

# Part Four

Demons

# CHAPTER 19

**FETCH**

FOOTAGE OF THE crash aired on the nine o'clock news of every local affiliate. No deaths but plenty of injuries, and only two passengers unaccounted for, though no one could remember what the couple looked like. Not a single reporter, crew member or viewer saw the circle of stones on the shore.

The standing stones only existed to those who wished to conceive, to the creatures who fed upon the blood of the innocent.

By the time the coast guard and first responders from Barrows Bay arrived on the scene, Martin and Sheila were long gone. They followed a clear path up the side of the wooded bluffs to County Road 8, the same road he'd walked the night Ruby St. John died, the same his birth mother had walked to escape her pursuers, with little premature Martin—then Stephen—cradled in her arms.

They continued in the opposite direction, away from the Savage house. No idea where they would go, only certain they couldn't go back to his childhood home, walking under a pall of silence for half a mile or more. Tired, confused, frightened.

Finally, Sheila spoke. She was worried—not just about the Midwives or the visions they'd had at the stones, but because she hadn't taken her birth control in days. She'd forgotten the pills on her bedside drawer, and Martin had come inside her.

She'd felt it trickle cold down her inner thighs as they hiked up the bluff.

"What happened back there, it can't be a coincidence, can it?"

"What do you mean?"

"I saw Helen Birch pass the car when we were waiting for the ferry."

"My car..." Martin said glumly, wondering if it had survived. Wondering if they would be able to salvage it from the wreck. Upset that he'd lost Tansy, their only protection against Barclay —and now also the Midwives. "Sorry, go on."

"No. No, you should take a minute to mourn. It was a beautiful car."

He laughed. Prodded her again to continue.

"When Helen went down the hill, she had a tray covered in aluminum foil. When she came back, the tray was gone."

"What are you thinking? She poisoned the ferry crew?"

"When I went to Geraldine's to return her Tupperware, she gave me this tea she said Helen made. It was delicious. But then I started hallucinating—bizarre, just terrible things. I was sure she drugged me. And she knew things about me it wasn't possible for her to know. About my sister. My mother."

"Well, okay. Let's say she did drug the ferry crew. To what purpose?"

"To keep us from leaving the island?"

"Why wouldn't they just poison *us*?"

He had her there. The motive completely fell apart the moment it was picked at.

"How about this," he said. "Do you think it's a coincidence the ferry crashed where it did? That *we* ended up there? I don't know about you, but it felt like we were *meant* to find those stones. That someone wanted us to."

"But why?"

"Maybe they needed to tell their side of the story? No matter what Ruby and the others have done since, you have to admit what happened to those little girls was tragic. Maybe more than the crash itself."

"It was awful."

"Maybe they needed someone to know? Outsiders. An impartial jury."

"Maybe... but how could they know the ferry would crash at that exact spot?"

"Yeah, I guess that's a little too convenient, isn't it?"

"A little. What I wonder, does everyone in town know what those women truly are? Are we dealing with a community-wide cult? Or are they completely oblivious?"

Her question triggered a memory. "The day we first got here, Nadine asked if I knew what a 'glamour' was. Something about making things look different than they were. 'Like the emperor's new clothes,' she said. She was talking about Ruby and the other midwives."

Sheila remembered lying on the rock in the waves, looking at a shore shimmering indistinctly, as if in the midst of creating itself. "Why didn't you tell me this before?"

"I thought she was a lunatic. I didn't want it to be true. But I think deep down I knew it was. Mavis Lynch was the woman I saw in the shadows when my house was burning down. I'm sure of it. She was parked outside the bookstore when Nadine said that about glamours, witch's spells."

"She was out front of the house when we first arrived. In her pink Cadillac," Sheila said. "Aunt Norma's Them was the Midwives. Every second we've been in this town they've had their eyes on us. Your mother. The other four. Watching us." She hugged herself, shivering against the chill. "Maybe even listening. Is anywhere safe? Can we trust anyone?"

"We need to get off this island," Martin said. "Now more than ever."

---

IT TOOK NEARLY an hour to reach the turnoff where Sheila had seen a sign for boat rentals on the drive to Dr. Mulligan's farm.

The sign directed them to a dirt road winding through the woods. The sun had set and they walked it in near dark, illuminated by a third quarter moon shining pale through the clouds. Their eyes adjusted quickly but with the forest still black as night, every snapped twig startled them, made them anxious.

Five minutes down the road brought them to a ramshackle cabin, the warm orange glow of an oil lamp flickering in its grimy windows. A fire crackled in a weathered stone hearth, smoke rising from the chimney. Patsy Cline's "I Fall to Pieces" trickled from an old radio on the mantle. Her haunting vocals seemed to echo in the dark.

Metallic thuds and clinks and wooden creaks arose from the dark water beyond the cabin. Boats on a wood dock. This was the place.

He turned to Sheila. She looked scared. He felt her fear mirrored in his own face. He reached out to knock on the cabin door.

"Wait," Sheila whispered.

"What's wrong?"

"What if he tells them where we are? What we're doing?"

"It's a chance we have to take."

"Is it?" She nodded toward the water. "We could just *take* a boat."

He considered it. She was right. The country music was loud enough they could reach the dock without alerting whoever was inside if they kept quiet. He didn't feel great about stealing, but if they ditched it on the other side of the sound the owner would get it back eventually.

"Okay." He crept toward the side of the cabin. Sheila followed. Their footfalls crackled on sticks and stones, and a soft carpet of pine needles, golden-hued in the lamplight.

They reached a stone path leading down to the water. Three badly beaten tin boats rocked against the dock. Only a small shed stood between them and escape, a half-circle carved in its door. Smelled like something had died in there and the owner used strong chemicals to lessen the stench.

He looked back up at the cabin as they passed the shed. No movement in the windows. On the radio, Johnny Cash sang in baritone about ghostly flying horsemen.

The shed door swung open on rusty hinges and a deeply tanned older woman with ropey muscles stepped out. A home-rolled cigarette bobbed between her lips, its cherry illuminating a leathery, weathered face. She saw them and raised the shotgun she held in both hands as the door clapped back against its frame.

"Who the hell are you? What gives yous the right to be on my land?"

Sheila responded quickly and admirably calm. "I'm so sorry, ma'am. Nobody answered when we knocked at the house. We wanted to rent a boat—"

"So yous thought you'd just *take* one instead, that right? Coulda just waited. Lady can't use her own crapper these days without some goddamn citiot wantin a whiff?"

Martin glanced over her shoulder at what was clearly, from its chemical and human waste stench to the crescent moon carving in the door, an outhouse.

"We were just hoping to find someone on the dock," Sheila said, recovering from a slight wince when she recognized the smell.

"Well, yous found someone," the woman said, still pointing the shotgun between them. "Who in the hell rents a boat after sundown, Pete's sake? Got someplace to be better'n right here?"

*Anywhere would be better than here*, Martin thought. *Even just two or three feet upwind*.

"An appointment," Sheila said. "Early morning appointment."

The barrels flicked toward her. She flinched.

"Too good for the mornin ferry, are yous?"

"I guess you didn't hear." Martin held eye contact with her despite the strong desire to keep his eyes on the gun. "The ferry crashed. There won't be service for at least a couple of days."

He had no idea if it was true, but it seemed to satisfy her. She lowered the shotgun so it pointed at the path between their feet.

"That so?" A grin creased her weathered face. "Guess business is gonna be boomin come sunup." She nodded. "All right, let's head on up the house. I'll need a major credit card, course."

"Of course," Sheila said.

They follow the woman up the stone path.

"You two don't seem like island folk. But yous got a familiar look to ya." She gave them a narrow-eyed glance over her shoulder. "'Specially you," she said, nodding at Martin.

"We're just a couple of citiots from New York," he said.

Sheila nodded vigorously.

The woman spat at her feet. "Never cared for the place." She jabbed her scrawny chest with a thumb. "Barrows Bay, born and raised, this gal."

"It's a lovely island," Sheila said.

"Wouldn't go that far. It is what it is. Plenty enough for Clarabelle Leigh." She opened the screen door, held it with her boot while she opened the inner door. "Head on in. Don't mind the mess. I sure don't."

The cabin was small and cluttered. Beneath the smell of the fire were hints of wet dog, creamed corn and a hundred other unpleasant odors. An old hound lying on a tatty dog bed near the hearth raised its head from its paws briefly before returning to doggy dreamland.

"That's ol' Rooster." The woman parked the shotgun against the doorjamb. "Barks come sunup every damn mornin, that's how come I call him that."

Sheila bent to pet the dog.

"Don't pet him!"

She drew back her hand from the sleeping dog as though it might bite her.

"Not 'less you want your fingers to stink like coon shit. Mutt's been rollin 'round in it all week. No idea from where." She grabbed an old credit card imprinter from the oak dinner table. Pushed aside some Barrows Bay *Islander* biweeklies, a jar full of pennies and a dirty hand towel, and set it down.

Martin and Sheila turned to each other, realizing in the same moment she hadn't rescued her purse from the car. And that this woman seeing his credit card would out him as Ruby Savage's son.

"Is it okay if we do cash?"

"Don't take cash. Can't trust you'll bring the dang thing back if I do."

Martin turned to Sheila. "You know what? Maybe we should just call the office in the morning and reschedule."

She nodded. "That's a good idea."

The woman eyed them suspiciously. "Yous two want a boat or not? You was pretty damn hot to trot a second ago."

He moved for the door. "We'll take a raincheck on the boat. Sorry about that." He took out his wallet, pulled a damp twenty out of the billfold and held it out to her. "For your time."

She took it. Scowling at it, she rubbed it between her fingers. "It's wet." If her eyes narrowed any further, she wouldn't be able to see.

"Ran it through the wash this morning." His lie felt feeble.

She tucked the bill down the collar of her shirt, into her bra. On the radio, Johnny Cash gave way to Dolly Parton's "9 to 5."

The woman's face suddenly fell slack, her hand settled on her breast like she meant to feel herself up. She was staring at the fire. Its flames flickered in her cloudy eyes. He was sure they'd been clear and green before. Probably her only attractive feature.

Sheila gave him a wary look.

When the old woman came back her eyes were pallid slits. "Hold on a minute. I *know* you."

"I don't think so," Sheila said.

"Oh yeah, I do. You're the writer. Ruby Savage's boy. I see it very clearly now."

Her voice had changed. Lost its hardness and much of its country cadence.

"I don't know who Rudy Savage is," he said, backing toward the door.

"Oh yes. You do." She grabbed an iron poker from the rack and started swinging it back and forth like she was conducting Dolly's band as she backed them to the door. "You know Ruby. You know her more than anyone. Seen things you shouldn't have seen."

He reached for the door. "Put the poker down."

Her eyes flashed. She presented her nicotine-stained teeth in a vicious grin. "What? This?"

She swung at him. Martin stepped back, reaching for the door. She struck out quickly. He pulled his hand back as the poker clanged against the door handle.

"Why are you doing this?" Sheila asked.

"Why? *Why*, my dear?" Rooster raised its head and growled softly up at its master. "Because the two of you can't seem to help yourselves from meddling in island business." The poker swished back and forth hypnotically in her hand. "Because *someone* has to deal with you before it's too late for all of us."

Martin backed into the door. He felt along the jamb. "Clarabelle, was it?"

She smiled. It might have been sweet if not for the menace in her eyes and her bad teeth. "That's right, dear. Clarabelle Leigh."

"I recognize that voice," Sheila said. "You're Ethel Kelly. Somehow you've... you've taken over her body."

The smile grew. "You really are quite a clever clog, my dear. Unfortunately, not a single soul in Barrows Bay would believe you."

"I believe her," Martin said, still reaching, bending ever so slightly at the hip for the shotgun against the jamb.

"Well, that comes as no surprise. After that foul business amongst the standing stones, I'd imagine the two of you are thick as thieves."

Sheila flashed him a fearful look.

"That's right, my dear. I know everything. I *saw* everything. I know about your filthy little dalliance and I know you've seen what we are. But I know something that you don't."

"What's that?"

"Geraldine spoke the truth, my dear. You've a bun in the oven. No bigger than pea at the moment, but that bun will *grow*. And I don't think you've got it in you to get the scrape this time, not after the last. No, you'll be *stuck* with this one." The brown teeth exposed further, as much a snarl as a smile. "That is, *if we let you live*."

Martin grabbed the shotgun by the barrel and swung it into his hands. The old woman—Ethel, Clarabelle or both—rounded on him with the poker.

"Put. The poker. Down."

He primed the weapon. No idea if it required it. Nor if he could bring himself to fire it on an innocent woman. He only intended for her to drop the poker.

She called his bluff, striking Sheila on the thigh with its iron hook.

Sheila cried out and grasped her leg. Blood oozed out from between her fingers.

"Put it down, or so help me..."

"So help you, *who*? The only god on this island is Mother. And she'll forsake her only begotten son, too. Just you wait, my dear."

"*I'm warning you...*"

"So you have." The woman stepped closer to him. Her milky cataract eyes regarded him as she raised the poker to

Sheila's throat. She didn't seem to notice or care that the dog's growl at her feet had grown fiercer.

"Do it, dear," Ethel said with Clarabelle's lips. "Pull the trigger. Shoot an innocent woman in her home. Become the killer they say you are."

Ruby's words again. He tasted blood on the back of his tongue.

"Shoot her, Martin," Sheila moaned, the sharp end of the poker against her larynx.

"Yes, *shoot her*. Shoot her right between her childless breasts." Ethel thumped a fist against the scrawny, leathery chest she wore. "Do it, *you naughty boy*."

The phrase stung him: it was the same phrase Tish spoke the moment before Barclay leaped from the closet and strangled the life out of her.

She must have been reading his mind, using it against him. He struggled not to pull the trigger. To paint the walls with her brains. The poker pushed deeper against Sheila's throat. The shotgun rattled in his quivering hands.

*Become the killer you* know *you are*, he thought.

With a wild snarl, Rooster leaped up from his bed, raising a cloud of dust, chomping down hard on his master's leg.

Clarabelle dropped the poker, kicking at the dog as he held on tight to her ankle, drawing blood.

"*Bloody thing! Vile thing!*"

Sheila made a double fist like a volleyball player and brought them down on the woman's head.

Clarabelle flinched, and the milkiness instantly faded from her eyes. They opened wide in pain and fear. She looked down at her leg, where the hound dog still held her in his teeth. Then to Martin, training the shotgun on her.

"What the hot shit is happenin here? Rooster! Bad dog!"

Rooster's sad eyes rolled upward at the sound of her voice and he promptly let go, backing away fearfully until he plopped back down in his bed.

Martin lowered the shotgun.

"*Give me that*," she snapped, grabbing it by the barrel and tearing it from his hand. "You even know how to use this?" She looked at Sheila's leg. "Dang. Rooster bit you too?"

"It wasn't the dog. You hit me with the poker."

"*I* hit you? I don't remember that at all." She scowled thoughtfully. "Felt kinda like I fell asleep there for a second or two..."

"Do you know a woman named Ethel Kelly?"

Clarabelle nodded. Squeezed her ankle where the dog bit her to stem the flow of blood. "One of the Midwifes."

"She was using you, speaking and moving through you. She wanted us to shoot you."

The woman looked to Martin for confirmation. He nodded. He'd been so close to doing just that. If the dog hadn't bit her just then, he might have.

*Woe betide me.*

"You people need to get the hell out of here."

"We need a boat," Martin said. "Please."

"I ain't about to get caught givin you a boat. If Ethel knows you're here, Mother does too. And you're her son. I knew I recognized you."

"She's not my mother."

"If they find us, they'll kill us," Sheila pleaded.

"I don't know that. And I don't know *you*. Alls I know is ya scared my poor boy somethin terrible and I gotta tend to this bite." The woman slumped into a chair at the table, fumbling to make a cigarette on a rolling machine. "Go on an' leave me be. I'm an old lady. Never hurt no one." She fired up the unfiltered smoke and took a drag, her hands shaking.

"*Please,*" Sheila said.

"You're not welcome here no more, don't ya get it?"

*And now that they know what we're doing*, Martin thought, *they won't just let us leave.*

"Come on," he said, ushering Sheila to the door.

She came away reluctantly. He held the door as she stepped back into the cool, dark evening.

"If they come here asking about us, please don't tell them anything."

Clarabelle spat a piece of tobacco. "If they come round here, I don't 'spect I got much of a choice."

He nodded. They had already pulled her deep enough into this. She was just trying to protect herself, her dog.

"I'm sorry I almost shot you."

"I'm sorry you didn't," the woman said without looking up from the fire.

# CHAPTER 20

## SANCTUARY

O N THE WALK back to town, they passed several beachfront houses against the black backdrop of the ocean and overcast sky. Most of the residents appeared to be home and not many owned boats. The few that did had kayaks, sailboats, canoes. Even if they could manage to steal one, it would be too dark to see anything out on the water. The harsh current would set them adrift.

"Do you believe her? That you're pregnant?" Martin asked, breaking a long, thoughtful silence.

"I don't have any reason to think she was lying. She *knew* things, Martin. At David and Laura's that night, Ethel Kelly knew the baby was breeched before anyone else."

"Maybe she's just got good eyes."

"She's *blind*. But she knew. And she knows what happened at the stones. What we did. She could *see* through that woman's eyes. How can we stand against that?"

He said he didn't know.

The beachfront houses were behind them now. Ahead, the lights of downtown brightened the night sky. It was almost as though the town was sparkling on the darkened horizon.

"There's got to be a way. Maybe we can convince Ruby to let us go."

"We can't go back to that house. Not after what Clarabelle said. If Ethel knows, Ruby knows too."

"But Ethel seemed to think Ruby was protecting me. She said she'll forsake me, remember?"

"A woman possessed by a demon had a poker to my throat. I don't remember much of what she said."

"Well, what if Ruby has been protecting us, like I thought? What if she's not like the others?"

"What do you mean?"

"I don't know. This is all so crazy."

Sheila nodded somberly. "I'm starting to think James Barclay doesn't look all that insane anymore."

"He could've been right, for all we know. Dark magic exists. Demons. Why not witches?"

"Murder is murder."

"Is it? The bible says 'thou shalt not suffer a witch to live.'"

"It also says 'he that smites a man shall be put to death.' Those were innocent women, Martin. Innocent *children*."

"Maybe. You're probably right."

They walked in silence until the first houses on the outskirts of town winked into view. Within all of that light was a darkness much blacker than the night. The awful truth of Barrows Bay rotted within the walls of every home, every business.

How many citizens knew its darkest secrets? How many had stood at the little St. John girl's funeral knowing her blood had been spilled to keep those evil women alive?

And what was the tradeoff? What did Barrows Bay receive for turning a blind eye to this madness? Why did they revere Ruby Savage as their tin pot savior? What were these creatures of the stones, these demons wearing human skin—the *Chadrach*?

Why was Ruby sent away to Saints of Mercy? And why did someone set his house on fire after she was gone?

He needed to know. It was no longer about his book. This was life and death.

County Road 8 became King Street as they reached the bungalows on the edge of town. The families within ate and conversed and watched television as Sheila and Martin passed by unnoticed.

"It's so quiet," she said.

No cars passed as they walked. No dogs barked. No

honking horns or raised voices from afar. At the first intersection it was quiet enough to hear the red four-way traffic lights flick on and off.

"Creepy," he said. "That's what it is."

She agreed with a cautious nod.

They passed darkened storefronts, most closed as early as six in the evening. Martin's shrine still stood in the bookstore window, though a FOR LEASE sign hung in front of his posterboard face. He glanced over the titles, books spanning his entire career. It all felt so distant and unimportant now. Like someone else's life.

At the center of downtown, boisterous laughter and muted rock music drifted out from the Legion Hall.

A man in cowboy garb stood on the steps, smoking a joint. Martin recognized him from the night Ruby St. John died. The cowboy looked up and scowled when he saw them. He tossed the roach on the sidewalk and ground it into the concrete with the heel of a snakeskin boot. AC/DC's "Dirty Deeds Done Dirt Cheap" thundered into the otherwise silent street as the man returned to the darkened bar.

"I guess the Rhinestoned Cowboy wasn't happy to see us," Martin said.

"Isn't it rhine*stone*?"

"It was a joke. Because of the weed."

"Ah," she said, not feeling much like laughing.

The little white Catholic church shone against the darkened sky up ahead, illuminated by two spotlights in the hedges on either side of the doors. It stood just off the main street, just before the road sloped up toward Sinjin's grocery store.

"Looks like the church might be the only other place open in the whole damn town," he said.

"Might be a good spot to lay low," Sheila suggested. "Aren't they obligated to provide sanctuary?"

"It's worth asking."

They continued toward it. The traffic lights overhead buzzed from green to red. Somewhere in the night, raccoons squealed, fighting over a tasty morsel of trash. What sounded like a garbage can lid hit the concrete and spun until it fell.

Sheila drew back the squeaky, weathered-brass door

knocker and struck it against the plate three times. It echoed within the small church.

A moment later, noise arose from within: a door thudding, footsteps crossing the sanctuary, stumbling, a groan of wood against wood followed by muttered curses. Until finally the locks and latches were drawn.

The heavy door came open and Reverend Atkins stood behind it, holding it in both hands like a large shield. He was bleary-eyed, reeking of whiskey. His sparse, snow-white hair hung in his face.

"Yes? It's a tad late for confession, if that's why you've come."

"We were hoping you could give us sanctuary for the night," Sheila said.

The old man blinked dazedly. His drunken gaze found Sheila and he gave her a tight smile, polite but far from friendly. "Sanctuary? My child, whatever would compel you to inquire of such an antiquated custom?"

"I'm Ruby Savage's son. Martin Savage."

The holy man's eyes bugged out momentarily. He covered poorly with a cough. "Why yes, of course. I do seem to recall the two of you sitting beside *la grande dame* during my service for that poor dear girl." He tutted. "Such a terrible tragedy. But why on earth would you require sanctuary?"

"We have no place else to go, Reverend," Sheila said. "Dr. Mulligan said we could trust you."

"He did, did he?"

"That's right," Martin said, although the doctor didn't seem to think very highly of the reverend at all. "He told us everything."

The reverend nodded with a heavy sigh, as if he'd always expected this time might come. He stepped aside and ushered them in.

"Well then, come in quickly," he said, peering out into the darkened street. "Before you let the dickens in with you."

---

"MY PARISH ISN'T QUITE what it once was," Reverend Atkins admitted, groaning as he took a seat behind the desk.

"There was a time when people turned to scripture for comfort. Now they turn on reality television."

The office smelled of wood polish, cheap cologne, sandalwood and the opened whiskey bottle. Photos covered the walls of the reverend, much younger, smiling in the midst of a children's choir, shaking hands with President Clinton and Bush Jr. Another with Mother Teresa, which appeared to be from missionary work in India, judging by the people surrounding them. In another he was crouched next to a dead buck alongside Dr. Mulligan and a third man with a dark mustache and bushy eyebrows. The three men were apparently good friends.

Reverend Atkins poured a round of whiskey in three mismatched coffee mugs. Sheila sipped from hers—the caption read *It's What's On the Inside that Counts: Coffee*—and the strong liquor warmed her from the inside out. Martin drank his in a gulp and set his *World's Greatest Dad* mug down on the reverend's desk.

"Dr. Mulligan said you might know something about my mother."

Reverend Atkins gave him a condescending smile. "My child, *everyone* in Barrows Bay knows about Ruby Savage."

"I meant my birth mother. I think he said her name was Rosalee?"

The reverend choked on his whiskey. He cleared his throat, wiping amber liquid from his rosy double chin. "Ryland told you about Rosalee, did he?"

"He said she died the same year Martin was born," Sheila said. "During childbirth. He told us to talk to her father, Michael Creemore."

"Yes, Michael." The reverend peered over his shoulder at the photograph Martin had noticed, the three men and the deer. "Terrible shame what happened with his little girl. And what became of him following her untimely death."

"We were on our way to talk to him when the ferry crashed," Sheila said.

"You were on the ferry? My goodness, gracious. I thought you looked a touch worse for wear but I had no idea—"

"We're fine," Martin said. "Just lucky to be alive. What can you tell us about Rosalee Creemore and her baby?"

He nodded. "Much of what I know was told to me in confidence. In confessional. Michael Creemore and I were close friends. I was Rosalee's godfather. I couldn't possibly reveal—"

"Tell us what you can. Please. All my life I thought Ruby was my mother. Now I find out she wasn't even related to me."

*And worse*, he thought. *Much worse*. But he didn't say it. No way to know if the reverend could be trusted, how deep he was in the Midwives' back pocket. Mulligan suspected the man had a dirty secret. Something he would sell out his closest friends to keep.

The reverend sighed. "Very well. Rosalee came to me when she discovered she was with child. We spoke very briefly about it. She was quite young and worried what her father would think. After what she told me, quite frankly, so was I."

"What did she tell you, Reverend?"

"Father, please."

Martin caught Sheila's gaze and tried not to react. Mother. Father. Structures of power, filling in for absent parental figures.

He indulged the man. "What did she say, Father?"

"I'm not at liberty to divulge that. What I can tell you is that the pregnancy was accidental. I can also tell you I convinced her to carry the child to term. In cases like hers it has become... an issue of contention, if you will, whether or not a woman should carry. The stance of the Catholic church is still quite firm. Abortion is a mortal sin, regardless of circumstance. The penalty in this life is excommunication. Without repentance, the penalty is Hell."

"Patriarchal bullshit," Sheila said.

The reverend offered an apologetic half shrug. "Be that as it may, I encouraged her to carry and she did. For Martin's sake, I'm sure you'd agree she made the right decision?"

Sheila conceded with a half-shrug and a nod.

"Who was the father, Reverend Atkins?" Martin asked. "Did she have a boyfriend in school? An older man?"

"The parent's name was told to me during confession. If I were to tell you that it would break the sanctity of the—"

"Reverend, I'm a psychologist," Sheila interrupted. "I know all about the ethics of confidentiality. But Rosalee Creemore is dead—"

"Her *spirit* is still with us, my child. Her father is still alive, albeit not of sound mind."

Martin struggled to contain his frustration. "Don't you think her spirit would want *her son* to know who his father is? And what about you? You've kept this secret for over *forty years*. The entire town believes I'm Ruby Savage's son. Why don't they remember my real mother? Doesn't your goddaughter's memory mean *anything* to you?"

The reverend's face reddened. He poured himself another drink, downed it and poured another. "Very well. You're right, of course. Rosalee's memory should indeed be honored."

Martin thanked him.

"You may want to retract your gratitude once you've heard what I have to say. I believe what she told me—what I revealed to her father after her service—is what drove my dear friend to insanity."

"What is it, Reverend? Please."

"Rosalee and her father were avid hikers," the reverend began. He sighed deeply through his nostrils, brushed a withered hand through his snow-white hair. "After her mother passed, the two of them explored the entire island from top to tail. One day, according to my goddaughter, they came upon something neither had seen before. There were *standing stones* below the bluffs."

Martin and Sheila shared a look.

"I'm not certain how much of her story is true or imagined. If I were an outsider considering the things she'd told me that day, I would say she made up the entire thing in order to cope with the truth of it, with the trauma. But since I know this town, and the many peculiar things that have occurred here over the years, I'm apt to believe her."

He peered inauspiciously first at Sheila, then Martin before continuing.

"Rosalee feared the stones, you see. She told me she *sensed* something wrong about them. Something perhaps *evil*. But Michael's curiosity got the best of him." The reverend swallowed another hard gulp of whiskey and grimaced. "She told me... he was *writhing* against the stones... almost as if he were in the throes of an unholy madness. Like a bacchanalian reveler in ancient Rome. And suddenly he began to seize. His eyes rolled back, so that only the whites were showing. The moment dear

Rosalee stepped into the circle to help him, she was consumed by their power. What happened next..."

The reverend trailed off, but their imaginations filled in the blanks, having experienced it themselves. The stones had appeared to them. Upon entering the circle a sort of orgiastic psychosis held them in its sway until the act it drew them there to perform was completed.

A fertility ritual.

The stones had been waiting for them.

Primed by the blood sacrifice of a child, like Ruby St. John.

"You're saying my father—"

"Is also your grandfather," Reverend Atkins said, his eyes lowered. "Yes, I'm afraid so."

BARROWS BAY HAD EXPERIENCED many deaths during childbirth over the years, the reverend told them. Far more than the national average for a town of its size.

"When you were born, Martin, it was almost as if the people of Barrows Bay forgot my dear goddaughter had ever existed. The Mother had borne a son. Never mind the fact that she was seventy years old if she was a day. Never mind that many of the town elders had been delivered by her themselves. Or the conspicuous lack of a father. Ruby Savage had a child—and it was a time to rejoice."

Sadly, Ruby's mental wellness had quickly begun to deteriorate, most noticeably at town gatherings—the funerals, the weddings, the Harvest Festival, the big Christmas gala at the town hall—and the people of Barrows Bay passed it off as "the blue feeling," which would later come to be called postpartum depression.

She had missed out on several births in the following years, choosing instead to stay home and take care of Martin. When she was taken away to Saints of Mercy Sanitarium, the entire town mourned. In her absence, Mavis Lynch filled the role. Though no one had ever dared call her "Mother," she had already been in charge of all births since Martin was born.

"Mavis was none too pleased when Ruby came traipsing back to town some years later, apparently all cured. Ms. Lynch had fashioned her own little fiefdom here on the island, and the town had grown into something Ruby Savage never would have condoned. It became a tourist trap. Mavis's Women's Weekends put Barrows Bay on the map. Ruby thought them gauche. *Decadent.* I must say I agree with her. But by then it was too late and much too popular to stop."

"So Mavis and my moth—" He still found it difficult not to think of her as his mother. He was still getting used to it, to being an orphan. "—and Ruby, they've been locked in a power struggle ever since."

"One could say that, yes. One could also say they despise each other. There's a term I've heard in working with school choirs on the mainland. I believe Ruby Savage and Mavis Lynch are what children these days call 'frenemies.'"

Sheila laughed.

The reverend excused himself to get blankets from the back closet and Martin attempted to absorb all that he'd told them. It was a lot to take in. His birth mother's unwitting rape at the hands of her father. Her death during his birth. His grandfather's breakdown. Ruby raising him as her own despite her deteriorating her mental health.

Barclay's "trail of blood" ran much deeper and further back than he ever could have imagined. He couldn't help but wonder if the killer had been right all along.

That his birth had been unholy.

That these deaths would only ever stop with his own.

Reverend Atkins returned a few minutes and several muttered curses later holding a stack of folded bedclothes. He laid them on the cot with a pained grunt.

"One of you will have to sleep on the floor, or among the pews. Though I suspect with what you know about Ruby Savage and her companions, it might be wise for you to stay together."

They agreed. Martin said he'd take the floor, leaving Sheila the cot.

"I'll be back first thing in the morning," the reverend said, standing in the doorway. "My little rectory is on the other side of the cemetery. I'd invite you to stay but I don't suspect our mutual friends would appreciate it very much. I like to believe what's said within these hallowed walls shall never reach their wicked ears, that God would prevent it. I understand that faith is a difficult concept to subscribe to in these troubled times of ours, particularly in light of what we know about those... *witches*, for lack of a better word. Those wolves in sheep's clothing. But it's all we've got to cling to, isn't it? That light will triumph against dark. Good against evil."

Sheila paused in laying out her sheet on the cot. "Can I ask you something, Reverend?"

"Of course, dear child."

"What happened between you and Dr. Mulligan? When we spoke, he seemed to imply you'd betrayed him."

Reverend Atkins contemplated the question for a moment, peering out into the bright hallway. "Ryland Mulligan is a kind and decent man, but he's also an old fool. He should never have returned to this island. He shouldn't have pushed against the Midwives. If I betrayed anyone, it was Michael and Rosalee Creemore. The whole town betrayed them. We'll all pay for it someday." He nodded gravely to himself. "Perhaps sooner than later."

# CHAPTER 21

## A TIME TO BURN

THE KILLER STOOD at the edge of the earth overlooking the black waters of the Rhode Island Sound.

In the few days since he'd left Qurban Youssef's remains to rot in the Hell's Kitchen alley, Barclay had kept a close watch on Detective Lumsden. Biding his time. But the cop was always on the move, at the station, with his lady partner or his family.

Ol' Jimmy couldn't exactly confront a cop in broad daylight. Too loud. Too messy. He needed to be stealthy, like a coyote on the prowl. For as much pleasure as it would bring him to have his revenge on the detective who locked him away in the nuthatch for the past six years, just cut his throat from ear to ear right in the middle of the cop shop in front of all his friends and colleagues, Ol' Gimme Jimmy needed information, not the cop's blood.

In the end it turned out he didn't need Lumsden at all. Providence smiled upon him once again, in the form of an article.

This morning he stood outside the Science, Industry and Business Library in the shadow of the Empire State Building, among a throng of homeless people waiting for it to open. He fit right in, dressed in a baggy gray B.U.M. Equipment hoodie he stole from a Goodwill bin, his salt-and-pepper scruff now a full beard, patchy and prickly as a porkypine.

When the security guard opened the doors at just past ten, he shuffled in unnoticed among an aromatic sea of unnoticeables. While others charged their old flip phones, found themselves a nice space to nap for the morning or watched videos on the computers, Ol' Gimme Jimmy logged on to the Google and typed in Marty's name.

That smug face and shit-eating grin of his popped up alongside his Wikipedia entry, and Jimmy clicked the News icon. After several articles about Marty's agent and Gimme Jimmy's "daring late-night escape," which made the killer smile thinking of how he and Tisha May pulled it off, the latest result was a *New Yorker* article titled "Crime Writer Hunted by His Past," written by an attractive Chicano woman named Izzie Medina.

The title made Jimmy grin. Not *haunted* by his past but *hunted*, as if the past was a living thing, a man-eating monster that would tear him apart when it finally caught up. The rest painted Jimmy in a poor light, far too much editorializing. But his witch-hunting days weren't the focus of the article. The "Past" of the title referred to Marty's hometown. Not Stratford, Connecticut but a small island called Barrows Bay in the Rhode Island Sound. And to think all this time Ol' Gimme Jimmy had Marty pegged as a Nutmegger, born and bred.

Jimmy slipped out of the library as unnoticed as he'd entered. He considered paying the Medina woman a visit. Make her the next breadcrumb on his trail of blood, get Marty and the headshrink bitch's fear juices really and truly percolating. But when destiny came calling Ol' Gimme Jimmy wouldn't just stand there gawping with the door wide open. Surprise was the key.

In that spirit, he washed up as best he could in a gas station toilet and bussed straight out to Hartford. From the Nutmeg State he hitched to Narragansett and down to the cape, where he now stood waiting on a water taxi with fifteen dollars in his pocket.

Sailboat riggings clanged against their masts like the cowbells he remembered from when he was a boy, living next to the Rockford farm, and with the gentle wash of waves against the rocky shore it put him in a mood of peaceful contemplation, knowing his work would soon be done.

This business with Marty was a pleasure but it distracted

him from his true purpose. He'd be glad to get back to cleansing the world of Satan's whores and their infernal spawn. Vanquishing women who partook of the *osculum obscenum*, the profane act of puckering up and kissing Ol' Scratch's scarlet-hued turdcutter.

The end of the world was nigh on coming. A fella only had to surf the world wide web for a few minutes or switch on the news to see it plain as day.

The high-pitched buzz of a motor perked his ears.

"Here I come, Marty," he told the darkness. "Can ya feel it? Can ya feel death creepin up on ya like a rattler? The past is a man-eatin monster, an' he gon' gobble you up tonight. Count on it."

A flashlight came on in the dark out on the water, scouring the shore. The beam swished past him and returned, catching him in spotlight, not quite as bright and blinding as the light he'd seen when the Lord anointed him one of His holy soldiers for the End Times.

Just like then, he raised a hand to shade his eyes.

The light drifted away again, toward the rocking dock on the shore below him. The driver—possibly the same woman he'd spoken to on the payphone, though he'd expected a man—brought the boat in tight and cut the engine. She snapped the back hook then jumped out, leaving the flashlight to illuminate the floor of the tin boat, the chipped red paint of the gas tank, a paddle, a life vest, a scoped hunting rifle and a rusty bailing can.

She snapped the front hook and bent to pick up the flashlight, considerately shining it at Gimme Jimmy's feet this time rather than right in his peepers. "Yous call for a lift?" the raspy voice inquired.

"That's right."

"Well, come on then. Time's a-wastin."

Jimmy sauntered out onto the wobbly dock. "That it is, ma'am."

She struck a match against the edge of the dock and lit a home-rolled cigarette. The cherry illuminated the weathered face of a woman who'd lived a hardscrabble life on a wind-blasted rock. "Name's Clarabelle, if it's all the same to you."

"That's a pretty name, darlin."

Clarabelle spat a flake of tobacco and waved a hand toward

the rocking boat, ignoring the compliment. "Welcome to the Barrows Bay Express. Please keep your hands in the boat at all times and enjoy your trip. If yous get queasy from all the rockin just go on 'n harf over the side."

They piled in and Clarabelle cast off.

"Y'always bring a huntin rifle along fer the ride, do ya?"

Clarabelle shrugged. "Fella rings at three in the damn mornin, you never know what kinda degenerate you gonna meet."

"Mm-hmm, reckon you're right."

Clarabelle wasted no more time conversing. She twisted the handle and pulled away from the dock, into the choppy water. Jimmy's teeth clacked each time the boat slammed down over another wave.

Out on the sound he spotted lights brightening the horizon in the distance, outlining what appeared to be the small island of Barrows Bay. The town itself wasn't visible from the sound, just some houses on the shore and higher up on the bluffs, and the ferry dock lit up like a landing strip.

Fella who gave him a lift to Narraganset said the Barrows Bay ferry got in an accident so there wouldn't be one running for another day or two. Short of hiring a water taxi like Clarabelle's Barrows Bay Express, most people would be stuck on the island. Which suited his purposes just fine.

He was watching the island against the black horizon when a flickering orange glow arose from the trees near its center. After a minute, he thought he could make out black smoke rising into the sky above.

"What's goin on up there?" he called back to the driver.

Clarabelle squinted into the dark, the cherry on her smoke glowing red hot, illuminating her hard face. "Looks like somethin caught fire. First the ferry, now this. What the hell next?"

Jimmy watched the blaze burn brighter, a smile spreading across his scarred and bristly face. He had a pretty good idea what came next. The only thing he wasn't sure of was if it would start right here in Barrows Bay or further on down the trail.

*The End Times're nigh on indeed*, he thought, flames flickering in his eyes.

SITTING in the backseat of Mavis's Cadillac, cane between her knees, sunglasses in her lap, Ethel Kelly's wrinkled eyelids fluttered against her milky white eyes.

Mavis looked at her sister in the rearview mirror. The woman had been born sightless. When she passed away during the birth of her first child in 1946, just after the Second Great War, she'd acquired a new sight, one that didn't require eyes. She liked to joke, once the phrase came into fashion, that it was her "women's intuition."

Whatever it was, however it originated, her second sight was powerful. Mavis realized now how wise it was to turn Ethel toward her side, away from Mother. The two sexless beings in women's bodies conspired together in Mavis's usual spot, while the suds and foam brushes splashed over her car windows.

Ruby Savage had a plan for Martin and his whore, a plan Helen and Geraldine seemed comfortable with. But that night at the car wash, the same night they had fed on the child, Ethel looked into the future. And like the times before, she saw nothing but darkness.

"What does it mean?" Mavis asked.

"It means the End of Everything," Ethel told her.

While Helen and Geraldine sabotaged the ferry, Ethel joined with Mavis to get rid of the meddlesome doctor. The pigs had been Ethel's idea, the rifle Mavis's. With their combined wisdom and glammers, the old fool hadn't stood a chance.

After the ferry crash, Ethel had lost sight of Martin for some time. The old woman's magic had shown them the way to the stones. It was her penance. An offering of peace to her daughters. One child's life for the other.

Mavis doubted the old witch could convince Martin's whore to stay in Barrows Bay while she carried the child to term, let alone give it up to the slaughter when the time came to feed. She and Ethel came up with a plan of their own. One that didn't rely on the whims and caprices of people from Away, who weren't steeped in the traditions and rituals of the Bay.

An hour or so after the crash, Ethel picked up their trail on the other end of the island with the sensation of a damp twenty-dollar bill pressed against her left breast. Martin had held it for a short period. He'd received it as change for a fifty from a gas station attendant in Upstate New York.

Ethel left her body then, projecting her fetch into the dockmaster Clarabelle Leigh. The smell of wet dog, stale sweat and secondhand smoke permeated the body she inhabited. In the backseat of the Cadillac, she coughed a lungful of acrid smoke, much to Mavis's amusement. Mavis had once seen the woman spit out a cherry that hadn't been in her mouth moments prior. It was like a carnival sideshow, something new every time.

But somehow the whore was able to see Ethel beneath Clarabelle's skin. When Sheila struck the woman on the head it had expelled her fetch from Clarabelle's body.

"Say what you will about the bitch, she's one smart cookie," Mavis said.

From there they waited. Ethel sat quietly, awaiting a sensation that would draw her fetch from her body. Mavis read one of Martin's books, trying to get a better grasp of what might be going on in his head. Some sort of psychological insight Ethel may have missed.

*Mirror Man* was as much Martin's story as it was the case against Nico Damiani. He'd thrust himself front and center into the narrative, taking much of the attention away from the serial killer's history. Was it any wonder a man like James Barclay wanted to murder him?

Martin was scared, that much Mavis knew. He'd been a frightened little boy and he was just as frightened now. An outside observer might not see it, but it was apparent in every book he wrote.

He'd always been running, ever since he'd seen her standing in the glow of the fire. Perhaps much earlier than that.

She supposed it was possible he remembered the moments shortly after his birth. The running. The struggle. Perhaps he even remembered watching his birth mother die.

Mavis smiled at the thought.

"They're in the church," Ethel said from the backseat.

It was just past midnight. The reverend shook Martin's hand, saying goodnight. Ethel felt the rough bandage wrapped around his palm.

"Should I fetch?"

"Not this time," Mavis said, adjusting the brim of her hat in the mirror. "I've got a better idea. Something not even the smart bitch will expect."

With a wicked smile, she turned the key in the ignition. The Pink Princess's engine rumbled to life.

*To everything there is a season, Padre*, she thought, pulling out of the car wash lot. *A time to kill and a time to burn.*

---

THE DOCTOR'S assistant called Sheila into his office. She stepped into a small, curtained vestibule and changed out of her damp clothes into a fresh green gown, opened at the back. Then she sat in the tiny exam room on the crinkly paper covering the table, feeling uncomfortable in the flimsy gown, waiting for Dr. Mulligan.

A calendar was flipped open on the doctor's desk, December 15 circled in red. Puzzling over this, she looked over the posters on the walls. One listed common gynecological disorders. A second showed the stages of growth of a human fetus.

Her gaze settled on a poster that seemed out of place in the doctor's office: a dozen piglets clamoring over a fat mother sow's teat. The poster said *SAVAGING: It's not just wrong—it's dangerous!*

She was still puzzling over its intent when she noticed the buzzing from somewhere within the small, closed room.

The paper crinkled under her as she slipped off the table, tracking the sound. It seemed to be coming from the corner of the room, beside the desk where the calendar stood open on December, even though she knew it was March.

The buzz rose in intensity as she neared, as if in response to her proximity. She peered over the rim of the trash can. The inside was sparkling.

It was only when she looked closer that the glittering revealed itself to be a thick coating of metallic-green blowflies, rising and falling like a living wave.

Something lay within, attracting the swarm. It had no smell. Cautiously, she reached out a socked foot and kicked the bin.

The flies rose in a chaotic mass, swirling around her head in a horrid black cloud. She swatted at them, swinging her arms frantically. Horrified by the thought of their hairy little feet touching her, spreading whatever filth they found in the trash on her bare arms and face and in her hair.

Finally, the cloud dissipated. The room quieted, aside from the hum of the air conditioning unit and the especially loud ticking of a wall clock. Printed it in a curve around the top of the clock was the word MATERNAL—a very Freudian sick joke.

She leaned over the trash can.

Revulsion crawled like insects on her skin.

A fetus lay within, nestled among the trash, covered in blood and thick, white clots of vernix caseosa. The girl was dead, her pallor a dark, bruised purple.

Sheila fought back her gorge, barely managed to swallow it before stepping out into the empty hall and calling for the doctor.

"Hello! Dr. Mulligan!"

A tiny cough answered her call. Startled, Sheila returned to the trash bin. The purple in the girl's face mellowed as oxygen reached her lungs. She *cried*—just a single whimper, but more than enough for Sheila to be certain the girl was alive.

Footsteps approached the door. She twisted around, suddenly frightened.

Dr. Mulligan stood in the doorway, dressed in stained overalls rather than his doctor's white. He smiled. "Hello, Dr. Tanner." Flies buzzed out of his mouth and circled his head like a malignant halo. "Feeling all right?"

"That baby is still alive," she said. It felt silly to have to say it. The baby was crying incessantly now. Only a deaf person could miss it.

"We'll get that taken care of."

He shouted for the nurse. She came promptly, lugging a Shop-Vac behind her. It was Geraldine McKenna, wearing an old-fashioned white nurse's dress and cap and her white silk gloves.

"The trash requires disposal," the doctor told her.

"No," Sheila said. "No, she's not dead. Someone threw her away but she's not dead!"

The doctor gave her a condescending glower. "Of course, she's dead. She was never *born*. You didn't want her. You asked us to *remove* her for you."

Sheila looked down. Her fresh gown was soiled by a dark, blooming stain. Her flesh felt saggy around her belly. How long had she been carrying the girl inside of her? Weeks? Months?

"No, she's not mine. I wouldn't do that—"

"Oh, but you *did*," Dr. Mulligan said as Nurse MacKenna crossed the room between them. A whiff of rot carried on his breath, bad enough to make Sheila gag again. "And she most certainly is *dead*. I should know. *I'm* dead too."

The vacuum roared in the small room. The nozzle made a solid *schoomp!* as the baby—*her* baby—was sucked inside.

The motor whined, struggling to suck the baby inside. The little girl squirmed, her head caught in the impossibly large nozzle, her tiny limbs kicking, fingers and toes curling reflexively.

Sheila grabbed Geraldine by the arms, trying to wrench the vacuum away from the old woman before she really did kill her baby. The girl *belonged* to her—no matter what Dr. Mulligan said. She wanted her, wanted to keep her. This time, she'd carry the baby to term.

The tiny shoulders sucked into the nozzle. The girl's fragile little arms stopped squirming and her fingers clenched into tiny fists. Her feet bicycled. The umbilical cord flopped and wriggled, and Sheila could see it was *attached to her own body*, the other end disappearing underneath her gown and she could *feel* it, a strong pressure in her abdomen, like something tugging on her internal organs. Dr. Mulligan cackled, exhaling a mouthful of grave rot and blowflies, and she fought harder against Geraldine, even though the woman had taken off her gloves and her hands were black as basement mold, and the vacuum's whine crescendoed, sounding more like some kind of awful siren—

MARTIN DREAMED OF BLOOD.

He stood under a hot geyser of blood, basking in it, letting it wash over him, pour over his face, into his eyes, his mouth and ears.

He *tasted* it, salty and rich. And he knew it belonged to Nadine Hinkley, to Letitia May Cotton, to Ruby St. John. Each swallow brought exotic new flavors: Paula Danlon, Tina Wozinski and Jessica Renault—James Barclay's victims. And

Margaret Abbey's: Allen Merritt, George Leon and Lorne Cullen.

And Nico Damiani's.

Gorging on their blood. Choking on it.

He screamed.

The old civil defense warning siren woke him, and for a moment he couldn't tell if it was his own scream following him out of sleep. He rose from the floor, sweating, his back and arms stiff. He moved around cautiously, looking for the lamp on the reverend's desk, the horrendous alien howl bleating in the darkness. He bashed his knee on the edge and uttered a hushed curse.

"What's going on?" Sheila said, sounding frightened. "What is that?"

"It's the air raid siren. For the volunteer fire department."

She shivered. The wail of the siren in the dark gave her a chill. She still felt the dream with her. The flies coming out of Dr. Mulligan's mouth. Geraldine the nurse and the baby trapped in the vacuum. She doubted she would ever forget it.

Martin found the lamp and flicked it on. The office brightened. Sheila sat up on the cot, wearing only her mismatched bra and panties. The office was overly warm and they'd removed everything but their underwear before bed. Their clothes and Martin's blankets made a tangled mess on the floor at her feet.

"Same goddamn siren they had when my house was on fire. Still gives me the creeps."

"You aren't kidding. How long until it stops?"

He shrugged. "When the fire department gets to the scene, I guess. Maybe not until the fire's out. We should try to get back to sleep."

"I can't sleep through that."

"Yeah, me neither. Tomorrow's gonna be rough. What time is it?" He glanced at his watch. "Three o'clock. Jesus."

"The witching hour," Sheila said.

He pulled his jeans out of the pile and shook them out. Still slightly damp, despite the long walk and the warm office, it took him longer than normal to get his legs through. "Why did you have to say that?"

"Psychologically speaking, this is the most common time of night for supernatural experiences. I had the strangest dream just now. Dr. Mulligan was dead. He was my OB/GYN, for some reason. They gave me an abortion but the baby was still alive. She was in the trash."

He frowned at her, still trying to get his right foot into the leg of his jeans. "That's a weird dream. Jesus, that's loud as hell. There's gotta be a coffee maker in this place somewhere, right?"

"I think he said there's a meeting room down the hall. Are we getting up now? Did you want me to go with you?"

"It's fine. I'll make a pot. Might as well get up. We had, what? Three hours sleep? Four?"

She yawned. "I think four."

He tugged his sweater over his head. At least it was dry. "Kay. I'll be right back then. Don't go anywhere."

"Where would I go?"

He opened the door to the hallway. Bright lights from the nave cast a dim glow on the bulletin boards, the framed photos of parish events and gatherings, the stacked chairs.

At the far end were the washrooms Reverend Atkins had pointed out earlier. Between them and the office was the meeting hall, where residents occasionally held group events, art classes, banquets and small weddings. Martin had looked over the postings before they settled in for the night and hadn't seen a single one for AA or NA or any other self-help group. It struck him as odd.

He opened the door and the light startled him. He'd expected to find the room dark. The far wall was all windows overlooking the cemetery and the woods beyond. For some reason the sky, the trees, the gravestones and all of the tables and chairs in the room were lit by orange flickering lights like a Hallowe'en horror night.

*Fire*, he thought, navigating the tables toward the windows. Watching the flames flicker on the glass brought back memories of the blaze that nearly burned his house to the ground. He felt an overwhelming urge to flee in terror, yet he couldn't turn away.

"Sheila! Come in here! Quick!"

She didn't reply. Probably couldn't hear him over the siren.

As he reached the glass, he heard the low, primordial roar of the fire itself.

The window was warm when he pressed his palms against it

to get a look at the blaze. Black smoke swirled into view on the wind, curling around the headstones like mist.

*It's close. And whatever it is, it's big.*

Aside from Sinjin's grocery store the church stood pretty much alone on Cavan Street. The only other building was the rectory. He'd seen it during the funeral, a cute little backsplit bungalow with a neatly manicured lawn and gardens. Both had been yellow-brown from the season.

The reverend would be asleep inside.

"Sheila!"

No reply. He thought about her dream, wondering if she was on the pill. They hadn't discussed it. He hadn't had the courage to bring it up and she didn't seem eager to discuss it after they left the stones. Sooner or later he supposed they would have to talk about it. If it became a much bigger problem, difficult to ignore.

*Maybe we'll die first if we're lucky*, he thought sardonically. *Then we won't have to.*

He returned to the main corridor. The bathroom door was closed, a bar of light under it. "Sheila, are you in there?"

"I'll be right out," she said, hoping he wouldn't notice the thick quality to her voice. She was sitting on the lid of the toilet with her face in her hands. Tears burned her eyes. The bad dream had shaken her more than she'd expected and the dam burst as soon as she closed herself into the washroom, faced with the toilet, reminding her of that afternoon at Geraldine's house.

"I think the rectory's on fire," he shouted from behind the door.

*"What?"*

"Reverend Atkins's house. I think it's on fire. Are you dressed?"

She was still in her bra and underwear. "No," she said, standing up and crossing to the sink. "I'll be quick."

"Okay." He sounded uncertain. "I'll wait for you in the pews."

She quickly splashed water on her face, tore a few sheets of paper towel out of the dispenser and dabbed herself dry.

When she opened the door, Martin was gone. The siren wailed eerily in the dark, empty hall. She hurried to the office, gathered her pants, sweater and shoes, stepped into her slightly damp, torn pants and put on her sweater as she headed out to meet Martin out in the nave.

He stood at the pulpit, leaning over it, frowning at the Bible. It lay open on the second Book of Kings. One of the more peculiar passages, concerning the Siege of Samaria, had been underlined:

**28** *Then the king asked her, "What is the matter?" And she answered, "This woman said to me, 'Give up your son, that we may eat him, and tomorrow we will eat my son.'"* **29** *So we boiled my son and ate him, and the next day I said to her, "Give up your son, and we will eat him." But she has hidden her son.*

Sheila knelt to tie her shoes. "What's wrong?"

"You really should come read this."

She stood, her shoes tied. "Martin, we have to go."

Reluctantly, he stepped away from the pulpit and met her in the aisle, wondering if the reverend had inadvertently left the bible open to the part about cannibalism, specifically about mothers savaging their own sons—or if he knew much more than he'd let on.

Whatever the reason, nothing about this felt right. He stopped mere feet from the doors, grabbing Sheila by the shoulder. She turned with a frown.

"I don't think this fire is accidental," he said.

"You think someone set it?"

"What if it was Mavis and the others? What if this is a trap?"

She considered it, her eyes narrowing. "We can't stay here, Martin. Even if the fire doesn't hit the church, Reverend Atkins might still be *alive* in there."

"Then we have to hope he's made his peace for whatever part he played in this."

"I'm going out there—"

"Sheila—"

"Martin, I know you're scared. I'm scared out of my mind. But we can't hide here forever, living off communion wafers and sacramental wine. We have to leave this place, leave *this island*—and if it's not on a boat, I'll fucking swim."

She turned and drew open the door.

The siren howled in the empty street. Chilly night air blew in, swirling with heat from the fire like warm spots in a cold lake. She stepped out, mounting the steps to the walkway, and turned to look at the blaze. Her eyes widened, caught in its flickering glow.

"Martin—?"

"What?"

He stepped out and saw what she had. There were no fire trucks, no emergency vehicles of any kind. Only dozens and dozens of people, a hundred or more, standing in the street in their pajamas and boots and winter jackets. Closer to the blaze, some of them had removed their heavy wraps and held them. They watched the rectory burn with wonder in their eyes, as if it was no more dangerous or sinister than the Harvest Festival fireworks display.

Reverend Atkins knelt on the yellow-brown lawn, dressed a nightgown and cap like Ebenezer Scrooge, hands clasped together in prayer, eyes squeezed shut, face red from the fire or crying or both.

Mavis Lynch and Ethel Kelly stood over him, Mavis in her forest green peacoat, Ethel clutching her cane against the breast of her striped coat. Firelight flashed on the old blind woman's sunglasses as she turned to face the church.

A murmur ran through the crowd. Expressions of wonder evaporated, becoming anger. Rage.

"Well, it looks like the guests of honor have finally arrived," Mavis said, shouting to be heard over the fire, the siren. "Sinjin. Marcus. Please do us the honors."

Sinjin and Marcus stepped out of the crowd. The bigger man wore *Superman* pajamas, his head hung low as if in shame. Marcus wore his fedora even while dressed in flannels and heavy boots.

Martin and Sheila shared a desperate look.

They were caught, with nowhere to run except back into the church. They might be able to hide for a while but sooner or later they'd be captured and Mavis and Ethel would be even more likely to torture them.

As Sinjin and Marcus crossed the church lawn, the charred roof of the rectory collapsed on the second floor. The fire blossomed, brightening the faces in the crowd. Martin and Sheila picked out people they'd eaten and laughed with at Sinjin's clambake: "Double-D" Darla and Dianne, the husky redheaded boy Sinjin suggested should try out for the football team, Pauline, who wore too much makeup and worked cash at the grocery store, the little curly-haired blonde girl, wearing a pink winter coat with fairy wings below the hood.

Not a single face turned to look as the blaze swelled. They were intent on the interlopers. Their prey.

Reverend Atkins wept plaintively as his house burned to the ground.

"I'm real sorry, Marty," Sinjin said, rising the steps.

Martin jerked away as Sinjin reached for his arm. Marcus grabbed Sheila by the shoulders. She struggled. He was stronger, held her firmly in place.

She chopped his forearms—a move she learned in a self-defense class—and simultaneously brought a knee up into his groin.

Marcus doubled over, grasping his balls, the breath knocked out of him.

Sheila ran, dashing down the stairs and darting across the lawn, away from the maddened crowd.

"You bitch!" Marcus groaned.

Martin hauled back and punched Sinjin in the jaw. The blow felt weak even before it connected, like punching someone in a dream.

The big man shook his head, clenched his teeth and struck Martin in the temple so hard stars filled his vision. He staggered back against the door, struggling to remain conscious.

"Why are you helping them?" he said when his vision cleared. "They killed your daughter!"

Sinjin rubbed his fist. "This is the best little island in the world, Marty. And we mean to keep it that way, whatever it takes."

Out on the lawn, Double-D and a man from the crowd had cornered Sheila. She scurried back and forth between them like a pinball in a machine, but she was outnumbered and out-matched and it looked like she knew it.

"Stop this nonsense!"

Everyone froze, turning toward the rectory lawn. The reverend stood shakily. His nightgown was soiled where his knees had ground into the damp lawn. Mavis watched him with a sly grin.

The sirens stopped suddenly, as if responding to his plea. A queer hush fell over the crowd.

"Can't you see what we've become? What would God think of us if He looked down upon our community now? My children, this is *insanity*!"

For a moment the words seemed to connect. People in the crowd blinked and looked around at each other as if waking from a dream.

Then a man shouted, "We're not your children!" Several people agreed to this, their heads bobbing up and down. "We belong to the Mother!"

"That's right," Mavis said, smiling beatifically. "And Mother says it's time for Martin and his whore to leave this place, whether they like it or not. It may once have been his home, but he no longer belongs here."

"Then let us go!" Sheila cried, caught between Darla and her husband in matching plaid pajamas. "We tried to leave, but you won't let us. First the ferry crash, then the boat rental and now this. We just want to go home!"

"The woman fibs!" Ethel said. "All she does is talk and talk, running that smart mouth of hers. If not for her meddling, the little St. John girl would be alive today."

"That's bullshit and you know it! That girl was alive. I heard her cry!"

"You did not!"

Sheila recognized the voice. The crowd parted again and Laura St. John emerged, her rosy cheeks wet with tears. Standing beside Martin, holding him put, Sinjin found something interesting to look at on the step between his boots.

"Ethel's telling the truth," Laura said, surveying the faces in the crowd. "She wouldn't stop interfering. If she'd just shut up and let them *work*—"

"Laura, don't do this—*please*."

"No! You're gonna shut up and listen now! If not for you, my baby would be alive! You—you distracted them! They could have saved her life!"

Before Sheila could argue Darla and her husband grabbed

her arms. She stopped struggling. Even if she could fight them both off, the crowd would tear her apart.

There was no way out.

"People, please!" the reverend cried, hands clasped in supplication. "Don't you see what we've become? 'The first to speak in court sounds right, until the cross-examination begins,' Proverbs, 18:17. Justice of the mob is no justice at all. Only the lord can judge these people. We must let them plead their case!"

Ethel swung out with her cane and struck the reverend's clasped hands so hard the crack echoed despite the roar of the fire.

The reverend fell to his knees with a cry of agony, fingers splayed, dripping fresh blood on gray snow.

"Stuff your proverbs, Padre," Mavis said. She nodded toward Sinjin and Darla. Marcus had gotten to his feet, clutching his testicles and looking ill. "Take them to the cenotaph."

Marcus hobbled along beside Sinjin, shoving Martin down the walkway.

They met Sheila and her captors in the street.

"*You will all be judged!*" the reverend shouted as two men who looked like accountants or lawyers hauled him to his feet again. "God's wrath will spare no one, especially infernal demons like Ruby Savage and her minions!"

The crowd pushed Martin and Sheila forward, herding them toward King Street.

"Martin!"

He looked back over his shoulder. The men held Reverend Atkins in front of his stoop as he struggled. Flame poured out of the front door. Sweat stood out on their foreheads.

"I lied to you before! What Rosalee told me! It wasn't Michael! It was Ruby! *It was Ruby!*"

The men pushed him into the burning house.

The flames swallowed the reverend whole. His screams carried in the night, rising in ecstatic agony. Then they stopped altogether.

As the people of Barrows Bay thrust Martin and Sheila toward downtown, shouting and laughing, the two of them shared a look of despair, knowing they had finally reached the end.

# Chapter 22

## Judgment from Above

THE CROWD DRAGGED them to the monuments of the *Ruby* victims overlooking downtown. They tied Martin to the emaciated man and Sheila to the woman, both statues taller than them by at least a foot. The bronze child clutching the father's leg appeared to look up at Martin beseechingly.

"Did they hurt you?" Sheila asked. She was out of breath from struggling. They both were.

"I'm okay," he said.

His breath caught as Sinjin cinched the knot tightly around his chest. His vision had cleared from the punch but it felt like it was going to be a goose egg on his temple in the morning.

If they survived the night, which didn't look likely.

"I'm sorry I got you involved in all this."

"How could you know about this, Martin? You were just a kid. And Barclay had just as much reason to come after me as you. If you hadn't been involved, he would have come for me right away instead of playing cat and mouse."

"I can't help but feel we'd have been better off if we'd stood our ground," he said.

She looked out over the angry faces in the crowd. "Something tells me we're not going to get a fair trial here."

Ethel tapped her cane three times on the ground beneath her feet. A reverent hush fell over the crowd.

"In olden times, people were prosecuted for practicing witchcraft," the old woman proclaimed. "During the so-called Salem Witch Trials, thirteen women and seven men were found guilty and executed."

"*Do it!*" a man cried.

"*Kill the bastards!*" a woman shouted.

Sheila thought she recognized the boisterous voice as one of the women from the St. Johns's house the night the baby was murdered. Rather than anger her, she felt sad. The *Chadrach* had held these poor people hostage for generations. She wondered what might have become of them if not for their evil influence, if not for their charms and glammers.

"Now, now," Ethel said calmly. "The good reverend was right about one thing. We mustn't punish them without first hearing their confession."

"There's nothing to confess!" Sheila cried. "If anyone should be confessing it's you two!"

The crowd booed. A crushed beer can hit her in the chest and clattered at her feet.

"Settle down now, people," Mavis said. "You'll have plenty of time to throw things after they've confessed!" Her eyes gleamed as a smile crossed her lips. "Perhaps we'll make this an old-fashioned stoning!"

The crowd cheered. They were agitated. Eyes wild. Fists clenched. Dangerously close to frenzy. The atmosphere was electric, like the air before a storm. Martin felt like all it would take to get the crowd to beat them both to death with anything close at hand was a single word from Ethel or Mavis.

"What exactly are we being accused of?" he asked, directing the question at the Midwives but projecting his voice the way he would at a book signing, so everyone in the crowd could hear.

The streetlamp above them glinted on Ethel's sunglasses as she turned. "*Murder,*" she said.

"Murder?" Sheila jerked against the ropes pinning her to the statue. "I didn't kill that girl! You did!"

"So you say," Mavis said. "Sadly, any proof is buried in the old church yard."

"Then dig her up! If you can prove it, let's see her remains."

"And desecrate a child's grave? Surely you can't be suggesting that!"

The crowd erupted with boos and murmurs of discontent. The old woman was playing it up for them.

"Then you've got no proof, just accusations," Martin said.

"Oh, but we do have proof of murder. *Premeditated*, in fact. Martin practically confessed to it in his book, isn't that right, Mavis?"

Mavis nodded with a devious smile.

"You've gotta be kidding me! Damiani would have killed me if I didn't get him first. I thought he could lead me to the killer, I didn't *know* he was the Mirror Man. You think I went there on a vigilante mission? He was a lead, that's all. I could have *died*."

"So you told the police," Ethel said. "But your thoughts tell a different tale."

Sheila was watching him, questioning him with her eyes.

"It's not true."

"Isn't it?" Ethel said.

Was there a part of him that wished it was true? A part that wanted to play the hero, who suspected Damiani was the Mirror Man and wanted the killer to reveal himself so he could justify the murder as self-defense?

"Even if it is, you can't prove it."

"You wouldn't think so, would you?" The blind woman approached him, holding her cane at her sternum. "But I *can*."

She rose on her tiptoes, bringing her nose close to his ear. He tried to shy away but Sinjin held his head. The old woman breathed in deeply through her nostrils. He smelled baby powder, Ivory soap—and lurking beneath it all a sickly-sweet mustiness, like an old corpse.

Pain throbbed in the center of his brain, like a loud buzz heard through earphones. The old woman was searching his thoughts. The pain blossomed. He struggled against Sinjin's grip but found he couldn't move an inch.

"Oh yes, I see you've got *plenty* to confess, dear boy," she said. Her breath stank of rot, hot in his ear. "So much guilt, it's practically eating you ali—"

A sudden crack shattered the quiet.

For a split-second, he thought the sound had come from inside his own head, that the old woman had broken his mind.

With the echo still ringing, Ethel's head obliterated, instantly severing the connection between their minds. The pain diminished. Blood and bone spattered his face.

Sinjin let go of his head, allowing him to turn away in horror.

The cane fell from Ethel's splayed fingers and clattered on the concrete pedestal. And somehow Ethel still stood, her body wavering, gore and chunks of brain dripping down the front of her shawl. The top of her head looked like a hollowed-out pumpkin. Her sunglasses hung from what was left of her nose, the lenses shattered.

The crowd all looked up at once and blinked in confusion, like people roused from their cell phones. The anger in their eyes evaporated. A woman screamed, causing a chain reaction of shock to ripple through them.

Mavis grabbed Ethel's lifeless body the moment gravity started to take hold and hugged her, blood smearing black on her forest-green peacoat. Her hat was coated with it. She resettled it on her head with a whimper of sorrow as she cradled her dead sister in her arms.

Another thunderous crack got the crowd running in all directions, ducking for cover, screaming, pushing each other. Diving behind parked cars and bolting down the sidewalks.

Sparks erupted from the statue of the little girl. The bronze gonged like a bell.

The bullet was closer that time. Close enough for Martin to feel the wind of it, for bits of shrapnel to pepper his lower legs.

He looked up to where he thought he'd heard the shot. A glint of light flashed on the bookstore roof. Not a muzzle flash but a brief reflection, likely from a scope. Two shadows lay huddled against the eaves.

Mavis caught his gaze and followed it. She blinked away tears and scowled at the shooter.

Ethel groaned softly. Her lips moved, as if she was trying to speak. A delicate bubble of blood formed between them and popped.

With her brains blown half out of her head and her eyes somewhere on the surrounding pavement, her mind was still alive. If any doubt lingered as to her supernatural origin, it was gone now.

Mavis leaned over her living corpse to listen.

Another blast cut through the night. The muzzle flash brightened the roof for a split second, making the shooter's partner visible. From the distance Martin still couldn't make out if it was a man or a woman.

The bullet struck Mavis's hat, launching it clean off her head, revealing the sparse white hair and pink scar tissue on her scalp.

Whoever it was had no intention of shooting either Sheila or Martin. They were after the Midwives. If Mavis hadn't lowered her head to listen to her friend, her brains would have painted the courtyard along with Ethel's.

She laid Ethel on the pedestal and stood. Stooped to pick up her hat, placing it on her head as she strode into the street.

"Big man with a gun!" she cried. Her voice was clear. Her stride straight and resolute. "Why don't you come down here and show us all how big you really—"

A bullet answered her taunt. It struck Mavis in the chest and exited through the back of her coat in a red spray.

The impact doubled her over. She spat a wad of blood between her patent leather shoes. Then she straightened, looking directly up at the shooter. Her gaze fierce. Her gait weaving slightly as she continued toward the bookstore, shouting despite the evident pain.

"Is that all you've got, Big Man? How brave, hiding behind a gun to put an old woman down like a dog in the street. How virile you must be—"

The next shot tore out her throat.

She spun on her heels, staggered two steps toward the monument, then dropped to her knees.

Her gaze fell on Sheila, then Martin. A gout of arterial blood splashed down the front of her coat. Her mouth opened as if she were about to speak.

Then she slumped forward. Her nose smashed against the asphalt, opening like an overripe fruit, but she was already dead.

Ten seconds of tense silence lapsed.

Then, a familiar voice.

"You still tickin' down there, Marty?"

Martin and Sheila turned to each other, both of them recognizing the twang of Barclay's voice from the rooftop.

"We're alive," Martin called back. "I'm guessing not for long."

"Well, that all depends."

The shooter and scout got to their feet, silhouettes against the moonlit sky.

A flicker of yellow light illuminated them. Impossible to tell who was who from the distance and low light, but the shooter appeared to be a woman. She brought the flame to her face for a moment, then let it die. The subsequent red glow indicated she'd been lighting a cigarette.

"Depends on what?" Sheila shouted.

"On if you can get us inside the lion's den without getting' all four of us kilt," Clarabelle Leigh said, the cherry on her cigarette bobbing as she spoke.

Before they could ask the woman what she meant the two shadows retreated.

In a few minutes or less they would be face to face with the man who'd murdered three or more innocent women and their unborn children without remorse or pity, who'd terrorized them and run them to ground for his own petty amusement.

Martin squinted out at the empty street—the perfect setting for a showdown. Most of the crowd had returned to their homes, likely as confused as they were frightened. He wondered what they would take away from tonight. If any of what was said or what happened here would be remembered in the morning.

"So this is it, huh?" Sheila said, only loud enough for Martin to hear.

"I guess it is."

"What do you think she meant by 'lion's den'?"

"They mean my house. They plan to kill Ruby. And I don't know if we should try to stop them."

Sheila looked out at the street as the rooftop shooter and the serial murderer stepped out of the alley. Clarabelle held a high-powered rifle, shuffling on the leg where her dog had bit her. Barclay held a bowie knife, glinting under the street-lamps, moseying toward them like a cowboy in an old Western.

"I don't know either," Sheila said, watching their provisional saviors. "But I don't think they'll give us much of a choice."

BARCLAY GAVE Mavis's prone body a solid kick in the ribs with his pointy-toed cowboy boot. The old woman moved easily and made no sound when her face hit the ground again with a solid smack.

"Always kinda figured they'd turn to dust," Clarabelle said, the cigarette bobbing between her lips. "Somethin like that anyway."

"If it'll make you feel better, sweetcheeks, we can come on back here when all's said and done and set these old bitches ablaze."

She nodded, still looking at Mavis's corpse. "I'd like that. Which one was it you said got in my head?" She directed the question to Sheila.

"It was Ethel. I recognized her voice."

"Makes sense," Clarabelle said, eying the woman whose head she'd nearly blown clean off. "Old bat's always had a keen eye even though she was blind as a... well, a bat."

She strode up to the old woman's body. Hocked up a good loogie and spat it right on Ethel's chest.

"Feel better, snookums?" Barclay said, grinning from ear to ear.

"Uh-uh. Not until we've roasted every last one of them evil bitches."

"Reckon so." Barclay leaped onto the pedestal beside Martin, regarding him on his haunches. "So here we are at last, huh, Marty?"

As he got to his feet he raised the knife, twirling it between his fingers, bringing the edge of the blade perilously close to Martin's face. Martin wouldn't give him the satisfaction of cringing. He didn't even flinch. After everything they'd been through today, Barclay's taunts seemed feeble.

"Found yourself caught in a pit of vipers here, did ya? Well, that's okay. I reckon we could put this grudge of ours on layaway for a minute."

"That's real gracious of you, Barclay."

"Hey, we're all friends here. Call me Jimmy. Ol' Gimme Jimmy's come to the rescue. Ain't that fuckin ironic?"

"Then cut me free or put me out of my misery. Your breath is killing me."

"Aw, it ain't that bad." The killer threw a look over his shoulder. "Is it, Clara?"

Clarabelle shrugged. She dropped her cigarette and crushed it into the asphalt.

"You an' me is gon' be friends for a while, Marty." Barclay grinned as he worked at the ropes behind Martin's back with the knife. "I'm not an unreasonable man. And I b'lieve you come to realize there are things in this world an ordinary man might attempt, rather feebly, to rationalize. Things like these old broads. Clarabelle tells me they got the whole town under a spell, ain't that right, sugarbush?"

Clarabelle grunted noncommittally.

"Some kind of supernatural phenomenon I have yet to ascertain. Looked to me like she was right, judging by the way those folks scattered once the spell lifted. What do you think about that, Marty?"

The rope snapped and Martin shook his arms loose, numb from the elbows down. "I think you got lucky. You can rationalize what you did to those girls, to Letitia May. To Qurban. You can call it your purpose or a mission from God. But the truth is, you *enjoy* killing. Whether you were born a killer or you grew into the role, I can't say. But you're a coldblooded murderer now, Barclay. That's all you'll ever be."

Barclay stood in silence a moment, while Clarabelle and Sheila watched him, awaiting his retort. Then he chuckled. "I guess it takes one to know one, huh, Killer?"

Martin drew back a fist but stopped when Barclay pointed the tip of the blade at his solar plexus.

"Come on, now, Marty! Let's put this feud of ours behind us. We have a common enemy, the four of us. Don't you just love those scenes in the movies when the good guy and the bad guy team up to take down an even bigger bad guy? Or lady, as the case may be?"

Clarabelle grunted or chuckled, Martin couldn't tell which.

"Okay, Doc's turn." Barclay took two steps toward Sheila. She leaned back as far as she could, trying to get away from him.

"*Stop*," Martin said. "Why don't you let me do that?"

Barclay grinned back at him. "You want me to just hand over my knife?"

"*My* knife," Clarabelle said.

The killer's face flashed with annoyance, then sweetened. "Excuse me. You want me to hand over this lovely lady's knife? So you can stab me with it, like you did to the Mirror Mask guy."

"She doesn't trust you. You've got a bad history with women, in case you've forgotten. Especially women close to me."

"Aw." Barclay pooched out his lower lip. "I ain't hurt a hair on Clarabelle's head, have I, hotlips?"

The woman shrugged, studying the long, sleek barrel of the gun. "Not without consent."

Barclay flashed a grin at Martin. "You see there? I ain't gonna hurt your little lady, Marty. Don't you worry that perty li'l head a yours."

As Barclay reached for the rope looped over her breasts, Sheila spat in his face. The killer grinned, wiped the spit from his face with the back of his hand and licked it like salt before a tequila shot. He smacked his lips and gave her a quizzical look. "You been foolin around with Marty's heart, Doc?"

Sheila stretched her neck as far as the rope would allow, getting right in his face. "Fuck you. You think we'll help you after what you put us through? *You're* the bad guy, Barclay. Not Martin. Not me. You understand that, right? You got that through your thick fucking skull?"

The killer grinned at Martin over his shoulder. "She's a wild mare, this one. Now, may I please cut these ropes for you, my dear, so we can get on with this?"

Sheila slackened against the ropes. Barclay moved around behind the statue and worked at them with the blade. In a moment she was free, rubbing her wrists to get the life back in them.

"Thank you," she said, not to Barclay but to Clarabelle. "I'm sorry we almost killed you back at your house."

Clarabelle shrugged and grunted. "I prolly woulda done the same, to be honest. C'mon." She nodded toward the bookstore. "Truck's in the lot back there."

The four of them walked to the alley between the bookstore and the café next door. As they passed the shrine of Martin's books in the window Barclay peered in and chuckled. "That musta got you all soppy wet, huh, Marty?"

The killer chuckled again and stepped into the dark alley. Martin hesitated. Clarabelle gestured ahead with the rifle, though the move held no threat.

"Go on. I won't let no harm come to ya, not so long as I'm around."

"You know you can't trust him," Sheila said.

A grin spread across Clarabelle's weathered face. "He ain't the first broken man to show me kindness. I can handle m'self, believe me."

Barclay turned back from the opposite end of the alley. "My ears're burnin," he said.

Martin and Sheila decided at the same time and stepped in side by side, followed by Clarabelle with the rifle. Within moments they stood around her beaten, mud-spattered red pickup. She got the keys out, climbed in behind the wheel and opened the passenger door. Barclay climbed in.

"You two okay in the bed?"

Barclay winked. "From what I hear they're more than okay."

Martin pulled down the gate and climbed in. He held out a hand to Sheila. She ignored it, climbing up easily beside him.

The engine rattled to life and Clarabelle pulled out of the lot, raising gravel dust. As they peeled out onto King Street, Barclay slid open the back window. "Clarabelle said you was there when the old broads killed that little girl, that right?"

"Sheila was," Martin said.

"An' you saw 'em kill her?"

"She wasn't dead." Sheila spoke in monotone, clearly not interested in conversating with the murderer. "They told us she was breeched. That she didn't make it. But when they swaddled the baby I heard her cry."

Barclay nodded. "That's witch magic. Some of 'em call it a glamour. A spell or illusion. Makes you see what they want you to see 'stead of what's there."

Clarabelle caught Martin's eye in the rearview mirror, glancing away from the road. "They can read minds," she said. "Force people to do stuff they don't wanna do. Make yous see whatever they want ya to see, and wear your skin like a people suit. But they can't all do everything. Seems like each one got a partic'lar trick they're good at. The blind woman could read minds. Geraldine can see things, make you see em too. The one with the hat and the pink Caddie and all them cats, she was what you might call an influencer." Again, her eyes left the road. "I don't know about th'other one, but your mama—" She shook her head. "—she's the meanest damn one of em all."

"She's not my mother."

"That's right, she ain't. I went to school with your real mama. Girl named Rosalee, friends just called her Rosy. We wasn't friends or anythin, me an' her. She was a year ahead of me. Pop'lar girl. Cheerleader. Always been an outsider, myself. Figure that's why I can see what most other folk from around here can't."

The killer watched her with the smile of a proud father.

"So how do we go up against something like that?" Sheila asked.

"*We* don't," Barclay said. "Not at first. Marty's gotta soften her up." He turned all the way around in his seat. "Clarabelle says the old woman took a shine to ya, must've from the second you popped your li'l head out of that pretty young cheerleader's hooha. That's how come she took you as her own 'stead of carvin you up and eatin ya for Christmas dinner, pass the gravy, God bless us everyone."

Barclay's patter grated on him, but Martin had to admit the story made sense. The Midwives—or the *Chadrach*, the creatures beneath their "people suits"—required a sacrifice. How often, he didn't know. The child provided sustenance, reinvigorated them, renewed their youth.

It explained why his mother had been so strong the morning after the ritual. He hadn't just imagined it. It also explained why Mavis—it could only have been her, the old woman in the hat—tried to burn down the house after Ruby was taken away to Saints of Mercy. Ruby was protecting him, for some reason. Once she was gone, the others could have their long-awaited feast.

*If not for Norma, I'd be dead*, he thought. *Poor, sweet Norma.*

He hoped she wouldn't get caught in the crossfire. He promised himself to do everything he could to get her out of that house in one piece.

"The other two," Sheila said. "Helen and Geraldine. How do we find them?"

"Way I figure," Clarabelle said, "you go after the Mother, the other two'll come runnin. In fact, I wouldn't be surprised if—"

She slammed on the brakes. The truck dovetailed, burning rubber and throwing Martin and Sheila up against the cab.

"Speak of the goddamn devil," she said.

Helen Birch stood in the headlights in the middle of the road, dressed in a tattered blue Snuggie that covered everything but her winter boots. Her heavy-lidded eyes glared at the truck but there was a dulled quality to them, as if she was sleepwalking.

"Mrs. Birch?" Clarabelle leaned out the driver's side window. "Whatcha doin in the road?"

Helen said nothing. Just stood there, grinding her teeth, nestled in her Snuggie.

"Aw, the hell with it."

Clarabelle pounded her foot on the accelerator. The truck swerved and lurched forward.

The old woman made no move to get out of the way. Clarabelle gripped the wheel so tight her knuckles went white, and the grille struck Helen dead on. The old woman didn't make a sound as her bones cracked and her body hurtled over the hood, tearing the passenger side mirror off as the pickup roared away from the scene.

Martin watched the old woman, supine in the middle of the wet street. She made no move to get up. He didn't think she was dead. Stunned, maybe.

"Jesus," Sheila said, mirroring his thoughts as the old woman's body receded in the gloom behind them.

# CHAPTER 23

## HOME IS WHERE THE HURT IS

CLARABELLE LEIGH STOPPED the truck at the corner of Martin's street and turned off the running lights. The big gingerbread Victorian at the end of the road stood with its first-floor windows bright against the dark trees and darker ocean. A sight once warm and inviting, now as sinister as a vampire's castle.

"We'll be keepin an eye on ya, so don't try anything funny," Barclay said. "Ain't that right, snookums?"

Clarabelle picked up the rifle from her lap and chambered a round. The killer grinned.

"Ya'll stick to the plan, hear? Get her in a window, unobstructed. Clarabelle'll take it from there."

Martin started up the sidewalk, Sheila at his side. The thought of the rifle scope at his back caused the hair on the nape of his neck to prickle. He wasn't sure if Clarabelle would shoot him if he screwed up but he couldn't take the risk.

Fortunately, the killer himself only appeared to be armed with the knife. And there were plenty of sharp things in the kitchen. Knives. Scissors.

*Ruby's scissors,* he thought. He hadn't thought of them in years, the silver shears she'd kept hidden in her sewing chest, tucked in amongst the bobbins and buttons and twists of multicolored thread. The ones she told him he mustn't ever touch.

"He won't let us live, you know," Sheila said.

"You don't say."

"So what are we gonna do? Serve up your mother on a platter?"

"She's not my mother."

They passed the bungalow where they'd seen the family playing board games on their first day in town, such a peculiar sight it stuck with him after all they'd been through since. The lights were out. Everyone asleep. Dreaming suburban middle-class dreams.

"Why couldn't I have had a normal family? Was that too much to ask?"

"Nobody has a normal family, Martin. It's a fantasy. Make-believe. And Ruby was a mother to you, once. She protected you from the other Midwives."

"Then she abandoned me. They almost burned the house down. I could have *died*."

"While Ruby was committed in a mental hospital."

"Right. You think trying to kill yourself isn't as bad as abandonment? Two hundred years old and suddenly she's a fucking emo kid with a death wish?"

"We can't possibly know what she was going through." Sheila gave him a sidelong look as they approached the house. "She must have felt guilty for what she'd been doing all those years."

"You're sympathizing with her? *They ate children*."

"Animals eat children in the wild. I'm not saying I condone it but context matters, Martin."

"*Context*," he sputtered.

They stopped at the foot of the walkway and looked back the way they'd come. The truck was still parked on the corner, the cab empty. Barclay and Clarabelle must have gone to find a better vantage point.

It was a little past six am and the sun was just beginning to appear above the trees, giving the street an eerie golden glow. Magic hour. Literally, if they weren't careful.

He wondered how many of their neighbors had been at the big show on King Street. It hadn't been the whole town. Couldn't have been. He'd only recognized a few of the faces among the crowd, mostly from the funeral and Sinjin's party.

That said, he didn't exactly know who any of his neighbors were, not anymore. And judging by what they'd just been through, he likely never had.

Nothing he remembered of his childhood home was the same. It had all been lies. Corpse worms festering just below the cheerful façade.

He looked up at the house again, remembering the day they first arrived. How ready he'd been to tell Sheila to turn the car around and drive them to the closest airport. Leave the country on the first flight to anywhere. He wished now that he had. A moment of cowardice could have saved both of their lives. Or at least postponed the inevitable.

No use speculating on what might have been. They had business to take care of now. There was no turning back. Ruby and the Midwives had to be dealt with, no matter what might happen to the two of them. Still, he wasn't sure he had the strength to go through with it. Despite her appearance of frailty, he was just as frightened of Ruby now as he'd ever been as a boy—more so, now that he knew what she was, and what she was truly capable of.

It was time to put an end to all the hurt and confusion and terror of the past. Ruby Savage would make amends for everything she'd done, or suffer the consequences.

He started up the path. Sheila took his cue, walking a few paces behind him.

As they drew near, Norma appeared in the kitchen window. She looked harried, moving around busily in her apron, likely making breakfast. Smoke or steam rose from the sink or the stovetop.

"We have to get Aunt Norma out of there," Sheila said.

"We'll figure something out. Signal her somehow, without getting Ruby's hackles up. It's not like they'll be able to hear us from outside."

Sheila nodded.

He opened the door.

The smell of frying bacon made his mouth water. He hadn't realized how hungry he was until just now. He'd just about kill for one of Norma's bacon and egg sandwiches, the bread fried in bacon fat, runny eggs with crispy edges and two slices of American cheese oozing down the crust.

Maybe Barclay would afford them the mercy of a last meal.

Sheila followed him into the kitchen, both of them moving cautiously, peering into empty rooms and darkened corners—as much for Barclay as Ruby.

Norma stood hunched over the sink when they entered, scouring something. She looked up and jumped at the sight of them. The pot clattered in the basin.

"Oh! You scared the bejesus out of me!" She looked them over. "What the H-E-double-hockey-sticks have you two been up to? We've been worried sick!"

"Is Ma upstairs?"

It felt off calling Ruby "Ma" with all they knew. But anything else would raise Norma's hackles. Better to keep up the pretense, for all of their sakes.

Though, considering what Barclay had in mind, maybe not for Ruby's.

"She's upstairs, dead to the world."

Norma stepped away from the sink. Martin took her by the shoulders and tried to guide her into a chair, away from the front window, out of sight from Clarabelle's rifle.

"Have a seat, you look tired."

Norma scowled at him. Her tears came suddenly, as if she'd been trying to hold them back. He couldn't remember the last time he'd seen her cry. Might have been the day they took Ruby away. It made him sad just to see it.

"Hey," he said, laying a hand on her shoulder. "What's going on? Are you okay?"

"I just wish I'd done better by you is all," she said.

"What? Aunt Norma, are you nuts? Come on, sit." She let him direct her to into a chair. "You did right by me. You did everything you could."

She shook her head, let out a pained sob as tears rolled down her cheeks. "I promised Ruby I'd protect you."

"And you did."

"No. You wouldn't be back here if I did. I should have told you, should've told you everything."

"Norma, it's okay." He hugged her around the shoulders. She leaned into him, her breath hitching.

Sheila pouted at him from the doorway and he suddenly had to hold back from breaking up himself.

"You know, when people ask about where I grew up, ask me about Ruby, I always say you're the one who raised me, you know that, right?"

She nodded softly against his chest. "But I should have *protected* you—"

"You didn't know—"

"I *knew*. I knew this place wasn't safe for you. Never was, especially not since that day—"

"Hey, we don't need to talk about this now, Aunt Norma."

"—the day Ruby left. And when you didn't show up by midnight your mother said you'd gone back to the city. Given us your typical Irish goodbye. But I thought for sure *They* got to you." She looked up at him, her eyes big and wet with fear. "They did, didn't they? That's why the two of you look so scared?"

He shared a look with Sheila, not sure how much he should reveal, how much Norma knew. "Nobody got to us, Aunt Norma, we just..." He didn't know where to begin, so he decided not to try. "We got in a little car accident. Spent the night at the mechanic's. I should have called."

"Okay." She sniffled. Took a tissue out of the apron pocket and gave her nose a good honk. "Well, I'm just glad you're alive. Help yourself to breakfast. I hoped I'd see you by noon if at all, heat it up in the mike for ya."

"Breakfast sounds great, Norma. I'll get Ma."

"Let her sleep. She needs her beauty rest."

"It's our last meal together. I'd really like her to join us. She can go back to bed once we're gone."

Norma untied her apron and slapped it on the table with a heavy sigh. "Well, I suppose it's for the best, even though I'll miss you like crazy."

"You could come visit us in the city sometime," Sheila suggested.

Norma sputtered, already back to her old self. "Not flippin likely."

Martin smiled. "I'll get Ma."

He gave Sheila a serious look and left the kitchen. He didn't realize his error until he reached the stairs. *Should have gotten a knife—if not for Barclay than for her.*

The steps creaked as he ascended. What would he say to

her? How would he explain their absence? Or did she already know everything? How much of the thoughts and powers did she share with the others?

Supposing she really was the first, as the vision at the stones seemed to recount, was she also the strongest? Or had her powers faded over time, with age and infirmity? Had her days spent in an aging human body withering away at the hospital dulled her powers, her extrasensory perception?

*Only one way to find out*, he thought. He knocked on her bedroom door.

"Ma? You awake?"

"I am now," she said, annoyed.

How easy it was to fall back into the old ways. *Ma this* and *Ma that*, like she'd said when she first saw him after twenty-something years apart. Back into the old pattern of hook and jab, as if the time spent away from each other had been days rather than years.

"Breakfast is ready. Sheila and I—we're leaving today."

"So I've heard."

"You heard?"

"I heard every word you said through the vent. I hear every-thing in this house, Martin."

He wondered how to process that. Was it a veiled threat? Had she heard something she shouldn't have?

"You want me to help you down the stairs or—?"

"I'll be fine. Let me get dressed and put on my face."

*Put on my face.* Was she taunting him now? Words he'd heard her say dozens of times had taken on sinister new mean-ings. Judging by the mess Clarabelle's rifle had made of Ethel and Mavis, it wasn't just a matter of putting on a mask. There was sinew and muscle and bone under her flesh. Brains and fluid.

Could the creature beneath be harmed at all?

"You don't need makeup, Ma. It's not a formal event, just —" He almost said *family*, and couldn't bring himself to finish the thought. "—just the four of us."

"Well, you never know when someone might pop by unan-nounced."

Again, he wondered: did she know?

She was coming down for breakfast. At least there was that.

"All right, we'll see you downstairs. Don't be long, it'll get cold."

"I'm not a child, Martin. You don't have to goad me."

"Okay, Ma."

He went back down. At the foot of the stairs, a hand shot out of the darkened living room and dragged him inside. He almost cried out but a second rough hand covered his mouth, reeking of cigarettes and Old Spice aftershave. He felt Barclay's hot breath on his neck as the killer whispered hoarsely, "Don't mess around, Marty. Play along and I'll let the other old broad live."

Martin shook his head free. The killer's bowie knife flickered in the dim glow of dawn. "I've got this under control, you didn't have to break in."

"Door was open. Heck, that's practically an invitation."

"Don't fuck this up," Martin said. "I'll get her in front of the window. But if you touch Norma I'll make damn sure to leave a permanent scar when you come for me."

Barclay winked. "I'm countin' on it, Killer."

Martin returned to the foyer. He heard Ruby's door open. When he peered back into the living room the killer had receded into the shadows.

Ruby seated herself in the chair lift and tucked her shillelagh into her lap. It had been years since he'd seen her use the black wood cane rather than her walker. Not since before the White Place, where it would likely have been considered a weapon. He'd always been afraid of the shillelagh, afraid she'd hit him with it, as he'd once seen her strike a mouse dead on the kitchen floor.

He wondered why she chose today to start using it again. Was she really that much healthier?

She pressed the lift button with a quivering hand and began to descend, the motorized whine loud in the otherwise quiet house.

As she reached a beam of early morning sunlight, he saw how much younger she looked than she had when he first returned. Like she'd lost a good twenty years. She didn't need as much makeup and the lines and furrows in her face and neck had softened.

If this was the effect of their ritual, he could see why they did it. He knew at least a few rich Manhattanites who would murder a baby or two if the result was eternal youth.

"Well? Too busy to call, were you? Don't you know you frightened poor Norma just about to death?"

"Sorry, Ma. We got in a little fender-bender. I would have called but—"

"Never you mind. You've been put through the ringer enough, by the look."

The lift stopped at the bottom and Ruby grasped her cane with palsied hands. His immediate feelings were sympathetic. Were the tremors an act? Did she even need the lift anymore? The cane? He thought again of dragging her to her feet and forcing her to stand on her own—but if he was wrong, he wouldn't be able to live with himself if she broke a bone.

Not that either of them had much longer to live, with Barclay in the living room and Clarabelle across the street, aiming her rifle.

"Here, Ma, let me help you with that."

"I've gotten along just fine without you all these years. Woe betide you for implying otherwise." Her fingers were less gnarled, he noticed. The grip firmer. She pushed herself up with a groan, but it seemed habitual, not a response to pain. Like when he bent deep to pick up something from the floor.

He glanced into the darkened living room. Ruby followed his gaze.

"Looking for something?"

"Just making sure I don't forget to pack anything."

She squinted into the dimness. From the angle, Barclay wasn't visible to either of them. She seemed not to see anything and turned away brusquely.

"Heaven forbid you had to come back for something. Norma would pitch a fit."

She shuffled toward the kitchen, lifting and lowering the cane with heavy thuds and taking tiny steps alongside it, her slippers swishing on the hardwood. He followed her. If she was faking it, she was doing a damn good job. Anyone who didn't know her as well as he did would have been fooled.

"Morning, Ruby," Sheila said, smiling cheerfully.

Norma rose in her chair. Sheila laid a hand on her shoulder.

"Sit," she said. "You've been on your feet all morning. It's about time we serve you for a change."

Norma didn't put up a fight. She smiled to herself as Sheila went to the cupboard and got some plates. Martin pulled a chair out for Ruby, one at the head of the table, in direct view of the window.

"I'll sit in my regular seat, thank you." Ruby set the cane aside and dragged a chair out. Eased herself into it, making a good show of quivering each one of her limbs and grunting as she eased her bony rump onto the frilly, flower-printed cushion.

Martin glanced at the window. It was difficult to tell if Ruby was visible from wherever Clarabelle had situated herself. Unless the woman was on the front porch of the house across the street, he doubted it.

"Wouldn't you rather sit in the sun, Ma?"

"It's six in the morning. If I was concerned about sunlight I'd have stayed in bed."

He sighed and helped Sheila with plating the food. "You want yours zipped, Ma?"

"I've put my teeth in. I'll avoid the mush today, thank you."

They brought the food over and everyone tucked in. For several minutes the only sounds were knives scraping on crisp toast, cutlery clinking on plates and Ruby's noisy chewing.

Sheila and Martin ate uneasily, aware this would be their last meal. The food didn't have much taste anyhow. Grease and salt and runny egg the texture of snot. It was all Martin could do to hold it down, and Sheila looked queasy herself.

He glanced again into the dark foyer over his mother's shoulder. Shot another fretful glance out the window.

"Are you expecting someone?" Ruby said, gobs of chewed toast on her tea-stained teeth that didn't look like her too-white dentures. "You keep looking out the window as if you're awaiting a package."

He was caught unaware. The lie sounded like it. "Oh, uh, the mechanic said he'd tow the car over once he was done with it. Kinda need it if we're gonna get moving."

"Quite eager to leave Norma and I in the dust, are you?"

He shrugged. "It's a long drive, Ma."

"If they even get a replacement ferry running," Norma said,

sopping up yolk with her toast. "You might be stuck here another day or two, depending."

Sheila gave him a fretful glance.

"Well, I guess we'll have to see."

Ruby watched the exchange with a glint of mischief in her eye, her lips pursed.

*She knows we're lying. She's just waiting for one of us to slip up and say something stupid. Does she know everything, though? Does she know about Barclay and rifle?*

A horrible thought came on the heels of this, so sudden it made him drop his fork.

Growing up, he'd always thought his mother had eyes on the back of her head. She seemed to have a preternatural sense of when he was getting into trouble with his friends, when he was tracking dirt into the house or trying to sneak cookies from the jar on the highest shelf of the cupboard, or an extra sliver of strawberry-rhubarb pie from the pan.

He'd assumed all mothers had such powers, as most children did. Everyone thought their mother was always one step ahead of them. But after what Ethel had done at the memorial he wondered, *What if she really can read my mind?*

"Sorry," he said, bending to pick up the fork.

The crack of rifle fire came the instant his head dropped below the table.

The window shattered inward. He rose too quickly, certain Ruby was dead, and banged his head on the underside of the table. Stars shot across his vision.

"What the heck?" Norma gasped, scooting back in her chair.

Sheila dropped beside the counter. Ruby was moving toward the window, almost gliding, her gaze flitting from the shards of glass on the floor to the singed hole in the fluttering terrier-print curtain.

"Ma, you really should—"

"*We've got your woman!*" The gruff elderly woman's voice carried in the early morning. "*Come outside so we can settle this face to face!*"

Norma scowled. "Is that Helen?"

"It *is* Helen." A sly smile spread across Ruby's face. "And who, I wonder, is she addressing? A friend of yours, Martin?"

She turned back from the window, catching him in her gaze

like a trap catching a wolf. He felt her working in his mind the way Ethel had earlier but the ache this time was swift and sharp. The confession spilled out of him: "James Barclay is in the house. The killer who was hunting us. They're planning to kill you."

Her fixed smile widened. "There. That wasn't so hard to admit, was it?"

He shook his head, fighting a strange urge to cry, like a little kid confessing to stealing from the church collection plate or calling her a swear behind her back.

The sound of bootheels on tile alerted them. Barclay stepped out of the shadows, twirling the knife in his hand. "I guess now the beans are spilled, no use me hidin."

"Ah," Ruby said, her smile so wide now her yellow teeth showed. "You must be the Witch Killer. 'Tis a pleasure to finally meet you."

"Witch *Hunter*, I b'lieve they call me. And I must say, I am pleased to meet you, Mrs. Savage." He pointed with the knife. "You're the genuine article. I could smell it the second I stepped inside this den of yours."

"*Miss*," Ruby said irritably. "And I could smell *you*, Mr. Barclay. Your woman across the street, too. Cigarettes and gun oil and hurried sex under the three-quarter moon. Don't you dare think for a moment I don't know what you did to my kin. Their blood is on your hands—isn't it, Jimmy?"

Barclay flinched.

"Ol' Gimme Jimmy," she said, smiling again. "That's what they called you, isn't it? Your old crew? The boys?" She crossed the room slowly as she spoke. Not a hint of infirmity anymore, the pretense entirely dropped. "Or so you like to tell yourself. The truth is quite sad. Pathetic, even. The other boys hated you. They *picked* on you. Beat you up and called you names. Gimme Jimmy Never Gets. Jimbecile. Jimmy the Fairy."

Barclay shook his head. "No, that ain't true. I was the king of that school."

"You were the king of *squat*. The girls picked on you, too, didn't they? Their words stung more than the boys and their fists. Ugly Jimmy. Always *staring*. Pervert. *Creep*. The ugly little boy who eats worms for attention."

He jabbed at her with the knife. "*No*."

"But the worst was when Mama beat you. You were filthy. Stupid. A foolish son is a sorrow to his mother. Spare the rod and spoil the child. Isn't that right, Jimmy Joe?"

She was close enough now he could easily cut her if he wanted to. Instead the blade drooped. The killer's hand quivered, as if she'd passed her palsy on to him.

"There, there, child." Ruby held out her arms to him, offering her embrace. "Let Mother take away your pain."

*Take away your pain.*

The phrase triggered Martin's memory. His palm red and angry, the flesh still sizzling where he'd touched the—*scissors*—furnace.

*Let Mother take away your pain*, she'd said, exactly as she did now. Only she hadn't been directing him away from the pain, she'd been pushing him *toward* it, the heat prickling his face, the smell of his own hair singeing in his nose—

Barclay stepped into her embrace, weeping openly, the knife an afterthought. She wrapped her arms around him. Patted his back as tears streamed down his face.

Martin held up his hands, both of them injured because of Ruby: the stigmata he'd borne from living with a monster for a mother.

"You did this to me, Ruby. I remember now."

"Oh boy," Norma said gravely. Hunkered beside her at the foot of the counter, Sheila gave him a puzzled look.

"When they sent you away, it wasn't because you tried to kill yourself. You tried to kill *me*, didn't you?"

The old woman's head flicked toward him but she didn't let go of Barclay, didn't stop whispering in the killer's ear.

Barclay's eyes had closed, still leaking tears. "Mama," he said, his voice weak and wet. Like a weeping child.

"You tried to push me into the furnace. I don't know if you were planning to burn me alive or to cook me to eat—" He remembered it all now. "—but I had your scissors. And I *cut* you with them. There was black smoke, like a snake slithering out of your wrist. And that's when you went crazy. That's when you lost your mind. Or maybe it was when the demon lost its hold on you."

Ruby stopped whispering. He had her full attention now, though she still hadn't turned.

"I heard the both of you screaming from upstairs," Norma said. "I ran down, almost broke my neck on the dang steps, and there was Ruby covered in blood and you with those silver shears in your hands. I had no idea what happened but I knew we couldn't let the police know the truth, whatever it was. And Ruby, you started babbling about your little sister. I never knew you had a sister. Something about a bedwetter, saying he smashed in her brains on a rock."

"Ledbetter," Sheila said. "The captain of the *Ruby*. The ship she traveled from Ireland on with her baby sister."

Ruby finally turned, letting go of Barclay. Glaring at Martin.

The killer blinked his red-rimmed eyes but still appeared to be under her spell.

"The stones told you this, did they?"

"We know everything," Sheila said. "They called you the *Chadrach*, but that's not what you call yourselves. You were the first people, long before the Pilgrims, even before the Manisses tribe settled here. You've been harvesting these people for almost two-hundred years. Eating their children. The ritual nourishes you. It makes you younger and stronger. It makes you *immortal*. And if it really was the children you needed, it might be understandable, from an ecological standpoint. But it's not. You feed on sadness and despair, but what you really crave is *revenge*. Because they killed one of your daughters. And now they've done it again."

"You're *wrong*." The smile returned to Ruby's face. "Ethel and Mavis live. Take a look out the window, if you don't believe me."

Cautiously, they peered through the shattered window.

The other Midwives stood in the street in the warm glow of sunrise. Bruised and bloody, Helen held Clarabelle's unconscious body, the woman's arms slack at her sides. Geraldine held the rifle in her gloved hands. On either side of them, Mavis and Ethel stood as if their wounds weren't still gaping, still oozing fluids, caught in the gray limbo between life and death.

"You see?" Ruby's smile widened. "We are *stronger* than you. We are the *first*."

She reached up and gestured with her finger, dragging it across her throat. Standing opposite her, Barclay mimicked the action, raising the knife. His flesh opened easily from ear to ear. Twin jets of gore spewed from the severed arteries.

Ruby stepped quickly into the spray. Pools of blood poured down her face and into her open mouth. They watched in horror as she tasted it, savored it, licking her lips, her eyes opened in ecstasy.

He remembered the dream that woke him a few hours earlier and wondered if Barclay's blood had a flavor particular to him. If she could taste his memories. His fears.

The killer's eyes sprang open in shock as if the fact of his death just struck him. Then he fell to the floor, the blood spurting from his wounds weaker with each diminished beat of his heart.

Ruby wiped her mouth with the back of her hand. She swiped her hands on the front of her dress, already soaked with the killer's blood, turned primly and sat. Picked up her teacup and saucer and took a generous sip of what was likely more blood than tea.

"There, that little problem's all taken care of," she said. "Spared you doing the bloody deed yourself. Don't you want to thank me, Martin?"

He didn't. He felt cheated, looking down at the lifeless body of the man who'd terrorized him for the past six years. The Witch Hunter's death should have been at his hands. Blood relations or not, the need for revenge ran deep in the Savage family's marrow.

"Now, whatever shall we do with the two of you? You obviously know far too much for us to let you on your merry way. But then, who would believe you?"

"I guess you'll have to kill us. Finally finish what you started."

"I don't want to kill you, Martin. I never wanted to kill you."

"Then explain this." He held up his left hand.

The creature wearing the old woman's body sighed. Nodded tiredly toward the window.

"My daughters, they believe you're bad news. Ethel saw nothing but darkness in our future. The end of the road. They think you will be the cause. I suppose they were right, in a way. I spared you because of your fairy mark, the little red splotch right on the top of your crown. My baby sister had the same birthmark. Poor, sweet Violet. I knew then the time had come to stop with all this bloodshed, all this petty revenge. Where had it gotten us? Perhaps I was being too sentimental. But maybe it's high time to shelve the past. Put it behind us, where it belongs."

She picked up the teacup and saucer again. Looked at its contents, then set them down.

"What if we were to sweep it all neatly under the rug, hmm? Just like Norma would, once she's already cleaned the entire house and discovered another dust bunny under the coffee table."

Norma looked guiltily at her shoes.

"How does that sound? I'll make it so your memories of us and this island and all that has happened to you here just—*poof* —disappears. Would you like that, Sheila? Martin? Norma—we can do it for you too, if you like. Though I'd prefer it if you stayed." She grinned again, showing her ancient, blood-pinked teeth. "A three-for-one special. What do you say to that?"

Martin shook his head. "And the five of you keep bleeding these people dry? No thanks."

"It would seem to me you cared very little for the people of this town, Martin. So little you turned your back and never once spoke of us. Not once in your career. Left us in the dust, so you did. Ancient history. Now you're petitioning for a key to the bleeding city?"

"*Do you need us, Mother?*" Helen called from the street.

"*I'll bloody tell you when I need you, woman!*" Ruby shouted back.

Sheila cringed. Norma covered her ears.

Martin stepped around the table toward her. Done with being afraid. Eager to end this, once and for all. "You killed Nadine Hinckley," he said. "You killed Ruby St. John and Reverend Atkins and God knows who else. You killed *my mother.*"

He slammed his fist on the table, so hard the wound split open and the cutlery jangled. Norma's glass upturned and spilled the last of her milk on the tablecloth.

"*I'm* your mother."

"You're not. You never were. You're a cuckoo bird, stealing other people's children."

"That's not true. I am your mother, Martin. I'm as much your mother as Rosalee Creemore. More so, considering I'm the one who raised you."

"Norma raised me."

*"No more bargaining, Mother!"*

Norma covered her mouth, surprised by the words coming from her lips. The hand dropped back into her lap and her eyes rolled up, the lids fluttering. *"Send out the boy and his whore, or you'll all pay the price."*

"It's Ethel," Sheila said, scooting away from her.

Ruby rose, gripping the edge of the table. "Get out of her, you treacherous witch! Your fetch is not welcome in this house! I most certainly *do not* invite you!"

Norma's eyelids stopped fluttering and her eyes regained their focus. "What just happened, Ruby?"

All of the fire left Ruby's eyes then. Her shoulders sagged and she slumped back into the chair.

"Bugger. I should have known they would turn on me. There won't be much time now, Norma. You must get to the basement. In the furnace, among the ash, you'll find them. Six objects made of silver. I tried to burn them but the filthy beggars wouldn't melt. I'll protect your mind from them, but you must be swift!"

Whether out of fright or distrust, Norma didn't move.

"Haven't I always been good to you, Norma?"

Norma nodded. "You have."

"Then trust me. One last time."

Norma eased herself up from the floor and moved in a crouch across the kitchen, slipping on the pool of blood, then into the foyer.

They heard the basement door latch click. The creak of the hinges. Norma's heavy footsteps thudding down the steps until they were gone.

"Where's Norma?" Helen called. "Ethel can't hear her thoughts!"

"She's fainted dead away!" Ruby called back. "You've done the poor woman's heart in, so you have!"

Out in the street, Helen had lain Clarabelle at her feet. Geraldine held the rifle in both hands, apparently trying to figure it out. She finally managed to pull the bolt and ejected the empty shell casing, chambering the next round.

"Get out of the window, Martin," Ruby said.

Geraldine raised the weapon and aimed down the barrel.

"*Martin*," Ruby hissed.

He ducked just as Geraldine pulled the trigger. The bullet caught the drapes and smashed the china tea kettle on the far counter.

"Send out the boy and his whore now, Mother!" Helen said. "This is your final warning!"

"Or you'll do what? Shoot me?" She uttered a derisive chuckle. "You'll have to do better than that!"

"Ruby," Sheila said. "Please. You have to let us go."

The old woman favored her with a sad smile. "All I ever wanted was a human grandchild of my own. Someone to pass on the family name. Pass on our legacy. All that led you to those stones was my doing. The child within you is as much a part of me as the two of you. Promise me you'll bear this child. Promise an old woman that much, and I'll make certain they don't harm a hair on your heads."

There was no time to discuss it. Norma returned from the basement then, the silverware jingling musically in a pouch she made with her sweater, her hands black with soot.

"I've got almost all of them. Couldn't find the second needle. Must've fallen through the grate. Everyone okay?"

"We're all fine, Norma. And what you've brought will do. You're a loyal friend."

"Thank you, Ruby."

"Bring them to me, but be careful. You mustn't let them see you."

Norma crossed to the table, careful to avoid the window. She dumped the silverware in front of Ruby. They clattered on the table in a cloud of ash. The ancient creature picked up a knitting needle and twisted back and forth in the kitchen light, staring at it in mystical reverie.

"Will you bear this child?" she asked Sheila. "Will you love her as I tried to love her father, in my way?"

"Her?"

"Oh yes." Ruby's smile was wistful. "A girl. She'll grow up strong and spirited, like her mother. Like her grandmother."

Whether she meant herself or Rosalee, Sheila didn't know. But she nodded. She'd already decided the moment she woke from the nightmare, and whether the dream or her hallucination at Geraldine's house had solidified her decision, there was no question now. "I'll keep her," she said.

"Good girl," Ruby said softly. "Now, I want the three of you—wait a tick. Where are my good shears?"

Norma's right hand shot out from behind her back. Before Ruby could react, the scissors plunged to the handles into her chest, and Norma stepped back, a hand to her heart, horrified by what she'd done.

The old woman coughed blood. Shock and pain in her eyes. A rivulet of black smoke escaped her lips.

She snatched out suddenly and grabbed Martin's left hand. Her grip as strong as the day he'd sat at her bedside. The flood of memories she passed to him hit with such force he collapsed into the chair beside her, his teeth coming together painfully—

*—He rises from warm water, gasping his first breath.*

*Faceless shapes surround him. So bright it hurts his eyes. He screams.*

*She takes him. Holds him. Love radiates from Her skin and the beating thing inside Her.*

*Raised voices. Words he doesn't yet know but senses the emotions behind them. Terror. Anger. Jealousy.*

*Sloshing water and hurried footsteps. They're moving into a much bigger place. A place with no above and no around.*

*Running, running in the dark. The sharp smell of—*pines, gravel, ocean—*things he has no words for.*

*Cold and wet.*

*Crying, because She is scared. Someone chasing them.*

*Something.*

*White shapes surround them.*

*They take him from Her arms. At first he's frightened. Then he's embraced by a fuzzy warmth. Being unable to move his limbs calms him.*

*He feels safe again.*

*They leave Her behind.*

*—He's in a new place now. Warm and comfortable. The space where he sleeps moves like when he was in Her tummy.*

*He cries less. When he does, the new Her shushes him and sings to him and makes funny faces.*

*He likes the new Her. He misses the first Her. But he can't remember what she felt like and he never knew what she looked like. The new Her is old. Her skin is dry and thin like paper that makes swishy noises like cloth when it touches him.*

*Other hers visit them. He always seems to know when they're near before they arrive. He senses their presence.*

*They look down at him with anger in their hearts, radiating through their false smiles.*

*They hide their thoughts from Her.*

*They look into the After and see only darkness.*

*He meets another boy and a young—her—girl. They play together. They are friends. They ask him about his Mommy and he's forgotten about the first Her, only remembers Mommy and Aunt Norma. They have Mommies and Aunts too but they also have Daddies. Mommies and Daddies live together and make little brothers and sisters for them to play with.*

*They ask where his Daddy is. They ask why his Mommy is so old.*

*The other old ladies don't visit anymore. He's glad. They scared him but he can't remember why. They were always smiling and their smiles felt wrong.*

*—He's bigger now. It's winter and he's drawing in his bedroom, sitting cross-legged on the floor. He drew a monster with a funny hat. He wants to cut it out to put over his bed but he can't find the scissors in the kitchen drawers. He knows where Mommy keeps her scissors. He saw them one time when he was looking for string but she said never to touch them.*

*Mommy is in the bathroom. He sneaks into her room. Quietly opens the sewing cabinet. The scissors are shiny. They go* snick! *when he opens the blades. He closes the cabinet and reaches the stairs just as Mommy steps out of the bathroom.*

*Her face changes. He doesn't see it change. He senses it, shifting behind her skin. It's the first time he's sensed something in forever and it scares him.*

*Mommy is fury.*

*She is the Wicked Witch.*

*The evil old hag from fairy tales.*

*He runs, tripping and almost stumbling headfirst down the stairs, hearing her footfalls on the stairs above him as he hurries down. He hits the ground floor and grabs the bannister to swing himself around on his sock feet, and races toward the kitchen—*

*Aunt Norma is washing dishes. She looks up as Mommy screams.*

*He unlatches the basement door, tears it open and dashes down the steps without even turning on the light. He can't see a thing but he's been down here before. Knows where everything is by heart because this place haunts his dreams.*

*The low, raftered ceiling. The smell of damp concrete and earth. The cement floor littered with small stones and the shells of dead bugs. The furnace in the darkest corner with a face like a squat black goblin and a mouth full of hot fire.*

*He runs straight for it. The heat bakes his skin but she knows he's afraid of it. She won't look for him there.*

*Mommy thunders down the basement steps.*

*She calls out to him.*

*He tries not to breathe. It's so hot back here, the scissors scald his hand.*

*Mommy sees him through the dark.*

*He can't hold it in any longer. The pain is too much. He cries.*

*She runs to him. The scissors are burning his hand and there's black smoke rising from his fist.*

*Mommy reaches out. Delicately, as though she's as afraid of him as he is of her.*

*The scissors open in his hand. He doesn't know if he did it or they did it on their own. She's still reaching out for them and he brings them toward her and the blades—*

*—slash across the Mirror Man's throat. A geyser of blood pours from the gaping wound and some primitive urge draws him into the flow. He sees red, blinks it clear. Tastes the tang of salt and copper. His gorge threatens but he swallows and it's like the world's biggest hit of cocaine, like jet fuel filling up his brain—*

*—as her blood pours into his mouth. His instinct is to spit but instead he licks his lips and swallows, and Mommy smiles and nurses him with the wound on her wrist, and the pain in his hand lessens and his heartbeat slows, and he's not scared anymore. He's safe. He's with his mommy and she loves him.*

*"I'm sorry, Mommy," he says, his lips sticky with her blood. "I won't be bad no more."*

*"What the H-E-double-hockey-stick is going on here?" Norma*

*says, breaking the spell, and Mother and Son turn with guilt in their eyes and blood staining their lips—*

—Martin drew a sharp breath, blinking awake to the sound of Sheila calling his name, drawing him up from the fog of unconsciousness.

He'd slumped over the table. The memories nearly crushed him under their weight. Everything he'd forgotten. Everything he'd once been. He shook his head clear.

Sitting next to him at the table, the scissor handles protruding from her scrawny chest, Ruby turned to him with a hint of a smile, removing her hand from his with a soft swish of dry flesh.

"Ah," she said, her lungs whistling. "You remember it all now, do you? The truth beyond magic?"

It took all of his strength to nod his head.

"Good." Blood trickled from her lips. Thin billows of black smoke flittered from the wound. "It's good that you remember. It will make what I have to do easier."

"I'm so sorry, Ruby," Norma said, a hand still held against her heart. "I'm so sorry."

"Don't be sorry, Norma dear. You're a good woman. A far better mother than I ever was. You did what was necessary. What was *right*. It's high time for me to do the same."

"What are you gonna do, Ma?" Martin asked softly.

Ruby smiled weakly. "I brought them into this world. I can just as easily take them out."

Outside, the Midwives began to shriek.

Sheila rushed to the window. Martin pushed himself up shakily and stood beside her.

The old women howled and writhed, their brittle old bones shattering, flesh sagging and falling off their bones like melting tallow. The screams grew to frantic, inhuman wails. Ribbons of black smoke curled from their bubbling tissue. The smoke eddied and swirled, seeming to form menacing, shrieking, vaguely human shapes with blazing green eyes briefly—then flittering away on an ocean breeze as the bodies they'd inhabited slumped to the ground, returning to dust.

Ruby's last breath wheezed out around the scissors as her ribcage collapsed.

Martin watched from the window as the old woman's body

crumpled and sagged like a rotting pumpkin, her shadow diminishing on the floor beneath her. With one last gasp the black smoke left her body and, like her daughters, dissipated in the breeze fluttering through the shattered window.

The silver shears thumped down on the frilly seat cushion as the flower-printed fabric regained its shape, the woman who'd been sitting there suddenly and inexplicably gone.

Martin stared at the purple flowers for several moments. He felt no remorse. No sadness or pain. Only relief. As if a great weight had lifted from his shoulders.

He'd lived under Ruby Savage's shadow for as long as he could remember. Now was his time to walk in the sun.

Norma laid a hand on his shoulder. Tears spilled down her face. "I'm so sorry, Marty."

"Don't be. You did great. Better than any of us could have."

He hugged her fiercely. Sheila embraced them both.

As they stood in the kitchen, hugging each other, drawing strength from one another, the wallpaper began to peel and curl as if it was burning. The floor tiles shriveled and bubbled and the boards beneath their feet split and charred. The sink fixtures cracked and the pipes groaned.

They stepped out of their embrace and watched the spectacle. No heat accompanied the change, only a strange shimmer that gradually dissipated as the house returned to its true state, the *Chadrach*'s glammer finally fading.

Out in the street, people left their suddenly ramshackle houses in robes and pajamas and winter jackets, blinking and smiling up at the morning sun as if it was the first time it had shone on Barrows Bay since the summer.

Clarabelle rose from the ground, holding her head, looking around in confusion.

Eventually, all eyes settled on the Gingerbread House across the street, the house that had somehow burned without fire.

---

THROUGHOUT THE DAY, dozens of people came with home-cooked food and condolences. Faces from the crowd the night before wore looks of guilt and sorrow. They offered apologies for their behavior, and Sheila and Martin accepted them. They had lived under the sway of the Midwives and the veil had finally lifted. The scales had fallen from their eyes. What happened the night before was no more their fault than the deer that killed Nadine Hinckley, or the pigs that fed on Dr. Mulligan's remains.

Sinjin and Laura offered their apologies with a toast. They told the gatherers they'd decided to try again. They would name the girl Sheila. If it was a boy, they would name him Martin. Theirs wouldn't be the first child in Barrows Bay born without the Midwives: that honor would be bestowed upon Frannie and Nathan O'Neill, who were due at the end of June.

As people came and went from the Gingerbread House word arrived of changes occurring all over town, like they had in the Savage house that morning. The downtown dilapidated. Roads cracked and riddled with potholes. Trees gnarled and craggy.

No one could quite understand what had happened overnight—most thought they had all somehow slept through a late-winter nor'easter—but plans already began to formulate. They would all chip in. They would work together and rebuild.

Barrows Bay would thrive again, without the need for dark magic.

Her citizens would bear many children and those children would grow to raise a generation of their own. Free of the past for the first time since the *Ruby* crashed upon its shores.

Free of the *Chadrach*. Free of the Midwives.

The dining room was filled with food in casserole dishes and Tupperware containers, with laughter and joy and the sound of happy children.

Sheila slipped her hand into Martin's and squeezed. He turned to her and smiled, uncertain what the future held for them, whether they would give each other another chance or share custody or go their separate ways, live separate lives.

But he felt the love radiating through her pores, and he tried to return some of it without words. He hoped the little life growing inside of her could feel the love radiating back to her, too.

# Epilogue

## Father

M ARTIN HURRIED DOWN the hall, the soles of his boots slapping on cold tile, leaving a trail of red behind him.

The bouquet struck his hip with each hurried step, freeing petals that fluttered in his wake to the hospital floor.

The nurse at the desk said Sheila was in room 321. The cab ride across the city had taken ages. He was late.

Sheila had gone into labor while he was pitching his latest book at a major New York publisher. It was sad taking a meeting without Qurban, with his new agent who didn't make him feel like he was her favorite fucking writer, but they'd made it work. The book was a hit. She sold it as *"Rosemary's Baby* meets *Midsommar* for the modern American reader."* It was tentatively called *The Midwives*, though the publishers weren't sure about the title.

Martin burst into the room. The trio of women gathered around Sheila's bed in scrubs and doctor's whites turned to the door. He'd never understood the idea of a pregnant woman being "radiant," but despite Sheila's sweat-dampened face and wet hair hanging in her eyes, he couldn't help thinking it at the sight of her. She was truly glowing.

Shimmering, even.

"Is this the father?" the nurse asked Sheila.

"He is." Sheila blew wet hair out of her eyes. "And he's late."

"To be fair, you were late first."

Sheila rolled her eyes. The doctor blinked at him behind her face mask.

"I'm just gonna put these down," he said, feeling awkward. He laid the red violets on the bedside table.

"Are those why you were late?"

"Yup."

She sighed. "Then I guess I have to forgive you." They were her favorite flower.

He stood by the bed. In the preceding nine months he'd learned a lot about delivering children, simultaneously dealing with Sheila's needs and cravings while researching and writing his novel. Almost enough to deliver the baby himself. "How close are we here?"

"Contractions are two minutes apart," the nurse said, looking at the clock.

The doctor glanced between Sheila's legs. "Dilated eight centimeters. We're very close."

Martin took her hand, the way they were taught in prenatal class. The classes felt somewhat cultish during the first session, but they had quickly gotten used to the eccentricities of the practitioner and the other new parents. They'd even made friends with a newly divorced couple from Yonkers who felt as out of place with all the hippy-dippy New Age weirdness as the two of them did.

They focused on their breathing.

Sheila groaned in pain as another contraction hit and her fingers clamped around his. He was prepared for the grip but not for its strength. For a moment he thought of his mother, handing down generations of memories and history from her ancient hand to his, nearly drowning him in the sins of the past.

"She's crowning," the doctor said.

Relief washed over Sheila's features, tears of joy replacing tears of pain. In the months leading up to today, she'd worried the baby would breech. That they would have to do a cesarean. Or worse, that she would die in the womb.

Martin had never told her any of his own suspicions.

"Push, mama," the nurse said.

"Push," Martin echoed.

Sheila pushed with all her might, cords standing out on her neck, the vein in her forehead that looked like the Missouri emptying into the Mississippi when she got angry bulging. The bones in his hand felt like they might break. Sweat dripped into her eyes and he wiped it away.

After what felt like an eternity, the doctor rose with a squirming little purple creature in her hands. A girl, just like Ruby had promised them. Immediately she began to cry, surprisingly loud, consistent wails that could probably be heard all the way down the hall.

The doctor handed their newborn baby girl to Sheila, who took her as the nurse and doctor began wiping the vernix caseosa from her soft flesh with fresh, damp towels.

Sheila opened her gown and laid the baby against her breast, skin to skin like the birth instructor suggested. She smiled up at Martin, tears shimmering in her eyes, and he realized his cheeks were also wet from tears.

They stood like that for several minutes, the baby finally calming, the delivery team busying themselves while Martin and Sheila held hands and looked into their daughter's squinty little eyes.

Finally, the nurse turned to him with a pair of scissors. "Does Daddy want to cut the cord?"

He blinked at the scissors. At the umbilical cord.

Flashing on two-and-a-half centuries of ritual killings. Bloodlettings. Feasts. Terror, grief and pain.

"Martin?"

He turned to Sheila. To his newborn child. Reality returned to him and he took the scissors. He positioned the blades around the umbilical cord and brought them together swiftly—

*Snick!*

He'd never heard such a beautiful sound in his life.

---

ONCE THE DELIVERY team had cleared and it was just the three of them in the room, Martin held out his hands.

"Can I hold her?"

Sheila smiled softly. "Of course, you can, Daddy."

She passed the baby over. He took hold of her the way he'd been taught, under the bum and cradling her head in the crook of her arm. She cooed and he bounced her softly. Her blue eyes—they would turn green soon, like her grandmother's—blinked up at him but she couldn't see her parents yet, just hazy shapes. She could sense their love, though. The love they had for her and for each other.

It had blossomed naturally during the pregnancy. They'd spent so much time with each other it would have broken them if there hadn't already been a connection between them. He'd cut down on the drinking—just a celebratory drink here and there—and she'd taken the last few months off of work to rest at the doctor's insistence. They hadn't moved in together but Martin had spent the night in Sheila's guest bedroom so often it seemed like they had.

She'd invited him into her bed many times. Pregnancy tended to raise the sex drive, according to their birth instructor. During the last trimester, Martin could surely attest to it.

Their baby reached up and grasped his index finger. He shook it lightly, as if to introduce himself. "Hello," he said softly. "Hello, baby Violet."

"Violet, huh?" Sheila said. They still hadn't decided on a name. He shrugged.

The baby smiled. It wasn't just gas. She liked the name. She felt like a Violet.

"I guess she likes it." Sheila smiled herself. "It's a fine Gaelic name," she joked, and Martin laughed.

Maybe theirs wasn't a normal family. But as Sheila once told him, "normal" was a fantasy. Make-believe.

Another side effect of the pregnancy, other than causing them to reevaluate the things that meant most and casting aside what didn't, was a heightening of the senses. He'd learned that women might experience a heightened sense of smell during pregnancy, some kind of evolutionary trait. What he hadn't expected was for his own senses to evolve.

He'd known, for instance, that Violet would not only survive the delivery but would be born with blue eyes and a full head of hair.

He knew she would grow up strong and empathetic and patient like her mother. He knew she would acquire a love of language like her father. That she would have a fiery temper like Ruby's, be fiercely loyal and brave like Rosalee, and have a deep interest in the human psyche, like both of her parents.

He knew that she would remember the past, but never be tempted to repeat it.

The Savage blood ran in her as it ran in him. The spirit of the *Chadrach*, passed from Ruby Savage to Rosalee Creemore at the standing stones, black smoke like a snake entering her body at the moment of conception and filling a new soul with life.

There were others like them out in the world. Ghosts wearing human skin. Eternal souls in ephemeral bodies.

Some were evil, like Mavis and Ethel and the others, feeding off weakness and despair. They craved human blood to stave off death and extend their lives if not forever, indefinitely.

Others had cast aside their immortality to live among humans, despite humanity's flaws. Had chosen to lift them up rather than tear them down. To show them they could be more than their pasts, their petty quarrels, their selfish desires.

Martin was the first Father in a long line of Mothers.

He would teach their daughter a truth he could have only ever learned from returning home: that the world was better with a little magic in it—but eventually even magic must return to dust.

# Afterword

From start to finish, this book took me the longest to write of all of my books.

*The Midwives* was the first novel I'd ever completed. I'd written dozens of false starts since I began writing in my spare time at the age of fifteen—over thirty years ago now—often as much as a hundred pages or more. But nothing ever came together in a way that felt like it could work as a cohesive story. It was clear I really didn't know what I was doing.

I wrote *The Midwives* in 2011 at the suggestion of a woman I was dating at the time and finished that first draft in about five or six months. It was pretty awful, but writing it proved I could actually finish something longer and more in-depth than a screenplay. From there, I was hooked.

I threw that first draft in a drawer—following advice from Stephen King's *On Writing*—and started writing what would eventually be my first published book, the horror collection, *Gristle & Bone*. I wrote a second novel, *Salvage*, which became my "first novel" upon publication. I wrote two more novels and several novellas and another collection. But every once in a while, I would think about returning to Barrows Bay and Martin and Sheila and Ruby and Aunt Norma. And of course, those mean old ladies I was certain I could make if not terrifying at least very creepy.

The initial concept came to me when I heard about the odd practice of consuming part of the placenta, and I was suddenly struck by the image of a teenage girl running in the dark, holding a newborn—running from entities that looked like sweet old ladies. Her midwives. I didn't know if it would be a short story or a screenplay or a novel. I waffled on that decision many times, as I often did back then.

In the first draft, I couldn't even keep track of the individual Midwives' names. They had no personality, no individuality. They had different physical characteristics but they all acted essentially as a single entity. Adding the rivalry between Ruby and Mavis Lynch gave the rewrite some legs the original draft lacked, a lynchpin on which the second half of the story hung. *wink*

So what changed from that first draft? Pretty much everything aside from the core concept and a few early scenes. Martin Savage was originally the district attorney who put James Barclay away. At one point the original draft featured a blood orgy at an old folks' home—yes, really. And I'm relatively sure the scene with Sheila and Geraldine (Martin and Geraldine in the first draft) was a pretty obvious rip-off of the scene in King's *IT* with Beverly Marsh and Mrs. Kersh, though I only realized it after seeing the 2017 film.

After publishing *Ghostland*, I flip-flopped between various different projects, as I often do when I finish a book, trying to decide what to write next. I knew I needed some time away from Rex Garrote and Ben and Lilian, to let the rest of their story gestate. So rather than start something entirely new, I decided to rewrite my silly, terrible first novel from scratch, into something I could be proud of. I'm pretty happy with how it turned out. I really enjoyed writing it, and I hope you enjoyed reading it.

---

As always, there are people to thank. First and foremost, I should thank my mother, who is absolutely nothing like Ruby Savage. She always reads those *first* final drafts, and while she sometimes doesn't appreciate the subject matter, she has always encouraged me to keep writing.

Thanks also to the amazingly talented visual artist François Vaillancourt, whose wonderfully macabre artwork graces the cover. He really captured the essence of what I was going for when I came up with these characters.

Thanks to Dallas Mayr (aka Jack Ketchum), whose comments about my debut collection gave me an extra boost of confidence just when I started feeling like I might be spinning my wheels. I wish I had known he'd read my stuff when he was still around—but it was a pleasure to speak with him briefly over email while discussing his contribution to the *VS:X* anthology I put together a few years back.

And of course, thank you to all the readers. I would still write even if no one was reading my books, but knowing people *are* reading what I write makes the process more of a pleasure than a penance.

Thanks for taking this trip to Barrows Bay with me. Until next time, and as always—keep it creepy.

DR
February, 2020

# About the Author

Author of the cult smash-hit *Woom* and *Ghostland* and more than 15 other books that aren't the cult smash-hit *Woom* or *Ghostland*. His debut collection was blurbed positively by the legendary Jack Ketchum. His novel, *Pedo Island Bloodbath*, was nominated for a 2024 Splatterpunk Award for Best Novel.

For 7 *free* dark fiction short stories/novellas including the prequel to *GHOSTLAND*, "The Moving House," signed copies of Woom, bookplates and merch, please visit www.dun canralston.com.

SHADOW WORK
- publishing -